BROADSWORD
Monthly

I0611805

Version 1.0 PDF February 2020
Version 1.0 Print February 2020

BROADSWORD

ADVENTURES FOR FIFTH EDITION **MARCH 2020 ISSUE 4** Monthly

COVER: This griffon rider of Kuzhuk wants to know why you're trespassing near the Sanctum Of Qaorr. Cover art by Justin David Russell.

Here we are at the fourth issue of BroadSword Monthly...

I'm especially excited with this issue since it marks the beginning of the ongoing campaign/worldbuilding exercise, *The Hand of the Eight*. Starting with this book, the stories and adventures will all feed directly into each other. Of course, the adventures can also be played as one shots, most taking no more than 3-4 hours.

This is all part of the world of Omeria that's being created with each story I tell there. Omeria is an exciting world that has a lot of shades of traditional Fifth Edition campaign settings but with a few major differences.

You'll notice that the stories also serve as mysteries for the GM. So if you just want to enjoy the fiction, you can do so without having surprised spoiled by too much exposition. Enjoy!

-Dave Hamrick

Special thanks to Jason Glover of Indie Conquest and Kevin Crawford of Sine Nomine Publishing for releasing some outstanding art assets for personal and commercial use. All artists have been duly credited.

-Scott Craig

VOL. I, NO. 4

EDITOR Dave Hamrick
MARKETING Dave Hamrick
LEAD DESIGN Dave Hamrick
DESIGNERS Scott Craig, Griffon's Saddlebag, Kyle Painter
TESTING The Halo Wheelman
PROOFREADING Benjamin Gilyot, Joel Graham
LAYOUT Scott Craig

ART DIRECTOR Scott Craig
CARTOGRAPHY Miska Fredman, Dyson Logos, Dave Hamrick, Watabou.itch.io
ART Fat Goblin Games, Dean Spencer, Miguel Santos, Nate Furman, Luigi Castellani, Jason Glover, Joyce Maureira, JD Russell, David Johnson.

"The witch approached it and pared its edges with a sword that she drew from her thigh. Then she sat down beside it on the earth and sang to it while it cooled. Not like the runes that enraged the flames was the song she sang to the sword: she whose curses had blasted the fire till it shrivelled big logs of oak crooned now a melody like a wind in summer blowing from wild wood gardens that no man tended, down valleys loved once by children, now lost to them but for dreams, a song of such memories as lurk and hide along the edges of oblivion, now flashing from beautiful years a glimpse of some golden moment, now passing swiftly out of remembrance again, to go back to the shades of oblivion, and leaving on the mind those faintest traces of little shining feet which when dimly perceived by us are called regrets."

-Lord Dunsany, *The King of Elfland's Daughter*

WORLDBUILDING THE DMDAVE WAY

By Dave Hamrick
Cartography by Watabou.itch.io

Worldbuilding is the process of creating a fictional, fantasy world in which to run your roleplaying games and adventures. Some GMs go all out. These folks create elaborate world maps, name every world leader, and even know what the weather is like on any given day. Others only build what they need—for them, they couldn't tell you what is beyond the next hill until their characters discover it.

I mix in a little bit of both.

How Omeria was Born

The campaign setting, Omeria is detailed in this book. Omeria is a high fantasy world that (so far) takes place on a single continent named Omeria. When I started creating Omeria, all I had was a map. The map was the same one I used in a Team Superhydra adventure, ***Hearth: Quest for the Shunned City***. Cze of Cze & Peku painted the map and filled in a few spots. But that was it.

Not one to waste assets, after finishing Hearth, I started Hand of the Eight using the same map. I focused on a small area of the map, roughly the size of Texas (in real life). That area became known as the Weysevain Coast. for the first adventure, ***Storm of Mega***, included in this book, I invented a small village, Haver, and gave it some details.

And that was it. When writing ***Storm of Mega***, I couldn't tell you what was east, west, north, or south of Haver. I hinted at some history in the characters and dropped a few random names. But

overall, I never made more than what I needed.

Expanding on Omeria

Chapter 2 of the ***Hand of the Eight*** expanded the world. It introduced the city of Castlegrasp and the island of Ghost Holm. Now, there were allusions to war and a majestic city to the south. Chapter 2 also dropped the all-too-important name Odonburg for the first time. Of course, if you've read the stories in this book, you probably know how important Odonburg is to the overall story.

Again, there wasn't much made beyond what I needed immediately. The blocks were starting to fall into place, though, and a world was being developed.

When I started writing Chapter 3, I knew that I wanted to learn more about the Weysevain Coast. Opening up fantasynamegenerators.com I started giving names to towns and villages in the area. I crowdsourced my patrons for cool landmarks, too. That's how I created Qola and Onorim's Palace.

At this point, it was important that I started using consistent

naming conventions. Because Haver, Castlegrasp, and Orbea were all at the edge of a vast desert overlooking a coast, I thought that it should have a Moroccan vibe to it. Going further north, I gave the towns of Arruqueta, Cabal, and Lacasa basque-sounding names. The names became places which gave me new ideas for stories which became more places and so on.

I'm Not Done

Keep in mind that this book only covers the first six chapters of the story that I want to tell. In all, I plan on having at least 35 chapters not including side quests. Future adventures will take the characters through new places such as Presson's Enclave, the Anorian refugee nation of Vaskil, or even across the Ocean of Warna to the east. So far, these places are just names.

If you ever find me on Discord and ask me a question about Omeria, chances are you'll get an answer: I don't know. But that doesn't mean we won't ever know.

It just means that soon we'll find out together. Ω

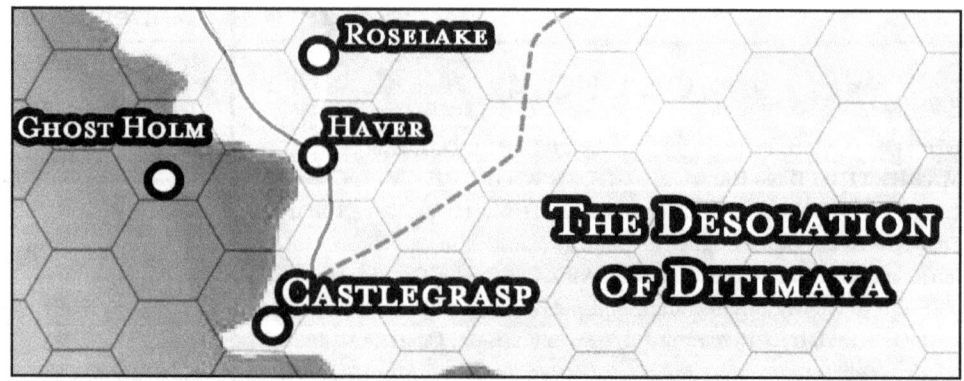

USING THIS BOOK
GETTING THE MOST FROM BROADSWORD MONTHLY

By Dave Hamrick
Art by Dyson Logos

Must-have Tomes
To run this adventure, you will need access to the Fifth Edition rules and associated rulebooks.

Understanding the Format

> Text that appears in a box like this is meant to be read aloud or paraphrased for the players when their characters first arrive at a location or under a specific circumstance, as described in the text.

In addition to the monsters included in the core rulebooks, you will also need to use the content found in the Appendices of this book.

When a creature's name appears in **bold** type, that's a visual cue pointing you to its stat block in the core rulebooks. If a stat block appears as part of this book, the adventure's text tells you so.

Spells and equipment mentioned in the adventure are described in the core rulebooks. *Magic items* are also described in the core rulebooks unless the adventure's text directs you to an exclusive item that comes with this book.

Abbreviations
The following abbreviations are used throughout this adventure:

hp = hit points
AC = Armor Class
DC = Difficult Class
XP = experience points
pp = platinum piece(s)
gp = gold piece(s)
ep = electrum piece(s)

sp = silver piece(s)
cp = copper piece(s)
NPC = nonplayer character
LG = Lawful Good
CG = Chaotic Good
NG = Neutral Good

LN = Lawful Neutral
N = Neutral
CN = Chaotic Neutral
LE = Lawful Neutral
CE = Chaotic evil
NE = Neutral evil

DELVING INTO DEEP DUNGEONS WITH DYSON

 Natural Wall
 Secret Trap Door
 Bars or Portcullis
 Stone Bridge

 Worked Wall
 Double Door
 Pit Trap
 Rope & Wood Bridge

 Archway
 Elevated Ledge
 Curtains or Tapestry
 Sloped Elevation

 Doorway
 Ledge with Ramp Down
 Trap or Trap Trigger
 Crypts

 Secret Door
 Ruined Wall
 Boxes and Barrels
 Sarcophagus

 Stairs
 Lake or Pool
 Bed or Cot
 Small Ledges

 Natural or Rough Stairs
 Battlements
 Table and Chairs
 Crevasse

 False Door
 Ladder
 Throne and Dais
 Cave Under Ledge

 Passage Underneath
 Statue
 Altar
 Debris, Rocks or Scree

 Trapdoor in Floor
 Pillars or Columns

See all of these icons interacting with each other at http://rpgcharacters.wordpress.com/maps

WELCOME TO OMERIA
A PRIMER

By Dave Hamrick
Cartography by Watabou.itch.io

Welcome to the long continent, Omeria. If you read the **Behind the Screen** section, you are probably aware that Omeria is a campaign world that is not quite done cooking. While many of the core assumptions and rules have been established in the content contained within this book, there is still a lot for both of us to learn about this fun, new world.

This introduction to Omeria will give you a little insight into the basic core assumptions. These are the guidelines that I've given myself when writing the story. You are in no way beholden to these rules. Please, feel free to change anything as you see fit. It's your world.

If you really want to get a sense of the world that is Omeria, I recommend reading through all of the adventures in this book. They will help you better understand the major players, customs, and important locations int he world. In addition, you will be given insight into how the fantastic elements of Omeria such as magic, undead, and even fiends, work.

Core Assumptions

Overall, the adventures set in Omeria are based on the following core assumptions about the world.

Omeria is Divided

There are three major sections of Omeria. To the north are the Knotsiders, most of whom are descendants of the Pressonian crusaders who crossed the Basilisk's Spine Mountains and conquered the Anorian elves. The Basilisk's Spine separates Northern Omeria from Central Omeria. Central Omeria's most striking feature is the colossal wasteland that consumes the majority of the land, the Desolation of Ditimaya. Dividing Central Omeria from Southern Omeria is a chain of volcanoes and lava flats called the Obsidian Plain. All of Southern Omeria belongs to the Nation of Odonburg, the most technologically advanced civilization in the world.

Gods Are Distant and Alien

Most of the gods of Omeria are conceptual and rarely if ever, interact with life on Omeria. What few gods have appeared were often seen as alien and too bizarre to understand. The non-aberrant gods and forces in the world, such as the sun, storms, and even the sky are seen as deities, but even then, they're just ideas. While clerics might be rare in Omeria, warlocks are common.

The Age of the World is Unknown

Man has had a presence in Omeria for at least three thousand years. However, it is only within the last one thousand years that man has celebrated its Age of Triumphs. Before the humans, the elves of Northern Omeria were the dominant species. But even they were preceded by another race, the mysterious dulons.

The Apocalypse is Coming

In the city of Castlegrasp in Central Omeria, stands a powerful magical artifact called the Amazing Clock. Like most clocks, the Amazing Clock can tell time. But the Amazing Clock

has more than three hands; it has eight in all. In addition to the hours, minutes, and seconds of the day, the clock provides information on the days, months, years, and seasons. Then, when its unseen eighth hand emerges, the clock predicts a coming cataclysm. Seven times in the last five hundred years, the eighth hand has appeared. And seven times, trouble followed. Now, the people of Omeria wait for the eighth appearance of the eighth hand, the infamous Hand of the Eight. It's believed that when the Hand of the Eight appears the world will end.

Magic is a Limited Resource

There are many ways to tap into magic in Omeria. The Striped Conjurers of Karmithyash derive their power from the evil that taints the Obsidian Plain. The evokers of Odonburg draw energy from emerald Odonburgite. And the Abjurers of Olyothyr use the fabric of the Other to protect themselves. No matter the source, all magic in Omeria is finite, some types more than others.

Gods of Omeria

There are religions and cults in Omeria, but the vast majority of Omerians consider themselves areligious. That's not to say that they don't believe in gods and higher powers. Omerians know for a fact that gods and goddesses exist. But they also understand that the deities of Omeria are strange and fantastic creatures that have little care for worship.

Notable exceptions include the worship of natural forces around Central Omeria as well as the divine worship of the Four Generals in Presson's Enclave.

In Omeria, warlocks are far more common than clerics. Warlocks derive their power from these forces, often through pacts that the sources may not even be aware of having. Clerics have a deeper connection to the alien gods of Omeria, but the line between cleric and warlock often blurs

Adventure Time

The events in this adventure start in late autumn in the year 1040 of the Age of Triumphs.

Historical Scrolls

The following pages include a number of scrolls from various archives with much useful information. You can find a list of the gods of Omeria, key Omerian historical events, important locations on the continent, and a rare scroll of the Aiquan king list. Ω

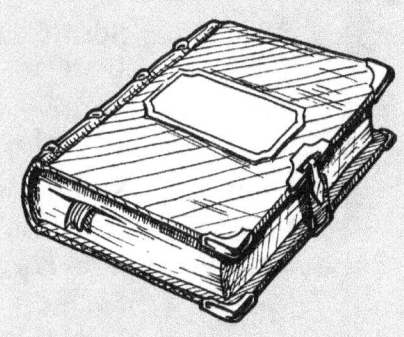

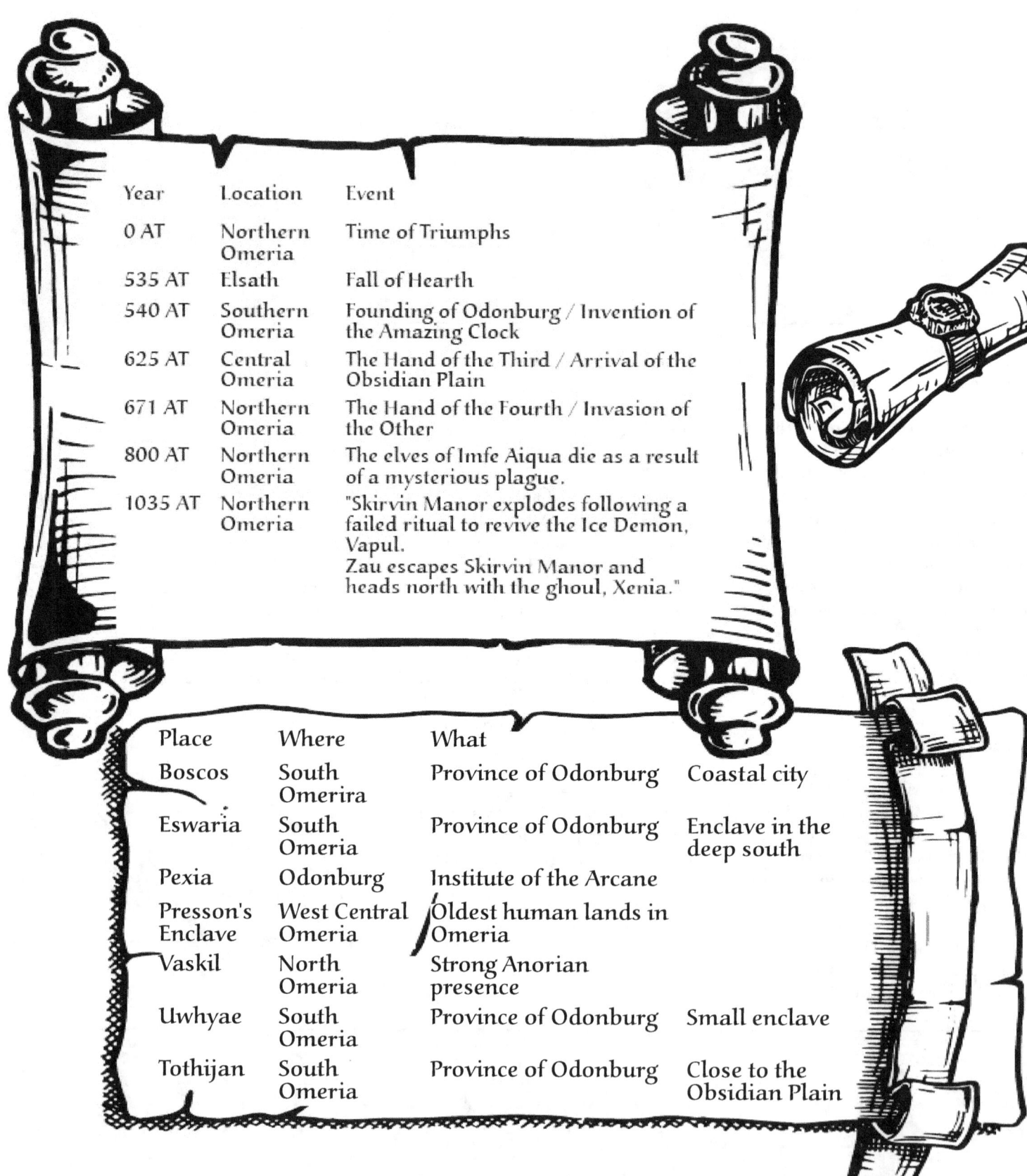

Year	Location	Event
0 AT	Northern Omeria	Time of Triumphs
535 AT	Elsath	Fall of Hearth
540 AT	Southern Omeria	Founding of Odonburg / Invention of the Amazing Clock
625 AT	Central Omeria	The Hand of the Third / Arrival of the Obsidian Plain
671 AT	Northern Omeria	The Hand of the Fourth / Invasion of the Other
800 AT	Northern Omeria	The elves of Imfe Aiqua die as a result of a mysterious plague.
1035 AT	Northern Omeria	"Skirvin Manor explodes following a failed ritual to revive the Ice Demon, Vapul. Zau escapes Skirvin Manor and heads north with the ghoul, Xenia."

Place	Where	What	
Boscos	South Omerira	Province of Odonburg	Coastal city
Eswaria	South Omeria	Province of Odonburg	Enclave in the deep south
Pexia	Odonburg	Institute of the Arcane	
Presson's Enclave	West Central Omeria	Oldest human lands in Omeria	
Vaskil	North Omeria	Strong Anorian presence	
Uwhyae	South Omeria	Province of Odonburg	Small enclave
Tothijan	South Omeria	Province of Odonburg	Close to the Obsidian Plain

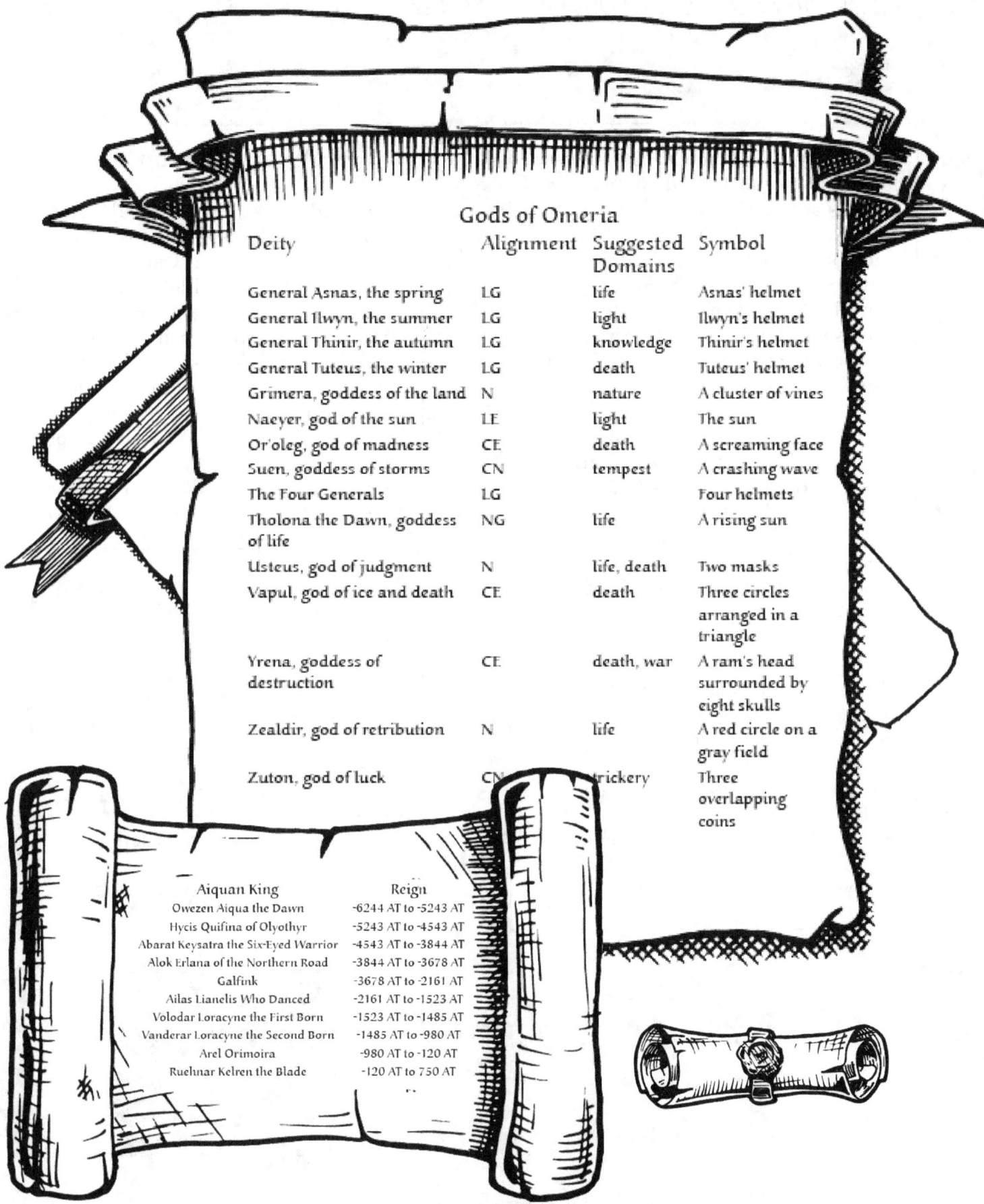

Gods of Omeria

Deity	Alignment	Suggested Domains	Symbol
General Asnas, the spring	LG	life	Asnas' helmet
General Ilwyn, the summer	LG	light	Ilwyn's helmet
General Thinir, the autumn	LG	knowledge	Thinir's helmet
General Tuteus, the winter	LG	death	Tuteus' helmet
Grimera, goddess of the land	N	nature	A cluster of vines
Naeyer, god of the sun	LE	light	The sun
Or'oleg, god of madness	CE	death	A screaming face
Suen, goddess of storms	CN	tempest	A crashing wave
The Four Generals	LG		Four helmets
Tholona the Dawn, goddess of life	NG	life	A rising sun
Usteus, god of judgment	N	life, death	Two masks
Vapul, god of ice and death	CE	death	Three circles arranged in a triangle
Yrena, goddess of destruction	CE	death, war	A ram's head surrounded by eight skulls
Zealdir, god of retribution	N	life	A red circle on a gray field
Zuton, god of luck	CN	trickery	Three overlapping coins

Aiquan King	Reign
Owezen Aiqua the Dawn	-6244 AT to -5243 AT
Hycis Quifina of Olyothyr	-5243 AT to -4543 AT
Abarat Keysatra the Six-Eyed Warrior	-4543 AT to -3844 AT
Alok Erlana of the Northern Road	-3844 AT to -3678 AT
Galfink	-3678 AT to -2161 AT
Ailas Lianelis Who Danced	-2161 AT to -1523 AT
Volodar Loracyne the First Born	-1523 AT to -1485 AT
Vanderar Loracyne the Second Born	-1485 AT to -980 AT
Arel Orimoira	-980 AT to -120 AT
Ruehnar Kelren the Blade	-120 AT to 750 AT

THE TARRASQUE TASK OF MOREEN TRASK

What do you do when a 1,200 foot long, 600-foot tall, hard-shelled lizard barrels across the desert headed straight for the tavern in which you and your friends are unwinding? Obviously, you let a strange, bushy-haired gnome woman use telekinesis to toss you inside a hole in the thing's side so you can wander around in its innards looking for a magic sword.

The Tarrasque Task of Moreen Trask is an 8th-level Fifth Edition adventure intended for 4-5 characters written by adventure creator DM Dave. A cleric—especially one with a ton of healing spells—will be a huge benefit in this adventure. Meanwhile, characters with poor Strength and Constitution scores will probably struggle. Also, if you or any of your players have a weak stomach you better avoid this one. There's a whole lot of gross stuff in it.

You can get the full adventure including all of the full-color battle mats, miniatures, magic items and more for FREE on DMDave's Patreon.

Features Creations By:

Cze and Peku - Neutral Party - Eightfold Paper - Crosshead - Maphammer - Tom Cartos - Dice Grimorium - Domille's Wondrous Works - Dungeon Mapster - Fantasy Atlas - John Stevenson - DrMapzo - Meditating Munky - Forgotten Adventures - 2-Minute Tabletop - J.Dungeonmaster - Venatus Maps - Afternoon Maps - Paper Forge - ItsADnDMonsterNow - The Griffon's Saddlebag - Music d20 - Tabletop Audio - DM Dave.

For more info, visit:

https://www.patreon.com/posts/32632654

HAND OF THE EIGHT CAMPAIGN

CHAPTER 1: THE STORM OF MEGA

BY DAVE HAMRICK

1st-Level Adventure for Fifth Edition

Cartography by Watabou.itch.io

"The Storm of Mega" is a 1st-level Fifth Edition adventure for 3-5 characters. Characters who survive the adventure should reach the 2nd level by its conclusion. This is the first chapter in the "Hand of Eight" adventure path. It can be played as the kickoff for the larger adventure setting or as a one-shot adventure for your players.

The campaign is intended to be set in the DMDave crowdsourced campaign world of Omeria. However, it can just as easily be inserted into any other large town overlooking a large ocean or sea.

Just off the coast of the small fishing town of Haver, a powerful storm churns. The Haverians have begun preparations for the hurricane, evacuating non-essentials to the nearby village of Roselake. Unfortunately, what they didn't account for is the sea-faring orc tribe of the Odzedoz. The orcish pirates plan to use the storm as the perfect opportunity to lay siege to the town. Led by Mega the Brash, a powerful orc chief known for his blood-thirsty, take-no-prisoners nature, the orcs are a true force to be reckoned with.

Background

Three weeks ago, a gnome sage from Knotside named Valcyrn Vorpos came into possession of an ancient tome. The heavy, leatherbound work was written long ago in a language that hasn't been read or spoken in over a millennium. Teetering on the edge of skepticism and intrigue, Vorpos sent word to the four wisest sages he knew, the fabled Oracles of Brezutism. They, too, were intrigued.

Unfortunately, one of the Oracles, Ruhmeid Nammod of Gilstead, knew exactly what the book was; the book was named *Prime* and within its pages it held dark, secrets. Nammod brought this information to the attention of his master, a vile fiend named Hulay.

Without hestitation, Hulay tasked Nammod to steal the book.

Nammod encouraged the other Sages and Vorpos to meet him in his hometown of Haver, just off the Weysevain Coast. There, the group would work together to decipher the book's meaning and learn its purpose. As Haver was a "midway point" for the Sages, they agreed.

From there, Nammod put his plan into motion. He'd use a ritual to call forth a powerful storm—a hurricane—to lock down the harbor and the town. Then, through back channels, he'd task a regional, sea-faring orc clan named the Odzedoz to attack Haver. But the raid wouldn't be just a distraction; he paid the raiders' captain, a mean-spirited orc named Mega, to attack and kill the other four sages. With no witnesses, Nammod could bring the book to Hulay with none the wiser.

The characters are passing through or just starting out in the town of Haver when the storm hits and the orcs attack.

Adventure Summary

The adventure begins when the characters are paid by local Haverians to help them protect the town from the coming hurricane; boarding up windows, making sure any refugees who need to escape to Roselake do so, etc. It's not exciting work, but the pay is decent.

Just as the storm is about to hit land, fishermen anchoring in the harbor report the presence of a small fleet of orcish ships sailing along the coast headed straight for the harbor. Low on men, the towns' burgomeister asks the characters to help the town against the invasion.

Once the assault begins, the characters must battle orc pirates throughout Haver. Eventually, they take notice of a group of orcs heading for the southern part of town, where the sages are. If the characters follow the orcs, they find them attacking the sages.

As an event-based adventure, there are many different ways that this adventure could play out. Before you run it, make sure you understand all of the events and the characters involved.

The Storm

Nammod used a scroll of *control weather* to summon the hurricane. Nammod is secretly concentrating on the spell the entire time and seems visibly distracted. As the adventure progresses, the hurricane intensifies, and the orcs of the Odzedoz attack during its strongest point.

Adventure Hooks

As a 1st-level adventure, there are plenty of reasons why the characters would be in Haver, either as a party that already knows each other or as individuals seeking adventure. Here are a few hooks that you could use to get the party involved in the storyline.

Trouble Sighted

A trusted sailor and Haverian, Nononlim Marblemantle told Rahl he saw a fleet of three orcish longships coming up the coast with the storm on their sails. Low on help and unlikely to get assistance from neighboring Castlegrasp in time, Rahl and burgomeister Mastid ask the characters to help, offering to pay 50 gp per character.

Important Meeting

Supposedly, a group of Omeria's greatest sages are meeting in secret at the Sparkling Lookout. Whispers abound that the graybeards possess a book with unreadable text; no one even can even read its title. Hardly an event for a sagacious or learned person to miss.

Just Passing Through

The journey north through the Lost Dragon Pass is an arduous one. But you've all heard that there are sailors in the village of Haver who can sail around the Beast's Horn. From there, it's a quick journey up the Tranquil River. Southern Omerians often talk about the adventures to be found beyond the Spine. Just gotta wait out this storm.

Haver

Haver is a large village of roughly 800 people. Most Haverians toil in the Omerian Ocean as fishers, traders, and sailors. For the most part, it's stayed out of the politics of greater Omeria (and the fiasco following the death of King Evadimus of Riva).

The majority of Haverians are humans of Ditimayan decent. However, around 20% of Haver's population is made up of Von Doral dwarves. Although they've lived with each other for nearly three decades since the fall of Von Doral, the tensions are still high. Much of Haver is segregated, with the humans living and operating in the town proper and the dwarves living just past the Eastgate in the ironically nicknamed Noble's Ward.

Long before it was a fishing village, Haver was a seaside fortress and the site of the Attack of Regrets. Surroundingthe edge of the harbor are the old ballista and canon ports facing towards the sea. Of course, an actual canon hasn't been in place for almost a decade, not since the signing of the Treaty of Hidden Goals fifteen years prior. The only siege weapon that remains is Old Beatty, a rusty mangonel at the north end of the docks.

Most travelers and Ditimayans know Haver for its piety and devout worship

Locations in Haver

1. Sisaboat's Gate

The gate takes its name from the town's first burgomeister, Oli Sisaboat. A garrison of three human **guards** works at the gate. With crime and trouble so low, it's rare they do more than drink and play dice.

Just beyond Sisaboat's Gate is Rirrearded Market where farmers and other homesteaders south of Haver arrive to buy fresh wares from the Haverian fishers and traders. Despite Haver's relatively small size, there is also a black market within the market, run by Graki (CN female half-orc **thug**).

2. Eastgate

The Von Doral dwarves use the Eastgate as their main gate in and out of Haver. They've supplied their own garrison of six dwarven **guards**. Unlike the human guards by Sisaboat's, they stay alert of goings-on at Eastgate, the Eastgate District just within the walls, and the Noble's Ward where the Von Dorals live. The dwarven garrison is led by Alfoghistr "Alfie" Sapphirebuster (LN female Von Doral dwarf **knight**), a veteran of the Attack of Regrets.

Many of the dwarven trade shops are in Eastgate proper, whereas their residences are just outside of the gate itself.

The dwarves have their own market named simply the Dwarven Market. It mostly caters to the wants and needs of the Haverian Von Dorals but does have a few goods Haverians and outsiders can't find elsewhere in the region.

3. Sunrise District

The Sunrise District is best known for the open-air Temple of Suen. Gifts of fish, crabs, and shrimp are laid at his statue by the fishers and sailors of Haver. Ubirlun Grumblebrow (N male Von Doral dwarf **priest**) maintains

the temple but spends most of his day lending a hand to the sailors down at the docks.

4. The Docks

Naturally, the docks are the center of commerce in Haver. At any given time, there are 8-9 sailing ships achored at the dock with another 4-6 just off the coast. Various warehouses and fisheries take up a good portion of this district. Although most Haverians are inured to it, the smell of raw fish is strong here. Rahl (NG male canid **commoner**) is the current master of the docks. Although Rahl spends most of his mornings hungover and most of his evenings chasing after the local ladies at The Wise Shirt, he's beloved by most in Haver for his tenacity, loyalty, and kindness.

5. The Wise Shirt

There are three taverns in town and two inns, but the most popular of the bunch, by far, is the Wise Shirt. This drinking hole is owned and operated by Aywin Luphine (LG male high elf **noble**), who most see as a bit of a snoot, but it's his star bartender Bezka Wells (LG female half-elf **noble**) who keeps everyone coming back night after night. Bezka drinks almost as much of the ale as she sells and loves to dance on the bar. Rumor around town is that she's in a relationship with the burgomeister, but neither will confirm or deny the allegations.

The Shirt has a small inn, too, with four beds. It's only 5 sp per night to sleep at the Shirt and that includes three square meals and stabling (if you're coming with horses).

6. The Sparkling Lookout

Situated by the water and a short walk from Rirrearded Market, the sage's guild makes its home in the long-decommissioned lighthouse, the Sparkling Lookout. In addition to

Ruhreid Nammod, there are three apprentice wizards here (LN male human **commoners** with proficiency in arcana that can cast *firebolt*, *mage hand*, and *prestidigitation* at will). Their names are Emar Cadel, Zuzen Mahran, and Nebrork Hallowpelt.

(As the Hand of the Eight campaign progresses, additional locations in the Haver will be developed.)

7. Townhall

The largest building in town is the townhall. Here, the burgomeister makes announcements concerning the welfare of the town. Any disputes and civil matters are handled here, as well. There is a small jail in the basement of the building capable of holding three prisoners.

8. Old Beatty

More of a decoration than a weapon these days, Old Beatty is a large, rusting mangonel that served during the Attack of Regrets. The weapon has stats typical for a mangonel (as detailed in Chapter 8 of the *DMG*).

Old Betty, Mangonel
Large object
Armor Class 15
Hit Points 100
Damage Immunities poison, psychic
A mangonel is a type of catapult that hurls heavy projectiles in a high arc. Haverians used Old Beatty to ward off raiding ships. Before the mangonel can be fired, it must be loaded and aimed. It takes two actions to load the weapon, two actions to aim it, and one action to fire it.

Old Beatty hurls heavy stones.
Mangonel Stone. *Ranged Weapon Attack:* +4 to hit, range 200/800 ft. (can't hit targets within 60 feet of it), one target. *Hit:* 27 (5d10 bludgeoning damage).

Haver

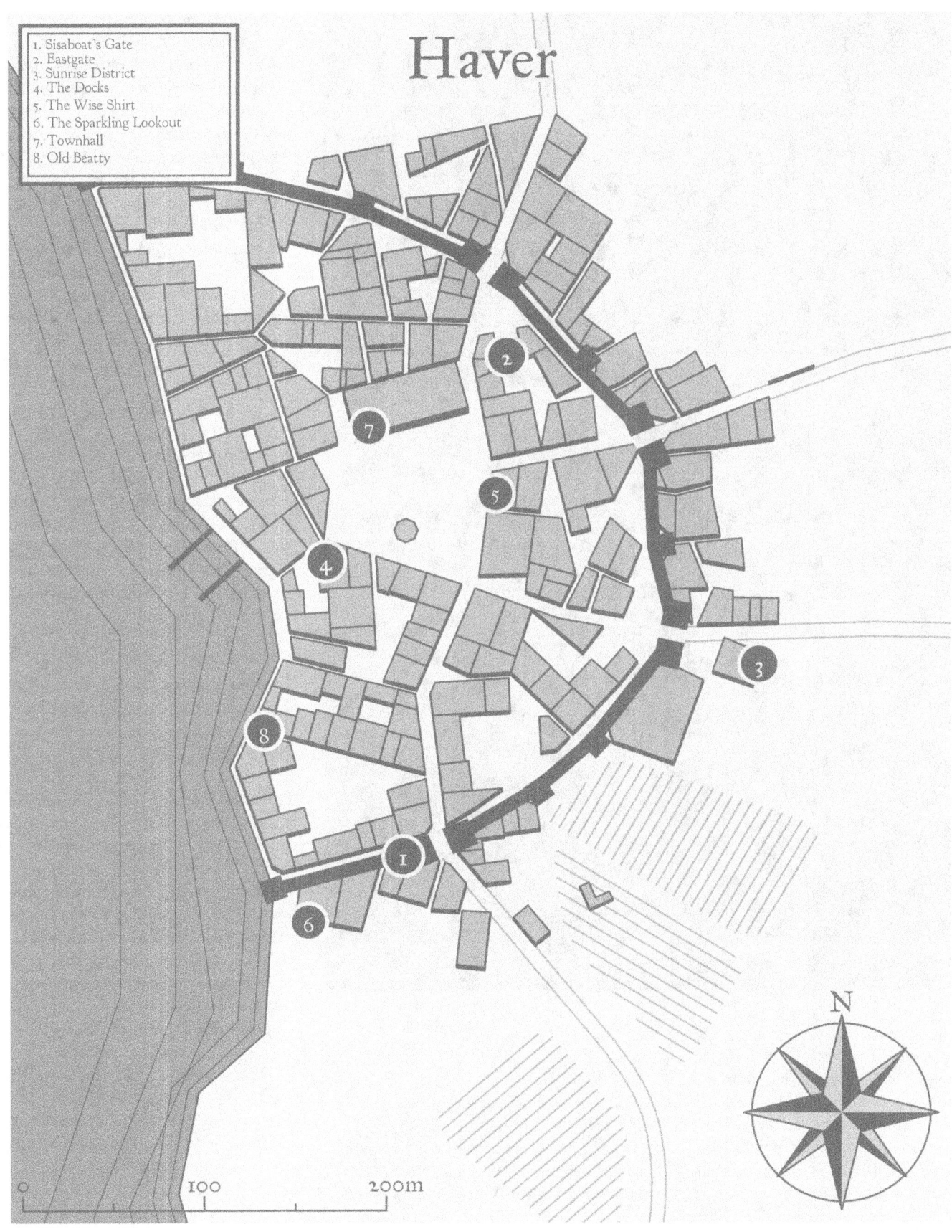

1. Sisaboat's Gate
2. Eastgate
3. Sunrise District
4. The Docks
5. The Wise Shirt
6. The Sparkling Lookout
7. Townhall
8. Old Beatty

100   200m

The humans believe he's too soft on the dwarves. They believe the dwarves steal jobs and opportunities from the native Haverians. Meanwhile, the dwarves believe Mastid gives favoritism to humans. Either way, there hasn't been a riot or major scuffle for the better part of the year and he hopes to keep it that way.

The Von Dorals have their own representative, Degnarlum Coppertoe (NE male Von Doral dwarven **commoner**), a sailor. Coppertoe's job is to protect the interests of the Von Dorals. Unfortunately, Coppertoe is easily manipulated and a cheap bribe. Since his election, he's damaged the reputation of the Von Dorals more than he's repaired it.

Finally, the local sages guild operates out of an decomissioned lighthouse named the Sparkling Lookout. Ruhmeid Nammod (NE male Ebrovellian human **mage**) works with three other sages. While they aren't politicians, per se, the sages do offer advice to the burgomeister and townsfolk when it's needed.

Haver Region

Haver rests on a rocky shore between the Weysevain Coast and the expansive Desolation of Ditimaya. It is a stopover point at the southern end of the Lost Dragon Pass before travelers reach Castlegrasp sixty miles to the south.

A fertile belt of green surrounds the large village allowing farmsteads to plant thriving plum orchards, apricot trees, and palms. The ocean air combines with the warm winds of the Desolation, providing perfect growing conditions for vintners, especially south of Haver. Castlegrasp wine is beloved across most of Omeria (despite their current political affiliations).

Go sixty miles or further east and the Desolation takes over: rocky badlands, craggy boulder fields, and sandy dunes dominate the landscape as far as the eye can see.

To the west of Haver is the wondrous and stormy Omerian Ocean. The

of Suen, God of Storms. Hurricanes and tropical storms aren't uncommon in Haver. Since the powerful storms often disable competition, they see these destructive natural forces as gifts from Suen. As such, Haver is exceptional at preparing for such events.

Politics of Haver

The iron-willed burgomeister of Haver, Rhukhim Mastid (LN male Ditimayan human **veteran**) does his best to keep the peace between the Haverian humans and Von Doral dwarves.

majority of the year, storms batter the Weysevain coast. Only during the dry summer months are Haverians spared the gifts of Suen.

(As the **Hand of the Eight** campaign progresses, additional areas in the Haver region will be developed.)

The Storm Cometh

After you've established the reasons why the characters are in the village of Haver and they've had a chance to explore and interact the village, introduce the coming storm with the following description:

> The warm air turns cool and a rumble of thunder echoes overhead. Westward, black clouds boil over turbulent waters—it's a storm, and a nasty one by the looks of it. A bell starts to ring at the center of town. The folks of Haver seem to know what it means and start following protocol. The fishermen call to their hands to unpack what they can and tie down the rest. Shop owners cash out their customers and start shuttering their shops. Parents coax their children away from the docks and back indoors.

Soon, the Haverians shutter windows, prepare sandbags in front of their doors, and remove any items outside of their homes or places of business that could get blown away during the storm.

Storm Conditions

The hurricane will make battling the orcs much more difficult than normal. You may want to review the section on Weather in Chapter 5 of the DMG before running this adventure. The two biggest components of the hurricane is its strong winds and heavy precipitation. During the storm, all ranged weapon attack rolls and Wisdom (Perception) checks are made with disadvantage. The strong winds and rain extinguish open flames, disperses fog, and makes flying by nonmagical means almost impossible. As a stormborn vulture, Cheeko can fly in the storm without penalty.

Helping Mastid

After the characters have had a few minutes to react to the coming storm, introduce the following scenario.

> "You there!" calls a tall fellow with dark hair and a crooked nose. "I'm the burgomeister here. Looks like we've got a hurricane brewing off the coast, likely headed this way. Could you assist?"

If the characters aren't driven by an innate desire to help the town prepare, Mastid offers each 5 gp for assistance and twice that if they do an exceptional job. From there, he's got a few chores he can help with. The characters can work as a team, or they can split up to handle each of the chores.

Shutter Townhall

Townhall is a large, rectangular building bordering town square. As most of the garrison is assisting in evacuations, there aren't many hands to help shutter its 10 huge windows. Mastid needs at least one character to assist.

Resolution. No checks are required to shutter the windows, just time. It takes 20 minutes for one character to board up the window, 10 for two, 7 for three, and 5 for four.

Catch Tibby

Venerable Mrs. Odette's white cat, Tibby, is on the loose and won't come in. Frantic, Mrs. Odette demands that Mastid help her, so Mastid deletages the task to the characters. If they agree, they follow Mrs. Odette to her small house in the Sunrise District.

Resolution. It takes three successful ability checks to catch Tibby. The checks must be made in order, and if one check fails, the characters have to start over with the first check. Each series of checks takes 1 minute to perform, even if the very first check fails.

- First, one character will need to make a DC 14 Wisdom (Perception) check to spot the cat.
- Next, once Tibby is spotted, a character must make a Dexterity check contested by Tibby's Dexterity check (Tibby gets +2 to the check).
- Last, the same character who succeeded on their Dexterity check must make a Strength (Athletics) check contested by Tibby's Dexterity (Acrobatics) check in order to catch her. Tibby gets a +2 to her check.

Once all three checks are successful, the characters can hand off Tibby to Mrs. Odette who retreats into her shanty for the duration of the storm—not a word of thanks, either!

Convince Darebumli Onyxbrow to go to the Wise Shirt

Darebumli Onyxbrow (CN male Von Doral dwarf **commoner**) is a stubborn, drunk sailor who lives on his small sailing boat in the harbor. Every storm, he refuses to go in. Typically, it requires Mastid and at least two members of the garrison to convince him—by force, bribe, or lies—to go to the Wise Shirt where he can stay through the storm. Not wanting to deal with it this time, Mastid turns to the characters for assistance.

Resolution. Getting Onyxbrow to leave his ship and go to the Wise Shirt takes some coaxing. Have the players roleplay the interaction with Onyxbrow. Onyxbrow is incredibly stubborn and has a bit of a foul mouth, spouting a surprising range of dwarven profanities through slurred speech. There are three things that will automatically motivate Onyxbrow to leave his ship for the Wise Shirt:

- *Gold.* If the characters offer up at least 1 gp as a bribe, Onyxbrow will head to the Shirt.
- *Alfie Sapphireburster.* Should the characters mention that Alfie Sapphireburster will be at the Shirt, he'll dash that way. The old man's got something of a crush on the guard.
- *Jokes.* Onyxbrow loves a good joke. Any character who demonstrates a keen sense of humor or razor wit (the more off-color the better) will convince Onyxbrow to head towards the Shirt.

The only other option to get Onyxbrow to the White Shirt is to knock him out cold (Mastid mentions that it's been the only solution on more than one occasion). The characters can fight the old man—who enjoys throwing things and cursing as he does—and knock him out with non-lethal force. The only trouble is that they'll have to drag the heavy, old coot to the Shirt if they do that.

Pirates!

As the waves begin to lap at the shore rocking the boats in the harbor, Nononlim Marblemantle (NG male Von Doral dwarf **commoner**) rushes to Mastid or the characters with reports that he saw the black sails of Odzedoz longboats galloping over the waves.

> "Odzedoz," sighs Mastid as he looks out over the black, cresting waves. "They're a nasty band of orcish pirates led by a cutthroat named Mega the Brash. Half the garrison's assisting with evacuations and with the storm coming, we won't be able to get word to Castlegrasp. You're fighters, right? Think you can help?"

MEGA THE BRASH
Medium humanoid (orc), chaotic evil

Armor Class 16 (chain mail)
Hit Points 45 (6d8 + 18)
Speed 30 ft.

STR	17(+3)	INT	11 (+0)
DEX	12 (+1)	WIS	14 (+2)
CON	16 (+3)	CHA	13 (+1)

Skills Intimidation +3, History +2
Senses darkvision 60 ft., passive Perception 11
Languages Common, Orc
Challenge 2 (450 XP)

Aggressive. As a bonus action, Mega can move up to his speed toward a hostile creature that he can see.

ACTIONS

Multiattack. Mega makes two attacks with his handaxes.
Handaxe. *Melee or Ranged Weapon Attack:* +5 to hit, reach 5 ft. or range 20/60 ft., one target. *Hit* 6 (1d6 + 3) slashing damage.
Battle Cry (1/Day). Each creature of Mega's choice that is within 30 feet of him, can hear him, and not already affected by Battle Cry again advantage on attack rolls until the start of Mega's next turn. Mega can then make one attack as a bonus action.

Should the characters agree, Mastid offers to pay each character 50 gp for their services. The fisherman told Mastid they were at least twenty minutes out, so there will be time to prepare. They also mention that it looks like there were three longships.

Mastid explains the orcs' typical tactics:

- Fortunately, the Odzedozi longships aren't (usually) equipped with siege weapons. However, each ship can hold as many as 50 orcs.
- It's likely that Mega is riding with them. Mega never misses the opportunity to join in a raid. Often, Mega rides first into the throes of combat upon his stormborn **giant vulture,** Cheeko.
- The orcs will use their overwhelming numbers to swarm the docks, preferring a frontal assault.

Assets

Fortunately, the characters and Mastid aren't the only ones around to fight the pirates.

- Alfie Sapphireburster has offered to stay with the noncombatants in the White Shirt along with Bezka and Aywin.
- Rahl always invites a good fight. The canid arms himself with a harpoon that's easily twice as long as he is tall.
- Despite her orcish nature, Graki takes up arms for Haver whenever danger is near. She will directly assist the characters and Mastid.

5 members of the garrison are still in town. They are all **guards**.

10 sailors have offered to help. They are all **commoners** armed with light crossbows (+0 to hit, 1d6 piercing damage).

- Old Beatty is the only mangonel left over from the Attack of Regrets that's still operational.

Strategy

Mastid looks towards the characters for a defensive strategy, as his chief concern is protecting the people of Haver. However, if he's asked for advice, he offers the following:

- It takes five people to effectively operate Old Beatty. He suggests that the characters help with it since they're more likely to understand its operation. If the characters don't wish to use the mangonel, the guards from the garrison will instead use it.
- The buildings surrounding town square offer plenty of excellent vantage points for snipers, especially the roof of the town hall.
- The walls around the town—while crumbling—also offer an excellent vantage point against the orcs.
- Should things turn bad, the White Shirt was once an old fortress. It's easily defendable and has an old smugglers tunnel that leads out of the walls.

Raid of the Odzedoz

You're free to play out the Raid of the Odzedoz as you see fit. For random encounters with Odzedoz orcs, have 1d4 **orcs** attack the characters as needed. In addition, below are a few important encounters that the characters should experience, especially "Sisaboat's Gate", "Following Mega", and the "Sparkling Lookout.""

500 Feet from Harbor

The first sign of the ships comes with a flash of lightning. The three longships bear the black banners of the Odzedoz orcs. The ships move 60 feet per round, so it will take it roughly a minute to get to the harbor. The ships are within the long-range of the mangonel at this point. It's possible that the mangonel can down one ship (or at least knock out a handful of orcs) in that time.

200 Feet from the Harbor

As the ships enter the mangonel's normal range, Mega takes off on Cheeko (Cheeko defaults to the Dodge action). Mega (see the Appendix) will fly straight towards anything that's capable of dealing heavy damage to his ships—such as the mangonel—and then turn his attention to the south section of the town.

Attack on The Harbor

Once the three ships land, 70 orcs leap from its side and march into town. From there, they split into groups of 3-4, each group raiding a different location. The western part of the town is the most dangerous, as fully half of the raiding party stays within 300 feet of the boats. Despite the chaos they cause, Mastid does not recommend going into that area. "It's certain death. The businesses will recover."

Town Square

A group of 6 orcs heads for The White Shirt. Led by an experienced raider named Haguk, the orcs know that many of Haver's citizenry will be holed

The Crushing Wave, Banner of the Odzedoz

up there. Haguk is an orc with 22 hit points. Sapphireburster and three commoners man the old fortress' arrow slits with light crossbows, but the orcs are determined to break down the door. The doors to the White Shirt, when barred, have an AC of 16 and 30 hp with immunity to poison and psychic damage. If Mastid notices the orcs attacking, he encourages the characters to stop them.

Among the 15 commoners, Sapphireburster, and the Shirt's the staff, Ubirlun Grumblebrow is in attendance as well. Grumblebrow offers healing to injured Haverians and the characters.

Rahl is Cornered

During the fray, Rahl bravely steps out and starts fighting a pair of orcs. Unfortunately, the canid is no match for them and is smote with a single hit, dropping to 0 hit points (but stable). Through the rain, the characters must rush to his aid, fighting off the orcs as they do. If Rahl is saved, the characters should consider bringing him to the White Shirt where Grumbebrow can apply healing. "Did I get 'em?" Rahl will ask weakly, once he comes to.

Sisaboat's Gate

After the orcs have been in Haver for 3-5 minutes, Mastid notices something

THE SPARKLING LOOKOUT

4. GALLERY

3. BEDROOM

1. ENTRY

2. GUILDHALL

unusual. Mega and a group of 4 orcs are headed for the southern part of the city. Their manner is determined—they're after something. The market is closed and there are no residential areas on that side of town, so why go there? The only thing of note is the sage's guild in the decommissioned lighthouse, the Sparkling Lookout. Curious to Mega's intentions, Mastid asks the characters to investigate.

Following Mega

Unless the characters are particularly stealthy, Mega tasks Cheeko to attack. Cheeko is intelligent and cruel and should offer Mega and his squad some time. Cheeko won't fight to the death, instead fleeing if his hit points are reduced by half or more.

The Sparkling Lookout

Unless the characters were able to cut Mega and his squad off, the orcs successfully made it inside the Sparkling Lookout. When the characters are within 50 feet of the building, read:

The door to the old lighthouse is off its hinges. As you approach, you hear a small explosion and hear the screams of orcs.

The lighthouse has four main areas described below.

1 - Entry

This large, octagonal room is 50-feet wide in diameter with 80-foot high ceilings. A staircase spirals along the walls up to the second floor. In addition to the entryway, there is a wooden door to the north that appears to

have been hacked open. The charred body of a dead orc raider lies twenty feet from the door. After a few seconds, a second orc raider stumbles out of the room to the north holding its bleeding face. After a gasp, it collapses to the ground. Sounds of a scuffle continue.

Both of the orcs were killed by the sages' magic.

2 - Guildhall

This 30-foot by 30-foot library is in tatters. You find three bodies on the ground, all humans with brightly-colored livery. They look dead, victims of axe attacks. Three orcs hover over a fourth human dressed in a similar manner who looks to be pleading for his life. The human holds a large leatherbound tome in his arms.

Mega and the two surviving orcs hacked into the guildhall and killed three of the Oracles of Brezutism. Only Ruhreid Nammod remains. If the characters approached the door to the guildhall carefully, they can hear Nammod begging Mega for mercy.

"You can't kill me!" the gray-haired man pleads. "We had a deal. You and your men would attack the town and kill the other Oracles and I would get the book to Hulay."

The large, mohawked orc snorts. "The deal has changed. As big a risk as you are taking, weak-sack, I imagine that book is worth more than what you paid me. I'm thinking much more."

"You will anger Hulay!" says the old man.

"Then I will anger Hulay," says the orc.

Unless the characters intervene before he can strike, Mega strikes Nammod dead and takes the book, Prime. From there, Mega and the two surviving orcs will make their exit. If Cheeko survived the encounter with the characters, the vulture waits at the gallery of the lighthouse. Once Mega has collected the book, he has no interest in fighting the characters and will try to make a hasty escape, using the other two orcs as a distraction.

3 - Nammod's Bedroom

The sage lives on the center floor of the lighthouse. The octagonal room is 40-feet in diameter with a spiral staircase at the center leading up to the gallery (**Area 4**) and another staircase leading down to the Entry (**Area 1**). The three apprentices and Valcyrn Vorpos are hiding here under Nammod's bed. If Mega runs through this area, he ignores the presence of the acolytes and the gnome and heads directly for the staircase leading up to the lantern room.

4 - Lantern Room

The top of the lighthouse is surrounded by thick, rain-battered glass. A 5-foot wide catwalk surrounds the lantern. If Cheeko survived his encounter with the characters, the vulture's broken one of the windows, exposing the lantern room to the hurricane outside. With his bird there, Mega wastes no time mounting the beast. He then flies back to his longships, sounding a horn to call the Odzedoz raiders back to sea.

Adventure Conclusion

At the very least, the characters should have encountered Mega and the orcs at the decommasterizissioned lighthouse.

Depending on how the characters handled the event, there are a few different possible outcomes.

Mega escaped with the book. If Mega escaped with Prime, he and his crew will sail back to the Odzedoz hideout in The Ghost Holm.

Mega survived but did not escape with the book. If the pirate lived, he's likely frustrated with the characters for ruining his chance at earning both the book and the gold Nammod promised. Even if Nammod is alive, he's not likely to pay Mega after the orc threatened his life. Mega will try to coax the characters into a trap.

Mega was killed. With Mega dead, the Odzedoz are without a leader. His toughest soldiers vie for the spot as the leader of the Odzedoz, demonstrating their leadership prowess through demonstrations of brutality.

Nammod survived and still has the book. Visibly shaken, but alive and with his prize, Nammod will try to flee the town. He has a horse tethered near the market that'll he'll use to ride south to Castlegrasp. If the characters cut him off before he can leave, Nammod asks the characters to help him secure the book, ensuring them that it is an artifact of great value.

"In the wrong hands, doom will fall on the land." Of course, if the characters heard Nammod's protests to Mega, revealing his hand in the storm and raid, they may have reservations

Nammod survived but lost the book. If Mega escaped with the book but didn't kill Nammod, Nammod is hysterical to get the book back. He'll offer the characters a small fortune to retrieve it from the orc's hold in The Ghost Holm. Even if the characters overheard Nammod's pleas to Mega, Nammod drives home the fact that Mega could sell it to villains far more dangerous than Hulay.

Nammod was killed by Mega. Most likely, Mega kills Nammod. Once Nammod is dead, the *control weather* spell loses its power and within 10 minutes it's back to blue skies and sunshine.

In addition to the sages at the Sparkling Lookout and any named NPCs that were killed during the incursion, two fishermen were killed at the hands of the Odzedoz. The Haverians spend the next couple of days cleaning up and making repairs. A funeral at sea is held for the departed, their bodies set upon flaming rafts with Ubirlun Grumblebrow offering them to Suen.

Mastid is true to his word and pays them the 50 gp promised. As he awards the characters for their hard work, he asks them one more favor:

> The Odzedoz are a growing threat here. And this is probably their boldest attack yet. With the political trouble brewing over Omeria, it's unlikely we'll get as much help as we like from Castlegrasp. What would it take to have you help us handle the Odzedoz problem?

If the characters agree to help, Mastid and the other surviving townsfolk begin to make preparations for an attack on the Odzedoz's fortress island of the Ghost Holm. The attack takes place in Chapter 2 of this adventure path, ***Assault on the Ghost Holm***. Ω

CHAPTER 2: ASSAULT ON THE GHOST HOLM

BY DAVE HAMRICK

2nd-Level Adventure for Fifth Edition

Cartography by Dyson Logos
Primary Art by Jason Glover

Assault on the Ghost Holm is a 2nd-level Fifth Edition adventure for 3-5 characters. Characters who survive the adventure should reach the 3rd level by its conclusion. This is the second chapter in the Hand of Eight adventure path. It can be played as part of the larger adventure or as a one-shot.

The campaign is intended to be set in the DMDave crowdsourced campaign world of Omeria, but can just as easily be inserted into another coastline in a high magic campaign setting. The campaign is intended to be set in the DMDave crowdsourced campaign world of Omeria. However, it can just as easily be inserted into any other large town overlooking a large ocean or sea.

The sea-faring orcs of the Odzedoz clan have grown more and more dangerous over the last few months. Just recently, the tribe attacked the fishing village of Haver during a hurricane.

Now, comes word that the meddlesome orcs have captured a respected Castlegraspian noble's daughter. Led by the loathsome Mega the Brash, the orcs make their home on a 200-foot spire of rock off the coast of an island called the Ghost Holm. Of course, the orcs aren't the horrible things that live on the forgotten island.

Background

Despite being a noble's daughter living in the coastal city of Castlegrasp, Nadia Mansouri's done well to distance herself from the luxurious lifestyle often associated with the Mansouri name. Instead, Nadia, one of Omeria's leading philologists, busies herself in the large libraries and scroll vaults of the city.

A few nights ago, as Nadia returned home from another night of reading through ancient Elsathian texts, two cloaked men approached her in the street. Without a word, the pair tried to grab her. Of course, Nadia is a noble's daughter and is well-versed in the use of a dagger. She got one in the shoulder and the other in the thigh and fled.

Unfortunately, the third—a massive, white-mohawked orc— caught her by surprise and knocked her unconscious with the butt of one of his black handaxes. A city guard walking his beat saw the trio load the girl on the backs of three horse- sized vultures then take off. The guard got an arrow off, taking out one of the riders, but the other two escaped with Mansouri. The captain of the guard immediately identified the felled rider: Odzeboz pirates.

Nadia's father Baariq flew into a frenzy at the loss of his daughter, swearing he'd put a bounty of 1,000 gp per orc scalp. But his advisors knew that the best course of action was to keep the matter quiet. All they had to do was wait for the orcs to send a ransom letter. Three days later, the letter came:

"If you hope to see your daughter alive, bring 10,000 gold pieces in a simple wooden crate to the old pirate caves at the Ghost Holm. Send only one man, unarmed in a rowboat. Once we have received and counted the gold, we will return the girl with your man. Any hint at soldiers, adventurers, or assassins, and the girl gets a spear through one of her pretty brown eyes."

Under advisement, Baariq Mansouri agreed to the terms. He would send his most trusted bodyguard Tazim Hajji with the gold. While his advisors comforted him repeatedly that he would see his daughter alive again, it didn't matter— Mansouri's pride was wounded. He would have vengeance for this crime as a clear message anyone else who would dare mess with the Mansouris.

Mega's Plan
Mega wants the gold, certainly. But Mega also wants the girl, especially if he's in possession of *Prime*. Within the last two weeks, Mega secured the services of a mercenary doppelganger named Vista. Vista was paid handsomely to assume the appearance of Nadia Mansouri following her capture. After the ransom exchange, Mega

---

What if Mega is dead?

This adventure assumes that Mega survived *Storm of Mega*. If this isn't the case, replace Mega with his younger brother, Xnath, using the same stat block and motivations. The plot remains unchanged.

(Oh, instead of a mohawk, Xnath keeps his long, white hair in a ponytail.)

---

would trade the Faux-Nadia for the gold (or book). Then, he would flee north with the real Nadia and the book to meet his brother at the western edge of the Basilisk's Spine.

Faux-Nadia, Vista would continue the ruse for as long as necessary. After all—who doesn't want to live the life of a wealthy noblewoman for a while?

Adventure Summary

Lord Baariq Mansouri of Castlegrasp travels north to the fishing village of Haver to seek Alfoghistr "Alfie" Sapphirebuster. Sapphirebuster carried the Mansouri banner during the Attack of Regrets fifteen years prior. Unfortunately, once he arrives, he discovers that Sapphirebuster is no longer interested in covert missions, no matter how much Mansouri wishes to pay her. If the characters participated in defending the town during the Odzedoz attack (see *Chapter 1: Storm of Mega*) three and a half weeks prior, Sapphirebuster recommends that Mansouri speaks with them instead.

Should the characters take Mansouri's offer, they must sneak into the orc's fortress atop Jando's Spire in the Ghost Helm, find his daughter, and rescue her. If the characters take the mission, they are given passage by boat to the western edge of the island. Soon, the characters discover that orcs aren't the only danger on the island. Animated suits of armor— relics of an old war— haunt the swamps and forests of the Ghost Holm.

From there, the characters must circumvent notice of the orcs and head towards the ruins of Jando's Spire. This is a particularly difficult mission as it requires the characters to use stealth to sneak past a small army of orc pirates without being noticed. Getting across the spire, they enter the town ruins, discover Nadia and her captives, and make an escape before they're killed by the Odzedoz orcs.

Adventure Hooks

If the characters are still in the village of Haver following the conclusion of *Storm of Mega*, then they will need to have reasons for staying there for the last few weeks. They're free to spend time performing downtime activities and helping the villagers rebuild after the storm. Then, once Lord Mansouri arrives, they might be eager to jump at the opportunity to take the clandestine mission. In addition, there are other threads leading from Storm of Mega and this adventure that the characters may follow.

The Ancient Book
It's possible that the orc pirate's leader, Mega, escaped with the ancient book *Prime*. If this happened, then the kidnapping wasn't random. As a philologist, Nadia Mansouri has the ability to translate the text. Mega, realizing the book's value, wants to know exactly what is inside the book and how he can leverage its power.

Even if Mega didn't flee with the book (or even survive *Storm of Mega*), and Ruhmeid Nammod had the book, the orcs kidnappers in Castleburg weren't there just to grab Nadia. Their first mission was to kill Nammod who fled with the book to Castleburg. Successfully accomplishing that—the old man's body appears in a gutter a week after Nadia's kidnapping—they grabbed Nadia and fled.

The Book for the Girl
If the characters stopped Mega in

Storm of Mega from collecting the book and went so far as to recover the book from Nammod (ideally, tossing the turncoat in Haver's jail), then Mega (or his successor) doesn't want 10,000 gp for the girl. He wants Mansouri to convince the characters to trade the book for the girl. If this is the case, when Mansouri arrives in Haver, he won't seek his old banner woman, Sapphireburster, but he'll seek the characters directly.

An Old Friend

It's possible to run this adventure without ever having run *Storm of Mega*. If this is the case, one or more of the characters knows Mansouri personally. When Mansouri arrives in Haver, he requests their help with the same mission: land on the backside of the island, sneak onto Jando's Spire and save Nadia. Keep in mind that you can incorporate this angle even if you are running the Hand of the Eight adventure path.

The Wise Shirt

It's been three weeks since a hurricane rocked the Weysevain Coast and the fishing village of Haver (see *Chapter 1. Storm of Mega* for details about Haver). During the hurricane, a band of orcish pirates named the Odzedoz attacked. Casualties were limited, but a handful of traveling sages on the south-side of the town was found murdered.

Celebrated heroes of the conflict, the characters have spent the last few weeks helping rebuild. They are free to participate in downtime activities. Refer to the *DMG* or *XGtE* for ideas on the types of downtime activities that they can take.

Also, during that time, Haver's popular drinking spot, the Wise Shirt's offered two of its rooms for the characters to rent- free for a month as a way for saying thanks for their assistance during the pirates' incursion.

When the adventure begins, the

> #### Replacing Vorpos with Nammod
>
> It's possible that Ruhreid Nammod (NE male Ditimayan human **mage**) is still alive following the orcish incursion from the first chapter and that no one knows he was involved. If this is the case, it might make more sense to place Nammod in the role of Vorpos.

characters are relaxing in the bar. The bartender, Bezka Wells (LG female half-elf **noble**) keeps the drinks flowing. While her attention is never fixed too long on one single guest, she has been seen chatting (flirting, really) with the town's burgomeister, Rhukhim Mastid (LN male Ditimayan human **veteran**). Also staying at the tavern's inn is a peculiar gnome named Valcyrn Vorpos (N male gnome **noble**). Vorpos hails from the north of the Basilisk's Spine in Knotside. He and a trio of apprentice mages narrowly escaped with their lives when the Odzedoz orcs attacked the local sages' guildhall at the south end of the village. The event left him deeply troubled. On more than one occasion, the characters have heard the gnome screaming in the night. Currently, he's quietly nursing a whiskey at the bar.

Baariq Mansouri

Eventually, Baariq Mansouri (LN male Ditimayan **noble**) enters the bar flanked by two well-armed bodyguards (LN male Ditimayan **veterans**).

> A figure steps into the light of the tavern door, the afternoon sun to his back. He stomps the wet sand from his riding boots and enters. Just behind him are two armed guards. The man is roughly six-feet tall and dressed in the blue-and-purple livery of a Castlegraspian noble. He strokes his well-trimmed beard and looks directly at you.
>
> "I believe it is you who I am looking for," says the man before walking over.

However Baariq heard of the characters, he introduces himself and explains the recent events that have led him here including Nadia's kidnapping at the hands of the Odzedoz and the ransom.

Then, in a lowered voice, he makes his offer:

> "These orcs have stolen my heart from me. And I am a Mansouri— we do not let such insults pass lightly. As my man delivers the ransom to the orcs, I want you to sneak onto their island, find my daughter, and slay the bastards who took her. Do this, and I will pay you handsomely."
>
> Mansouri places a fat coin pouch on the table in front of you.
>
> "That is a downpayment of 800 gold pieces. I will double it when you bring me back my daughter. Triple it if you bring me the head of the orc who leads the Odzedoz. What say you?"

Mansouri will give the characters as much time as they need to consider his offer, but no more than an hour. He can be found near the Eastgate chatting with the Von Doral dwarves, many of whom served under his banner during the Attack of Regrets.

Either way, this is where Mansouri wishes to discuss how the assault on Ghost Holm will transpire.

What Vorpos Knows

Unless the characters and Mansouri took the conversation somewhere else, it's likely that the gnome scholar, Valcryn Vorpos heard the entire thing. What intrigues him most about the kidnapping isn't the who or what, but more the why. After Mansouri departs. Vorpos gets the characters' attention.

> "Nadia Mansouri! Nadia Mansouri!" the gnome says, his eyes wide with anxiety. "She's not just some noble girl. She's central Omeria—if not the entire continent's—most sought after mind in the field of philology. It all makes sense! It all makes sense!"

Wherever the book, *Prime*, currently is, Vorpos knows that Nadia's kidnapping has something to do with it and its contents. She is one of the few people on the entire continent who could decipher the book's ancient languages.

"With the orcs recently attacking the sages' guildhall at the Sparkling Lookout and now this high-stakes kidnapping, it's simply too big of a coincidence!"

At this point, the characters may want to know more about the book and its origins. Here is what Vorpos learned about the book in the short time he possessed it:

- The book is written in an ancient language that has not been read or spoken for over one thousand years.
- No spells can decipher the language. Spells and effects such as comprehend languages have no effect. In fact, such spells have the opposite effect, making the words even more indecipherable.
- It's possible that the book is the long-lost tome, *Prime*. Although *Prime*'s true function is not totally clear, the book is said to be unspeakably evil and capable of granting any who can understand it great power.

> "If the book is in the hands of the Odzedoz orcs and they are using Nadia Mansouri to decipher its contents," the gnome says, "it's possible that all of the Weysevain Coast could be in grave danger."

The Ghost Holm

The ransom exchange is set for sunrise three days from when the characters meet Mansouri. After the characters have agreed to Mansouri's rescue mission, he secures them a ride on a fishing boat the very next morning. He also gives the characters a *wand of fireworks* and 2 *potions of healing* each.

The boat, piloted by a grumpy, old drunk friend of Alfie Sapphireburster's named Darebumli Onyxbrow (CN male Von Doral dwarf **commoner**) sails for a day along the outskirts of the Ghost Helm. Once Onxybrow's ship is roughly 15 miles west of the island, Onyxbrow sets the characters out in a rowboat under the cover of night. Mansouri paid Onyxbrow to keep his boat there for two days. With a case of Castlegraspian win—*Alnab min alma'Mansouri 1071*, no less —it's unlikely that Onyxbrow will go anywhere anytime soon.

It will take the characters 5 hours to reach the island in the rowboat, arriving approximately one hour after midnight.

Once on the island, the characters have five hours to cross the seven-mile stretch of the island, sneak into the Odzeboz camp, cross over the Janto Spire, and rescue Nadia. After she is safe, they must give a signal, firing a flare from the wand of fireworks that Mansouri gave them.

Chewing his nails to the point of bleeding, Mansouri will be standing by on a Castlegraspian warship 20 miles south of the Ghost Helm. Once the signal is given by the characters, he and a militia of 50 **guards**, 8 **veterans**, and 2 **knights** will attack the Odzedoz's anchored ships. Otherwise, he will have to surrender the ransom as requested.

General Features

Unless otherwise stated, the Ghost Holm has the following features.

Coastline. The coastlines are rocky and have plenty of boulders. Except for the two-mile stretch that travels through the swamps, they're one of the easier ways to get around the island. Of course, the chance of getting spotted by an Odzedoz patrol increases significantly.

Forests. Like much of the Weysevain Coast, palms, willows, and poplars grow here. The floor itself is covered in thick shrub. Because of the coverage that the forest canopy offers, the chance of the Odzedoz lookouts spotting the characters is reduced. The trade-off, however, is that much of the forest counts as difficult terrain.

Mountains. The Ghost Holm's mountains have been well worn by age and are passable on foot. Regardless, they are still difficult terrain. Furthermore, Odzedoz orcs watch the island from watchtowers.

THE GHOST HOLM

1 HEX = 1 MILE

Swamps. The southwestern corner of the island near the Lagoon of Wisps is covered in muddy, insect-infested swamps. The swamps are difficult terrain. In addition, the chance of encounters with wisps and suits of animated armor increases while traveling through the swamp (see below). Fortunately, the Odzedoz will go nowhere near the swamp.

Random Encounters

As the characters travel from the western side of the island to Jando's Spire, there is a chance once each hour

that they could encounter something. To determine if an encounter happens, determine which of the four types of terrain described above that the characters are traveling through.

Then see which set of encounter dice you must roll.

Terrain	Random Encounter Dice
Swamps	1d6
Forest	2d6
Mountains	3d6
Coast	4d6

Roll the dice to determine the nature of the encounter on the Ghost Holm Encounters table below. Encounters marked with an asterisk are described after the table.

Result	Encounter
1	1d2 will-o'-wisps
2-4	Animated armor*
5-11	No encounter
12-15	Spotted by orcs*
16-18	Orc patrol*
19-24	No encounter

Animated Armor. Fifteen years ago, Ghost Holm and Jando's Peak, in particular, were the staging ground for northern warships during the Attack of Regrets. Knowing the strategic importance of Jando's Peak and the island, an armada of warships from Odonburg landed on the west coast. They magocrats had their fair share of humanoid soldiers, but their elite ranks were filled by suits of animated armor. Outside of the explosion that destroyed the Bridge of Dreams, the Odonburg incursion was mostly a failure. The mages escaped, leaving behind dozens of mindless automatons. Now, the animated suits of armor wander the western end of the island looking for their masters. When they are unable to find their masters, the default to their next course of action: attack. There is usually no more than a single suit of **animated armor** encountered at a time. And they are varied states of disrepair and malfunction. Before the encounter begins, roll on the Animated Armor Malfunction table below to determine what special circumstances there are. On a result of "No malfunction," the animated armor operates as normal, attacking any creature it finds.

Animated Armor Malfunction

d6	Malfunction
1-3	No malfunction.
4	The armor is heavily rusted. It acts as if under the effects of a slow spell. Its CR is 1/2.
5	The armor is missing its lower half. It is considered prone and its movement is 5 ft (as it crawls). Its CR is 1/2.
6	The armor has gone berzerk. It has advantage on all of its attack rolls and attacks made it against are with advantage. Also, it can use its bonus action to take the Dash action on each of its turns. Its CR is 2.

Orc Patrol. A group of 1d4 orcs with 1 wolf patrol the area, looking for trespassers. Being creatures with darkvision, they don't use light, so unless the characters are moving at a slow pace, it's unlikely that they will notice the orc patrol until it's right upon them. Patrolling orcs have been ordered by Mega to rush to the nearest post (see Spotted by Orcs below) and raise the alarm. Otherwise, the characters have a chance to hide until the patrol passes.

Spotted by Orcs. At regular intervals, especially on the coast and through the mountain passes, the orcs have built lookout posts o 20-foot high watchtowers. There are two orcs per post. If the characters are traveling at a slow pace, there is a chance that the characters may spot the orcs before the orcs spot them. If the characters have a higher passive Perception check than the orcs (the orcs have a 10 for Passive Perception), they can see the orc before they are spotted and have 1 round to react. Otherwise, the orcs spot them first. On the spotter orc's turn, it rings a bell attached to its tower. The bell can be heard for a mile. From there, alarms raise throughout the entire island eventually reaching Mega and the rest of Jando's Spire.

Keyed Encounters
There are four notable locations on the island, their positions marked on the map of The Ghost Holm on page 4.

1 - Landing
Unless the characters wish to specifically do otherwise, the characters land in this hex on the western end of the island. The western coast is unpatrolled, so the characters can safely leave the rowboat onshore.

2 - The Gorgon
While it may be one of the most dangerous spots on the island, the Wisp Swamp is virtually free of orc patrols and spotters. However, the signs of war are still here. When the characters arrive at the edge of the mire, read the following:

> For the last ten minutes you've been traveling, the ground has grown increasingly muddier and wet. Soon, you're surrounded by a gray swamp. After traveling a few hundred feet, the willows part, revealing quite the sight: a ship of some sort, likely a magic-powered airship, in ruins. Time and the salt weather have not been kind to the ship. Its balloon lies in tatters among the trees. The hull is split open like a ripe cantaloupe, the swamp's waters filling its innards. Painted across the stern is the ship's name: The Gorgon. If there was anything worth discovering among the wreckage, it will be impossible to find it.

The Gorgon's job was to offload animated suits of armor onto the island. Before it could find a safe spot to land, its balloon was hit by a fireball. The ship crashed into the swamp, killing almost all of its crew. Meanwhile, the animated suits of armor sunk to the watery depths of the Wisp Swamp.

As the characters approach the Gorgon, 4 **animated suits of armor** rise from the mire. They're heavily rusted from years of sitting at the bottom of the marsh. Treat them as if they are all under the effects of a *slow* spell. Their CR is 1/2.

3 - Stratego Pass
What was once a goat path now acts as an important trail for the Odzedoz. When the characters enter this hex, read or paraphrase the following:

> Sixty feet ahead of you, you see what looks like two thirty-foot- tall watchtowers bookending a narrow passage through the crags. Atop each of the watchtowers are two orcs. A ship's bell has been hung on a pole at the center of the watchtower.
> Clearly, it's an alarm system set up by the orcs.

Here, the characters are faced with a tough decision. They can fight the four **orcs**, or they can go around it. Going around the pass adds an extra hour of travel time to their quest. This could make or break the mission as time is running out.

If one orc is taken out, chances are that the second orc in the roost will notice and raise the alarm. If both orcs in one watchtower are taken out, the two orcs in the companion tower will notice the others' absence at the end of their next turn. Once the alarm is sounded, there's no going back.

Should the characters best the orcs, they can travel through the pass. The pass makes traveling through the mountains easier—it's no longer difficult terrain. However, the chance for an encounter increases. While the characters travel through the pass, roll once every thirty minutes for a random encounter instead of every hour.

4 - Jando's Spire
Jando's Spire is detailed in the next section.

Jando's Spire

Jando's Spire was once a community of sailors, traders, and smugglers. Its strategic location and fog-swept spires made it the perfect spot for warships to mount offensives. During the Attack of Regrets, northern warships used the Spire as their base of operations. The bridge that once connected the Spire to the rest of the Ghost Holm, the Bridge of Dreams, was destroyed by Odonburgian warblimps. The remains of the homes and businesses that covered its flat top now lie at the bottom of the bay in the channel.

The characters are sure to arrive in Jando's Spire in one of two spots, either the southern coast (**Area 1**) or the northern cliffside (**Area 2**). Regardless, read the following:

> The trees break, revealing a clearing. Lit by the dim light of pale Ricoanus and crimson Yuduyama, you can that 100-feet in front of you the clearing ends with a sheer drop overlooking the crashing waves below. 200-feet from the cliff face you see

it: Jando's Spire. While this side remains encased in darkness, the Spire has a few torchlights throughout the ruined buildings that were once home to the citizens of Jando's Spire fifteen years ago. The biggest point of interest on the Spire is the large castle at the far eastern edge.

There are Odzedoz orcs everywhere.

The Spire itself is 200 feet above sea-level. It's climbable, certainly, but the easiest way into the Spire is through a set of caves in its southern base. The only trouble is, that's how the Odzedoz enter the spire as well.

No matter what the characters do, they will have to sneak to the spire, find a way to its top, then make their way to the crumbling castle where Nadia is held.

Travel Through Jando's Spire
Using the map on page 29, the characters can move 6 hexes per minute if they move at a normal pace. They can choose to move stealthily at 4 hexes per minute, or they can move quickly and suffer a -5 penalty to their passive Wis-

JANDO'S SPIRE

1 HEX = 50 FEET

SIDE VIEW

dom (Perception) checks. See chapter 8 of the *PHB* for details on travel pace.

Getting Spotted
Every minute that the characters travel through Jando's Spire, roll a d20.

- If the characters are moving at a **normal** pace, they are spotted on a result of 17-20.
- If the characters are moving at a **slow** pace, they are spotted on a result of 20.

- If the characters are moving at a **fast** pace, they are spotted on a result of 13-20.

  When spotted, the orcs raise the alarm (see below). Then, 1d4 + 1 orcs arrive in 1d4 rounds.

Climbing Down the Western Cliff

The biggest challenge the characters will face is climbing down the cliff to the water below without being noticed.

With a rope, the characters can rappel down the western cliff to the tumultuous water below the Spire at a rate of 30 feet per round.

If the characters move at a slower rate of 20 feet per round, they descend using Stealth, using the cliff's rocks to hide.

The characters can also move at a rate of 40 feet per round, quickly rappelling down the cliff face. This makes the group easier to spot. They are spotted on a roll of 10 or higher.

Climbing Up the Spire

If the characters forego the Pirate Caves, they will need to climb the spire. Of course, climbing the Spire is a lot more difficult than rappelling down the western cliff. There are no ropes and the cliffs have been worn smooth by the winds and waves of the might Omerian Ocean. Each round that a character climbs up the Spire, they must make a DC 15 Strength (Athletics) check. If they fail their check, they make no progress. And if they fail their check by 5 or more, they fall, landing in the rough ocean waters below, taking 2 (1d4) falling damage for every 10 feet they fall. From there, they will need to make a DC 13 Strength saving throw. Failing that, they are pushed 100 feet out to sea by the riptide.

High Alert

If the island is on high alert (from the character's being spotted and the bells sounding) all checks to spot the characters are made with advantage. Plus, it's unlikely that any of the orcs standing guard around the Spire and the western cliff will be surprised. Still, be sure to reward player ingenuity.

Keyed Encounters

The following locations are keyed to the map of Jando's Spire on the page 29.

1- Southside

A collection of abandoned residential homes looks over the nearby cliff. Anything of value that these buildings once had have long since been looted by the Odzedoz. There are two orcs standing guard on this end of the cliff.

2 - Northside

An old manor building sits atop a hill overlooking Jando's Peak. It was once the home of a powerful Jandorian smuggler. Now, it acts as a barracks for the Odzedoz orcs. There are two **orcs** outside, and three more **orcs** inside. The rest of the orcs that would normally be sleeping here are making preparations for the exchange in the morning.

3 - Collapsed Bridge Channel

Once the characters are in the water at the bottom of the cliff, they can hide in the water. The water here is extremely rough, made worse by the ruins and rocks. Each round that a character moves through the water without some sort of support, they will need to make a DC 13 Strength (Athletics) check each turn to swim against the powerful riptide. If the character sidles along the rooftops of the houses and debris of the collapsed bridge, they can make the check with advantage. Failure results in them being pushed 100 feet out to sea, and if they fail the check by 5 or more, they're pulled under and begin to

suffocate. On their next turn, they can make another DC 13 Strength (Athletics) check to resurface.

4 - Pirate Caves

The Spire's old smuggler caves are still very much intact and in regular operation. Refer to the Pirate Caves section below for details.

5 - The Quackling Lute Tavern

Should the characters make it through the pirate caves, they will emerge through an old secret entrance in the basement of the Quackling Lute Tavern. The orcs have maintained the Tavern and kept it in relatively good shape. Guarding the exit from the Pirate's Caves below are two **orcs**.

6 - Jando's Spire Proper

Much of the old town lies in ruin, although there are a few lanterns hit here and there lighting the way to the Griffinwatch Ruins at the eastern end of the Spire (**Area 7**). If the characters should get distracted from their mission and decide to search the buildings, there's a 5% chance that they find something of value in each of the old homes or businesses. Refer to the *DMG*'s individual treasure charts (0-4) for details on what they find.

If Mergigoth is traveling with the characters, he can surpass all of the guards here—there's no need to roll for being spotted.

7 - Griffinwatch Ruins

Once a mighty fortress at the eastern edge of Jando's Spire, this keep is now the center of operations for the Odzedoz orc clan. It is detailed further in the Griffinwatch Ruins section below.

The Pirate Caves

Originally a loading zone for the smugglers who called the Spire home, now, these old caves are used as the main access point into the Spire. If the characters can't or won't climb the Spire, they must go through these caves. This will be a bit like running the gauntlet as a heavy concentration of Odzedoz orcs are working here.

General Features

Unless otherwise stated, the Pirate Caves have the following general features.

Ceilings. Within the man-made chambers and corridors, the ceilings are 10-feet high and made of hewn stone braced with wooden timbers.

Doors. The doors are wooden doors braced with iron and hung on iron hinges. Most have staining from salt deposits.

Floors. Within the complex, the floors are hewn stone with overlaid limestone tile. Many of the tiles are cracked.

Lights. Lit torches are hung all throughout the caves. Even so, there are still plenty of shadowy recesses.

Sound. Noises and voices travel far in the cave, echoes bouncing off walls. Any orc that yells out will instantly be heard by all other orcs in the complex.

Walls. The walls in the man-made complex are brick and masonry.

Keyed Locations

The following areas reference the Pirate Caves map on page 32.

1a - North Tunnel Entrance

It's assumed that characters entering this way do so by swimming across the Collapsed Bridge and the turbulent channel between the Spire and the western cliffs. If this is the case, read the following:

> Just a few feet ahead, a 40 foot-tall, 15-foot wide opening in the face of the spire stands before you, the ocean water lapping into it. Torch lights flicker within the cave. Even over the waves, you can hear the guttural speech of orcs.

Anyone who understands Orcish hears a pair of orcs discussing the sun-

set ransom exchange. A few jokes are made regarding the "condition" for the girl after she's handed off.

Of the two ways to enter, this is the most difficult, as there are two lookouts posted by a campfire roughly 70 feet from the entrance (**Area 2b**), then another on the cliff just above them (**Area 5b**).

The tunnel itself is only large enough to fit rowboats and the smaller karvis used by the Odzeboz.

1b - South Tunnel Entrance

Although more turbulent, the southern entrance in the pirate cave is a safer bet for entering unseen by the Odzeboz. If the characters enter by swimming through the Collapsed Bridge channel, read the following:

> Just a few feet ahead of you you see a wide, flat opening in the eastern face of the spider. It seems that it opens into a large, torch-lit cave in the underside of the spire. A small bay inside the cave hosts two tethtered Odzeboz karvis, their Crushing Wave flags flying high.

It's hard to hear anything over the crashing waves from this point in the cave. Furthermore, the current pushes against any who try to enter the cave this way. If the characters wish to swim into **Area 2a** from this entrance, they each must succeed on a DC 15 Strength (Athletics) check. Failure

results in them being pushed back out into the Collapsed Bridge channel and failing by 5 or more means that they are pushed 100 feet from the Spire into the dark waters of the Omerian Ocean.

2a - Cave Harbor

Torches keep most of the area well-lit except for the southern portion of the cave, just beyond the karvis. Read:

> The cave's small harbor is approximately 50 feet by 70 feet. Two Odzeboz karvi longships are tethered to a narrow dock at the center of the cave and a rowboat with supplies—likely ill-gotten gains—is tethered to another dock against the southern wall. A wooden-door connects the southern dock to a man-made complex. At the east end of the cave is a sandy beach with another, long dock. The beach is approximately 30 feet deep before it hits the naturally hewn stone wall of the cave.
>
> There is a mined tunnel at the center of the eastern cave wall. In the northern cave wall, there is a 10-foot-wide by 10-foot high hole that overlooks the entire area.

The water in the harbor is 10-feet-deep at its deepest point. A half-blind **giant octopus** nicknamed Wobbly by the orcs lives in the water. While wobbly doesn't particularly enjoy the taste of humanoid flesh, any creature that swims through his lair is likely to disturb him enough for him to see what's going on. Once he discovers that it's a humanoid—especially if it's a humanoid that's attacking—he'll retreat to a narrow pocket at the bottom of the lake. Still, the surprise should be enough to make a character yelp, thus drawing the attention of the orcs.

If the characters enter through the southern tunnel (**Area 1b**), they will be able to use the parked karvis as cover as they move through the water. Plus, the shadows against the southern wall make it easy for them to get onto

THE PIRATE CAVES

1 SQUARE = 5 FEET

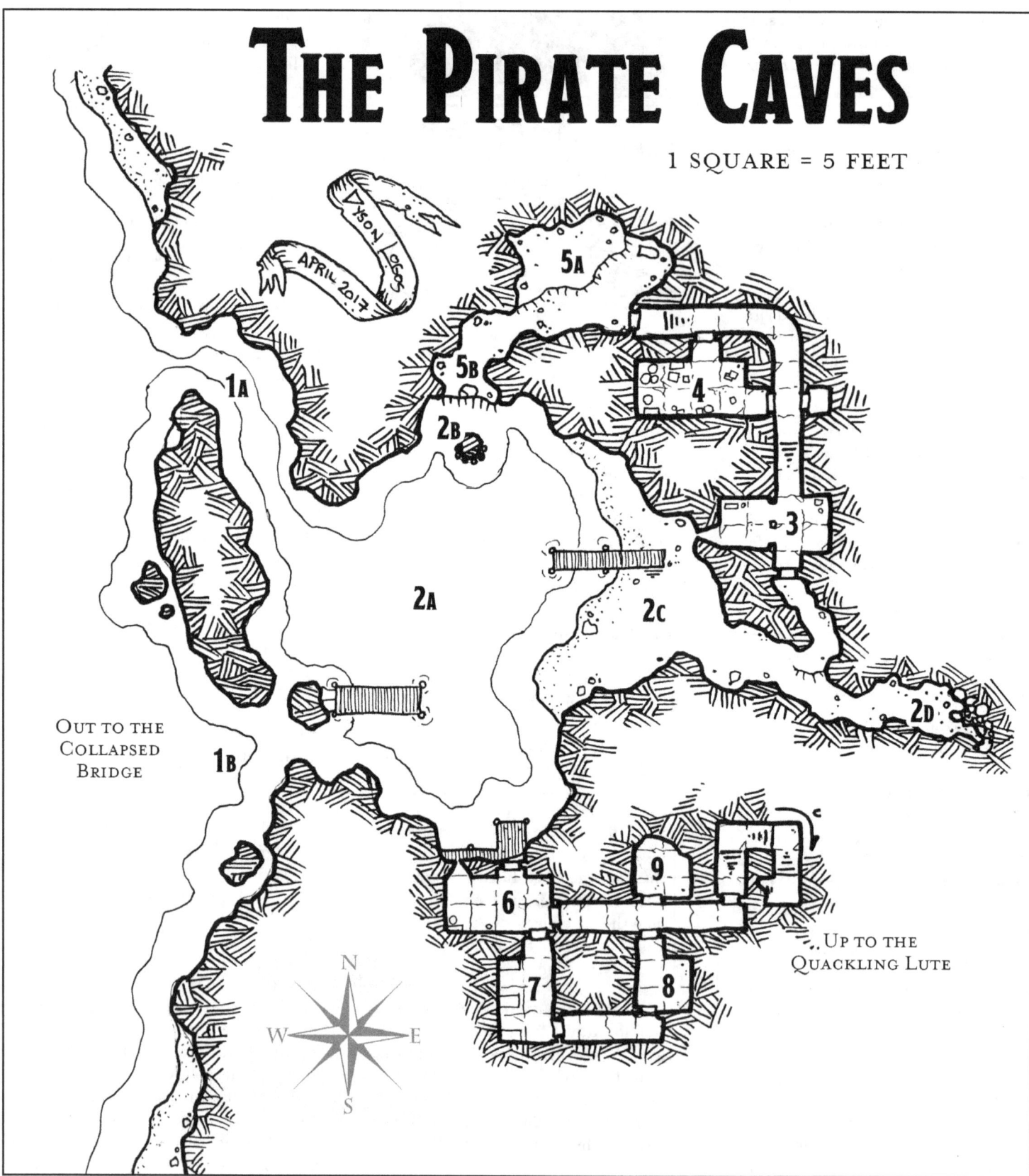

DYSON LOGOS

APRIL 2017

5A

5B

1A

2B

2A

4

3

2C

2D

OUT TO THE
COLLAPSED
BRIDGE

1B

6

9

UP TO THE
QUACKLING LUTE

7

8

N
W E
S

the dock and move through the door leading to **Area 6**. A single orc guard watches from the arrow port in Area 6. She is the only complication that the characters will face.

2b - Campfire

A pair of orc guards tend to a campfire at the northern part of the shore. With lookouts to the north and south, they spend most of their time chatting. Occasionally, Mergigoth from Area 5a steps to the ledge to chastise and remind the pair to keep watch.

Anything that happens in this area is likely to be noticed by the orc guard in **Area 5b**.

2c - Harbor Beach

The beach at the eastern edge of the cave is free of guards, however, it is well lit. It's nearly impossible for the characters to come onto the beach without being noticed by the orcs in **Area 2b, 2c**, or the arrow slit at **Area 6**.

If the characters haven't met Brìl yet, they can hear her crying from the beach.

2d- Brìl

If the characters haven't encountered Brìl yet, read the following:

> This rough-hewn tunnel is barely 5-feet wide and 5-feet tall. Fifteen feet in, another tunnel branches off to the north. From there, the torch lights end and there is only darkness beyond. From within the darkness, you think that you can hear someone crying, pleading in an unusual language.

The language is Sylvan. Brìl, a **selkie** (see Appendix B), is chained to the wall of the end of the tunnel. She begs the orcs to free her, promising she won't tell anyone who captured her. The orcs captured her a week ago as she was swimming through their harbor looking for fish. Amused by her transformative nature, the orcs have kept her chained

in the cave. They feed her fish heads and command her to sing with false promises of emancipation.

Brìl is friendly but somewhat child-like and naive. Upon meeting the characters, she promises them great rewards, telling them that her father is a "powerful and just king of the sea" (although this isn't true, Brìl believes that it's true).

Brìl isn't much of a fighter, nor does she wish to stay in the cave any longer than she needs to, so it's unlikely she'll join the party. If freed, she immediately makes for the harbor and leaps into the water, immediately transforming into a seal. From there, she swims away.

3 - Empty Room

> This room is 20-feet wide east-to-west and 10-feet wide north to south. There are two exits from the room. In the center of the north wall, a corridor leads to a flight of stairs. At the south is an exit blocked by a wooden door. Other than a few bits of jetsam, the room appears to be empty.

4 - Mergigoth's "Office"

Whether the characters raise the alarm or not, read the following description when they enter this room:

> This room is roughly 20-feet wide east-to-west and 10-feet wide north-to-south. There are two exits, one to the north and one to the east, both blocked by wooden doors. A cluttered mess of barrels, chests, random furniture, and other oddities fill nearly every inch of the room. In the north-west corner, an obese orc sits on top of a table peeling a potato. "So you are here to save the girl," he says to you in Common, in a tone that sounds like he's been expecting you.

Mergigoth was once one of Mega's captains. Mega saw Mergigoth as too ambitious and decided to demote him. Mergigoth was no longer allowed to sail with the rest of the Odzedoz fleet, and would instead watch over the pirate caves. With a well-developed taste for pillaging, Mergigoth saw this as a grave insult—possibly worse than death. He's been waiting for the perfect opportunity to get back at Mega and take over the Odzedoz.

Mergigoth introduces himself. He's a typical **orc**, however, like Mega, Mergigoth is a little smarter than other orcs of the Odzedoz (he has an Intelligence score of 11). Without deceit, he explains his situation to the characters. He mentions that he can get them to Mega and Nadia Mansouri without drawing attention to themselves, but will only do so if they promise to kill Mega no matter what.

In the storage room that Mergigoth calls his "office", there are three chests filled with Odzedoz clothing and armor, as well as the black, curved great axes the orcish pirates are famous for carrying. Here is Mergigoth's plan: Under the cover of darkness, Mergigoth can escort the characters dressed as orcs through the Quackling Lute upstairs, through the orc- laden Jando's Spire Proper, and into Griffinwatch ruins. From there, Mergigoth will lead the characters directly to Mega and Nadia.

If the characters agree, Mergigoth lets them get dressed. He then does exactly as he stated. Mergigoth can easily get past all of his subordinates, introducing the disguised characters as recruits from the other end of the island who claim they spotted something. "They saw adventurers on the island," he repeats. "We're headed straight for Mega to report."

Mergigoth can get past every sentry until he reaches the vultures (see **Area 2c** in Griffinwatch Ruins).

5a - Rubbish Cave

> This dark, natural cave is roughly 20-feet by 20-feet. There are two exits. The first is a natural tunnel that leads into a well-lit cavern to the southwest. The second is set into the eastern wall and blocked by a wooden door. There is litter everywhere.

5b - North Lookout Point

A lone orc stands in this chamber looking out over the underground harbor. The orc is armed with a light crossbow. It is a 20-foot sheer drop from the southern edge of the chamber to the beach below (**Area 2b**).

6 - South Lookout Point

> This room is 20-feet wide east-to-west and 10-feet deep north to south. There are three doors out of the room, one in the north wall, one in the east wall, and one in the south wall.

A single orc sits on a stool looking through an arrow slit that faces the underground harbor. He's armed with a light crossbow.

7 - Barracks

> This room is 15-feet wide north-to-south and 10-feet wide east to west. There is a door to the north and one to the south. Four unmade bunks take up the majority of the room.

Normally, there would be sleeping orcs here. With the Spire making preparations for the ransom drop, it's all hands on deck, so these barracks are empty.

Treasure. If the characters spend at least a minute tossing the room, they find 2d12 sp among the orcs' possessions.

8 - Lounge

This room is 10-feet by 10-feet with exits to the north and south. There is a table with stones bearing strange runes at the center of the table. It smells strongly of rotten meat and spilled beer here.

The runes are part of a popular orcish game called Krighurgradh. The gaming set is worth 5 sp.

9 - Spoils Room

This room is locked. A character can make a successful DC 12 Dexterity check using proficiency in lockpicking tools to pick the lock, or it can be broken down with a successful DC 15 Strength check. The latter will undoubtedly draw the attention of any living orcs within earshot. Mergigoth (see Area 4) has a key to the area. However, he will dismiss it as nothing more than a storage room, hardly worth looking in.

> This small 10-foot by 10-foot square room holds barrels, crates, and chests filled with goods. They all seem to be in good shape and all seem to bear the symbols and crests of different Weysevaini cities and townships.

The trade goods weight approximately 700 lbs. If turned into Castlegrapsian authorities, the characters will earn a 10 gp reward. Otherwise, the goods are worth 100 gp in the open market and will take at least a week of downtime to offload (with a heavy chance of complication, no less).

Griffinwatch Ruins

Once a powerful fortress at the eastern end of Jando's Spire, this old castle now sits in ruins, its walls and rooves toppled by the Odonburg magic during the Attack of Regrets. Mega has claimed the main meeting hall as his audience chamber and throne room. It's there he keeps Nadia Mansouri.

General Features

Unless otherwise stated in an area's description, the ruins have the following features.

Ceilings. In the few rooms that still have rooves, the ceilings are made of wooden slats braced with timbers. For the parapets, rooves, and towers, stone tiles are laid over the top of the wooden slats, providing an additional layer of support.

Floors. Within the keep itself, the floors are made of laid stone tiles. The courtyard was once paved, but time and heavy use have worn away most of the tiles, revealing the dirt and stone of the Spire. Aggressive shrubs and vines grow over everything.

Light. There are a few torches lit through the keep, but most of the light comes from a massive bonfire at the center of the courtyard area 2a.

Walls. The walls that still stand are made of heavy limestone blocks and set into place with mortar. The castle's outer walls are 3-feet-thick, and the inner walls are 1 1/2-feet thick.

Vines and moss grow over everything. Because of the age and weather to the outer wall, they are easier to climb than the Spire itself. A character lacking a grappling hook needs only a DC 12 Strength (Athletics) check to climb. Just as before, a failure results in no forward progress, and failure by 5 or more results in the character falling.

Wind. The keep sits at the top of a hill on the eastern edge of the Spire, overlooking crashing waves 200-feet below. Wind pushing through the ruins sometimes makes an eerie, low- pitched whistling sound.

Keyed Encounters

The following area descriptions are keyed to the map of the Griffinwatch Ruins on page 36.

1 - Entrance

> The massive keep looms overhead. Walking up the steep path to where the fortress's front gate once stood, you see that much of the north side of the keep remains intact whereas the southern side is mostly destroyed. It's dark outside the keep, but through the rubble of the destroyed southern gate tower, you see a massive bonfire blazing in the courtyard.

Two **orc** guards stand outside the gate and a third keeps a post in the still-standing northern gate tower. All three are armed with light crossbows. If the characters are traveling with Mergigoth, he informs them both that they are to report sightings of adventurers directly to Mega.

2a - Western Courtyard

> A massive bonfire at the center of this 45-foot by 35-foot courtyard illuminates everything. The area where the keep's gate once stood is at the western end of the courtyard. To the south, much of the keep's outer wall

> has collapsed down the south side of the keep's motte, leaving only boulders and debris. At the north are a collection of buildins, some destroyed, other inact. To the east stands the impressive keep itself. While the forty-foot high keep's walls western side remains intact, it's clear that the front of the keep has taken considerable damage. It appears that the entry to the keep itself is through another gate to the east of the bonfire. Unlike the gate to the east, both of the gate towers by the western gate are still standing, as is much of the outer wall there.

Four **orcs** wander around the courtyard. The light of the huge bonfire makes it easy to spot any trespassers sneaking into the courtyard.

Two more orc guards are posted in the watchtowers by the inner gate (**Areas 5a** and **5b**).

If the vultures are still in their roost (see **Area 2c**), they can smell the characters from the courtyard, recognizing that they aren't orcs, especially if Cheeko is among them (see *Chapter 1* for details on Cheeko).

If Mergigoth is with the characters and they are outed— either through actions of their own or by one of the vultures— he immediately turns on the characters and reveals their presence, knowing that he'd rather give them up than face the axes of his brothers and

sisters (nevermind the fact that he led them to the keep in the first place).

2b - Inner Gate

There are no guards standing outside the inner gate, however, two orc guards armed with light crossbows watch from the two gate towers (**Areas 5a** and **5b**). The large door that divides the courtyards is unlocked and unbarred, but makes an incredibly loud noise when opened. While many of the orcs are used to it, the orcs in **Areas 5a** and **5b** will immediately take notice if it opens.

2c - Vulture Roost

Three **giant vultures** fight over the carcass of a seal. If Cheeko survived during the Storm of Mega and interacted with the characters, the moment the characters step into the courtyard he smells them—even if they're disguised. Cheeko flutters into the courtyard to find the characters. Although Cheeko can't form complete sentences, he can utter a few orcish words such as the words for human, elf, and hero.

Cheeko wastes no time to reveal the presence of the characters and attack. He seeks revenge against any character who dealt damage to him. Cheeko will try to grab one of the characters then fly over the keep and deposit them in the ocean. A character that Cheeko drops over the ocean must make a DC 10 Dexterity saving throw. On a failed saving throw, the character falls 200 feet into the ocean, taking 50 (20d4) damage from the fall. On a successful saving throw, the character grabs a hold of Cheeko's legs, preventing the bird from dropping them again.

2d - Kitchen Ruins

This was once the Keep's old kitchen. It's one of the few sections of the western courtyard that isn't bathed in light from the bonfire. If the characters make it to this section of the courtyard and successfully hide, they can use their action to watch the movements of the orcs in the courtyard from the van-

GRIFFINWATCH RUINS

1 SQUARE = 5 FEET

tage point. If they do, the next check they make to move stealthily is made with advantage.

3 - Dining Hall

This room is roughly 20-feet by 20-feet. Two large, oaken tables with multiple benches take up the majority of the chamber's center. There are three exits. In the center of the eastern wall is a wooden door. Direct-

ly opposite of the door is an archway that exits into a collapsed building that looks like it may have once been a kitchen. Finally, part of the southern wall is destroyed, giving you a clear view of a large courtyard beyond. At the center of the courtyard is a huge bonfire.

A pair of nude, drunken **orcs** snore under one of the benches, their armor and gear scattered haphazardly around

the room. Nothing short of an explosion will wake the couple from their post-co-ital slumber (blech!).

4 - Eastern Courtyard

Only the light of the twin moons light this 40-foot by 30-foot court-yard. Most of the keep's old wall is still intact save for a large hole in the southwestern corner that overlooks the ruined rooftops of buildings south of the motte. There is an exit to the west—a door flanked by two 30-foot tall towers. At the north side of this courtyard, the keep looms over the rest of the fortress. There is a lowered portcullis that blocks entry into the keep, however, that doesn't matter. The keep's northeastern tower is a crumbled mess, exposing the illuminated interior within.

There are no guards in this courtyard as the guards in **Areas 5a, b,** and **c** are more concerned with attacks from outside. The portcullis hasn't worked in years. Mega and his orcs enter Griffinwatch through the collapsed southeastern tower. They pass through the northernmost point—a character who makes a successful DC 10 Intelligence (Investigation) check that there are no footprints that lead through the rubble at the southern edge of the ruined tower.

Trap. Any creature who walks through the southern part triggers an explosive device hidden against the keep's southern wall. Any creature standing in the area where the tower once stood must make a DC 12 Dexterity saving throw. A target takes 10 (3d6) fire damage on a failed saving throw or half as much damage on a successful one. The explosion causes a thunderous boom audible out to 300 feet.

5a - Southern Guard Post

A lone orc stands in this tower. Its attention is on the southwestern portion of Jando's Spire and anyone who passes through the inner gate (**Area 2b**). The orc is armed with a light crossbow.

5b - Inner Guard Post

A lone **orc** stands in this tower. Its attention is on the courtyard beyond. There is a winch inside this post that used to operate the portcullis to the keep; it's broken. The orc is armed with a light crossbow.

5c - Southwestern Guard Post

A lone **orc** stands in this tower. It stares out at sea through a spyglass built onto a bolted-down turnstile in the center of the room. The spyglass, if removed, is worth 1,000 gold pieces.

Despite knowing its value, Mega felt it was more valuable doing what it was made to do.

6 - Griffinwatch Keep

If the characters enter the keep stealthily, read the following:

> As you sneak into the keep, you see a trio of long shadows on the wall cast by a pair of creatures just out of sight. The two are having a conversation. The largest creature—from the sounds of it, an orc—says to one, "Tomorrow, we will hand you over for the ransom. Get your rest tonight. You'll need it." The second voice—likely a human female—replies, "Yes, I understand."

After the characters hear this, or if they were not able to sneak into the keep, read the following:

> The huge chamber before you is 40-feet deep north-to-south and 35-feet wide east-to-west. The ceilings are 40-feet high and mostly intact. A wooden throne sits near the northern wall. Behind it, hung with nails, is a flag depicting a white wave overcoming a human skull on a black field. The first is a tall orc with a white mohawk.

At the center of the room, lit by a single torch hung on a partition 5-feet from the easternmost wall, stand three figures. The centralmost figure is a large orc. He wears a long, blue coat like that of a sea captain and two wicked-looking black handaxes on each hip.

Two human women flank either side of him. Both look exhausted and downtrodden, wearing matching dull gray clothes. What's most interesting about the women, however, is that they appear to be identical twins. Both have the same dark hair, same brown eyes, same olive complexion that match the description of Nadia Mansouri.

The orc, of course, is **Mega** (see Mega's stats in *Chapter 1*). The woman to his right is Nadia Mansouri (NG female Ditimayan human **noble**) and the woman to his left is a **doppelganger** named Vista that has assumed Nadia's appearance. Using its detect thoughts ability, the shapeshifter is a near-perfect copy of the noblewoman, going so far as to mimic her exhaustion and traumatic stress.

If the characters sneak into the room without Mega or the doppelganger noticing them, they witness Faux-Nadia grab the real Nadia by the arm and pull her towards a closet in the northwestern corner. Nadia meekly pleads as the doppelganger shoves her inside, shuts, and locks the door.

From there, it should be obvious she's an imposter.

Otherwise, if the characters are noticed by Mega or the doppelganger, this is how the scene plays out:

> "By the Gods!" gasps the woman to the right of the orc. While the orc and the other woman seem surprised by your appearance, she starts sobbing and runs towards you.

At this point, the characters will need to roll for initiative to decide what to do. On her turn, the real Nadia will use her action to run to the characters for assistance. Mega, thinking quickly, grabs the fake Nadia and puts the blade of one of his axes to her neck.

> "You shifty doppelganger!" the large orc yells at the woman who ran to you. "How dare you try to save your own neck!" He then turns to you, "This is the real girl, fools. That one is a doppelganger trying to con its way out. One false move and I'll slash the real girl's throat."

Mega's goal is to make the characters think that the Nadia that ran to them is the fake Nadia and not the real deal. Of course, the real Nadia immediately protests as the fake-Nadia pleads to the characters as Mega's hand axe comes dangerously close to her/its neck.

The orc chief hopes that during the confusion, he can use Faux-Nadia to escape. While he wants to possess the real Nadia, he isn't willing to lose his life for the girl. There are other philologists in the world. The doppelganger, Vista, continues to play its role as Nadia, going along with Mega's escape plan. Mega hopes to find the quickest way out of the situation, either by finding a large group of orcs to distract the characters, a giant vulture he can mount, or even his ship. Worst case scenario, he'll leap from the spire into the ocean below. His coat is a seafarer's jacket which might help him survive the fall (at your discretion). You can learn more about the seafarer's jacket on the Griffin's Saddlebag (**https://www.patreon.com/posts/seafarers-jacket-24836707**).

If all else fails, Mega and the doppelganger will fight their way out of the situation. Both have a keen sense of self-preservation and would rather flee than die at the hands of a group of adventurers. Mega isn't above surrendering himself to the authorities, either, especially if the real Nadia survives.

Adventure Conclusion

There are a lot plot threads potentially open at the adventure's conclusion. Here are a few outcomes to consider:

- It's possible that Mega and the doppelganger's deception paid off and the characters killed the true Nadia. The doppelganger, seeing a fortunate opportunity, continues its ruse and "rejoins" Baariq Mansouri in Castlegrasp as the nobleman's daughter.
- Mega may surrender himself to the Castlegraspians. If he does, he's interred in the Castlegraspian dungeon. Having escaped prisons before, Mega's hardly afraid of a city dungeon.
- There is a possibility that Mega started the adventure in possession of *Prime*. If this is the case, he played it smart. The day before the characters snuck into Jando's Spire, Mega entrusted the book with his first mate, Gluronk.
- Gluronk's instructions were clear: she was to camp on the northside of the island. If Mega didn't contact her twenty-four hours after the ransom drop, she was to take a boat from the island and head north to find Mega's old brother, Gradba.
- If Mergigoth is still alive at the adventure's conclusion, he assumes leadership of the Odzedoz. Knowing that the Castlegrapsians would never let the orcs remain in the area, Mergigoth and the Odzedoz evacuate up north up the Weysevain Coast to find a new home.
- Once the characters give the signal with the *wand of fireworks* (if they saved Nadia, that is... or whoever they think is Nadia), in four hours the Castlegraspian warship arrives at the Spire and starts pelting the ruins with its catapults and ballistas.
- In the rare case that Nadia survived and the characters are in possession of *Prime*, she's intrigued by the na-

ture of the book and hopes that she can study it (this is even more so the case if Nadia is actually Vista, who recognizes that the book must have quite a bit of value attached to it.)

The characters can leave the island the way they came, rejoining Onyxbrow. They can also find a place to wait and watch the Castlegraspian ship lay waste to Jando's Spire. Afterward, Mansouri sends a rowboat to retrieve the group.

Baariq is true to his word. He pays 800 gp for the rescue of his daughter and another 800 gp for the head of Mega. He then gives them an additional 200 gp for their discretion in the matter.

The adventure is continued in the next chapter of **Hand of the Eight, The Black Bird**.Ω

Discover new worlds.

Become a DMDave patron today and you'll receive over 170 PDFs, new campaign settings, player options, adventures, and more.

Get access to all of the adventures that appear in BroadSword monthly in full color PDFs.

Plus, subscribers at certain tiers get BroadSword Monthly PDF and physical coopies at no extra charge in addition to other types of swag.

SEE WHAT HUNDREDS OF PATRONS ARE TALKING ABOUT:

www.patreon.com/dmdave

CHAPTER 3: THE BLACK BIRD

BY DAVE HAMRICK

3rd-Level Adventure for Fifth Edition

Cartography by watabou.itch.io
Art by Luigi Castellani, David L. Johnson, Miguel Santos, Joyce Maureira

*Black Bird is a 3rd-level Fifth Edition adventure for 3-5 characters. Characters who survive the adventure should be two-thirds of the way to level 4 by the adventure's conclusion. This is the third chapter in the **Hand of Eight** adventure path. It can be played as the kickoff for the larger adventure setting or as a one-shot adventure for your characters to follow.*

The campaign is intended to be set in the DMDave crowdsourced campaign world of Omeria, but can just as easily be inserted into any other large city overlooking a large ocean or sea.

One of the most notorious criminals ever to be interred in Castlegrasp's dungeon has escaped, leaving almost no trace behind. A powerful, authoritarian noble has placed one of the largest bounties ever seen on the man's head: 20,000 gold pieces dead or alive. This incredible sum draws adventurers, rangers, and bounty hunters from all corners of Omeria. And the race is on. Of course, those who seek to collect the reward aren't the only ones hunting the escaped prisoner. A dark being known only as the Black Bird is also hunting the prisoner, but for a different reason. Rumors persist that the prisoner knows the whereabouts of a powerful tome of ancient evil and the Black Bird's masters wish to collect the book and destroy anyone who knows about it.

Background

Two weeks ago, the notorious criminal, Mega the Brash, leader of the Odzedoz pirates of the Ghost Holm, was arrested and interred in the dungeons of Castlegrasp. His crime? The abduction of Nadia Mansouri, daughter of an important Castlegraspian noble. If Mega is found guilty of the crime by Castlegrasp's jury, he will be turned to stone and placed in the city's Yard of Deterrents.

Of course, Mega always has a plan

in place. Two nights ago, one of the dungeon guards was murdered by a doppelganger on Mega's payroll. The doppelganger assumed the appearance of the guard, took his position at the jail, disabled the second guard, and freed Mega from his cell. The doppelganger gave Mega a *hat of disguise* which he used to assume the appearance of the second guard. With a *silent image* scroll, the doppelganger created the appearance that Mega and both of the guards were still in place. By the time the illusion ended, Mega had escaped the city through the eastern gate and the doppelganger assumed another role in the city.

Once the body of the first guard was discovered a day after Mega's escape, the authorities determined that a shapeshifter was at work. Baariq Mansouri, the noble whose daughter was kidnapped by Mega, immediately put out bounties on Mega and his associate. "Mega the Brash, Wanted by the Royal Jury of Castlegrasp. Alive or Dead, 20,000 gold pieces." Bounty hunters, rangers, and adventurers from all over central Omeria answered the call.

Inevitably, the characters learn of the bounty placed on Mega. One would assume that their having a history with the orc would give the characters an edge. Unfortunately, the competition is steep and the hunt has already begun.

The Black Bird

Bounty-seekers are the least of Mega's worries. A creature known only as "The Black Bird" seeks the orc as well. The Black Bird suspects that Mega knows the whereabouts of an unreadable ancient text called *Prime*. It is the Black Bird's mission to find Mega, learn what the orc knows about the book and its current location, then destroy him.

The Black Bird is a force of nature, leaving a trail of bodies in its wake. Likely, he will be the most dangerous

creature that the characters have faced so far in their journeys thus far.

But what if Mega is dead (or not in prison)?

This adventure assumes that Mega survived the first and second chapters of the *Hand of the Eight* adventure path and was taken into custody. However, it's possible that Mega died at some point in either adventure or escaped. If that's the case, don't worry: It's still possible to run this adventure.

First, if Mega died or escaped, replace the imprisoned orc with either his brother Xnath (detailed in Chapter 2) or, if Xnath died, too, substitute an appropriate associate. You can use Mergigoth, or another orc who was part of Mega's organization (such as the orc felled from its giant vulture in the Background of part 2).

If Mega survived and escaped, Mega arranged the escape of one of his associates, instead. Knowing that the escaped criminal will lead any who follows him/her to Mega, Baariq offers

the same bounty. The only difference is that the characters and NPCs tracking the escaped prisoner will follow them to where Mega is located.

If Mega died but the book was given to his first mate Gluronk, the escaped criminal knows where Gluronk and the book are and can lead the way.

In the rare instance that Mega has been dead since Chapter 1 and the characters have had *Prime* this entire time, the adventure can still play out the same way. However, The Black Bird wants to find the remaining members of the Odzedoz in order to learn what happened during their assault on Haver. It's from the orcs the Black Bird learns that the characters have the book. During the final battle with the Black Bird, the Black Bird focuses his efforts on the characters and the recovery of Prime instead of killing Mega.

Adventure Summary

The adventure starts when the characters are called to the coastal city of Castlegrasp by the noble, Baariq Mansouri. They are informed by Mansouri that Mega the Brash has escaped Castlegrasp's dungeon and is likely headed north towards Lost Dragon Pass. Unfortunately, Mansouri has no other clues for the characters to follow.

From there, the course that the remainder of the adventure takes relies heavily on the characters and the choices they make. While he's been careful, Mega has left numerous clues along the way. Craftier characters will be able to follow them to Mega's ultimate destination.

Through their travels, the characters encounter various bounty hunters, rangers, and other adventuring parties who seek the reward. They also cross paths with the mysterious and dangerous Black Bird who seeks the ancient book rumored to be in Mega's possession.

The climax of the adventure takes place at in the abandoned city of Qola as Mega atempts to escape on a Dinzer cargoblimp.

Adventure Hooks

If the characters partook in the first two chapters of this adventure, then they should have enough incentive to chase after Mega. Not to mention, a 20,000 gp reward is nothing to scoff at. If you are running this as a one-shot adventure, here are a few hooks you can employ to get your characters interested.

Massive Bounty

Easily the biggest motivator for the adventure is the sizable bounty placed on the head of Mega by Baariq Mansouri. While the characters won't have the same edge over the competition they would have had they worked for Mansouri in the past, it's still a reward that's worth pursuing.

Something Wicked

Rumors persist across the Weysevain Coast that an evil creature known as the "Black Bird" is on the trail of an orc who escaped the dungeon in Castlegrasp. As the creature moves up the coast, it leaves a trail of bodies in its wake. The characters are tasked to stop this creature before it can kill more humanoids.

Ancient Tome

The characters learn the real reason why so many are after the escaped orc, Mega: supposedly, he carries an unreadable book said to possess power that eclipses even the Redstone Dinzers of Odonburg. Although not much else is known about the book—not even its title is known—it's considered priceless by those who want it. Only trouble is, anyone who's been in the possession of the book has either died, gone insane, or been imprisoned.

The Wise Shirt

The adventure starts when the characters are relaxing at the Wise Shirt tavern and bar in the coastal village of Haver. Haver is a popular stopover point for southern Omerian sailors headed north. The bar is owned by an uptight and anxious elf named Aywin Luphine (LG male high elf **noble**). Fortunately, Luphine mostly stays out of the way, allowing his star bartender, Bezka Wells (LG female half-elf **noble**) to act as the face of the tavern. The food is hot, the drinks are stiff, and if the characters need, there's even a few beds in the rear. You can learn more about the Wise Shirt and Haver in Chapter 1 of this adventure path, ***Storm of Mega***.

Whatever reasons the characters have for being in The Wise Shirt, eventually a messenger from Castlegrasp arrives carrying a satchel full of posters. After a quick word with Luphine, the messenger pastes one of his posters on the wall.

Read the following description:

> You watch as the blue-and-purple-clad messenger pastes a huge poster on one of the walls of the tavern. Immediately, everyone stops what they are doing and stares at the poster. Even Bezka stops drying a freshly-washed mug for a moment to stare at the poster. "Suen's wrath," she gasps.
>
> There is an pen-and-ink drawing depicting a sour-faced orc with a white mohawk on the poster. Below the image, the poster reads:

(See below)

Wanted!

Mega the Brash, orc pirate and scourge of the Ghost Holm, for murder, theft, extortion, sabotage, kidnapping of a noble's daughter, and prisonbreak.

20,000 gold pieces. <u>Dead or alive</u>.

Seek Baariq Mansouri of Castlegrasp for details.

"20,000 gold pieces? That's the biggest bounty I've ever heard of!" comes a voice from the rear of the tavern. A bald-headed man with a horizontal scar on his brow stands and puts his finger between the eyes of the drawing of the orc.

"Guess I've just found my next job!" the bald man says, hiking up his sagging trousers over his comically round gut.

If the characters helped Baariq rescue his daughter (in Chapter 2. *Assault on the Ghost Holm*), then they should immediately recognize not just the name of the orc pirate, but also Mansouri. In fact, the messenger was tasked to find them once he passed through Haver.

"Excuse me?" asks the Castlegraspian messenger. "But Lord Mansouri asked me to specifically find you. He thanks you for helping him in the past and hopes that you are able to take this bounty on his behalf. If you are available, he hopes that you can meet him in Castlegrasp before the week is through."

Should the characters decide to take the bounty and Mansouri's offer, they must travel south to the city of Castlegrasp. It's two days' journey by horse or one day by sailing vessel. The characters can book passage on a sailing vessel for 10 gp each.

Castlegrasp

Castlegrasp, the City of Granite, is the last major city before the Desolation of Ditimaya and the Obsidian Plain divide the rest of Omeria from the southern end of the continent. Ruled by Khan Hayyan Harrak XI (known by his people as 'Fair Eleven'), Castlegrasp keeps the peace thanks to its strong military and strict, but just, laws.

Castlegrasp is home to some 12,000 humanoids, the majority of which are Ditimayan humans. Indestructible granite walls surround the whole of the city. The mighty Castlegraspian Stonearms (LG any race **knights**) protect the city and keep the peace while the legendary Castlegraspian Navy patrols the turbulent waters of the Bay of Suen and the Omerian Ocean.

Thanks to the Castlegraspian navy's watchful eye, southern merchants feel safe traveling along the Scorched Coast. And as the connecting point between southern and central Omeria, Castlegrasp is a major trade port. Goods from Odonburg, Qey, Yraka, and more touchdown in Castlegrasp.

There, the merchant houses pur-

chase and issue the goods caravans for journeys north along the Arrow Road. Castlegrasp itself exports the unusually durable granite from which it earns its nickname as well as plums, sheep, and of course, its famous wines.

Due largely to Fair Eleven's just and (some would argue) liberal attitude towards criminals, most of the crime that existed two decades prior has vanished from Castlegrasp. Still, it has its fair share of black hat organizations. The city's biggest criminal organization, the Crystal Toad handles black market trade and is rumored to have many of the city's nobles on their payroll. Meanwhile, the shadowy cadre of assassins known as the Owls earn heavy purses of gold as murderers-for-hire. In the Low Ward, a new devilkin crimelord named Light Beyond the Hills invokes terror among the ward's citizens.

Not only does Castlegrasp act as the starting point for the adventure, but it could also function as an exciting base of operations for characters adventuring in Central Omeria.

Arrival in Castlegrasp
When the characters arrive, read the following:

Castlegrasp, the City of Granite juts like a sand-colored fist at the edge of the Bay of Suen. The unbreachable forty-foot walls that surround the city wrap the city like the arms of a protective mother. At the center of the city on a great mound is the infamous Violet Qsar, the royal palace and home to the city's eleventh Khan, Hayyan Harrak. He's commonly known as "Fair Eleven." Castlegrasp's blue and violet banners flutter in the warm breeze escaping from the south where the haze of the Obsidian Plain lingers; a stern reminder of the city's original purpose.

Even before you even enter the city, you find yourself surrounded by foreign merchants hawking their wares along the road. A Dinzer seller offer rare, brightly colored birds and other strange critters in locked cages. Yrenkan fruit vendors pressure you with odd, yellow fruit shaped like crescent moons. You even come eye to eight-eyes with a mysterious krig; he deals in leatherwares—"studded leather from Orbea, very good, yes!" clicks the man-spider.

Also among the crowd, you see the legendary Stonearms, the royal templars of Castlegrasp. Most cover their faces with blue and violet keffiyehs or wear ivory masks carved to look like tigers. However, there is no mistaking the rocky limbs from which they derive their honorifics.

Another surprising feature of the city are the wild tigers that roam its streets. The great amber, black, and white cats seemingly pay no mind to the city's inhabitants. However, many of the Castlegraspians make sure to bow their heads in the presence of the city's most sacred animal. A girl, no older than seven, ties a bow made of flowers to one of the beast's tails—no protests comes from the feline.

Bariq Mansouri lives in the section of town known as Sweet Olive Ward (**Area 23** on the map). He has asked those who seek more information on Mega's bounty to seek his assistant, Tree by the Lake at a small shop at the north edge of the Dek Baazar (**Area 14**). While the sense of urgency should be high, the characters are free to spend time exploring the city. In addition to the locations mentioned on the map of Castlegrasp in the Important Locations section, there are many opportunities for adventures, sidequests, and random encounters. Some suggestions are detailed below.

Side Quests

Castlegrasp offers plenty of opportunities for the characters to encounter NPCs who may need help. Of course, the characters are under no obligation to do so, potentially getting sidetracked from their mission. However, these side quests may provide additional rewards, experience, and discoveries for the characters.

1 - Bounty Hunters with a Debt. One of the bounty hunters that's trying to collect on the Mega bounty has a few enemies in Castlegrasp. He or she thought they could enter the city and get the information without notice, but they were wrong. Eros Mulopoulos (NE male human Knotsider **thug**), a heavy working for the Crystal Toad, noticed the bounty hunter immediately. Not wanting to get the Crystal Toads' hands dirty, he hopes that he can contract the characters—who should look stick out like sore thumbs in Castlegrasp—to collect on the debt. If they collect the debt—1,000 gp—he'll pay them 10 percent of the take. The bounty hunter has been seen drinking at the Armed Lavender (**Area 5**). To determine the name, personality, and stats of the bounty hunter, refer to the Bounty Hunter section later in this adventure.

2 - Chase off Cockatrices. Two brothers, Sufyan and Ayoub (LG male Ditimayan human **commoners**) approach the characters while they are traveling in or near Castlegrasp. The pair own a fox farm just outside of town that they inherited from their mother who passed away last winter. If that wasn't enough to deal with, their foxes have been consistently attacked by cockatrices every night. Now, the brothers are worried they won't have enough foxes to earn a living selling their pelts. The Stonearms won't handle it as cockatrices are considered holy animals in Castlegrasp. The brothers can't offer much more than a warm meal and a space to sleep in their barn. If the characters agree to help, they must stake out the fox pens at the brothers' farm. Some point during the night, the cockatrices arrive. There are six in all. Killing one or two of the monstrosities is enough to permanently drive off the whole brood.

3 - Rescue One-of-Eight. While the characters are traveling through the northern section of the city, they discover a group of five young men beating an old, blind man in an alley. The young men are easy to run off (all N male Ditimayan human **commoners**). The man, who tells the characters his name is One-of-Eight, is a blind seer (NE male Ditimayan human **mage**) who works at the temple of Yrena (**Area 8**). He asks that the characters escort him back to the temple. Any character born in or near Castlegrasp or who passes a DC 10 Intelligence (Religion) check, immediately recognizes who the old man is and the controversies surrounding Yrena's temple. He has no money to pay the characters, but thanks them for their assistance.

4 - Stop a Thief. As the characters make their way through one of the city's many bazaars, they hear the unmistakable cry of "Stop! Thief!", from Jibbran (LG male Ditimayan human **commoner**), a dried meat vendor. Jibbran turned away from his stall for a moment and a thief swiped his change pouch full of the days' earnings. The characters see the thief running through the bazaar. The thief's name is Roundabout Jen (CN female Knotsider human **spy**). She's quick and will try to outrun the characters—and possibly even a Stonearm or two—but if they catch up to her, she will immediately surrender the pouch. Unfortunately, if she's caught by Stonearms, she will immediately be arrested and taken to Castlegrasp's dungeon.

5 - Return a Book for Nadia. If the characters met Nadia Mansouri in the last adventure, she will be pleased to see them again and will send one of the family servants to invite them to her home in Sweet Olive Ward. Since her abduction, and especially since Mega's escape, she is afraid to leave the home. In addition, a pair of Blueguard girls (LG female human Ditimayan **guards**) stay at her side at all times. She asks that the characters return a book for her at the Maktaba (see **Area 19**). The book is The Legend of Hearth, signed by its author, Grovalder Hewpillar.

6 - Catch a Cheater. Hamza Belghiti (N male Ditimayan human **commoner**), a vendor for the merchant House Benjelloun, suspects that one of his stall neighbors, Reema Toufiq (NE female Ditimayan human **commoner**) of Ibn Al-Hasan is padding her numbers during The Big Game (see **Area 14**). He offers the characters 5 gp per hour if they will sit at the kabob cafe near their stall and keep an eye on her. If the characters agree, each hour they sit in bazaar, have them make a group DC 15 Wisdom (Perception) check. If half of the party or more are successful on their checks, they notice that the same person keeps coming to her stall and purchasing fruit, typically once every 20 minutes. The buyer is another member of Ibn Al-Hasan. If the characters reveal this to Belghiti, Belghiti exposes her to the referees. Ibn Al-Hasan is a powerful merchant house in Castlegrasp with connections to the Crystal Toad. The characters could end up making enemies during their short stay in the City of Granite.

7 - Load the Statue Cart. Two dwarves, Kobol and Lilac, drag a large cart through the city pulled by a **red-striped thornfoot**. Kobol and Lilac (LN male and female Von Doral dwarf **commoners**) shout at the characters, "You! You all look strong. With us! There's a silver or two in it for you." If the characters go along with the dwarves, the dwarves lead them to the Yard of Deterrents (see **Area 18**). There, the characters get a glimpse of Castlegrasp's infamous criminal-justice system. Six of the statues at the center of the grotesque statuary have blue paint stripes across their back. These criminals served their time but were not claimed by family and friends. The dwarves need help lifting the bodies onto their cart. From there, the dwarves will carry the statues north and deposit them in the Petrified Labyrinth. The statues are heavy, each weighing 900 pounds. Once the

Castlegrasp Encounters

d20	Encounter
1	A wandering **tiger** rubs its head against one of the character's legs.
2	A red-striped thornfoot breaks its restraints and traps a shop keeper in their stall as it thrashes about.
3	A child pickpocket (unarmed **commoner**) tries to pilfer one of the characters' coin purses.
4	A destitute devilkin woman (**commoner**) lies in the street and weeps. She claims that she has visions of the Black Bird every night. "He is coming! She warns! And when he does, the eighth hand will move once more!"
5	A runty **xorn** hobbles down the street. Considered a holy creature, the locals won't mess with it, but they do their best to remove any gems or jewelry they are carrying. The characters may not be so lucky.
6	Walking past a bordello, a devilkin woman (**commoner**) encourages one or more of the characters to join her.
7	While walking through a crowded street, someone intentionally runs into one of the characters. It's one of their bounty hunter competitors. Refer to the Bounty Hunter section for details and stat blocks.
8	A prankster (**commoner**) tells a Stonearm (knight) that he thinks he saw the characters steal fruit from a fruit vendor's stall. The Stonearm accosts the characters.
9	"Move, fools!" shouts a burly man (**veteran**) to the crowd as four tiger-masked men (guards) carry a litter down the street. Within is an important Castlegraspian noble.
10	The characters walk past a suit of an ornate **animated armor** that seems to be operating on its own. In the center of its helmet is the golden Eye of Worlds, the royal symbol of the Omerian Throne. The armor is a remote traveler from Odonburg.
11-20	The characters meet an NPC with a side quest (see "Side Quests" above).

characters have helped the dwarves, the dwarves pay each one 1 sp for their help.

8 - Find Echo in the Wind. In the Low Ward (**Area 16**), a devilkin mother named Breeze in the Pines (LG female tiefling **commoner**) is hysterical. Her daughter, Echo in the Wind is missing. The fear of all parents in the Low Ward is that if their child goes missing, the Light got them. She begs the characters to investigate, swearing it must be Light Beyond the Hill who took her daughter. Other devilkin **commoners** beg her to keep her voice down and not blame the Light until they know better. Fortunately, Echo wasn't taken by the Light or any of his lackies. Echo was playing around the petrified dragon, Grytias (**Area 11**), and got stuck on the dragon's ridged

back. As usual, there are no Stonearms or militia to be found in the Low Ward. Therefore, one or more of the characters will have to climb up the dragon, retrieve the devilkin girl, and deliver her safe to her mother.

Random Encounters

In addition to the side quests that characters can take on, there are plenty of strange, wonderful, dangerous, and amazing encounters in the City of Granite. Roll a d20 three times per day of game time, checking for encounters each morning, afternoon, and evening or night. An encounter occurs on a roll of 16 or higher. Roll a d20 and check the Castlegrasp Encounters table to determine what the encounter, or simply choose an encounter you like.

Tree by the Lake

Tree by the Lake (LG male tiefling **commoner**) is taking inventory at one of the Mansouri wineshops at the northern end of the Dek Bazaar. The short, squirrelly devilkin has been meeting with bounty hunters for the last two days. By the time the characters arrive, he's exhausted but willing to answer questions for them, especially if the characters are the ones responsible for rescuing Nadia Mansouri in Chapter 2.

Tree outlines the details of Mansouri's bounty:

- The bounty is 20,000 gold pieces to be paid in Castlegraspian din. The reward is the same dead or alive.
- If Mega is killed, the orc's head must be brought back to Mansouri and identifiable through divination enchantments.
- While there have been a lot of people asking about the bounties, there are only eight well-known bounty hunters and bounty hunting groups involved in the hunt. Their details are described later in this adventure.
- Mega and his associate were crafty and didn't leave many clues during their escape. However, he suspects that the associate was likely a shapeshifter of some sort and used illusions to smuggle Mega out of the prison.
- The city went on lockdown after the escape. This means that Mega and his associate only had the duration of an illusion spell to escape the city.
- Ten of the Odzedoz orcs that lived in Jando's Spire were captured and put into the city's dungeon. They are all sentenced to petrification in the Yard of Deterrents on the Day of Tigers (the last day of the week).

That is all of the information that Tree has for the characters. He recommends that they try to find clues by gathering information. If they can find more clues or associates of Mega's,

then it's possible that they can follow the orc's trail from there.

Tree answers any other questions he can to the best of his ability but eventually recommends that the characters get started as soon as possible, especially considering the number of interested parties there are.

Tracking Mega

The hunt for Mega begins in Castlegrasp. With little to go on, the best place for the characters to start is the city itself. Gathering information in Castlegrasp presents itself as a two-fold challenge. First, most Castlegraspians are lawful citizens, so they are unlikely to have connections to figures in the underworld. And the figures of the underworld that do operate within Castlegrasp don't exactly share their identity with those outside their organizations. Second, there are bounty hunters who already have a headstart on the characters asking the same questions and speaking to the same people. Even if the characters find an important clue, it's likely that one of the hunters heard it first and are already on their way to finding the next clue.

For each hour spent talking to people in the city, a character can make a DC 15 Charisma (Persuasion or Intimidation) check. If they choose Persuasion, they can add a +1 bonus to the check for every 1 gp that they spend (to a maximum bonus of +5). Characters with the criminal background make this check with advantage. If the check succeeds, roll a d20 and consult the Mega Clues table to determine what the character learns. It's possible that the characters can learn the same rumors more than once. Some of the clues direct characters to locations in and around the city. Refer to the area mentioned in the Important Locations section for what happens when the characters follow up on the clues.

Important Locations

The City of Granite is a thriving metropolis with hundreds of homes, shops, and places of interest. Below are some of the popular destinations found in Castlegrasp, keyed to the map of Castlegrasp on page 48.

1 - The Violet Qasr. The Violet Qasr is the royal palace of Khan Hayyan Harrak XI (N male Ditimayan human **noble**). Off-limits to outsiders and guarded by the Stonearms' most elite fighting force, the Granite Nine (all LN Ditimayan human **knights**), there are whispers of great treasures hidden within the Khan's palace. It is rumored that hundreds of feet below the palace, Uve the Harrow's ring is locked in a vault of permanent ice and protected by dao Gasta-Harrak's greatest warriors.

Mega Clues

d20	Rumor
1	"A rare creature—a doppelganger—was seen shifting at the docks three weeks ago. If a doppelganger is in town, it may have been the one that helped Mega escape."
2	"The Crystal Toad is a dangerous criminal organization in the city. It's possible that Mega and his associate were smuggled out by one of the Crystal Toad's runners." **(Area 13)**
3	"If Mega and his associate really wanted to avoid the attention of the Stonearms, he probably dealt with the devilkin in the white hat (Light Beyond the Hills)." **(Area 16)**
4	"The day after the lockdown, the Yard of Deterrents was swarmed by hundreds of blackbirds. It was inexplicable, but many who saw it think that it's an omen." **(Area 18)**
5	"There used to be ancient tunnels that ran out of the city, some were converted to sewers while others have been sealed off by the Stonearms. The orc pirate might have escaped through one of those tunnels." **(Area 12)**
6	"During the lockdown, only one of the gates remained open—the Sunrise Gate in the Sweet Olive Ward. Only city citizens carrying identification could leave through the gate during the lockdown. If Mega had another associate that was a noble living in the city, he may have escaped through the Sunrise Gate." **(Area 15 and 20)**
7	"The day after Mega disappeared, three people were killed at a house north of El Asoufi vineyard. Rumor has it that it was a freak occurrence that killed them all. Still, it's believed that Mega's escape had something to do with it." **(Area 21)**
8	"During the lockdown, a Knotsider gnome threw a fit because they wouldn't let her leave. They arrested the woman and impounded her ship. She was let off with a warning. Supposedly, she's been drinking at Temple of Suen until she can afford to get her ship out of the Bay." **(Area 10)**
9	"It seems crazy to travel along the Leash and through the Lost Dragon Pass with such a large bounty on his head. A less-traveled and much more dangerous journey through the Desolation of Ditimaya to Qola might make more sense."
10	"There is a list of banned magic items in the city. It's likely that they used one of those items, probably something to change their appearance."
11	"The last person to break out of the Castlegrasp Dungeon was a krig named Ivyn Kozer. He just got stone-to-fleshed three weeks ago and is now working in the sunflower fields south of the city. He may have insights to share with you regarding escaping the dungeon." **(Area 22)**
12	"The girl, Nadia, claims that she was captured to translate some ancient book that the orc stole off a group of sages. You might talk to the sages at the Maktaba about the book and what course of action an orc with a book like that might take." **(Area 19 and 23)**
13	"A pair of halfling bounty hunters seem to have found out the orc's next destination. They were seen heading through the Sunrise Gate to the north of Sweet Olive Ward." **(Area 20)**
14	"Just this morning, a fight broke out between some muscle-headed dwarven bounty hunter and a group of devilkin down in the Lower Ward." **(Area 16)**
15	"Need a smuggler? Stavros Nanakos is the person to talk to. You can find him down in the docks. And you didn't hear this from me." **(Area 13)**
16	"If it really was a shifter that broke the orc out of prison, then you should talk to Parody. She's one of Alzahra Nedali's girls at the Beautiful Tigress. I bet she knows the identity of the one who broke the orc out." **(Area 4)**
17	"If the Khan had an interest in this matter, he would send one of the Granite Nine to track the orc. Hard to know if this is true or not since their identities are all kept a secret, but someone who would know is Fayaaz Salem. He's a historian that works at the Maktaba." **(Area 19)**
18	"When it comes to evil, the eight blind seers at the Temple of Yrena can find what you're looking for. Fair warning, however—their divinations comes with a steep price." **(Area 8)**
19	"The sewage system of Castlegrasp leads to the harbor and the harbor is heavily guarded, so it's doubtful he got out that way. But if he was truly daring, he may have entered the March of Stonearms and escaped through one of the old tunnels there." **(Area 12)**
20	"Am I the only one who thinks he flew away? It's how he got into the city and kidnapped that girl in the first place. Who's to say he didn't do that again?"

The Khan often makes public appearances from the front of the Qasr upon the great, circular Dais of Khans where he takes answers directly from the people of Castlegrasp in a townhall format. It's the Khan's openness and frank manner of speaking that's earned him the nickname Fair Eleven.

2 - Orchard Park. The Violet Qasr overlooks a two-acre olive orchard at the center of the city. In addition to the olive trees which give the park its name, the park has many open fields for recreation and lounging, as well as a large, cold-water pond named Uve's Ire.

Statues of nine of the ten previous Khans are carved to look as if they are hiding among the park's trees. The only Khan whose statue is missing is Khan Hayyan Harrak III, also known as Forgotten Three. His statue is found two miles outside of the city at the edge of the Desolation, half-buried by the sand.

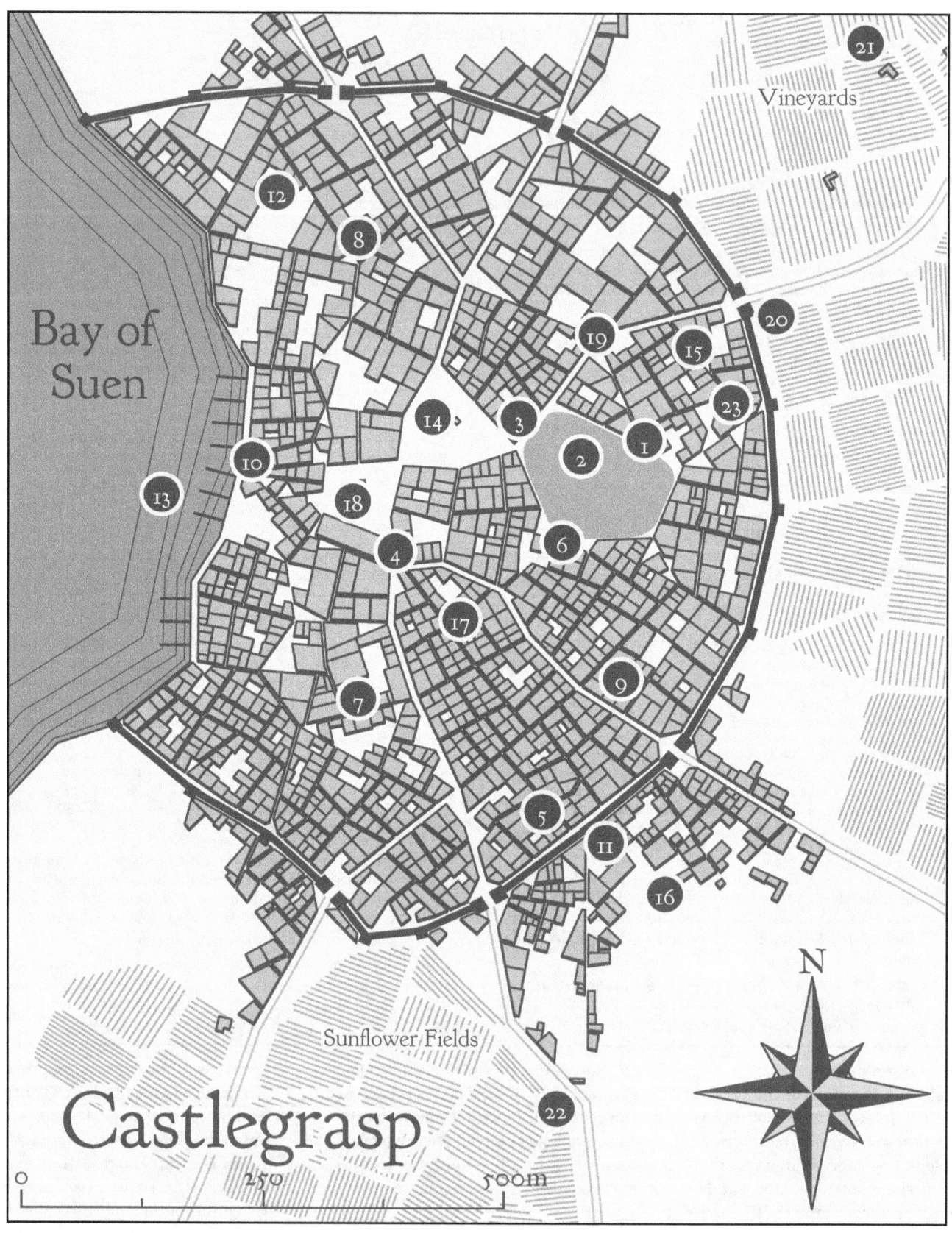

Bay of Suen

Vineyards

Sunflower Fields

Castlegrasp

N

500m

3 - The Vague Olive Inn. Also known as the Inn of Many Bridges, the Vague Olive is an inn, restaurant, tavern, market, and, of course, a popular gateway into the Orchard Park. The inn itself consists of eight separate buildings, all painted different shades of blue and violet each connected by ornate, crisscrossing bridges illuminated by willow-lights.

During the Autumnal Equinox (commonly referred to as Ditimayan New Year), the Olive celebrates with its popular Festival of Blue, where the citizens of Castlegrasp don blue masks and robes to celebrate the cooling of the Desolation and the return of the Weysevain wet season.

The Vague Olive is owned by Kashgar Rapos (N male **krig**). Having lived in the city almost since its inception, Kashgar is one of Castlegrasp's wealthiest and most influential citizens. The eight-eyed noble has a close relationship with the current Khan, as well as five of the khans before him. After all, it's no coincidence that his mighty tavern sits at the edge of the Olive Park with a clear view of the Violet Qsar.

4 - The Beautiful Tigress. If there is one thing that all Castlegraspian nobles love to do, it's outdoing one another. Seeing the elaborate design of Kashgar Rapos' Vague Olive, Alzahra Nedali (LN female Ditimayan human **noble**) went the other direction with her inn. The tallest building in Castlegrasp, the Beautiful Tigress is less an inn than it is a tower with many bedrooms. And the further one climbs the Tigress, the higher the room fee.

Supposedly, the suite at the very top costs a tenant as much as 2,000 gp per night. But it comes with many "perks."

Despite displaying a public persona of a bitter and uptight wine heiress, Nedali is actually one of the most beloved people in all of Castlegrasp. On more than one ocassion, the citizenry of Castlegrasp have suggested that were the city to elect its next Khan, Nedali should be next in line. Seeing as

how Fair Eleven has no heir—male or female—it just might happen.

Tracking Mega. If the characters heard a rumor that Parody might know something about the Shifters, they can find her here. Parody is a **doppelganger** who provides escort services for the Tigress. She's already been visited three times by bounty hunters and she's tired of telling everyone the same thing: "I don't know anything and it's racist to think that all shifters know each other."

5 - Armed Lavender Inn. Not all of Castlegrasp's inns are works of art or demonstrations of power and wealth. The Armed Lavender inn, a box-of-a-building pressed close to the city's outer walls, is a warehouse-sized fest hall that caters to Castlegraspians of all stripes. Its proprietor/bartender/entertainer, Rolf Anderberg of Jovelnot (NG male Knotsider human **scout**) delivers his northerner attitude and charm night after night. No one's ever seen Anderberg sleep. So, a frequent joke heard in the Armed Lavender is that Anderberg is secretly a Dinzer construct disguised as a northerner. "Splash a little water on him, and he'll likely rust."

Of course, the Armed Lavender comes with plenty of controversies. Its lack of security makes it one of the Crystal Toad's favorite places to do business.

6 - The Amazing Clock. Truly a sight to behold, the Amazing Clock is just that—a gargantuan clock. Fashioned by a silent mage named Oxon nearly 500 years ago and gifted to Castlegrasp shortly after its founding, this eight-handed clock does more than just tell time. It can predict phases of the moon, eclipses, and even seasonal weather patterns. But its greatest function is its ability to predict catastrophic events.

Whenever the clock's eight hands align as one, catastrophe follows. So far, the clock's hands have aligned themselves seven times in the last 500 years. Each ominous alignment was given a name: the Hand of the One, the Hand of the Two, and so forth. Because the alignments rely on the clock's unpredictable eighth hand for its forecasts, no one knows when the next alignment, the Hand of the Eight, will occur. And since this alignment will be eight on eight, many think it will be the clock's final alignment which will signal the end of the world. Hence the popular middle-Omerian expression and toast, "Until the Hand of the

Eight" (in essence, "seize the day.")

At all times, the Amazing Clock is protected by the final Dinzer Gear Golem, Constant. Not that anyone could harm the clock if they tried, mind you; Oxon's enchantments are unbreakable. Still, Constant stands guard as a reminder of the Castlegraspian-Dinzer alliance that has kept central and southern Omeria united for over a century.

7 - The Magic Dart. Looking for magic items? Look no further than the Magic Dart. Outside, the Magic Dart looks like an ordinary shop. Other than a simple wooden sign with its name painted in blue and purple, there's nothing special about it. Step inside, however, and right away you'll notice that the Dart is impossibly deep. The first thirty feet or so of the Dart is where most of the typical common and uncommon magic items one expects to be sold in a magic shop can be found. But the further you walk towards the back of the shop—of which you will never find the end—the stranger and more unusual the offerings become. Because of its neverending nature, a tradition known as "Running the Gauntlet of Dreams" has attracted adventurers and arcane scholars far and wide. To run the gauntlet, a visitor to the shop must see how far back into the shop they can travel before they wish to return. A gauntlet-runner can walk for miles into the rear of the shop without

ever finding the end. Most turn back in fear of the dangers that hide deep within the bowels of the Dart. Fortunately, the moment someone turns back, they discover themselves within the front of the shop once again as if they had traveled no further than a few feet.

The shop has only one known employee, Gudner. Gudner sits behind the counter at the front of the shop reading tomes day and night, pausing only to collect gold from customers for their purchase. Even those who've Run the Gauntlet and returned with legendary items have received little more than a "thank you, come again" from the tired-looking old man.

8 - Temple of Yrena. One would think that Castlegrasp's position on the border of the Obsidian Plain would make its citizenry shy away from the worship of Yrena, Goddess of Destruction, but quite the contrary. Having seen the effects of her wrath, Castlegraspians hold great respect for Yrena.

Yrena's temple is a circular building with a large circular courtyard at its center. A statue of the ram-headed goddess towers at the center of the courtyard, standing over the broken body of her lover, Zealdir, also a statue.

The temple is cared for by eight blind seers, Yrena's Witnesses (LE male Ditimayan human **mages**). In addition to their eyesight, the Witnesses have given up their names and personalities, each referring to himself as 'One-of-

Eight.' Although murder is illegal in Castlegrasp, Khan, despite being a skeptic, allows for the Temple of Yrena to make the eight sacrifices required by the Witnesses' tenets. In recent years, a movement calling for the end of the tradition has gained strength.

Tracking Mega. As the characters may have heard, the seers do have methods in which they can find Mega, but it comes with a very high price. One of the city's nobles, Tara Mounir (NG female Ditimayan human **noble**) is responsible for the movement to end the temple's practice of sacrifices. The seers argue that their sacrifices are the only thing that keeps the Hand of the Eight from happening. In three days, Mounir is meeting with Khan to discuss the situation. Popular opinion suggests that Mounir will succeed in having the law changed. If the characters can stop Mounir and offer evidence that it was they who did it, the seers will perform a scrying ritual to discover the current location of Mega. The group actually possesses a strand of hair recovered from the city dungeon they can use to pinpoint his location. The result of the ritual is similar to a *scrying* spell with a +8 bonus to the spell save DC.

9 - Shrine of Naeyer. "At Naeyer's feet!" is the worst curse a central Omerian can throw at his or her enemy. Naeyer, the Sun God, is feared more than both Yrena and Suen combined. Only by the care and wisdom of the

Children—the water sprites—are central Omerians protected by Naeyer's cruel hand.

As the god of fire and ifrits, Naeyer is identified by most central Omerians as an evil god. Those who worship him are called the Cracked, as their faces are often a blistered mess of damaged, bleeding skin. Despite the presence of the shrine, none of the Cracked are allowed in the city. The small, ramshackle shrine only exists to appease the cruel, chaotic god.

When the first rains fall on Castlegrasp following the Autumnal Equinox, Castlegraspians travel to the shrine to mock and shame the god, believing that once again the Children have once more protected them from Naeyer's wrath.

10 - Temple of Suen. Suen is the goddess of storms and worshiped primarily by sailors, fishermen, and others who work in or around the sea. Seen as neither god nor bad, the neutral goddess Suen can bring destruction just as quickly as she can bring great fortune.

The Temple of Suen in Castlegrasp is more than just a place of worship. It's also a popular tavern overlooking the Omerian Ocean and Bay of Suen. The high priest of the temple/tavern Barsumlin Coinminer (LG male Von Doral dwarf **priest**) serves drinks and issues prayers. Half the time he's drunk on his own supply, though, and passed out on the floor of the temple.

Ten years ago, the worshippers of Suen tried to erect a statue dedicated to the goddess in the harbor. Unfortunately, a southerner fishing boat accidentally bumped into the statue, knocking it onto its side. Later that year, that same boat was capsized by a colossal wave.

Tracking Mega. Isoniana Folli (NG female gnome **commoner**) has been getting plenty drunk since her arrest. When the characters find her at the Temple of Suen, she's singing old shan-

ties with Coinminer. Isoniana doesn't know anything about the orc's escape. She's just frustrated that her ship is still in lock-up. With drunken giggles she'll ask if the characters can loan her 500 gp to get her ship out of impound.

11 - Grytias' Fall. Fifteen years ago, five ivory dragons fought on behalf of the northern armies during the Attack of Regrets. Four of the dragons were killed south of the Obsidian Plain by Dinzer warblimps. But the fifth, a one-eyed grump named Grytias, turned his attention to Castlegrasp. Dozens of Castlegraspian Stonearms fell to the beast's breath during the battle. Finally, a knight named Thawab El Khouri

saddled a griffon and flew directly towards the beast. Grythias' caught El Khouri's mount in its jaws, but El Khouri was able to dodge its teeth and cling onto the dragon's dewlap. El Khouri stabbed Grytias through he neck with his spear, and in seconds, the dragon turned to stone and crashed into the city's Lower Ward. Sadly, El Khouri perished in the fall, too. The petrified corpse of the ivory dragon remains hunched over the city's southern wall. During the Day of Spoken Regrets in the summer, El Khouri's widow, Zayna, embraces visitors who come to pay their respects to the fallen hero.

12 - The March of Stonearms. Castlesgrasp was founded upon a granite quarry two hundred years ago. Today, the granite stones pulled from the quarry make up much of the city's walls, buildings, and even the Violet Qsar. But the granite did not come free. Soon after the mine was opened, the earlier Castlegraspians discovered that the terrain was inhabited by earth elementals. The elementals' queen, a might dao named Gasta the Pure, confronted the Castlegraspians, questioning their presence in Central Omeria. The city's founder, Khan Hayyan Harrak I, met privately with the dao. In a move thought unusual by many of his peers, Harrak surrendered his soul to the dao in exchange for access to the granite. Initially surprised by Harrak's offer, Gasta the Pure agreed to the exchange. Not only could the Castlegraspians mine the granite from her kingdom, but she would enchant the stone as well. Thanks to Gasta's magic, no man-made weapon would ever penetrate Castlegrasp's mighty granite walls. In addition, Gasta blessed the first nine Castlegraspian soldiers with her touch; she turned the soldiers' right arms to solid stone. But much to their surprise, they could still move these stone arms as normal. In addition, any bladed weapon they held with their stone arms would petrify any enemy it pierced.

Years later, as the Khan grew ill, he tasked the Nine to bring him before Gasta. As promised, he surrendered himself to the dao. Gasta, cherishing her long, peaceful relationship with the Khan, placed his soul within a sky diamond. She then set the diamond next to her heart, forever keeping him close. Their souls merged and the king and the genie queen became one.

When a Castlegraspian soldier proves his or herself during training, demonstrating immeasurable virtue, they are encouraged to take the March of the Stonearms. The soldier must enter the first mine and seek the dao Gasta-Harrak. From there, he or she must kneel before the dao and offer his or herself to the dao just as the first Khan did two-hundred years prior. If Gasta-Harrak detects the spirit of the Khan within the soldier, they are granted her blessing—an arm of stone. However, if she senses any impurity within the soldier's heart, she commands the earth to devour them.

Tracking Mega. More than a few Castlegraspians theorize that Mega and his associate escaped through the tunnels within the March. Trouble is, the March is guarded at all times by two Stonearm guards who allow no one to enter. They would have noticed if anyone tried to enter without permission from the Khan himself. Furthermore, the tunnels are incredibly dangerous, filled with territorial elementals and ravenous xorn. It's ultimately a dead end.

13 - Docks. The epicenter of commerce in Castlegrasp, the docks are alive with the sounds of fisherman shanties, laughing children, gulls, and the crashing of the Omerian's mighty waves. Easily one of the safest harbors in all of central Omeria—if not all of Omeria—Castlegrasp's docks are protected by the undefeated Omerian Navy. Its twenty-four warships have earned the nickname, the Azure Curse. They're fast, tough, and heavily armed, capable of sinking armadas twice their size.

The docks are also the center of operations for the Crystal Toad, where their three merchandise runners smuggle illegal products into the city. Stavros Nanakos (NE male Knotsider human spy) oversees the operations on behalf of his father, Daevid. Stavros has seen the inside of Castleburg's Dungeons on more than one occasion. Fortunately for the young noble, his father is an important player in local politics. Still, Captain Allah is determined to see young Nanakos entered into the Yard of Deterrents.

Tracking Mega. Stavros Nanakos has earned quite a bit of coin from Mega's escape, mostly from bounty hunters that have heard rumors that he can smuggle people out of town. His reaction is the same each time. First, he acts like he doesn't know what the bounty hunter is talking about—he does this in front of guards so he doesn't get roughed up by the bounty hunters. Then, once the bounty hunter leaves, he tracks down the bounty hunter in the city. "Listen," he says each time, "I didn't want to say too much because there were too many people listening at the time. But I'm not the one who got him out. But I might know who did." Of course, that information comes with a price: 50 gp. Once paid, he points the bounty hunter in the direction of Light Beyond the Hills in the Low Ward (**Area 16**). Stavros has no idea whether or not Light was involved but dislikes Light, so he has no issue sending hotheaded bounty hunters the devilkin crimelord's way.

14 - Dek Bazaar. In Castlegrasp, a mercantile lifestyle is more than just a way to earn a living; it's a competitive sport of sorts. Seven mercantile houses call Castlegrasp their home. And while the seven are fierce competitors, they also respect and admire one another.

Each day when Naeyer's eye banishes the twin moons, the seven houses play

what they call "The Big Game." Once the shops open in Dek Bazaar, it's a race to 7,777 gold coins. As the day progresses, the vendors shout their numbers so the housemasters can hear. The housemasters then mark their earnings in chalk on a large column of slate at the center of the bazaar. Once a house reaches 7,777 coins—typically in the early afternoon—the gamekeeper rings the bell, double-checks the numbers, and announces the winner. While all seven of the houses have shared one or more turns as The Big Game's winner, by far, House Ibn Al-Hasan has claimed the most victories. Ibn Al-Hasan trades in wine.

Tracking Mega. The Bazaar is a fascinating place filled with the most diverse collection of Castlegraspian and Central Omerians. While the characters are in the bazaar, read the following:

> The energy in the bazaar is mesmerizing. Everywhere you look, transactions are made, jokes are told, children play, vendors argue—this is no doubt the heart of the city. But you notice something unusual, too. About ten feet from you, a black-bird sits on the roof of one of the stalls. While your eyes may be playing tricks on you, it seems like the bird's eyes are glowing red. After a moment, the bird takes off, flying to the east.

The moment the characters got involved with the bounty on Mega, the Black Bird tasked one of his birds to keep a close eye on them. At this point in the adventure, the Black Bird is hundreds of miles away from the city, hunting Mega.

15 - Sweet Olive Ward. The majority of the city's nobles live in Sweet Olive Ward, north of the Violet Qsar. The ward itself was built into a rocky hill from which a cold-water spring gushed. Afraid to spoil the path of the water, Sweet Olive's streets and homes were

built around the natural flow. The waters terminate in a waterfall that fills a large well at the southwestern side of the ward. Then, the well's underground streams then flow out to the Bay of Suen and eventually join the waters of the Omerian.

The streets of Sweet Olive Ward are lush with greenery. Sleepy willows, plum trees, and of course, venerable olive trees flank the narrow streets of the ward. Although one of the shadiest areas in the city, it also has the largest security presence. In addition to the usual assignment of Stonearms and city militia, Sweet Olive has its own volunteer defense force called the Blueguard. While most of these young noblemen and women are thought of as "weekend warriors" by Castlegrasp's professional defenses, they have pledged their lives to the protection of the Granite City. During the Attack of Regrets, they joined the Stonearms on the front lines. Seven Blueguard boys died fighting for the City of Granite. The Blueguard's leader is a retired Stonearm named Safura El Khouri (LG female Ditimayan human **knight**). Her

brother was the great dragonslayer, Thawad.

16 - The Low Ward. The newest section of the still-growing Castlegrasp exists just beyond its southern gates. Many of the locals have dubbed the low ward "the Oven" as it catches the heat waves rushing up from the Obsidian Plain to the far south. As such, it's home to the city's growing devilkin population. Still untrusted by many Castlegraspians, the devilkin (called "tieflings" by northerners) have eked out a comfortable existence in the City of Granite. Despite the constant racism most Castlegraspian devilkin face each day, they are loyal to their home. Recently, the Low Ward celebrated the induction of the Stonearms' first devilkin, Ember in the Dark (LG male devilkin **knight**).

Unfortunately, Low Warders are frequently exploited by a despicable devilkin crimelord named Light Beyond the Hill (LE male devilkin **bandit captain**). Light, who masquerades as a simple baker, extorts and torments his brethren. When Light is crossed, he doesn't go after the one whom he

felt wronged him. Instead, he removes the heads of one of his enemy's family members and leaves it for his enemy to find.

Ember has tried, repeatedly, to bring Light to justice. Unfortunately, he is alone in his war against Light and his gang.

Tracking Mega. Stavros Nakanos (see **Area 13**) keeps sending bounty hunters to question Light Beyond the Hill as to the whereabouts of Mega. Just this morning, a dwarf bounty hunter attacked Light in broad daylight. Light escaped, but two of his men were injured in the attack. Since the incident, Light has locked himself in his home in the Low Ward. However, anyone that starts questioning where Light is located in the Low Ward will draw the attention of four tiefling thugs. The thugs are not kind to curious adventurers. Light was not involved in Mega's escape.

17 - Tiger Borough. There is a legend that Khan Hayyan Harrak IV once went for a walk in the lands south of Castlegrasp unarmed and without his guard. Three miles from the city, the Khan heard a low growl from behind a group of boulders a few feet in front of him—a hungry tiger. Khan turned and ran. Alone and without a weapon, he knew he was likely doomed. In desperation, he climbed a tall boulder. The Khan could not escape from the boulder and the tiger could not reach him, no matter how hard it tried.

The day turned to night and the desert grew cold. Eventually, the tiger grew tired and laid its head down.

"Man," spoke the tiger in perfect Omerian Common. "Why do you stay on top of that boulder? I wish to catch you so I may feed you to my children."

"Tiger," the Khan answered back, "I am the king of a great city and I must return to my people and ensure their prosperity. If you eat me, I cannot do this."

The Khan and the tiger knew they

were at an impasse. They remained silent for a short time after that. Eventually, Naeyer's eye reappeared in the sky. The tiger, even hungrier than before, sighed, "If you remain on that boulder and I remain here, then surely both of us will die. Then my children will die. And your people will not know prosperity."

"Yes, that is correct, tiger."

"Then we must make a deal. Allow me to bite off one of your legs and feed it to my children. I will then let you ride on my back to your city."

The Khan considered the tiger's proposal. Finally, he nodded, "Very well. You may bite off my right leg. After all, I have two. Am I so greedy as to desire both?"

Slowly, the Khan lowered himself

from the rock and approached the tiger. As they agreed, the tiger bit off the Khan's right leg and brought it to its children. Once its children were fed, it picked up the Khan and placed him upon its back. Then, the tiger raced the Khan back to Castlegrasp.

The Stonearms raised their spears at the sight of the tiger and the wounded Khan. But the Khan protested, "No. The tiger and I made a deal. I upheld my end of the bargain and the tiger has upheld its. It is free to go."

The tiger thanked the Khan for his sacrifice and returned to the desert and the Khan returned to the Violet Qsar. From that moment on, the Khan was given the nickname Tiger Four. Following the incident, Tiger Four led Castlegrasp to an era of great prosperity. He also passed an important law: "No tigers shall be killed within three miles of the city. They are our friends."

The Tiger Borough at the heart of Castlegrasp takes its name from this legend. Residents of the ward pay their respects to the legend of the Khan and the Tiger by leaving food at the doorsteps for wild tigers who enter the city. When tigers do enter the city, they do not attack, lending credence to the tale. Quietly, the tigers walk to the borough, eat the offerings, and exit the city as Castlegraspians watch in awe.

18 - Barracks and City Dungeon. When the laws are broken in Castlegrasp, criminals are placed in the city's dungeon below the militia's barracks. The leader of the militia, Captain Farida Allah (LG female Ditimayan human **veteran**) personally oversees every arrest and incarceration.

All criminals are given a fair trial by a jury of four representatives and the Khan. Those who are found guilty by the jury, are all given the same punishment: petrification and temporary residence in the Yard of Deterrents.

The Yard of Deterrents is a large courtyard filled with the petrified statues of the city's convicts. Convicts sit on one of the yard's stone benches. Then, one of the Stonearms touches their spear to the convict's spine and, within seconds, the convict turns to stone. The statue must remain in its petrified state until the criminal has served its time, typically a year, but sometimes longer depending on the severity of the crime for which they were charged. Once the time is served, the family of the convict can pay to have he or she returned to flesh. However, if no one claims the body within a year, the stone body of the convict is placed on a cart and delivered to the Petrified Labyrinth where it continues its mission as a deterrent—this time to the armies of the north.

Tracking Mega. If the guards and caretakers at the Yard are asked about the blackbirds that appeared the day after Mega escaped, they all vividly recall the event. Literally, hundreds of blackbirds touched down in the courtyard and remained for 10 minutes before flying away towards the east. What made it so unusual was that blackbirds aren't common this far south of the Spine. Supposedly, the blackbirds were later seen at a vineyard east of the city (see **Area 21**).

19 - The Maktaba. The outside of this long, narrow building betrays the awe and wonder within. Once one passes through the tall, arched doors of Castlegrasp's main library and scroll vault, their breath is quickly ushered from their lungs. Arranged almost like a honeycomb, the Maktaba is home to thousands of scrolls, texts, and books, some of which predate even the Desolation itself.

The Maktaba is not a public building.

To gain access, one must apply for one of the 1,000 available memberships, then go through rigorous background checks and tests of intelligence. Once accepted, one must pay an annual fee of 1,000 gold pieces. Even then, the Maktaba's rules are very particular.

Fortunately, the Maktaba's scholars are willing to perform research on behalf of those with the right amount of gold to spend. The price is steep, of course. Hiring one of the Matkaba's scholars costs 2 gp per day (for a minimum of 10 days), and often, research can take as long as a year. "We are neither cheap nor fast. What we are is thorough," the scholars fond of saying.

Tracking Mega. The official historian of Castlegrasp, Fayaaz Salem (LN male Ditimayan human **mage**), works at the Maktaba. If one of the Granite Nine are tracking the orc, he will know the answer. Of course, like the other scholars employed by the Maktaba, he will not answer a question for less than 20 gold pieces.

Once his fee is paid, he answers immediately: it's not one of the Granite Nine, but Ember in the Dark, the newest member of the Stonearms. He left the day after the orc escaped, heading north along the Leash. He traveled light and alone.

20 - The Sunrise Gate. The eastern gate has multiple nicknames: The Noble Gate, The Purple-Foot Gate, Third's Path, Naeyer's Curse, Little Naqqad, and, its true name, The Sunrise Gate. Situated east of Sweet Olive Ward, it's one of the most popular gates in the city as it offers Castlegrasp's sister villages, wineries, and desert borne merchants the most direct path in and

out of the city.

The nobles of Sweet Olive Ward lobby to keep the gate's exterior free of merchants and homes. Regardless, Naqqadi refugees congregate around the gate, using it as their favorite camping spot. Because it faces the direction Naeyer's eye rises each morning, anyone who stands near the gate can hear Naqqadi prayers at sunrise.

Jaul Serhane (LG male Ditimayan **knight**) is the Stonearm captain of the Sunrise Gate and easily one of the most beloved templars in the city. Jaul doesn't look like a typical Stonearm. He's overweight, balding, and loud. But his heart is as large as the Violet Qsar and his passion is deeper than the Omerian. During the festivals, he loves to dress up as The Tiger and chase the children who dress as the Tiger Khan. He's also a unrequited flirt, and loves to hand all of the women who pass through his gate lilacs.

Tracking Mega. The characters may have discovered that the Sunrise Gate was open during the lockdown. Also, it's possible they heard two halfling bounty hunters left through the gate a few days ago. Interviewing Jaul and the guards who work the gate (usually 10 guards at any given time) does not turn up too many leads. Captain Jaul is very forthcoming about any mistakes he makes, and this isn't one of them.

The Naqqadi refugees who gather around the gate similarly have not witnessed anything unusual, although a few do recall the halflings heading up the road, east towards the vineyards.

21 - Attiq El Aoufi's Winery. "Purple Foot" Attiq El Aoufi (N male Ditimayan human **veteran**) is the wealthiest independent winemaker in Castlegrasp. His vineyard, El Aoufi Msanie Alkhmr, is the best selling Central Omerian wine on the continent. While some of his competitors—especially Ibn Al-Hasan—refer to his wine as "cheap dog wine", El Aoufi's is truly a wine of the people, a bottle of Sweet Fruit Red available for as little as 2 gp

at most wine-sellers along the Weyse-vain. El Aoufir's winery covers nearly 20,000 acres of the verdant belt that borders the Desolation.

El Aoufi enjoys walking around his property, examining the grapes and making conversation with the devilkin pickers. A victim of racism himself in his youth due to his mother's Naqqa-di heritage, El Aoufi understands the plight of the Castlegraspian Low Warders.

Tracking Mega. The first place that Mega stopped after escaping the dungeon was the vineyard of Attiq El Asoufi. With his *hat of disguise*, Mega took on the appearance of a devilkin calling himself Wave over the Mountain. Mega's doppelganger companion arranged a meeting between Mega and one of the devilkin servants working the vineyard, Tale of the Dragon. The doppelganger remained in the city. Mega acted as Tale's cousin, traveling north from Southern Omeria. As not to draw suspicion to his sudden arrival, Mega remained with Tale and his family for two days. The plan was for Mega to stay with Tale's family for a month

until the excitement died down and the bounty hunters were off his trail, then head northeast to Qola. Unfortunately, his plans changed when a flock of hundreds of blackbirds assaulted

Tale's home. Tale, his wife, and one of his children were killed in the attack as Mega escaped. The only survivor was Tale's daughter, Tears in the Rain who has been living with El Aoufi since the strange encounter.

Following the bizarre attack, two hal-fling bounty hunters named Odeos and Ahmeego (see the section on Bounty Hunters) showed up at the site of the murders suspecting that the attack may have something to do with Mega's escape. The pair also spoke with the guards at the dungeon about the black-bird swarm that appeared there.

Tale of the Dragon's Home. The home of Tale of the Dragon is two miles north of the vineyard. The small home, no larger than a room with a connected outhouse and pen for chickens, is in tatters when the characters arrive. The home's windows are smashed open, the door has been pulled from its hinges (and tossed some 30 feet away into the

grapevines), and there is blood and bird feces everywhere. The dead bodies of blackbirds also litter the home inside and out. A DC 10 Wisdom (Animal Handling) check reveals that many of the birds died by smashing their bodies against the walls, windows, and doors of Tale's home.

The characters can spend as much time as they like investigating the home and its surroundings. For each hour that the spend searching, have one of the members of the party make a DC 15 Wisdom (Perception) check. If the check is successful, they find something stashed in the grapevines: a *hat of disguise*. Mega lost the hat while he was running from the birds.

Without a *hat of disguise*, it would be difficult for Mega to travel along major highways and through large population centers without being noticed.

Speaking with the Staff. Just as the characters can spend time inves-tigating Tale of the Dragon's home, they can talk to the other servants on El Asoufi's property. You can roleplay each individual interaction with the wine pickers, or for each hour that the characters spend speaking with the wine pickers, have one of the members of the party make a DC 15 Charisma (Persuasion or Intimidation) check. If the check is successful, one of the devilkin servants, Grass Between Your Toes recalls that she saw a man run-ning over a hill headed directly north. Shortly after he ran away, hundreds of blackbirds flew overhead in the same direction. When she heard about the blackbirds that destroyed Tale's home, she knew there was a connection, but was too afraid to share it with the oth-er bounty hunters.

Talking to Tears in the Rain. The only survivor of the massacre at Tale of the Dragon's home was his 8-year old daughter, Tears in the Rain. Tears was adopted by El Asoufi's daughter, Min-hat, and now lives in the estate. Since the event, she has said little. El Asoufi has prevented anyone from speaking to

her, excluding the Stonearm, Ember in the Dark who visited two days previous. A character with the noble or folk hero background might be able to convince the El Asoufis to give them access to Tears, but they must pass a DC 17 Wisdom (Persuasion) check in order to do so. Outside of enchantments, there are no other ways to gain access to the girl outside of direct violence. El Asoufi is a capable fighter, and at any time, there are 1d6 + 1 thugs (mostly tiefling) who will come to El Asoufi's aid. El Asoufi only wishes to protect the girl, and believes that all of these lines of questions will only harm her further.

While Tears doesn't remember much about the traumatic event, she does remember that Mega (as Wave) could sense something was wrong before it happened. "He just stood up from dinner and ran out the door. Then they came." She also says she remembers seeing a figure in all black standing watching from far away. "His eyes glowed red and he had a big spear that also glowed red and he stood in a tree with giant birds and watched me."

Area 22 - Sabbag Farm, The Farm of the Penitent. Once the daughter of a wealthy trader, Amina Bouzfour (NG female Ditimayan human **bandit**) committed murder seventeen years ago. She was found guilty by Khan Hayyan Harrak IX and sentenced to four years in the Yard of Deterrents. Sadly, once her sentence was up, Amina's family had left the city. There was no one to claim her. Just as she was being loaded onto the statue cart, an aging sunflower farmer named Mutah Sabbag paid her stone-to-flesh fee and gave the young girl a job on her farm. Mutah died two years later and left the farm to Amina. Paying Mutah's kindness forward, Amina spent the last eleven years managing Sabbag's sunflower farm. Using the funds from her crop sales, she purchases expired statues from the Yard of Deterrents, and like Sabbag, gives the restored ex-convicts jobs working the fields.

Bouzfour is extremely intelligent and heavily involved in Castlegraspian politics. She was one of the leaders who pressed for the introduction of a jury to try criminals versus the sole decision being left to the Khan. And while she believes that the current Khan is a fair man as his name implies, she feels that the Eleventh Khan should be Castlegrasp's last and that the city should turn to democracy as many of the northern kingdoms have.

Tracking Mega. One of the freed prisoners on Amina's farm, a **krig** named Ivyn Kozer, just started working at Sabbag's three weeks ago. He served a five-year sentence for burglary and escaping custody. Many of the underworld's criminals have since given Kozer the—somewhat unoriginal—nickname The Spider. Not so much for his krig nature, but his status as one of the only people ever to escape the Castlegrasp dungeon. Since Mega's escaped, he's been contacted by a few bounty hunters who consult the man-spider for methods of escape. While Kozer's method of escape was different than Mega's—and he won't share it to anyone—he did not anticipate the heightened security during the proceeding lockdown. As a krig, he was too easy to find with divination spells, especially since he lacked a magical way to disguise himself. He suspects that Mega used enchantments to make himself look different. Furthermore, he's probably stayed indoors and away from landmarks, knowing that if scrying sensors focus on him they may be able to determine his location by looking around the setting.

23 - Mansouri Estate. Baariq Mansouri lives in the Sweet Olive Ward with his third wife Aalia and his three daughters, Nadia, Rashida, and Lina. Mansouri is one of Castlegrasp's most important nobles and politicians. He sits on the jury as a representative for Castlegraspian commerce and has a close, personal relationship with the Khan. Politically and economically

conservative, many of Mansouri's campaigns within the city have made him a target for progressives. Although Mansouri hopes for the continued tradition of Khans and authoritarian rule in the city, he does believe that Fair Eleven should introduce a senate or committee of representatives to "unburden" the Khan with many of the day-to-day decisions. Naturally, he proposes that he should be a member of such a board were it to be formed.

Tracking Mega. Of course, Baariq is the one who placed the bounty on Mega's head. As a member of the city's jury, he would have undoubtedly sentenced the orc to a long tenure on a bench in the Yard of Deterrents. Now that Mega has escaped, he only wants death for the orc and has shared his thoughts openly with many.

If Nadia is secretly Mega's doppelganger associate (either in this new adventure or as a carryover from the last), then obviously, she will know Mega's whereabouts. Of course, the doppelganger is extremely good at playing the role of Nadia Mansouri, and nothing short of magic will cause it to reveal its presence. While Castlegrasp is nowhere near the magical utopia that a place like Oxonburg is, it does have its fair share of mages and creatures who possess truesight. All it takes is one person to notice her true nature.

If the characters discover Nadia's true nature, the doppelganger will trade the information it has on Mega for its own freedom. The doppelganger explains how the entire escape went down (ass detailed in the Background section above) as well as the steps they took following the escape and the arrangement with Tale of the Dragon to the east of the city. After Mega connected with Tale, that was the last it saw of Mega. It does know that Mega is headed to the far north, beyond the Spine, to find his brother Gradba. Gradba is rumored to live somewhere on the Qerno Peninsula.

The Weysevain Coast

Originally named for the explorer Duda Weysevain, the Weysevain Coast is the westernmost edge of Central Omeria and the Desolation of Ditimaya. Almost 60% of the population of Central Omeria lives along the coast. The villages and towns on the coast are connected by the Leash, a road that stretches from Castlegrasp to the south to Cabal to the north.

The locations described in this section appear on the map of the Weysevain region of Central Omeria found on page 61. Not depicted on the maps are tiny hamlets, villages, and homesteads too small to be seen at the scale. Assume that there are around 3d6 villages or hamlets near the larger cities (Arruquetta, Cabal, Castlegrasp, Gar

Wabrizz, and Tadju), 2d6 village or hamlets closer to the towns and large villages and along the major roads, and then 1d6 on hexes lacking major roads. While these locations are too small to be of consequence, adventurers traveling through may come across a settlement. Some of these opportunities are built into the random encounter guide later in this section, but you're free to add them as needed.

Some location entries include a suggested encounter that occurs when the characters pass through or first arrive. You can ignore the encounter and create your own activity based on the information given in a location's description. For example, the "Dreadfields" section mention the Dinzer pylons and the mire tyrants that stalk the lands, which might make for an interesting encounter of your own design.

Arruqueta

The city of Arruqueta is home to 15,000 living souls. Roughly 60 percent of Arruqueta's population are human, with another 30 percent taken by Von Doral dwarves. Like most of the refugee destinations for Von Dorals, tensions are high among the dwarves and humans. Arruqueta is presided over by the teenage Queen Daria Emagavel, a despicable tyrant, who is known as the Spear of Weysevain.

Despite the totalitarian nature of Emagavel's rule, the Great Equinox Library is an important destination for sages across all of Omeria. Recently, its greatest sage, Asorin the Black was murdered during an orc raid in the southern village of Haver. Asorin's acolytes have recovered the body and brought him back to Arruqueta in order to perform a revival ritual on their dead master.

Basilisk's Spine Mountains

The colossal mountain range that spans the width of Omeria and divides the northern end of the continent from the central end is the nearly impassable Basilisk's Spine Mountain. The mountain range originally had many names depending on the culture that lived near it. When Duda Weysevain traveled through the mountains and along the coast that now bears his name, he noticed on his map that the range resembled a large, multi-legged lizard, hence its modern name. Many of the geographical features that Weysevain recorded around the range take its name from the Spine.

A newer mountain range, the snow-capped peaks are treacherous and difficult to cross. In addition, it is a volcanic range rife with earthquakes, landslides, and other geological calamities.

Blood Drip

Perhaps the second most important road in the northern part of Central Omeria, the blood drip runs from Mighty Tadju through the Wounded Pass and into the goblin held lands of Gar Wabrizz. The road is incredibly dangerous for most humanoids as there are no patrols to protect travelers.

Cabal

The City of Daydreams, Cabal blankets the majority of Tusk Island. Once the largest city in Central Omeria, the Attack of Regrets reduced its population by nearly half. Now, it is home only to 8,000 souls, mostly human. Admiral Covadonga Carballo, like her bitter enemy Daria Emagavel, is a cruel and petty despot whose insatiable greed has nearly bankrupted this once-great city. For many, the most troubling aspect of Cabal is its rejection of all Omerian Gods, north, central, or southern. Religion is illegal on Tusk Island and any caught worshipping Gods or casting divine magic are sentenced to death.

Castlegrasp

Castlegrasp has a storied history as one of Central Omeria's greatest cities and one of the few in the land that hasn't fallen apart from catastrophe, civil war, or poor leadership. Castlegrasp is detailed earlier in this chapter.

Desolation of Ditimaya

No one knows how the Desolation of Ditimaya became the desert that it is today. One thousand years ago, it was the hunting grounds for the Ditimayans Tribes, the culture from which many Central Omerians can draw a lineage. Most of the Ditimayans disappeared following the Unlimited Eruption (the Hand of the Third) which created the Obsidian Plain and brought forth the Qhesori Hordes.

The Desolation of Ditimaya spans over one million square miles. While a green band surrounds either side of the desert and regular springs appear throughout, for the most part, the desert is almost completely uninhabitable. Nearly all Central Omerians recognize Naeyer, the God of the Sun, as the villainous culprit responsible for the arid wasteland.

Dreadfields

Fifty years ago, massive, 200-foot high obelisks of Pabradian steel were erected as fence posts by a cadre of Dinzer conjurers. The purpose of the fence was two-fold. First, the fence was supposed to be a deterrent for the ivory drakes of the north. Its second purpose was to conjure elementals to fight on behalf of the Central Omerian armies. These elementals were supposed to be drawn from the sand and fire of Ditimaya itself. But there was a grave miscalculation. What was supposed to be a mode of defense turned the land into a spawning ground for evil aberrations. Dinzer reinforcements were able to contain the majority of the horrors that rose from the pillars. Most of the creatures were destroyed. Still, mire tyrants, warp boars, and vexbrutes haunt

the land now known as the Dreadfields. Most who choose to travel through the Desolation of Ditimaya know that once they see the warning posts to turn back. "If you see the sign, you can still turn around. But if you see an obelisk, it's probably too late."

Gar Wabrizz

The hobgoblin kingdom of Gar Wabrizz thrives under the leadership of their queen, Glonkad the Unkillable. Visible for miles, the sprawling metropolis is infested with hundreds of thousands of goblins, bugbears, ogres, orcs, and of course, hobgoblins who have pledged their unwavering allegiance to the Gray Banner. While Glonkad's imperial tendencies have subsided since she and her ilk drove the Von Dorals from their homelands, the crafty queen has instead turned to economics and influence to control her neighbors.

Gar Wabrizz (roughly translated to "The Gray City") is not as dangerous for humanoids as one might imagine. Although Gar Wabrizz is by far the dominant power in Omeria, the Garrish know the value of peace over war, especially when it comes to the races of man. And since the north and south are content prolonging their decade-spanning cold war, the Garrish know it's only a matter of time before they make another move. After all, this strategy worked on the dwarves.

Gradba's Lodge

Mega's older brother, Gradba, lives in a cabin at the north edge of the Qirno Peninsula. His home is detailed in a later adventure.

Ghost Holm

Once home to a Knotsider colony named Jando's Spire, much of the Ghost Holm was destroyed by Dinzer warblimps during the Attack of Regrets. Since that time, it has become a safe haven for pirates, escaped criminals, and other scum. Rumors persist that the island hides many treasures and secrets. Ghost Holm and Jando's Spire are detailed in Chapter 2. *Assault on the Ghost Holm*.

Haver

Haver is a large fishing village two-days ride from Castlegrasp. It's mostly home to fishermen, sailors, and the occasional smuggler who hopes to avoid the attention of the Castlegraspian Stonearms. Haver is detailed in Chapter 1, *Storm of Mega*.

Lacasa

If you ask a Lacasan who their ruler is, they probably won't be able to tell you. An important crossroads between the road to Cabal, the Leash, and the passage through the north, Lacasa grew quickly thanks to its strategic location. That location brought trade and trade brought the guilds. With no true ruler and no ties to nearby Cabal, the city is run by its guild heads who (mostly) act in accordance with each other. Recently, however, a southern wizard named Unitor moved into the town and has started to "stir the pot."

The Leash

Spanning from Castlegrasp's northern gate to Daydreamer's Bridge in Cabal, the Leash is the most traveled road in Central Omeria.

For the most part, the Leash is safe, thanks to the presence of the Phantoms, a guild of nonpartisan knights and rangers who patrol the road and keep it safe from bandits, monsters, and other troubledoers.

Loqasoa

Loqasoa is the sister town to Scroas across Beiydark Channel. The bugbear-dominant town is ruled by a shadowy cabal of assassins.

Lost Dragon Pass

When Duda Weysevain crossed through the Petrified Labyrinth into the Central Omerian lands north of Lacasa, he spotted a carnelian dragon leaving its cave. Exhausted from a grueling trip through the wood elf lands of Sabalona, he wanted a break from travel and decided to be a naturalist for a few days. From a narrow ravine, he watched the dragon for days coming and going from its cave, feeding its young, and living its life, untouched by the hand of civilization. Then, one day, the dragon stopped leaving its cave. Weysevain waited for another week. The dragon never returned.

Weysevain knew better than to enter the dragon's cave to check on it—after all, the dragon wasn't even aware of Weysevain's presence—so instead dubbed his temporary passion as the "lost dragon." The Weysevain Coast from Cabal to Orbea now bears the name of Weysevain's dragon.

Olyothyr

Most of the true elves of Omeria are gone, having departed to the After. Only one of the great nations of elves remains, the pale, xenophobic Olyothyrians. The elves rarely leave their great home on the Qirno Peninsula. The few that do are usually of mixed heritage, so they do not feel the Attraction, the incurrable mental illness elves who stray too far from their homes feel.

Omerian Ocean

A turbulent, angry ocean, the Omerian pounds the cliffs and sands of the Weysevain Coast. Storms batter the coast almost year-round, making direct travel across the ocean trying for all but the mightiest sailing vessels.

Onorim's Palace

Onorim the Perpetual, once one of the Seven Eyes of Odonburg, grew tired of the constant warring between northern and southern Omeria. The wizard retreated to Stavfal Slope where he crafted a palace of ice and retired. Within its icy chambers, Onorim started to build the machine he calls the Tower. While he has not shared what he intends to do with the machine, he has told his old colleagues that it "will hopefully save the world someday."

Orbea

Also called the Maze of Orbea, this vast network of channels, canyons, caverns and natural bridges carved by the Orbean tributary is home to the enigmatic spider-humanoids, the krig. All krig are born from the same progenitor-diety, the unseen Matriarch. Krig are not born with names, gender, or any other identifier. Only through their relative position, location, or any scars, marks, or clothing they have gained during their time in Omeria can a non-krig tell one krig from another. Some believe that the krigs are sent throughout Omeria to gain positions of power in order to extend the reach of the mysterious Matriarch.

The Petrified Labyrinth

Ironically, the Petrified Labyrinth had its name long before it became a literal maze of petrified humanoids. The Castlegraspian tradition began after the War Of The Burning Forest. "Legendary Nine" Khan Hayyar Harrak IX captured 1,000 northern troops and had them turned to stone at the Petrified Labyrinth as both a warning and obstacle for the northern nations. Now, Castlegraspian criminals whose bodies go unclaimed following their tenure in Castlegrasp's Yard of Deterrents are deposited in the labyrinth. Currently, the labyrinth holds an estimated 3,000 statues.

Qirno Peninsula

Called "The Beast's Horn" by many who live in the western edge of the Basilisk's Spine, this damp, untamed forest region is mostly inhabited by Olyothyrian elves.

Qola

Once a sprawling metropolis and trade center at the northern edge of the Desolation of Ditimaya, Qola, the City of Welcomes, is now home to less

N

GRADBA'S LODGE

QIRNO PENINSULA

SERPENT'S TEARS

OLYOTHYR

SKIOUT

TROUBLED RUN

WALLINGMIOTA FOREST

SCROAS

SCHÄR

THE TEETH

SABALONA

LOQASOA

SABALONA TIMBERLAND

MOGRESZ

GAR WABRIZZ

THE PETRIFIED LABYRINTH

ONORIM'S PALACE

TRENROK BASE CAMP
X TRENROK MOUNTAIN
THE BASILISK'S SPINE MOUNTAINS

CABAL

WOUNDED PASS

THE LOST DRAGON PASS

THE WOUND

LACASA

TADJU

UQAMARTE

RUINS OF VON DORAL

ARRUQUETA

OMERIAN OCEAN

ORBEA

DREADFIELDS

QOLA

ROSELAKE

THE GHOST HOLM

HAVER

THE DESOLATION OF DITIMAYA

CASTLEGRASP

MAP KEY

LACASA	SETTLEMENT	TRAIL
	MEGA'S PATH	FOREST
	MAJOR ROAD	MOUNTAINS

1 HEX = 25 MILES

than 1,000 humanoids. This is mostly due to the infamous Hole at its center and the resulting evacuation. The Hole was born of a magical battle between a Dinzer Eye and a Dorethellian Sahir. The Dinzer, Shirick the Door, a danaavrakt, lost control of his power and created a "blip" at the center of the city. The blip slowly grew into what is now known as "the Hole." Interestingly, Shirick is also responsible for Dreadfields.

Qola is described in greater detail later in this adventure.

Roselake

Roselake is a village of 600 Central Omerians in the foothills of the basilisk. It's most well known for being the town where the last king of Von Doral, Aranmaic the Quiet lived following the evacuation of the city.

Sabalona Timberland

For centuries, the Sabalona Timberland has been the battleground for conflicts between the elves of Olyothmyr and the goblin hordes of Gar Wabrizz.

When the elves' numbers started to dwindle and the hobgoblins took control of the Garrish, it then became the site of many battles between the forces of the North and those of Central Omeria. There is a common expression in the north, "When Sabalona stops burning..." which means "that will probably never happen."

Schär

Schär is the second largest city in the goblinoid empire of Gar Wabrizz. It is governed by the goblin Duke Stogz, Grandmaster of the Lakes. Stogz openly contests the rule of Glonkad, although, many agree it is more of a show than a true contest. After all, goblinoids are expected to be ambitious and a lack of contest would surprise Glonkad. Regardless, Stogz sends at least one assassin every six months or so to kill Glonkad. Naturally, Glonkad lives up to her reputation and stops the assassin, then happily sends the assassin's removed head back to Stogz. Stogz collects the heads. "Politics as usual," he wryly replies to anyone who asks their purpose.

Scroas

Duke Widemouth Newton is the governer of Scroas the Swamp, the fourth largest city in the Gar Wabrizz empire. Although there are many goblinoids who live in Scroas, Scroas is predominantly lizard and frogfolk. Widemouth Newton has a tenous relationship with Queen Glonkad and doesn't "play the game" the same way his fellow lords do. Instead, he's content to guard the eastern edge of the empire quietly and away from the rigors of Garrish pomp and circumstance.

Serpent's Tears

The bay between the Qirno Peninsula and the Gar Wabrizz empire is called the Serpent's Tears. Nearly a century ago, it rose to fame as the site of a naval incursion by Glonklad's predecessor, Kleldruk the Fat. That battle turned the tide of war against the Olyothyrians. Supposedly, banshees haunt its mossy, green waters.

Skiout

High Priestess Faerstra Hun'iryn oversees Skiout, the third-largest city in Queen Glonkad's empire. A rare dark elf, Faerstra is the religious mind of the Garrish goblin hordes. She teaches the goblin clans the worship of Grimera, Goddess of the Land.

Skiout is also a satrapy, the home to the conquered elven tribes of Mythlalune, upon whose city Skiout was built. While free men and women all, the Mythlalune elves who still call Skiout home fear Faestra's Hun'iryn's wrath.

Tadju

The Tribal Confederacy of Mighty Tadju is the oldest civilization in all Central Omeria, just over 600 years old. Although Tadju itself is a city at the shores of the Wound, Tadju's influence covers the whole of the Tadjuuni Peninsula and much of the lands across. The Tadjuuni also swear that Ugash is part of its Confederacy, but the Ugashian Merchant Princes strongly deny those claims. Although their conflict is still somewhat cold, in recent years it's bloomed into skirmishes. And as Tadju finds itself with less and less arable land to grow fields, the more it looks to Ugash's verdant belt as its manifest destiny.

To make matters worse, the Tadju election draws near and the governors of the eighteen Tadjuuni states are all after the high position. Disappointed by the leadership of the current President, Awf al-Awan, the Tadjuuni people want new blood to oversee Tadju's future.

The Paragons of the True Emperor, a cult of some notoriety, use Tadju as their home base, quickly spreading their religion throughout the troubled lands. With each new convert, they gain a little more power in Mighty Tadju.

The Teeth

The Teeth are a collection of rocky islets, holms, and jagged rocks at the western edge of the Qirno Peninsula. Zen Kik merfolk call the waters around the Teeth their home.

Troubled Run

The raging, white water Troubled Run is the natural border between Gar Wabrizz and the neutral territories that buffer the hobgoblin empire and the human lands of the north.

Uqamarte

A satrapy of Cabal, the small city of Uqamarte is close to civil war with its imperial leaders and Admiral Covadonga Carballo. Cabal's taxation of the City of Storms has pushed Uqamarte to its limits. Recently, the city's satrap official Torkuato Beuba was targeted for assassination. The much-hated bureaucrat has since gone into hiding. Light on resources, Cabal received a loan of 200 militia from its southern ally, Castlegrasp, to tighten control over Uqamarte. Now the Martians are openly protesting Fair Eleven for his involvement.

Weysevain Coast

The western edge of Omeria is named for the northern explorer who first discovered it, Duda Weysevain, 400 years ago.

Von Doral

Perhaps the greatest dwarven civilization ever, Von Doral and the Infinite Gem Halls now lies in ruin. Fifty years ago, Queen Glonkad's father, King Gloat the Unbearable secured the southern borders of Gar Wabrizz by leading an assault into the labyrinth of mines below the Spine. There, the goblinoids conjured dark creatures from the recesses of the mountain. Unable to fight the horrors, the Von Dorals were forced to retreat.

Central Omerians recognize Von Dorals exodus as divine retribution for their failure to assist during the north-ern battles. Likewise, the Von Dorals blame the human Omerians for the loss of their ancient homelands. Tensions are high.

The Wound

The Wound is an abyss-like sea fed by the rivers and channels that pour off the Basilisk's Spine. Certainly beautiful in some places, the Wound is cold year-round. Furthermore, its steep waters give it an almost black appearance. Still, many important Central Omerian cities cling to its mighty shores.

Wallingmiota Wood

The Wallingmiota remains mostly unclaimed by both the Garrish and northern Omerians as it is the neutral lands that divide the two nations (thanks to Treaty of Clean Hands). Untamed and largely uninhabiteted, the wood is home to many large beasts, including the world-renown terror lizards of Wallingmiota. Scientists from all over Omeria are given the privilege to study and travel in the Wallingmiota thanks to an amendment to the Treaty of Clean Hands. Perhaps some may see it as a sign of improving relationships, but many goblinoids and humanoid scientists work together within the Wallingmiota despite the centuries-old rivalry.

Wounded Pass

A century ago, the Tradjuuni and Garrish united to develop a passage through the mountains. This tunnel was created to improve trade relations between Gar Wabrizz and Tradju, and for a time, it did just that. Unfortunately, the events that lead to the evacuation of Von Doral also affected the safety of the tunnel passage. Still, Garrish and Tradjuuni who have the resources to travel through the mountains do so. After all, it's safer than going over the Spine and faster than going through the circuitous route through the Elegant Valley to the east.

The Desolation of Ditimaya

The clues the characters find in Castlegrasp should lead them north from Castlegrasp and Mega's trail (the dotted lines on the map of the Weysevain Coast on page 61). Still, it's likely they won't know exactly where to start looking for Mega. Afterall, it's possible he could have gone north along the Leash, east through the desert, caught a ship in the Omerian, or something completely different. A criminal and born tracker himself, he's good at covering his tracks and knows how to avoid divination magic.

How to Find Mega
There are a few methods that the characters can use to track Mega.

Follow Another Bounty Hunter. The bounty hunters detailed in the Bounty Hunter section on page 71 have picked up on clues leading to Mega and likely have a headstart over the characters. By following one of them, the characters will eventually find Mega. Of course, they have to escape the bounty hunter's notice, too.

Track Mega. If the characters discovered that Mega was holing up at Tale of the Dragon's home outside of Castlegrasp, then they can start following his trail through the desert.

Find Mega's Contacts Throughout the Weysevain Coast. It's possible that Mega makes it difficult to follow his trail. If this is the case, the characters can search for his companions throughout the Weysevain Coast. While taking this particular path may lead the characters on a much different adventure path, it is the fastest way to find the book, Prime.

Travel Through the Desert
On the map of the Weysevain Coast, each hex measures 24 miles across. While traveling at a normal pace off-road, it takes two days to travel through 1 hex. If the characters are traveling on a major road, it only takes only one day to travel through 1 hex. Travel by sea is much faster as most sailing vessels can travel 4 hexes per day.

If characters traveling by foot or mounted move at a fast pace, roll a d6. On a result of 5 or 6, the number of days it takes to cross a hex is reduced by 1. Characters moving at a fast pace take a -5 penalty to their passive Wisdom (Perception and Survival) scores, making them more likely to miss clues and walk into ambushes. This includes checks made to follow Mega's trail.

If characters set a slow pace, it takes them three days to travel through 1 hex off-road and two days to travel through 1 hex on a major road.

Following the Trail. Have the players designate one party member as the tracker. The tracker might be an NPC, such as a guide or befriended bounty hunter, and the party can switch its navigator day to day.

At the start of each new travel day, the GM makes a Wisdom (Survival) check on behalf of the tracker. The result of the check determines whether or not the party loses Mega or the bounty hunter's trail over the course of the day. The DC of the check is based on who the characters are following.

Tracking DCs	
Quarry	**DC**
Ember in the Dark	10
Jacob Harlow	16
La Main de la Mort	11
Mega	12
Odeo and Ahmeego	14
The Onyx Triad	12
Tiriana Philen	11
Xion	12

Apply a +5 check if the group sets a slow pace for the day, or a -5 penalty if the group is moving at a fast pace.

If the check succeeds, the navigator knows exactly which way the quarry went. The GM tells them which hex to head towards (following Mega's path on the map).

If the check fails, the party loses the trail. They must spend another day trying to find it, or try to find another clue.

Random Encounters

The Desolation of Ditimaya is aggressively hostile towards most forms of life, especially humanoids. All manner of strange and deadly creatures live among the dunes. That's not to say it's completely devoid of intelligent life, either. At regular intervals, there are hamlets, nomad caravans, and oases to be discovered in the desert.

While the characters are traveling through the Desolation of Ditimaya, roll a d20 three times per day of game time, checking for encounters each morning, afternoon, and evening or night. An encounter occurs on a roll of 16 or higher. Roll percentile dice and check the Desolation of Ditimaya Encounters table on page 66. If the characters are in a hex that contains Mega's path and they have not lost his trail, use the Mega's Trail column. Otherwise, roll on the Off the Trail column. Random encounters marked with an asterisk are detailed below.

Abandoned Campsite (Mega). Mega used the area as a campsite and left clues that he was there. The next check that the characters make to follow Mega's trail is made with advantage.

Abandoned Campsite (Bounty Hunter). One of the seven bounty hunters following Mega used the area as a campsite and left clues. If the characters are already trailing a bounty hunter, this was their campsite. Otherwise, roll randomly on the Bounty Hunter table or choose one that is appropriate.

The next check that the characters make to follow the Bounty Hunter's path is made with advantage. If so, the next check that the characters to make to track Mega is made with advantage.

Bounty Hunter. The characters come face-to-face with one of the bounty hunters/bounty hunter groups. If they are trailing a specific bounty hunter, the bounty hunter has noticed that he/she/they are being followed and confronts the characters. Otherwise, roll for a bounty hunter or choose randomly from the table in the Bounty Hunter section. The nature of the encounter depends on the bounty hunter.

Bounty Hunter Trap. To discourage anyone from following him/her/them, one of the bounty hunters left a trap on the trail. As the characters are traveling, roll a Wisdom (Perception) check on behalf of the navigator. On a failed check, the party stumbles into a trap. Choose or roll randomly to determine the nature of the trap. The bounty hunter left no sign or trail as to which they went, but they did leave a note: "Stop following me."

d6	**Bounty Hunter Trap**
1-3	*Pit trap.* The navigator automatically falls into a 10-foot deep it and takes 3 (1d6) damage from the fall. Every other character must make a DC 10 Dexterity saving throw to avoid falling in as well.
4-5	*Spike trap.* Each character must make a DC 12 Dexterity saving throw. On a failed saving throw, a character takes 7 (2d6) piercing damage and must make a DC 12 Constitution saving throw. On a failed saving throw, the character is poisoned until they complete a long rest.
6	*Explosion.* Each character must make a DC 13 Dexterity saving throw. On a failed saving throw, a character takes 10 (3d6) fire damage. On a successful saving throw, a character takes half as much damage.

Dead Blackbirds. Similar to the scene at Tale of the Dragon's home, the characters discover dozens of dead blackbirds. There is a 50% chance that Mega was at the scene and fled.

Dinzer Pylon. One of the mysterious, 200-foot tall pillars of Pabradian steel looms over the landscape. While the pylon itself is not dangerous, those who camp near one or within sight of one at night notices that the sky above it takes on a strange green hue.

Hermit. A **druid** lives in a shanty or lean-to in the desert. Roll a d6. On a result of 5 or 6, the hermit is friendly and offers assistance. Plus, there is a 10% chance that the hermit saw Mega or one of the bounty hunters pass through. If so, the next check that the characters to make to find the trail is made with advantage. On any other result, the hermit keeps to itself and politely (or impolitely if you like) asks the characters to leave.

Merchant Caravan. Three wagons pulled by 3 **red-striped thornfoots** cross the desert. Playing it safe, the merchant caravan stops as soon as it sees another sign of a humanoid, then sends a rider (**scout**) ahead. The caravan is bringing spices from Tadju to Castlegrasp to trade in the Den Bazaar. The caravan is led by a noble who is accompanied by 5 **commoner** accountants. There are 8 **guards** present led by a **veteran**. There is a 10% chance that the caravan saw Mega or one of the bounty hunters pass through the area. The chance doubles if the characters offer gold in exchange for information. If so, the next check that the characters make to find the trail is made with advantage.

Nomads. A large group of nomads moves through the desert. There are 50 **commoners** protected by 10 **riding horse**-mounted **bandits** and 1 mounted **bandit captain**. They have over 100 sheep with them as well, and are using 2 **red-striped thornfoots** to pull their supplies. They are friendly and will gladly trade for water and supplies, of which they have plenty (standard *PHB* rates). There is a 10% chance that the nomads saw Mega or one of the bounty hunters pass through the area. If so, the next check that the characters make to find the trail is made with advantage.

Village. The characters discover a small village around a well or oasis. The village has a population of 1d6 x 100 people. To further detail the village, refer to the section on Settlements in Chapter 5 of the *DMG*. There is a 20% chance that the villagers saw Mega or one of the bounty hunters pass through the area. If so, the next check that the characters to make find the trail is made with advantage.

Village (Bounty Hunter Present). Similar to the entry for a village above, the characters discover a small village. However, there is a bounty hunter in the village. If they are trailing a specific bounty hunter, the bounty hunter has noticed that he/she/they are being followed and confronts the characters. Otherwise, roll for a bounty hunter or choose randomly from the table in the Bounty Hunter section. The nature of

Desolation of Ditimaya Encounters		
Encounter	**Off Trail**	**Mega's Trail**
Abandoned campsite (Mega)*	01-03	01-07
Abandoned campsite (bounty hunter)*	04-07	08-11
1 pseudodragon	08	12
1d3 giant scorpions	09-12	13-14
Nomads	13-17	15-19
Dead blackbirds*	18	20-23
Merchant caravan*	19	24-25
1d6 gnolls	20-24	-
2d6 tribal warriors	25-26	26
1d4 giant vultures	27-29	27
Dinzer pylon*	30-33	-
2d6 + 3 bandits	34	28-31
Village ruins*	35-38	32-35
1 ettin	39-41	-
Hermit*	42-43	36-39
1 red-striped thornfoot	44	-
1d4 berserkers	45-47	40
3d4 swarms of insects	48-50	41
1d3 manticores	51-52	42
1d4 + 1 giant hyenas	53	-
1 fire elemental	54	-
1 earth elemental	55-56	-
1 wraith	57	-
1 air elemental	58-59	-
1 hill giant	60	43-44
1d4 + 3 griffons	61	45-46
2d6 cultists	62-64	47
1 bandit captain with 2d6 bandits	65-66	48-49
1d6 orcs	67-69	-
Bounty hunter trap*	-	50-54
Bounty hunter*	70-74	55-64
Village (bounty hunter present)*	75-84	65-74
Village*	85-00	75-00

the encounter depends on the bounty hunter.

Village Ruins. The remains of a hamlet lies half-buried in the sand. there is a 25% chance that 2d4 **ban-** dits with 1 **bandit captain** hide among the ruins, waiting for passersby to make camp. The bandits have 3d10 gold hidden in the ruins, loot from previous victims.

Qola

Mega's trail eventually leads to the ghost city of Qola. As the characters approach the abandoned city, read the following:

> The titanic statue of Jerar, explorer and founder of Qola, stands 400-feet over the desert, the first sign that you are near Qola. Once called the City of Welcomes, Qola is now known as the Abandoned City. Hundreds of homes, businesses, and points of interest within the unwalled city have slowly evacuated over the last 50 years as a catastrophic 700-foot-wide hole of literal nothingness slowly swallows the city from the inside out. The city isn't completely empty, of course. There are still a few who remain: the stubborn, the curious, and the insane.
>
> The briny, unpalatable Qolan mire surrounds you, its glassy waters reflecting the ice-blue sky above. It's in those waters you first notice an exciting sight ahead. A red-and-blue Dinzer Cargoblimp crosses the sandy wastes to the south headed directly for the city. Judging by its speed, it looks like it's about to slow down and drop anchor.
>
> To signal its presence, the ship emits its ear-shattering foghorn, easily heard for miles.

Since Mega's arrival in Qola, he's kept himself hidden from the locals. The powerful magic that exudes from the Hole makes divination nearly impossible in Qola. Already, he's had two run-ins with bounty hunters in the city, killing one (your choice). But with the characters and bounty hunters arriving—not to mention the deadly Black Bird—Mega has few options. Until he learned about the incoming Dinzer cargoblimp, the *Postboy*, that is.

On instructions from Dinzer naturalists, the *Postboy* was to touchdown in Qola and coordinate with a Knotsider zoologists working in the city. In the early years of the Hole's appearance, the zoo was a low priority. Qola's previous rulers were more focused on addressing the Hole itself and removing it. When those efforts failed, the evacuations began. Now, as the Hole comes close to swallowing Qola's zoo, Omerian conservationists are trying to remove the animals and transport them over the mountains.

The *Postboy* is still 30 minutes out when the characters first notice it, and the characters are roughly 2,500 feet from the center of the city. Unless they've been killed, disabled, or otherwise sidetracked, all of the bounty hunters detailed in the section on Bounty Hunters close in on Qola the same time the characters do.

General Features

Qola is a ghost city. Nearly all of its buildings are abandoned and empty, many of which for decades. Most are falling apart due to neglect and the harsh conditions of the Desolation of Ditimaya that surrounds it on all sides. Sand, briny mire water, animals, and rubbish cover most of the ground, inside and out. Sand creepers, a yellow-green vine, is prevalent everywhere, making some areas almost completely impassable. The few natural Qolans who still live in the city are quiet, cold, and unfriendly. They have little to share and don't care for the reasons why the characters, or anyone else for that matter, are in the city. Many refuse to leave simply because it's the only home they've ever known.

Because of the strange effect the Hole has on the atmosphere, the sky directly above Qola rapidly changes colors during both the day and night. One moment, the sky is brilliant blue, the next light green, and then suddenly muddy red as if the sun was setting. At night, stripes of green, blue, and violet streak the black sky. Clouds swirl clockwise above the Hole, almost as if they were going down some unseen drain. With the exception of the Black Bird's flock,

beasts won't come within one mile of Qola.

Perhaps the strangest feature of Qola is the low hum the Hole makes. As more and more Qolans have fled the city, taking the ambiance of a living community with them, the hum's become much more noticeable. Some have been driven mad by the sound, claiming that they can hear the voice of aberrant gods from within it.

Of course, there are no gods in the Hole, nor are there creatures, or worlds, or portals, or *anything*. The Hole is nothing. Literally nothing. And it is *growing*.

Important Locations

For this particular adventure, these are the points of interest in Qola, as marked on the map of Qola on page 69. They are by no means all of important locations in the city, so feel free to alter and add more as you need.

1 - West Tuttahem Garden. The westernmost part of the city was once its wealthiest section, West Tuttahem Garden. The empty multistory buildings still stand, but nearly all have been broken into, looted, and vandalized. The only living creatures within are tiny to small monstrosities, sand creepers, and humanoid derelicts.

The cobblestone roads are covered with sand, only a few stones surfacing here or there. Wrecked carts, broken barrels, and even the occasional horse or red striped thornfoot skeleton tell a story of quick evacuation, chaos, and rioting.

A DC 13 passive Wisdom (Perception) check reveals that there are many fresh footprints entering the city from this ward, likely bounty hunters.

No matter which end of the city the characters enter, read the following;

> As you pass through the ruins of the once-prosperous city, over the wind you hear the songs of birds. On withered tree limbs and atop the cracked rooves of abandoned homes and

shops you see them: literally hundreds of blackbirds along the path you travel.

Anyone who makes a DC 10 Intelligence (Nature) check will know that for this many blackbirds to be found south of the Spine is almost unheard of. They can be scared away briefly with an area of effect spell like fireball or lightning. But always return. Their presence should invoke a sense of dread within the characters.

2 - The Terrific Lion. Sets of tracks leads through the courtyard towards a large building that was probably a tavern sometime ago. The blackbirds that you have seen everywhere are here, too, outlining the buildings surrounding you. Their chirps and songs make talking tiresome.

For a time, the Terrific Lion was the most popular tavern in Qola. Minstrels, performers, and exotic dancers traveled from all points of Omeria to perform on the lion's famous stage. Even after the Hole appeared, its popular remained, especially among those who wanted to see the dreaded Hole in person. Eventually, the curiosity turned to horror, and Qola's name became synonymous with dread. Then, five years ago, the Lion finally shut its doors, and its owners moved to Ugash.

The tracks were left by one of the bounty hunters (your choice), who is patiently waiting in the bar having a drink. The bounty hunter invites the characters in for a drink—"no gimmicks, no traps, just a drink at the end of the world, friends." The hunter, having seen the Hole, has taken a moment to collect his/her thoughts.

"I thought it would be like looking into the face of a god," [the bounty hunter] says, setting their glass down. "But no. It was worse than that. It was like looking at... nothing. Nothing at all. Life, hope, our future? All down that hole."

It's clear that seeing the Hole had a lasting impression on the bounty hunter. Their desire to fight—and even collect on Mega—is all but gone.

"Did you know that the Ditimayans believed that blackbirds were guardians of the underworld? They were supposedly servants of Yuduyama. Ol' Yuduyama would read the dreams of sleepers across the land, then signal the birds to collect the souls of those whose hearts were impure. When the morning came, the birds brought their cacophony to the ears of the wicked."

The bounty hunter motions to the birds outside. "Good thing it's just an old legend, right?" [The bounty hunter] laughs and pours [him/her] self another drink.

The bounty hunter has put his or herself out of the fight, content to sit in the bar and drink. Only if attacked, will he or she fight back.

3 - Dario de Luca. As the characters approach a clearing where the ruins of an old temple rest, they hear someone speaking to themselves thirty feet ahead.

Over the wind, the blackbirds, and the low hum of something just beyond the buildings that you can't see, you hear a man speaking. "One... two... yes. Damn. Okay, think think think. 700 feet now. 699 last week. Very small, but very big, too. But fifty years before that... fifty-two. Yes."

As the characters step into the clearing, they catch a glimpse of the man who is speaking. Dario de Luca (CN male Knotsider human **noble**) is a scientist and arcanist who has been studying the Hole for the last year. The obsession drove him mad. His hair and beard are a tangled mess and his clothing is in tatters. Forgetting to eat most days, he weighs no more than 90 lbs. His skin is leathery and blistered from constantly being out in the sun and

his eyes betray a lack of sleep. Using chalk, coal, paint, or anything else he can get his hands on, Dario's covered the walls of abandoned buildings, sidewalks, and even his arms with numbers, questions, runes, diagrams, and more.

Dario loves to explain his passion with anyone who will listen. He especially loves to mention how time is running out and explain his math. By his estimations, the Hole grows a little more each year. Currently, it's too subtle for anyone to notice. Less than an inch each year. But its growth is accelerating. Each year, the diameter grows by the amount it previously grew, but by times a factor of 1.5.

"It's nothing now! Nothing, really. Just a little more sand falling in. But! But!" he excitedly rushes over to a wall with a graph painted on it. "In eight years, the Hole grows by a full foot in one year. Then—THEN!— two years after that, it's growing by two feet per year. This continues, you see—SEE! In twenty years, it's over 800-feet-wide. 800-feet! That's right where we're standing. In just twenty years!"

He then pauses, looking for an answer. If none comes, he sighs.

"You don't get it either. No one gets it. No one cares. You just care about yours wars and pylons and cities and magics. No one cares."

4 - The Hole. As the characters approach the infamous Hole, read the following:

What you see before you defies all description. Certainly, it is a hole—a very large hole, in fact. That much is true. But it is not a pit or a chasm or an abyss. It is only a hole. Gently, the sand at its edges moves towards it, tumbles over the perfectly round edge, the vanishes into nothing.

The Hole, as it continues to grow,

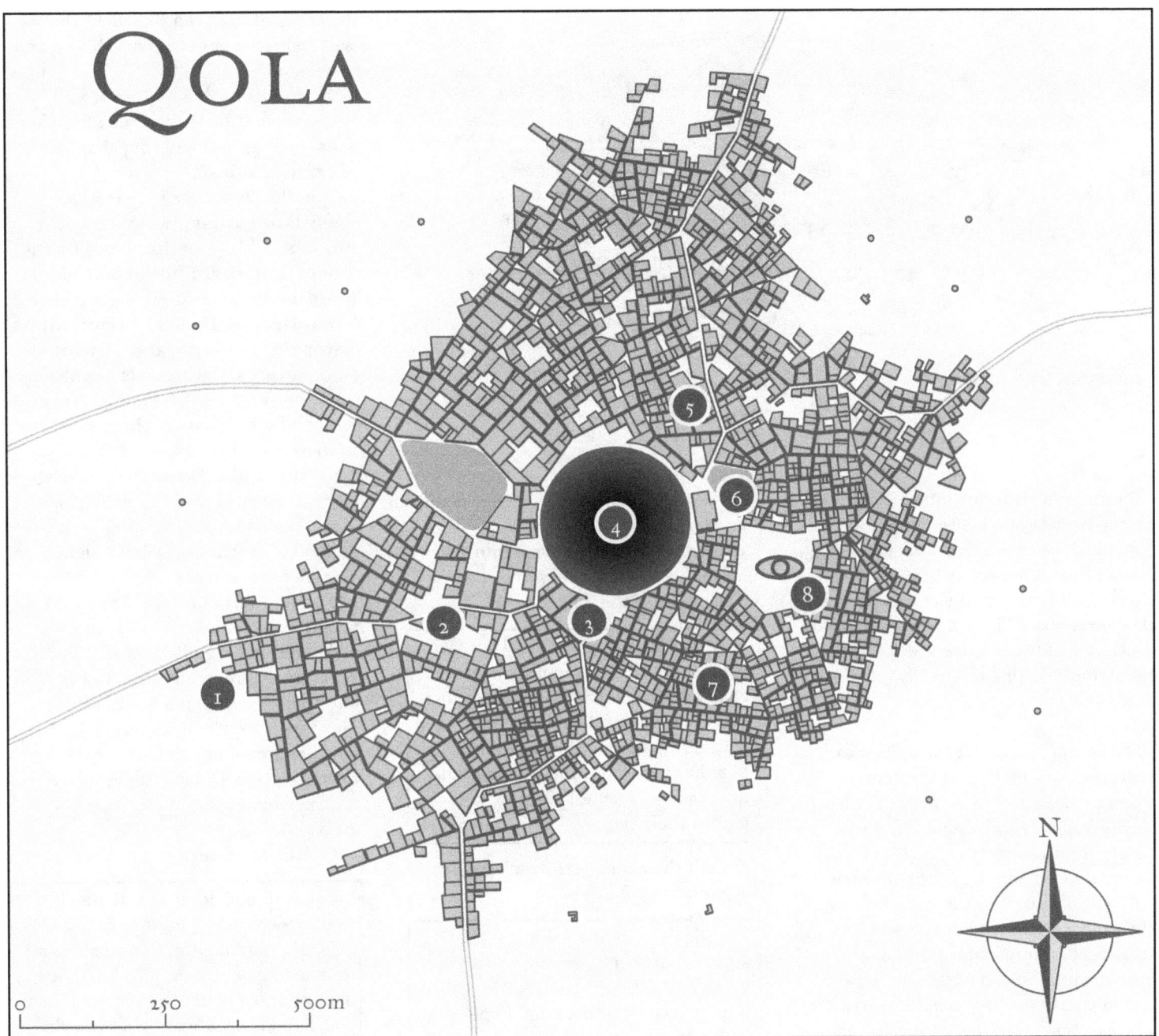

QOLA

erases more and more of Qola. There are hints that buildings once stood where it is, but they were either demolished or fell completely into the hole. And like the bits of sand, they, too, were erased.

It does not seem innately chaotic or destructive, as that would indicate it had consciousness or a sense of self.

Instead, it just is and isn't at once.

After reading the description to the players, each character within 300 feet of the 700-foot wide Hole that can see the Hole must make a DC 15 Wisdom saving throw. On a failed saving throw, a character becomes frightened of the Hole. The character can repeat its saving throw each hour, ending the effect on itself with a success. If the character fails their saving throw three times in the row, they gain a form of indefinite madness (see the *DMG*).

Any character who makes the mistake of coming into contact with the Hole is immediately disintegrated. Nothing can bring the character back from the dead, not even a *wish* spell or divine intervention.

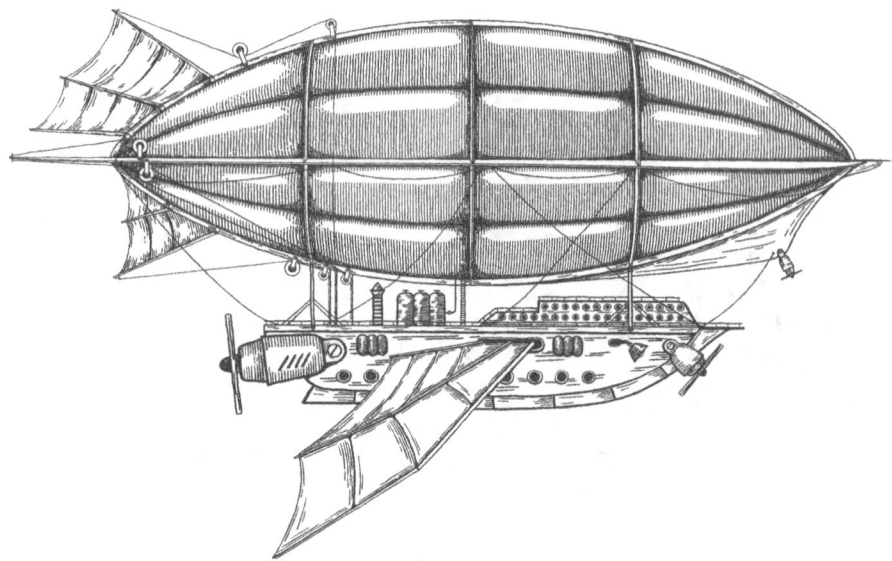

Jerar's Statue (**Area 8**), where they will be loaded onto the cargoblimp and evacuated.

The zoologists and porters are all non-combatants. Only if the animals seem endangered will they make an effort to fight back.

From the front cage to rear, the animals are: 2 **harpies** (muzzled), 1 **ankheg**, 2 **hippogriffs**, 2 **axe beaks**, 2 **hook horrors**, 1 **bullette**, 1 **black pudding** (in an acid-proof glass cage), 2 **manticores**, 1 **grick**, 1 **triceratops**, 1 **woggle**, 1 **otyugh**, and 3 **owlbears**. In their cages, the animals are harmless. But if released, a creature recklessly attack anyone or thing that gets in its way of them escaping the city.

7 - New Qola. The sound end of the city is a maze of shanties called New Qola. The shantytown's inhabitants are a blend of evacuated Qolans, sightseers, Hole-worshippers, and scientists. It's a rambunctious area. The mood is both remorseful and celebratory at once. And the area is lawless. Bandits roam freely, mugging is not uncommon, and there have been a few notable murders throughout the year. As the Dinzer cargoblimp glides over the town, the New Qolans cheer, dance, play instruments and celebrate its arrival.

8 - Statue of Jerar.

> The statue of Jerar is a 400-foot tall limestone idol built to praise Qola's original founder. It resembles a cloaked mage. In its right hand, it holds Jerar's walking stick, and its left hand is open and held towards the sky, welcoming travelers. The statue stands on top of a 50-foot tall, 80-foot wide pedestal. A single flight of steps rises from the park surrounding the statue to the top of the pedestal and the walkway surrounding the statue's feet.

If the characters approached from the south side of the city, through New Qola (**Area 7**), the cargoblimp is

5 - Mega's Hideout. Since his arrival in Qola, Mega has been hiding inside a small closet in an abandoned warehouse. If the characters tracked Mega this far, they find that the trail ends at the warehouse. There are clues that he was camped there, but no Mega. (Mega is currently hiding on the Statue of Jerar.)

The characters aren't the only ones there. One of the bounty hunters (choose one or roll randomly) has also discovered Mega's hideout. How the bounty hunter reacts to the other characters depends on the bounty hunter.

6 - Qola Zoo. What it lacked in size, the Qola Zoo made up for in wonder. It carried an unusual collection of animals from all over Omeria, some friendly, others dangerous, all exciting. The caretaker, Halim Saleem (LG male Ditimayan human **veteran**), stayed with the zoo as long as he could. Just as he was about to abandon it, a Knotsider zoologist named Buman Zenor (LG male Knotsider human **noble**) approached Saleem, offering to help. Together, the two made arrangements to have the zoo carefully evacuated and the animals transported over the Spine to Knotside. Zenor connected with an air transport company in Odonburg

who provided a specially equipped ship for their needs.

When the characters come into the park or area surrounding the zoo, read or paraphrase the following:

> Unlike the rest of the city that feels mostly empty, this old park seems to be alive with activity. Twenty animal cages set on wheels and tethered together line the nearby street. Each cage has a strange and unusual animal inside. They all seem to have fear in their eyes.

Even if the characters aren't in the zoo, at some point, read:

> To the east, by the goliath mage statue that casts a shadow over much of the city, the Dinzer cargoblimp prepares for docking. Ropes descend from its gondola. Two humanoids wearing costumes of blue and red leap from the blimp and slowly drift to the ground on floating discs.

While the blimp is docking, the zoologists scramble with the 6 local porters (**commoners**) to prepare the animals. The cages are tethered to a **red-striped thornfoot** that waits at the front. Once ready, the thornfoot will pull them down the street to still on its way into the city, sounding its impossibly loud landing horn as it comes closer.

Otherwise, the blimp begins to make preparations to dock. Two Dinzer porters (LN human Dinzer **thugs**) standing on levitating platforms (they are functionally similar to brooms of flying) drift to the ground holding onto the blimp's grappling anchors. Fifty feet from the pedestal a circular blimp dock has been set into the ground. The porters connect steel latch hooks to the blimp dock first. From there, the blimp moves closer to the statue of Jerar, its nose docking at the statue's outstretched hand. A third Dinzer porter climbing the underside catwalk tethers the blimp's nose to the hand, securing the blimp.

If the characters witness the docking procedure, read the following:

> A shout comes from above you. You look up to the top of the statue of Jerar where the blimp has docked. Although it's nearly 450 feet ahead, you can see one of the blimp's porter's fighting a second person at the top of the hand. Although it's hard to make out, you're pretty sure that it's none other than Mega. He's trying to get onto the blimp!

Of course, the characters aren't alone. The fight with Mega continues in the next section, Mega's Final Stand.

Mega's Final Stand

At this point, the characters should notice that Mega is trying to breach the cargoblimp. To get onto the blimp, he will have to get past the Dinzer porter, cross the catwalk, and step into the gondola. The characters have a chance to stop him before this happens. Unfortunately, they aren't alone. Including the characters, there are five factions at work during this battle. Before running it, be sure you review the details of each faction as well as the motivations for the individual bounty hunters.

The Bounty Hunters

The following seven NPCs are a part of the Hand of the Eight adventure path and are introduced in Chapter 3. ***The Black Bird.*** If you need to choose one of the Bounty Hunters at random, roll 2d4, then refer to the number next to their name.

2 - Jacob Harlow and Bruce
Jacob Harlow (NG male Knotsider human **scout**) lives in the wild with his husky, Bruce (use the **wolf** stat block). Contracted by a Castlegraspian's noble son to find the escaped orc, Jacob uses Bruce's keen senses to follow the trail. Jacob is not interested in working with the characters or any other bounty hunters but will bring no harm to his competitors.
  Ideal: "I work towards the greater good."
  Bond: "Bruce is my best friend; we protect each other."
  Flaw: "My arrogance turns many off."

3 - The Onyx Triad
Gundo, Ozek, and Lokai (all CE male Ditimayan human **cultists**) are members of a secret society known as the Onyx Triad whose headquarters are in a small village at the edge of the Obsidian Plain. The three are dangerous and savage. Not only will they attack competitors, but they will leave the remains of those they encounter as warnings to others who hope to collect on their bounties.
  Ideal: "We only hope to cause pain."
  Bond: "Each of us carries a special item gifted by the high priest of the Triad. We are very protective of the item."
  Flaw: "We are prone to rage."

4 - La Main de la Mort
A loner who hunts only for the opportunity to kill, La Main de Mort (CE male Knotsider human **berserker**) paints blue handprints onto the corpses of those he kills. He does not like being followed and will go out of his way to stop anyone who is on his trail.
  Ideal: "Change is beautiful."
  Bond: "I am drawn to the Desolation of Ditimaya and its savage, inhospitable nature."
  Flaw: "I often lose advantage in combat because I get cocky."

5 - Ember in the Dark
Ember in the Dark is the first devilkin (tiefling) Stonearm in Castlegrasp. He uses a **knight** stat block, except any creature he hits with a sword must make a DC 12 Constitution saving throw. On a failed save, the creature magically begins to turn to stone and is restrained. It must repeat the saving throw at the end of its

next turn. On a success, the effect ends. On a failure, the creature is petrified until freed by the greater restoration spell or other magic. Ember is not following Mega for the bounty. Therefore, he is willing to work with others to track and capture the orc.
Because of his status, many of the other bounty hunters are unwilling to attack him out of fear of retribution by the other Stonearms.
  Ideal: "All life is precious."
  Bond: "I am dedicated to the cause of being a Stonearm, and I am fiercely protective of all my colleagues (even if they don't extend the same courtesy)."
  Flaw: "I anger easily."

6 - Tiriana Philen
Tiriana Philen is a LE half-elf **noble** whose parentage traces back to Olyothyr, Tiriana uses her good looks, charm, and a whole bevy of disguises to get close to her bounties. If she discovers that she is being followed, she uses the same tactics on competitors.
  Ideal: "All must surrender their will to me."
  Bond: "I seek revenge against someone who wronged me many years ago."
  Flaw: "I am wanted in numerous cities across Omeria."

7 - Xion
Xion is a **drow** but with the following changes. He can cast the spell *shocking grasp* at will and will use that ability to subdue his quarry. True to his neutral evil nature, Xion has no qualms attacking and killing competitors.
  Ideal: "I enjoy causing pain."
  Bond: "I am in love with Tiriana Philen, although she is not in love with me."
  Flaw: "I once angered Queen Daria Emgavel. I cannot set foot in or around Arruquetta."

8 - Odeos and Ahmeego
Odeos and Ahmeego are two halfling brothers (CG male **spies**) from northern Omeria. They have no interest in working with others. However, they won't kill others on the trail as it goes against their moral code. If anything, they will try to slow competitors down by leaving traps, manipulating law enforcement, or creating deceptions along the trail.
  Ideal: "We are strongly independent."
  Bond: "My brother is the only person I can trust."
  Flaw: "I have a blindspot for my brother; if he is in danger, I can focus on nothing else."

Bounty Hunters

All of the bounty hunters in Qola converge on the courtyard surrounding Jerar's statue (minus any dead bounty hunters or those who've quit, such as the one at the Terrific Lion). Most of the bounty hunters are focused on stopping and capturing Mega. Remember that Mega's bounty is paid regardless if the orc is dead or alive. However, the bounty hunters would prefer that they didn't have to pull a crashed blimp off the orc's corpse to claim it.

Dinzer Porters

There are two Dinzer porters on the ground, one fighting Mega in Jerar's left hand, one in the blimp's cargo bay, and two more piloting the blimp. They are all **thugs**. The two on the ground are equipped with fully-charged wands of magic missiles and levitating platforms.

Unaware of the situation with Mega, the Dinzers believe that all of the bounty hunters and characters involved are raiders working together. They fight back at any that come close to them, the blimp's anchors, and the blimp's ropes.

Mega

Mega has been hiding in Jerar's left hand for nearly two days. He used a *potion of climbing* to reach the hand and hid within its fingers. His plan is to get onto the blimp, remove any nonessentials, and take the pilots hostage. Once he has control of the cargoblimp, he plans to fly over the Basilisk's Spine, preferably landing somewhere in the Wallingmiota.

During this battle, these are the actions he takes. You do not have to roll for results. Instead, allow Mega to accomplish each action in the round it appears. If accosted by bounty hunters, characters, or the Black Bird, he will not deter from his mission, and instead use his action to Dodge or Disengage rather than fight. If all else fails, he will fight, using his strength to over-power and throw his opponents off the statue or blimp. The following actions assume that Mega escapes without difficulty.

Round	Mega's Actions
1	Mega grabs the Dinzer porter in the Jerar's hand and tosses the man off the statue, 400 feet to his death. He then runs 30 feet across the catwalk.
2	A porter steps out onto the catwalk armed with a quarterstaff. Mega charges the porter and grapples him.
3	The porter and Mega fight, neither one able to defeat the other.
4	Mega overcomes the porter and throws him over the edge of the catwalk. The porter hits the ground and dies. Mega enters the gondola.
5	Mega enters the cockpit of the blimp and fights one of the Dinzer porters.
6	Mega continues fighting the porter.
7	Mega kills the porter and turns to the pilot: "Fly!" he commands, threatening him with a short sword.
8	Fearful, the pilot starts to pull the blimp away from Jerar's statue. If it is still attached to the blimp dock, it cannot move more than 60 feet in any direction.
9	If the blimp is still attached to the blimp dock, Mega uses a scimitar to hack away the ropes.
10	Mega frees the blimp of its ropes. The blimp flies north.

The Black Bird

As the combat continues into its fifth round, the final faction enters the fray: the mysterious Black Bird. Read or paraphrase the following:

> In a matter of seconds, the sky dims, turning from blue to green to yellow then orange and finally to red, as if the sun were setting midday. The songs of the blackbirds rise to their highest volume yet, drowning out all sound. You glance around: what was previously hundreds of blackbirds have now become thousands. They cover every surface within 200 feet of you and their eyes glow with red, radiant energy. Their song builds and builds and builds until finally they all go silent at once.
>
> And that's when you first see him.
>
> The man appears to be nothing more than a silhouette, his back to the sun, features indiscernible. You can't make out the features of his face, but like the birds enveloping him, his eyes glow with the same red, radiant energy. In his left hand he wields a four-foot-long spear with two blades. The first blade is a wickedly sharp point, typical for a spear, while the second is curved like a scythe. The entire weapon crackles with the same red energy.
>
> The dark figure's attention is on you briefly before he gazes up to the blimp above. Without a single utterance, he points with his free hand to the blimp. Immediately, the entirety of the blackbird horde vaults into the sky towards the blimp.

The **Black Bird** (see Appendix B) only cares for capturing Mega. He will defend himself if needed but spends most of his actions Dodging and Disengaging. Only if he truly feels threatened will he fight back. He will spend each of his actions climbing the statue (using his Cunning Action feature, he can climb 60 feet per turn).

His swarm of blackbirds is less a creature than a force of nature. He can use his action to command the entire swarm as if they were created through his Summon Murder action.

It will take the birds four rounds to reach the blimp. Once they do, they immediately attack the windows of the cockpit. Then, it takes them another round to break the glass. After that, they kill the pilot and corner Mega. Black Bird should arrive shortly thereafter.

Crash Landing

Black Bird does not need the blimp, he only needs Mega. After he's used his swarms of birds to corner and disable Mega, then uses his birds to carry him and Mega away from the scene.

If the control room of the blimp is disabled and all of its pilots killed, the blimp will start to veer out of control. One of two things happens:

If it is free of its tethers, the blimp slowly drifts towards the north. Like a released balloon, it travels until its gas dissipates. It then sinks, eventually landing in a lake, mountain pass, or forest somewhere north of Qola (GM's discretion).

If the blimp is still tethered, a catastrophe occurs. The tethers won't allow the blimp to head north. Instead, they anchor the blimp to the ground, forcing it to fall to the ground in a 90-degree arc, straight toward the Hole. It only takes the blimp two rounds to reach the Hole. Touching the hole, the blimp is instantly destroyed, erased from reality. Even the explosion caused by the destruction of its balloon is absorbed into the great, empty nothingness.

Next, the Hole starts to pull at the tethers with so much force it tears the entire dock from its place in the ground. Any creature standing within 15 feet of the dock when this happens must make a DC 13 Dexterity saving throw. On a failed saving throw, a creature takes 14 (4d6) bludgeoning damage and is knocked prone. From there, the Hole slurps up the ropes and the dock plus any debris it carries with it.

But that's not all. The amount of mass the Hole devours causes a chain reaction. One round after it destroyed the balloon, the tethers, and the ground dock, purple energy belches from the Hole. Each creature within 100 feet of the Hole is instantly disintegrated. Then, creatures within 500 feet of the hole must make DC 20 Constitution saving throw as a blast wave of purple energy rushes through the ruins of the city, destroying nearly everything in its path. A creature takes 35 (10d6) necrotic damage and is poisoned on a failed saving throw, or half as much damage on a successful saving throw and isn't poisoned.

Before this occurs, give the characters plenty of opportunities to escape. Explain that the ground is shaking and the hum the Hole creates is getting louder. As epic-heroes-to-be, they should be able to escape the wave in just the nick of time.

Adventure Conclusion

It's highly unlikely that Mega gets away this time. He either dies at the hands of bounty hunters or characters, dies in blimp's crash, or is carried away by the Black Bird and his swarms.

The characters should have many questions at this point, chief among them, who is the Black Bird and why did he capture the orc?

The characters won't have the reward, but what they witnessed is enough to make Baariq Mansouri interested. After the characters give a complete recount of what transpired in Qola, the noble pays them a total of 1,000 gold pieces, thanking them for their efforts. He also offers a single night's stay at the Vague Olive at no expense.

Along the way, the characters have met many interesting characters, especially the bounty hunters. At your discretion, they can continue their involvement in the mystery surrounding Mega and the book or go their separate ways. When rumors come out that the characters were paid when the others weren't, the bounty hunters might even feel resentment and demand a portion of the reward, even if it's small.

If the blimp crashed into the Hole, resulting in a destructive wave, hundreds died in the event. Fortunately, the zoologists Buman Zenor and Halim Saleem escaped with the animals intact (unless, of course, the characters got involved for some reason). The pair and their collection will return in the 1st-level adventure, *Flight of the Predator.*

After the characters spend time recovering, they are once again contacted by Baariq Mansouri. This time, Mansouri has a new lead he hopes that they can explore. "What do you know of an ancient tome named *Prime*?" he asks. The story continues in Chapter 4. *Secrets of the Book.* Ω

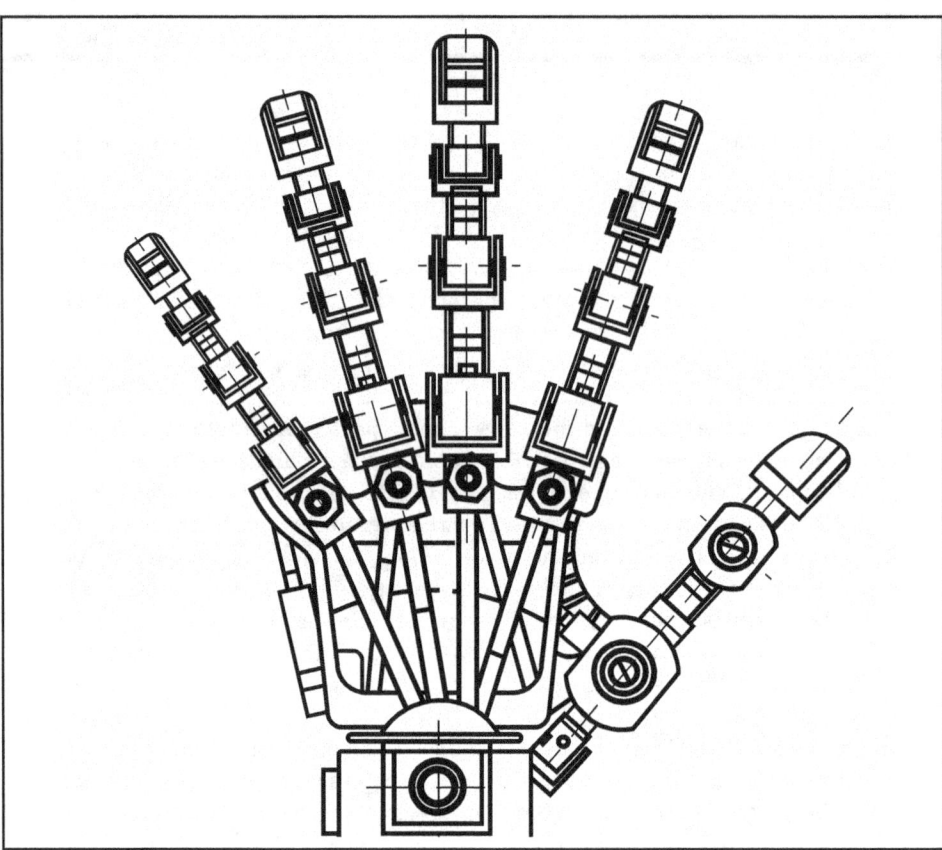

CHAPTER 4: THE SECRET OF THE BOOK

BY DAVE HAMRICK

3rd-Level Adventure for Fifth Edition

Cartography by Watabou.itch.io
Primary Art by Miguel Santos, Nate Furman, and Luigi Castellani

The Secret of the Book is a 3rd-level Fifth Edition adventure for 3-5 characters. Characters who survive the adventure should be two-thirds of the way to level 4 by the adventure's conclusion unless the characters first played Chapter 3 of the adventure path, The Black Bird. In that case, they will reach the 4th level by this adventure's conclusion and be 25-33% of the way to the 5th level.

The campaign is intended to be set in the DMDave crowdsourced campaign world of Omeria, but can just as easily be inserted into any other large, mysterious town overlooking an expansive ocean or sea.

Orbea, the Maze-like home of the krig, was the last place that the gnome scholar Valcryn Vorpos was seen alive. Supposedly, he knows the secret of the mysterious, unreadable book called Prime and why so many are interested in getting their hands on it. Of course, the characters won't be the only ones looking for Vorpos and the book. A vast conspiracy begins to unfold in this fourth chapter of the **Hand of the Eight** adventure path, **The Secret of the Book.**

Background

A little over two months ago, a gnomish scholar named Valcryn Vorpos came into possession of an ancient, unreadable tome. Unsure of what to do with it, Vorpos traveled to the fishing village of Haver to meet with a group of scholars to discuss the nature of the book. However, one of the sages, Ruhmeid Nammod was secretly working for a vile fiend named Hulay. Under the cover of a powerful hurricane of his own summoning, Nammod contracted a gang of orcish pirates called the Odzedoz to raid the village, kill the sages, and collect the book. Ironically, Nammod did not expect a doublecross from the leader of the orcs, an intelligent orc chief named Mega the Brash. Mega stole the book and fled to his island fortress in the Ghost Holm.

Interested in the book, Mega kidnapped Nadia Mansouri, an expert on dead languages, with the hope she could translate it to determine its value. Mega's plans were disrupted when Nadia's father, a powerful Castlegraspian noble, named Baariq, hired a group of adventurers to sneak onto the island, disable the orc, and reclaim Nadia. The pirate, Mega, was arrested by the Castlegraspian Navy and brought to Castlegrasp's dungeons. Before he could be arrested, Mega hid the book with his first mate, Gluronk. Gluronk escaped up the Weysevain Coast with the book.

Shortly after his capture, Mega escaped the dungeons of Castlegrasp thanks to a doppelganger. On the run, Mega planned to hide out at a nearby farm until the heat died down. That is until a powerful sorcerer known only as The Black Bird discovered him, forcing Mega to flee north through the desert. With adventurers and experienced bounty hunters hot on his trail, Mega entered the abandoned city of Qola. There, he attempted to hijack a cargoblimp from Odonburg, hoping he could ride over the mountains in it. Just as he was about to escape the bounty hunters and adventurers, the Black Bird appeared again. The sorcerer subdued Mega and wrecked the blimp. Then, in the confusion, the Black Bird and its swarms carried Mega away.

Now, investigators from Odonburg are involved. They've sent one of their best mago-detectives, Omnaweahl (or just "O" for short) to learn more about the incident in Qola, the orc, Mega, and the location of the book that's caused this whole mess. She has already flown to Castlegrasp aboard a Dinzer peregrine and spoken to both Baariq Mansouri and Khan Hayyar Harruk XI, ruler of Castlegrasp. Now, O hopes to speak with the enigmatic group of people who have been involved from the start: the characters.

Adventure Summary

The characters are asked to join Baariq Mansouri, Khan Hayyar Harruk XI, and Omnaweahl at the Violent Qsar in Castlegrasp. Omnaweahl explains that she has been dispatched by the Seven Eyes of Odonburg to learn more about an ancient book that was at some point rumored to be in possession of the orc pirate named Mega. Omnaweahl questions the characters' involvement and asks them for any clues they may have that could lead to the book. If the characters have trouble remembering, she mentions the Knotsider gnome, Valcryn Vorpos, who the characters should remember. Whether the characters work with the Dinzer Omnaweahl or not, they should head back to Haver to learn the direction Vorpos went. There, they learn that Vorpos traveled to the krig city of Orbea.

While the characters explore Orbea looking for Vorpos, they come across Gluronk, Mega's first mate, who has hidden a book with her friend, a powerful casino owner. Before their rendezvous with Gluronk, the characters learn that Vorpos was murdered. Plus, whoever killed the gnome framed the characters for the crime.

During the final scene, just as the characters retrieve the book from the casino owner, a deadly construct attacks the characters, trying to capture the book. Just in the nick of time, Omnaweahl arrives in her peregrine and helps the characters escape the nearly indestructible machine.

Adventure Hooks

While many of the descriptions and background elements assume that the characters are playing through the **Hand of the Eight** adventure path, it's possible to play this adventure as the starting point for the **Hand of the Eight** or as an unrelated one-shot adventure. Here are some suggested adventure hooks to help get the characters involved in the story.

Find the Gnome

The Dinzer mago-detective, Omnaweahl hires the characters to find the gnome Valcryn Vorpos. Supposedly, the gnome has information regarding the last known location of an important artifact. Not only does O fear for the gnome, but she fears that if the artifact falls into the wrong hands, all of Omeria could find itself in grave danger.

Legendary Book

Asorin the Black is the grand sage of the Great Equinox Library in Arruquetta. He was one of the sages killed during the Odzedozi raid on Haver. Fortunately, his acolytes secured his body and revived him. Now, he wants to learn more about the book and why it was important enough to have him and the others in his pact murdered. He sends the characters to Orbea to find and protect the sage, Valcryn Vorpos and learn the location of the book, *Prime*.

Keep the Book Hidden

If the characters have the book (which is a possibility) they must find somewhere to offload it. Knowing that Vorpos was once in possession of the book and knows more about it than anyone else alive, they go to Orbea to find the gnomish sage. If this is the hook, chances are the story plays out a little differently. The characters never meet Gluronk. Instead, they learn from Meros Scarletfoot that Vorpos was staying at the Tame Cave. Just as they enter Valcryn's room, they arrive just after Vorpos' murder, and the remote traveler alpha-class is still present. The alpha-class attacks the characters and they flee as O saves them at the last minute.

The Violet Qsar

The story begins when the characters are invited to the royal palace of Castlegrasp, the Violet Qsar. A squad of four elite Stonearms (LG Ditimayan human **knights**) escorts the characters from wherever they are currently located in the city to Orchard Park. As they pass through the Park, they notice something unusual.

> As you walk past the olive trees lining the stone paths through the park, a glint of brass catches your eyes. Resting in the grassy knoll 100 feet from the front of the Khan's palace is a huge, metallic bird, easily 75 feet long and 30 feet wide. Its body is seemingly made of equal parts polished brass and dark wood. Its eyes are made of dense, tinted glass. Getting closer to the bird, you recognize that it is actually some sort of flying vehicle designed to look like a falcon. Painted over its wing span are the red and blue colors of Odonburg.

The vehicle is a **Dinzer peregrine**, a magical flying vehicle. Omnaweahl used it to quickly cross the Obsidian Plain from Odonburg.

The Stonearms kindly announce that the characters are set to enter the Violet Qsar and meet the Khan. However, there are specific rules which they must follow.

- They must hand over all weapons, spellbooks, magic component bags, arcane focuses and holy symbols, familiars and animal companions, plus any other items that the Stonearms view as "troublesome" (lock picks, wearable magic items, etc.)
- Absolutely no magic may be cast within the Violet Qsar unless it is performed by those the Khan deems worthy. (No, the characters aren't worthy.)
- The characters cannot come within 30 feet of the Khan unless the Khan approaches them first.

- There must be at a minimum two militia members or Stonearms accompanying each character at all times. The Khan is always guarded by at least three of his personal bodyguards, the Granite Nine.
- They are not to directly address the Khan. Instead, they must address the Khan's personal bodyguard, Youssouf El Hajjam, who will then relay the message to the Khan. However, if the Khan addresses them directly, they are free to speak with the Khan.
- Failure to follow any of the rules results in immediate arrest and incarceration. Breaking any of the Qsar's rules is considered high treason by the jury of Castlegrasp. The minimum sentence for treason in Castlegrasp is one year in the Yard of Deterrents.

The Stonearms do not take these rules lightly. As some of the characters are likely to scoff at such rules and attempt to circumvent them those who do not wish to comply are politely asked to wait outside. Be sure to drive home the fact that while the Khan is Fair Eleven, those who violate the Qsar's rules will be severely punished.

Meeting the Khan

After the characters relieve themselves of their weapons and magical items, they are escorted into the Violet Qsar by 2 **guards** per characters led by the 4 Stonearm **knights**. At the front door to the Qsar, two members of the Granite Nine greet them and introduce themselves. Their names are Ghariba Skali and Chama Sabbag. Both of these young women have short, dark hair, and caramel-colored eyes. Like the other Stonearms, the right arms of the women have turned to solid stone. However, the rock surface extends beyond their shoulders, to their collar bone, neck, and jawbone like an earthy rash. Both women are friendly, but deadly serious about their duty to the

Khan. At all times, they are prepared to fight—assume that they have already rolled initiative, scored 20s, and are constantly using the Ready action each round to attack anyone who attempts to make a move on the Khan.

Similarly, the militia and Stonearms who accompany the characters are trained to reflexively act. If a fight breaks out, they roll initiative as normal. However, any initiative roll that they make that is lower than 10 + their Dexterity modifier is considered to be 10 + their Dexterity modifier.

Should an attack break out, the Khan's personal bodyguard Youssouf El Hajjam will quickly escort the Khan from the greeting chamber and through a secure door, which he will lock behind him. If that is not enough, the Qsar has many secret tunnels below it. Youssouf never leaves the Khan's side.

Still, despite their tense nature, all of the Khan's militia, Stonearms, and even the three members of the Granite Nine are always polite, friendly, and kind. "Rudeness invites conflict," was a common saying of the original master of the Granite Nine, Zamen Fadel, that all Stonearms now live by.

> The greeting chamber is a 60-foot wide circular room with 40-foot high ceilings. Against the north wall, two staircases rise to a balcony 15-feet above the floor. The balcony is filled with impressive artwork of immeasurable value.
>
> A glass skylight 60-feet above you bathes the room in natural light. A water fountain carved to look like the second Khan, Violet Two, is at the center of the room. On the left and right sides 20-feet from the fountain are two separate seating areas.
>
> After a moment of waiting, the tall, white double doors at the center of the north wall open and a large, man with a head that appears to literally be carved of rock enters. In a booming, gruff voice, the man announces, "All please kneel in the presence

of his Excellency Khan Hayyar 'Fair Eleven' Harrak XI, Khan of Castlegrasp, its satraps, colonies, and retainers, Defender of Central Omeria, Watcher of the Obsidian Plain."

All of the stone arms kneel and expect you to do the same.

Finally, a man wearing a long kandora made of white silk steps through the doors. He is a handsome man with dark skin and curly dark hair peeking out from beneath his violet keffiyeh. Judging by the confidence he exudes, this is no doubt the infamous Fair Eleven, Khan of Castlegrasp. Standing just behind the Khan you see two more figures. The first is an older Castlegraspian noble dressed in dark violet livery. The second is a young woman, perhaps no older than thirty, with dark skin, close cut hair, and a gold chain headpiece. Her robes are deep blue with bright red details.

The stone-faced man stands and turns to you, gesturing. "Behold, Fair Eleven, the ones you have requested have arrived."

"Thank you, Youssouf," the Khan says with a smile. He then approaches each of you extending a hand. "Thank you for coming." Youssouf seems taken aback by the Khan's gesture.

Khan Hayyan Harrak XI (N male Ditimayan human **noble**) is friendly, warm, and above all, an excellent listener. When he speaks, it's usually in the form of a question. And he never makes a quick decision.

Joining the Khan are Baariq Mansouri (LN male Ditimayan human **noble**), an important political figure and friend of the Khan, and Omnaweahl (N female Dinzer **mage**), a mago-detective from the southern nation of Odonburg.

Baariq is a no-nonsense authoritarian who rarely jokes. If the characters have had pleasant dealings with Baariq in the past, he is friendly and welcoming towards them.

Meanwhile, Omnaweahl (or just "O" for short) is a fast-talking Dinzer who frequently sprinkles conversation with nervous laughter. She has little respect for Castlegraspian traditions, despite receiving the same rules presentation that the characters did. Plus, she is extremely intelligent—and she knows it. And she wants others to know it, too.

Odonburg became interested in the book following the destruction of a Dinzer cargoblimp in the town of Qola just a little over 100 miles northeast of Castlegrasp. Omnaweahl was sent by Odonburg's leaders, the Seven Eyes of Odonburg, to learn as much as she could and report back to them. If what the Seven Eyes suspect is true, and the book is, in fact, *Prime*, they must secure it before it falls into the wrong hands.

Before the Khan can introduce her, she steps forward.

"Hello! I am Omnaweahl of Odonburg. You can call me O. Most folks do. It's easier, right? Ha! Anyways! I am told that you know the location of a powerful artifact."

Baariq clears his throat, trying to quiet Omnaweahl. The young woman glares back at the older gentleman, "What? Why all the unnecessary pomp and circumstance? This book is very important and we must find it immediately." She turns back to you. "So where is it?"

From there, the characters chat with the Khan, Mansouri, and O. Fair Eleven listens while Baariq fact-finds with strategic questions. Meanwhile, O cuts directly to the chase, asking any question she can that helps learn more about the book.

Baariq frequently apologizes for the young woman, who, in turn, gets offended by the older gentleman. Meanwhile, the Khan sips wine and watches in silence.

Eventually, someone drops the name of the last person known to have the book that's (hopefully) still alive: the gnome sage from Knotside, Valcryn Vorpos. The characters may recall that Vorpos filled them in on the book's most important details. If not, O repeats the same information:

- The book is written in an ancient language that has not been read or spoken in over a thousand years.
- No spells can decipher the language. If a caster uses a spell such as *comprehend languages* on the book, the book actually gets harder to read.
- It is commonly believed that the book is *Prime*, a long-lost book said to imbue any who can understand it with unlimited power.

Find the Gnome

As the conversation winds down, the mission should be apparent: find the gnome sage Valcryn Vorpos and learn the location of the book. The last place anyone saw him was the town of Haver, where he and a group of sages were attacked by orcs. That's where Baariq and O recommend the characters start their search.

Haver

The journey to Haver is quick: it's two days on the main highway, the Leash, or just one day by boat. Haver is described in greater detail in the first Chapter of the **Hand of the Eight, Storm of Mega**. There are two locations the characters should investigate while they are passing through.

The Wise Shirt

After **Storm of Mega**, Valcryn Vorpos spent his days and nights drinking

at Haver's most popular tavern, the Wise Shirt. At night, he retired to one of the rooms in the rear for restless sleep punctuated with nightmares from which he awoke screaming. The owners of the bar and patrons noticed that the gnome's sanity was starting to slip. Then, just last week, he packed a bag and left. The bartender, Bezka Wells, confronted Vorpos as he left. She tells the characters:

> "All he told me was that he had to go north. Said he thought of something and that he had to talk with someone there. But that's all he would say."

Bezka says he purchased passage on a sailing ship about five days ago. Before he left, he stopped by the Sparkling Lookout, a sage's guildhall at the south side of town.

The Sparkling Lookout

Once a lighthouse used to guide sailing ships through the dangerous fogs and storms over the Omerian Ocean, the Sparkling Lookout now acts as a guildhall for a trio of young mages named Emar Caden, Zuzen Mahran, and Nebrork Hallowpelt (all three are LN male Ditimayan human **commoners** with proficiency in Arcana and the ability to cast *firebolt*, *mage hand*, and *prestidigitation* at will). The mages' master, Ruhmeid Nammod was murdered by orcs during an incursion nearly two months ago. Since then, they've worked to rebuild the hall and their guild. Although they no longer have Nammod's teachings to guide them, they've since turned their attention to the study of the undead.

As soon as the acolytes learn that the characters are there to investigate the book and its connection to Nammod and Valcryn Vorpos, they are eager to assist in any way they can. They give the characters full access to Nammod's old bedroom and study at the top of the stairs. They also share with the characters that Valcryn Vorpos came to the Lookout five days ago. Saying very little, Vorpos took a book from one of Nammod's shelves and shoved it into his bag. Emar remembers the title of the book: *Glyphs and Scripts* by Aruxius.

> "Valcryn kept yelling over and over again 'stupid, we were all so stupid,'" Emar tells the characters. "He seemed really disturbed."

Emar shares that the book Vorpos took from Nammod's library is one of the most boring tomes he's ever read, focused solely on the practice and application of the 1st-level *illusory script* spell. The author, Aruxius, was a stodgy, old mage from Odonburg who taught enchantment and illusion courses at Pexia, Institute of the Arcane. It's said he was a *danaavrakt*, a descendant of the Striped Conjurers of Karmithyash. (The same ones who destroyed Hearth.)

The characters are free to search the study and the rest of the lighthouse. The three acolytes have nothing to hide. Beyond Nammod's old book collection, there is little of value. Although the characters aren't allowed to take any of the books with them, they can spend as much time as they like doing research. The books provide no more clues for the characters, but a character who spends at least a week of downtime in the lighthouse's library performing research on subjects arcane makes their resolution checks with advantage (see *XGtE* for details on downtime).

The Docks

Five days ago, Valcryn Vorpos booked passage on a sailing ship. When the characters ask around whose ship he

left on, they're pointed in the direction of Darebumli Onyxbrow (CN male Von Doral dwarf **commoner**). Onyxbrow is a cranky, red-nosed dwarf, whose attitude is just as salty as the sea on which he sails. Already halfway through his second bottle of *El Aoufi Sweet Fruit Red* for the day, Onyxbrow won't speak unless he's paid to do so. For 2 gp (the price of a third bottle of *El Aoufi*), he admits that he gave the gnome sage a ride to Orbea, the home of the krigs. "And for 15 gp each, I'll bring you all there, too!" he adds, hiccuping. Onyxbrox tells the characters that during the two-and-a-half-day journey, the gnome spent most of his time reading some book about glyphs. Onyxbrow didn't catch the full title.

The Maze of Orbea

It's a two-and-a-half-day journey by boat to Orbea or a four-day journey on foot or mounted. Regardless of the method the characters travel to the krig town, once they are within 1 mile of the town, read or paraphrase the following:

> Framed by the golden majesty of the Basilisk's Spine Mountains, the expanse of canyons, jagged plateaus, and bizarre natural rock formations known as the Maze of Orbea slides into view. At the highest part of the town, the east end, seven 200-foot tall airship docks stand; three blimps bearing the red and blue banners of Odonburg are parked there.
>
> Going west, the main roads and highways that enter the city either climb over its crevasses with expertly engineered bridges or descend into its depths via smooth, wooden ramps. Odd grey and green buildings with curved, crimson rooves decorate the plateaus and cliffs that surround most of the town. Within the maze itself, the raging Zheree River thunders through the center of the city before it crashes into the Keqrab Bay below.

> In addition to the Dinzer blimps overhead, sailing craft from all over the Weysevain Coast tread into the docks via the Omeria Ocean. You see banners from all over: Arruqueta, Castlegrasp, Odonburg, and even distant Murktown to the north.
>
> The roads in and out are cluttered with caravans, riders, and wagons coming and going north, south, and east.

At any time, roughly 6,000 humanoids call Orbea home, and only a third of those are actually krig. Humans, dwarves, elves, goblinoids, Dinzer automatons, canids, orcs, and others live and operate in the Maze. The remainder of the 10,000 or so krig estimated to be in existence lives elsewhere in Omeria. A popular conspiracy theory suggests that those krigs are an extension of the krigs' progenitor-diety, the Matriarch.

The characters know that Valcryn Vorpos was in Orbea at least a week ago (or longer, if they took a long time to get to the Maze from Haver). The only bit of knowledge that Onyxbrow had to share about Vorpos' location in the city was that he dropped the gnome off at the docks. "He seemed to know where he was going," the dwarf shrugs.

The characters will have to find clues and visit various locations in the town to learn Vorpos' current location—if he is even still there.

Gathering Information in Orbea

Orbea is a big place with a whole lot of people living and operating within and around its canyon walls. To follow the clues that point to Valcryn Vorpos as well as other potential mysteries (see Side Quests below), they will need to gather information. To simplify the process, use the following rules for gathering information in Orbea.

Resources. Gathering information requires a character to spend one hour or more talking to people and following up on leads.

Resolution. The character declares

		Gathering Information in Orbea	
Check Total	Outcome	Example	
1-5	Nothing important learned	-	
6-10	Basic information	"The Cords are a secret police force from Arruqueta who operate on Gadran's Plateau."	
11-20	Advanced information	"The leader of the Cords is Captain Santxa Goytino, one of Queen Emagavel's most trusted military advisors."	
21+	Confidential or classified information	"The Cords made a deal with the Tribunal to allow them to freely persecute Arruquettan Separatists while they turned a blind eye."	

the focus of the information gathering attempt—a specific person, place, or thing. After on hour, the character makes a Charisma (Persuasion) check with a +1 bonus per 1 gp spent, to a maximum of +6. Determine the type of information that the character learns using the Gathering Information in Orbea table at the top of this page.

Each outcome presents one or more NPCs who can answer questions depending on the level of the information learned. As the GM, you are the final arbiter concerning exactly what a character learns.

Complications. Some subjects may draw undue attention to the characters. For example, if the characters start asking too many people in Khikzux about the Crocodile Crew, they may find themselves the target of a lizardfolk hitman.

Each hour spent gathering information on a single topic brings a 10 percent chance of a complication. Create a complication that best suits the situation.

Side Quests

The Maze of Orbea is probably like no other location the characters have ever been to. It is a town of canyons, bridges, roads and elaborate tunnels, covered in multi-story buildings and walkways. Above all, Orbea is a town of mystery and exploration. A humanoid can spend a lifetime in the town and never see all it has to offer. As such,

there are plenty of opportunities for side quests while in the Maze.

The characters are under no obligation to participate in any of these side quests. However, these side quests can offer valuable opportunities for clues, experience, rewards, and discoveries during their time there.

1 - "Make me look good." As the characters are traveling through the town's streets, they're approached by a forlorn Knotsider human **knight** named Danyll the Lion. Recently, Danyll's had bad luck in wooing a local girl named Tanya. He believes that Tanya sees him as weak, despite his rank. He asks the characters if they will pretend to lose a fight to him and offers each of them 10 gp for their help. The set-up is simple: the characters pick a fight with Danyll, and Danyll tells them to back away. From there, the characters "attack" the knight. After 3 rounds, Danyll gets the "upper hand" and "defeats them all."

"If you don't mind, knick me with one of your blades just over the eye. I've got to really sell this."

Whether or not the knight's plan works is up to you.

2 - Quest for the Cure. The characters watch a man collapse in the streets. When they run to assist, they discover that it is an elf who is incredibly ill. His name is Galather Dorxidor. Galather is a traveling historian (**mage**) from Olyothyr who hopes to meet with a local geologist,

Graunder Diamondeyes. Galather believes that the source for the sickness that's plagued him and the elves of Olyothyr for the last few decades is in the actual soil of the land. When the characters first meet Galather, he has five levels of exhaustion (see the *PHB* for details) and can no longer move on his own. Long rests do not remove the exhaustion, however, a greater restoration spell will remove one level. If the characters can't cast greater restoration themselves, they can pay to have a high-level priest at one of the city's many temples cast it. It costs 450 gp per casting. Each week the elf fails to return to Olyothyr, he gains an additional level of exhaustion. If it seems like he will not be able to complete his quest, he hands the characters a box of soil and asks them to find the geologist, Graunder Diamondeyes in Khikzux Ward (**Area 10**).

The geologist is relatively easy to find if the characters spend a little time fact-finding (see the section on Gathering Information above). Graunder is not only a geologist: he's an **earth weird**. As a weird, he can touch the soil and sense any unusual qualities about it. Once the characters hand over the box, Graunder places his stoney paw into the soil. Immediately, he recognizes something unusual about it.

"It's tainted," he frowns. "But not as if something has been added to it, but more like something was taken from it. This isn't the first time

> I've felt this, either. Many years ago, someone brought me a box of soil from a tomb on the northside of the wound. It, too, had the same feeling of... absence."

Graunder isn't able to provide any more details than that. He does ask, however, that the characters leave the box with him so he can continue to learn more about it.

3 - The Parcel. As the characters are settling in, they meet a woman named Voh (**commoner**) who asks if they are looking for some easy work. She mentions that there is a parcel service over in Khikzux Ward (**Area 10**) that needs people to run errands. If the characters agree, they will have to go to the address the woman gives them. Outside of the building, via a magic mouth spell, the characters are asked to identify themselves and state their purpose. If they explain that they are delivering a package, a slot opens and a black, wooden box slides out. The magic mouth asks them to deliver the package to an address in the Eight Gems Ward. The recipient's name is Osma Jaroh, a retired adventurer and Knotsider ex-patriot (N male Knotsider human **mage**). He will pay the characters 5 sp when the package is delivered.

If the characters open the parcel, they discover shards of dull, green gems. The gems emit faint evocation magic but otherwise seem to have no known use. If sold, they fetch no more than 1 sp for the entire set.

4 - "Fancy a game of Banzo?". A man with a black eye and bloody nose bumps into the characters. He immediately raises his hand up, as if he is about to be struck, pleading, "Please! I haven't gotten the money yet! Give me more time!" When he realizes that the characters aren't the gangsters he fears, he introduces himself as Briyan and explains his situation. Only a few hours ago, Briyan bet everything he had in a game of Banzo at The Mys-

tique, a gambling hall in the Zhalruvox Channel (**Area 13**). The person who took his money was a high stakes gambler named Hydrius Suenborn. Briyan begs the characters to help him, claiming that if they don't, Hydrius and his gangsters will come after Briyan and his family.

The entire act is a ploy. Briyan (a **bandit**) actually works for Hydrius. His job is to look for "marks" around the city, sell the story about how he and his family are in danger, and then get heroes and adventures to help out.

The Mystique is simple to find and doesn't require information-gathering checks. It's a seedy joint filled with all manner of scum and villainy. Hydrius plays at a table towards the back of the Casino. Hydrius is a NE **water elemental** with an Intelligence score of 11 and a Charisma score of 13. He can speak Common. At all times, he wears a leather diver's suit so he can maintain his consistency without concentrating. While in the diver's suit, he loses Water Form trait and Whelm action. He can use half of his movement to open the face mask of his diver's suit and escape through the hole and vice versa.

Hydrius surrounds himself with a gang of six **thugs**. If Briyan's name is brought up, Hydrius laughs and makes them an offer: if they can beat him at three hands of Banzo, he will return all of the money he won off Briyan. But if Hydrius wins, he wants something of value from the characters. Choose an item that is special to one of the characters, such as a family heirloom important to the character's backstory, a powerful magic item, etc.

If the characters agree, they must choose among them who will enter the Banzo contest. Hydrius' thugs take the stake for safekeeping (within sight, so the characters don't get antsy).

During each round of Banzo, the character must make three checks: Wisdom (Insight), Charisma (Deception), and Charisma (Intimidation). If the charac-

ter has proficiency with Three Dragon Ante or any other card game, that tool proficiency can replace the relevant skill in any of the checks.

During the first round, the Charisma (Deception and Intimidation) checks are ringers. Hydrius purposedly throws the round. However, the character can use their Wisdom (Insight) check contested by Hydrius' Charisma (Deception) check; Hydrius makes his check at +7. If the character sees through the Deception, they are free to confront Hydrius about the bluff or ignore it, and possibly, use it to his/her advantage.

The second round is the same as the first, with Hydrius trying to bluff the character. This time, he feints frustration, slamming his fists on the table, cursing the characters for their absurd luck. Losing 0-2, Hydrius ups the stake:

> "If you win the next hand, in addition to what is already on the table, I'll give you something of great value." The water elemental claps his gloved hands together. One of his thugs steps forward with a chest and opens it for you to see. Within the chest is an ancient, golden amulet with two gashes carved into it. Strange runes decorate both sides. "This is the Herald's Key, a long lost treasure. These runes are written in the ancient tongue, Celestial.
>
> "They say that this medallion will reveal the location of the hidden city of Hearth to anyone who holds it. Within this lost city, you will find untold treasure. In fact, the medallion itself is said to be priceless. Easily worth millions in Castlegraspian din."
>
> He then leans forward. Behind the glass of his helmet, his water form creates on a distorted grin. "But if I win... *I own you.* You will do *whatever* I ask, *whenever* I ask it. Not as slaves, no, but let's just say: perpetual business partners? Do we have a deal?"

If the characters agree, the third hand of Banzo requires the character to make the same three checks. However, Hydrius cheats this hand. The character must first make his/her Wisdom (Insight) check contested by Hydrius' Charisma (Deception) check to catch the cheat.

If the character's check is successful, the character notices that Hydrius' expression changed for a moment—one of Hydrius' thugs is a magic initiate. He casts a subtle *minor illusion* spell on Hydrius' cards, changing them to Hydrius' benefit.

If the character does not notice Hydrius' expression change or makes no move to confront Hydrius, he/she must play his/her hand using their Charisma (Deception) and Charisma (Intimidation) checks. This time, however, the DC for each check is 20. The character must pass both checks in order to beat Hydrius.

Should Hydrius still lose the third hand or get caught cheating, he flips the table and attacks the characters. Hydrius hates losing more than anything. And as an elemental, he knows that his destruction will only result in his return to the Elemental Plane of Water—a temporary inconvenience. (So much for the thugs, though.)

Otherwise, if and when Hydrius wins, he immediately takes what is his and tells the characters that at some point in the near future he will call upon them to perform a task. What the task is and when it's called on is up to you.

5 - Catch the Litter of Canid Pups.
A canid mother (**commoner**) chases one of her pups in the street, cursing. She's already got two pups under each of her arms. Exasperated, she asks the characters to help her find the rest of her children. When asked how many children she has, she responds, "Seven total." The characters must find and catch the other four. To do so, a character must spend 1 minute searching for a pup. At the end of the minute, have the character make three ability checks in the following order: a DC 10 Wisdom (Perception), followed by a DC 10 Dexterity, and finally a DC 10 Strength. Each time a character succeeds on all three checks, they find one of the pups and grabs it. Otherwise, they have to spend another minute searching with another series of checks. Once all the pups are returned, the mother is thankful, but, unfortunately, has no reward to offer.

6 - "Oho! My hat!". While walking down the street, a stiff breeze knocks the hat off an elderly Knotsider **mage** named Ka Kazar the Confounding. "Oho! My hat!" Ka Kazar exclaims. "Help me get it back, would ye?" he asks the characters, feigning a bad back and 'even worse knees.' The old man's hat slides into a nearby alley. As the characters enter the alley, a gang of 3 **bugbears** stops the hat. "Zoomer Territory" they warn. While the bugbears hope to roll the characters, if they recognize a threat, they immediately surrender, instead offering information. While the bugbears don't know anything about Valcryn Vorpos, they can offer some insight into the three major gangs that claim ownership of Orbea: the Crocodile Crew, the Salvation, and the Boars. All three gangs are detailed further in the forthcoming one-shot *War on the Zheree.*

Meanwhile, Ka Kazar forgets that he even asked the characters to help him in the first place.

7 - Put the Krig Down. Two men in white robes are carrying a semi-conscious krig by its arms to a horse-drawn carriage 30-feet away. There is a third man, also in white, at the reins. If questioned, the men explain that the krig is sick and that they are taking him to a temple to receive medical attention. The krig, through its haze, gazes at the characters through its many eyes and weakly asks for help. If the characters intervene, the men in white robes attack. All three men are **thugs** who work for a terrorist organization called the Burning Web. The Burning Web believes that the krigs are all part of a vast, global conspiracy that wishes to take over Omeria by putting krigs in positions of power. They were taking the krig to a warehouse by the docks (**Area 6**) to perform experiments on it. After they save him, the krig thanks the characters, then leaves. If the characters decide to get involved, they must go down to the docks and find the Burning Web's warehouse. This side quest plot continues in the forthcoming one-shot adventure The Burning Web.

8 - Turf War. As the characters are entering a shop, restaurant, or tavern somewhere within Orbea, a **lizardfolk** dressed in a green cloak enters with them. Suddenly, a cry goes up outside the location: "This is Salvation!" Five halfling **bandits** chuck vials of alchemists fire at the location, setting everything ablaze. Characters caught in the crossfire must make the appropriate Dexterity saving throws (see the *PHB*). However, they are not the intended targets. The lizardfolk shouts back in Draconic, "Crew Forever!", pulls a heavy crossbow from under his cloak, and fires back. The lone lizardfolk and the halfling gangsters then trade fire as the place burns.

The lizardfolk is a member of the Crocodile Crew and the halflings are members of The Salvation. Both gangs have a bitter rivalry.

After 2-3 rounds of combat, the local militia (**guards**) shows up and all of the gangsters flee the scene. The lizardfolk is actually an important member of the Crocodile Crew named Draozax. Draozax's death could lead to an all-out war between the rival factions. If he is killed, the guards' captain immediately realizes the trouble the lizardfolk's death could bring Orbea. The guards ask the characters to help them deal with the issue.

The Crocodile Crew's turf is Khikzux Ward (**Area 10**) and the Salvation's turf is in Azen'qod Ward (**Area 17**). The war between the two crews continues in the forthcoming one-shot War of the Zheree.

9 - Family Matters. As the characters are traveling through the Eight Gems Ward (**Area 14**), they are accosted by Wind in the Valley, the devilkin servant (**commoner**) of an important noble named Makrino. Makrino is a member of the wealthy Urquiza family that lives in western Orbea. Recently, the patriarch of the family, Millan, died, leaving his entire estate to his two sons, Makrino and Maioriano. The brothers were each left a key to their father's treasure vault at his mansion in the Eight Gems Ward. To open the vault and retrieve the treasure, each son must use his key in synchronicity with the other. However, the two refuse to share the treasure. The servant offers the party 500 gp if they will break into Maioriano's home in the Eight Gems Ward and steal Maioriano's key. This side quest continues in the forthcoming one-shot Maioriano's Key.

10 - Something in the Tunnels. Three children have gone missing near a series of tunnels that run under Laris Ledge (**area 16**). The town militia has sent guards into the tunnels, but they, too, have yet to return. Finally, the militia's captain asks the characters if they will enter the tunnels to find out

what is responsible for the disappearances. Within the tunnels, the characters discover that a **roper** has climbed up from the Under and is eating anything that enters its territory. If the characters defeat the roper, the guards pay them 100 gp for their help.

Random Encounters
The Maze of Orbea is loaded with mystery, intrigue, danger, and excitement. It should seem like everywhere the characters turn, there is a side quest or encounter waiting to happen. Roll a d20 three times per day of game time, checking for encounters each morning, afternoon, and evening or night. An encounter occurs on a roll of 16 or higher. Roll a d20 and check the Orbea Encounters table on page 84 to determine what the encounter is, or simply choose an encounter you like.

Important Locations
The map of Orbea reveals the most important locations in the city detailed below. Of course, Orbea is a mess of buildings, canals, streets, and sidewalks and is easy to get lost in. Assume that almost any type of building or business one would find in a large city also exists in Orbea. Furthermore, Orbea is crowded. While only 6,000 or so humanoids call the Maze their home, 8,000 to 10,000 more are visiting the city for business or pleasure or sometimes both.

Many of the locations have interconnecting clues that lead back not only to finding Valcryn Vorpos but also to some of the Side Quests mentioned above. These clues are detailed at the end of the location's description. **1 - Orbea Airfield.**

Seven 200-foot-tall blimptowers organized in a triangle line either side of the main roads heading west out of Orbea. The towers are spaced roughly 250 feet apart. The main control tower is at the center of

the towers; through the use of illusory magic, a loud, echoing voice issues commands to the blimps' pilots and porters. Bright, red lights tip each of the towers, no doubt used to help guide blimps entering Orbea's airspace to their docks. Currently, there are three blimps docked in Orbea, all bearing the blue and red colors of Odonburg. At the center of the tower's framework, you see levitating platform discs lifting cargo up to the blimp's catwalks.

The blimps currently stationed in Orbea are *The Predator*, *Good Hope*, and *The Red-and-Blue Gentleman*. *The Predator*, a retooled warblimp, is currently on a mission to collect a group of evacuated animals from a village a few miles outside of Qola (detailed further in the forthcoming *Flight of the Predator*).

The Red-and-Blue Gentleman is a leisureblimp where wealthy nobles from across Omeria can gamble freely. And Good Hope brought important delegates from Odoburg to meet with the Krig Bairns (see **Area 3**).

The airfield itself is unguarded. The four towers not in use are locked up and the control modules for their levitating discs have been removed. The three towers currently in use are guarded by four Dinzer **guards** each. Each guard is equipped with a personal *evitating platform* (functionally the same as a *witch's broom*) and a *wand of magic missiles*. The guards for *The Predator* and *Good Hope* have instructions to only allow their respective blimps' pilots and crew members into the tower. And the guards for *The Red-and-Blue Gentleman* must see a ticket before they allow a passenger on board, and loading times won't start until an hour past sunrise the next day anyways.

2 - Qiassith Cliff. The industrial hub of Orbea hugs the northwestern cliff of the town. Not nearly as well lit as

Orbea Encounters

d20	Encounter
1	A **dust mephit** flies past the characters, sneezing as it goes. Each time it sneezes, it launches a cloud of dust into the air.
2	A **mage** strolls down the street pulling a treasure chest with legs (a **mimic**) on a leash like it was a dog. The treasure chest snarls at the characters as they walk past it.
3	Two **thugs** shove a devilkin **commoner** into the mud and start kicking him. If the characters intervene, the devilkin becomes a valuable source of information about locations in Orbea.
4	The characters catch a glimpse of a gnome wearing Knotsider livery, just like Valcryn Vorpos wore while he was in Haver. When they catch up to it, it turns out that it's a female gnome **commoner**. She hasn't seen Vorpos and mutters something about "racist Ditimayans" under her breath.
5	An old woman (**commoner**) hugs onto one of the characters. She smiles and whispers in his ear, "Tall and glowin' green, ain't they? Tall and glowing green." She then wanders off, muttering to herself.
6	A **commoner** merchant pushing a large cart accosts the characters. The cart has the heads of dead young dragons of all colors on it. "Dragon brains! Eat just a scoop and you'll become a sorcerer just like the great beasts! Only 1 sp a spoonful." He holds up a spoon for each character.
7	Three **water elementals** swim through one of the city's canals headed for the river. As they go, they leap like dolphins, splashing the characters as they go. The locals laugh.
8	A nude **krig** approaches the characters and asks in a demanding tone, "Have you seen Reverence?" The krig waits a few minutes for a reply, grunts, then pushes past the characters. A few seconds later, the krig stops another traveler asking if they've seen Reverence.
9	Two canid jugglers (**bandits**) begin performing tricks for the characters. Their trick is a distraction. Make Wisdom (Insight) checks for the characters contested by the canid's Charisma Performance checks (+3 to the roll). The character who fails the check and gets the worst result in the entire party has their entire coin pouch stolen by the jugglers' assistant (another **bandit**). If all of the characters pass their checks, they notice the third man trying to rob them. When the jig is up, all three take off in different directions.
10	The characters almost stumble into a suit of **animated armor** bearing the Golden Eye of Odonburg as it walks down the street. The suit is a remote traveler whose pilot is likely thousands of miles away.
11+	The characters meet an NPC with a side quest (see Side Quests on page 80)

the other parts of the town, Qiassith is filled with flat, ugly buildings where mostly krig and kobold factory workers labor to build technological commodities. These goods are then carted to one of the four 200-foot-tall blimptowers along the road leading northwest out of Orbea and then transported to its final destination.

3 - Shirzosh Commons. Although the krig call Orbea their home, they are not the rulers of the city. Or at least that's what the Tribunal of Orbea would have the populace believe. The Tribunal consists of three governors who make all of the decisions for the city and its people. The three governors are Sress of Elsath (N female **lizardfolk**), Clurt Justclurt (LN male **goblin**), and Veronia Winterhunt (LG female Knotsider **knight**). The three reside within Shirzosh commons at their own governors' mansions. Once per week, the Tribunal meets at the House of Records, where they parlay with guild lobbyists and vote on important issues. Of course, most Orbeans are hardly aware that the three even exist. Although they pass many laws, very few of them actually go into effect. And three almost never make public appearances. In fact, no one even remembers how the three got the job in the first place.

The main road that pushes through the Commons becomes a tunnel that leads into the Undermaze, the true home of the krigs. While the tunnels are not off-limits to non-krigs, they are rumored to be dangerous. Furthermore, non-krigs who wander too far into the tunnels eventually get lost within the maze. Dying of starvation and hunger, the trespasser is found by krigs and brought back to the surface where they are given over to one of the temples. This is the only warning the krigs ever give. The second time a non-krig gets lost within the maze, they are left ot die.

If there are krig leaders in Orbea,

THE SECRET OF THE BOOK

those leaders are likely the 15-20 krig who the Orbeans have dubbed the Krig Bairns. On rare occasions, leaders from other nations come to Orbea to connect with the Matriarch. While the Matriarch's true location is never revealed by the krigs and those who try to find her inevitably become lost in the Undermaze, the Krig Bairns represent her interests and desires.

In addition to the government buildings in Shirosh, the ward is home to many of the city's finest restaurants and taverns, including the Colossal Spider Tavern and Inn, a favorite stopping point for visiting dignitaries, ambassadors, and VIPs who wish to meet the governors or the Krig Bairns.

4 - North Ward/Zatiketa. North Ward has long been the middle-class residential section of Orbea. In recent years, however, the ward has turned into the home of separatists from Arruquetta, trying to avoid civil war and death at the hands of the Cord, Daria Emagavel's secret police force. As their numbers grew, the separatists began calling the region Zatiketa. Naturally, Orbea's acceptance of what Emagavel considers "war criminals" has harmed relations with Aruquetta to the north, but not even the Spear of Weysevain is willing to go against the krigs and their mother. Plus, the toll on Gadran's Plateau is one of her most profitable ventures.

Along with the Martians came the Boars, a clan of criminals led by a warlock named Hogan Zul (NE male Ditimayan human mage). The Boars are recognized by the black tusks they tattoo over their jaws and the thick pelts they wear over their shoulders. Hogan operates from his mother's house in a multi-tiered hovel built into the northern wall of the Yivu plateau. His mother treats visiting members of his gang like they were Hogan's childhood friends. They lovingly call her Mama Zul.

Despite their ready-to-rumble appearance, the Boars prefer intrigue over direct confrontation with the other two gangs of Orbea. Still, when pressed, the Boars' aptitude for violence is rarely contested.

5 - The Blinding Bridge. Its name comes from its position relative to both the eastern and western horizon. Those traveling out of the maze in the morning catch the rising sun, then, in the evenings, as they return, they're met with the setting. Superstitious Central Omerians believe it was built as a playful offering to Naeyer. Others think it's lousy engineering.

A natural divider between Khikzux Ward and Zatiteka, the bridge acts as a border between the Boars and Crocodile Crews' turfs.

6 - Salt Ward. Salt Ward is home to Orbea's cluttered docks and warehouses. Despite its proximity to the Obrean militia's barracks to the north in Shirzosh, the Salt Ward is thick with crime. There is not a week that goes by where a body isn't found floating face down in the Keqrab Bay. Most of the warehouses in the Salt Ward are owned by wealthy smugglers and merchant houses from all over Central Omeria. They use Orbea as a place to store illegal wares. As such, the warehouses are heavily guarded by well-paid professionals. So brazen are the landlords, they put their clan and tribe symbols on the doors of the buildings they own as a warning to those who would dare enter: "you steal from here, you steal from me."

A narrow flight of steps climbs 500-feet up to Sevari Tower (**Area 7**). Other than ramp leading into the Zik'thath market (**Area 8**), the steps—dubbed the Killer—is the only way up the plateau. Unlike the other plateaus in Orbea, there does not seem to be any tunnels leading through or even into the base of the tower.

Valcryn arrived at Orbea via ship. Therefore, the docks and the Salt Ward are the best locations to start looking

for him and gathering information. See the section on information gathering for details.

7 - Sevari Tower. The plateau that divides the docks and overlooks the harbor is called Sevari Tower. Once upon a time, the tower was not decorated with the red beacons lining its walls today. As such, the Tower had another nickname—ship smasher. Were you to dive into the Bay at the western front of the tower, you'd likely find the remains of dozens of destroyed ships.

The Tower itself is one of the few plateaus in Orbea that isn't hollowed out and littered with dark tunnels. It is also isolated from much of Orbea. There are only two footpaths onto the tower's surface. First, there is the 500-foot climb of steps from the Salt Ward. Lacking any sort of railing, the exhausting staircase has been nicknamed The Killer by the locals. The second way up is the unnamed ramp that descends at a steep angle into the rear of Zik'thath Market (**Area 8**). Both make travel and transportation enormously difficult for anyone who lacks a mode of flight. Because of its natural exclusivity, Sevari Tower is a paradise of high-dollar casinos, inns, restaurants, and high-end shops.

Its most famous casino is the Long Shadow, a four-story building that hangs over the tower's western edge. The minimum deposit at the Long Shadow is 1,000 gold pieces. Plus, most games have a minimum buy-in of 100 gold pieces. Like most of Orbea's casinos, the Long Shadow's most popular game is Banzo. Its current Banzo champion is a Knotsider gnome named Felgim Trumda. The casino's owner, a devilkin named Prayer in the Morning is loved and celebrated (and feared) by all who enter the casino's pitch black doors. She also offers a house specialty which she extends to anyone short on luck. "1,000 gp loan. Due in one hour with ten points on top. Or? You get the drop!" In other words, Prayer loans the

sap 1,000 gold pieces. The loan is to be repaid with a 10% interest on the principle in one hour. If the borrower can't pay up, Prayer's pit bosses open up a hole in the showroom floor and drop the borrower over 500-feet into the Bay below. If the borrower survives, they're debt-free. So far, no one has survived.

8 - Zik'thath Market.

> Alive!—there is seriously no better word to describe the place you're looking at other than "alive." Stacks upon stacks of shops, stalls, street vendors, and hustlers crowd the intersecting streets. The three largest natural columns of the town surround the bustling market on all sides, casting it in perpetual shadow. Regardless, the entire place is incredibly well-lit. At every turn, perpetual light spells have been cast upon the signs, posts, strands of bulbs, and even the railings throughout the area. Each tower of rock is wrapped in a web of scaffolding, then, haphazardly interconnected with natural and manmade bridges. Huge crowds of humanoids of all sorts haggle for goods and services all over. Stray dogs, cats, and infantile grick roam under the feet of shoppers and into stalls. Meanwhile, massive carts pulled by ornery-looking red-striped thornfoots shove their way past the people as their riders shout at passersby in strange dialects. You smell roasting meat and the sweet smoke of hashish pipes. You hear the squawks of rare birds and jingle of traded coins. What a place!

From run-of-the-mill weapons, armor, and equipment to curiosities from afar, anything and everything can be purchased at Zik'thath Market. The characters can expect to find any magic item of common or uncommon value here, as well as the occasional rare magic item, too. Plus, most of the vendors are willing to haggle. On the same token, street vendors can be incredibly pushy. And with all the commotion, theft is common.

Like much of Orbea, the presence of law enforcement in the market is low. If any is here, they only work if it looks like they can collect a "reward" from those they save (aka a shakedown).

9 - Yaqut Heights. Because it's a popular stopover for travelers on the Leash, Yaqut Heights is crowded with shops, bars, and hostels. In fact, it's home to the most popular inn in all of Orbea, The Married Couple, a pair of buildings connected by an underground tunnel. The western half of the Married Couple is the Restless Groom, a tavern and restaurant known for its spicy Arruquetan cuisine. The eastern half of the Married Couple is the Sleeping Bride, a reasonably priced inn with plenty of space. The Married Couple's owners, a married couple by the name of Ixaka and Ezker Arroquy (LN male Ditimayan **commoners**) are faithful supporters of Queen Dariah Emagavel. As such, no separatists are allowed at either end of the establishment. Cords looking for information on separatists often turn to the Arroquys. Both Arroquys have received numerous death threats, many considering the pair turncoats and traitors to Arruqueta's freedom.

10 - Khikzux Ward . The easternmost ward north of Zheree River is Khikzux Ward. Many of the locals give it the insulting nickname, Demi-human Town. It is home to lizardfolk, orcs, and frogfolk. Because the river is at its strongest point where it emerges from Zheree Canyon, the ward easily floods. Mold and biting insects are common. To account for the conditions, canals have been built into the streets. Some of the residents own gondolas, but most choose to walk along the narrow walkways or on the rooftops of the ward.

Khikzux is ruled by the Crocodile Crew, a tribe of lizardfolk led by an albino lizardfolk **druid** named Old Rat. Old Rat is worshipped by the Khikzuk as their prophet and savior. The glass-eyed leader often speaks before the members of the Crew—whom he labels "disciples"—with vaguely-worded predictions, which he later uses to prove his value as a diviner.

Currently, the Crocodile Crew is at war with the Salvation.

11 - Lenoro's Wall. Pressed tightly against its sister plateau, Yaqut Heights, Lenoro's Wall is the largest and shortest natural rock formation in the Maze of Orbea. Similar to the Heights, Lenoro's is a stopover for travelers entering Orbea from the west and North. Those who hope to avoid the toll to the south also hang a left to take the circuitous route around the town's borders. For this reason, many of the shops, inns, and taverns on Lenoro's Wall have names that play on the convention: the Go Left Inn, The Shop-Lefter, and Left Arms & Armor just to name a few.

A small park overlooks the east end of the Wall, a favorite spot for Orbean youths to gather and watch the Dinzer blimps as they enter the town. Meanwhile, the constant churn of the Zheree rages below.

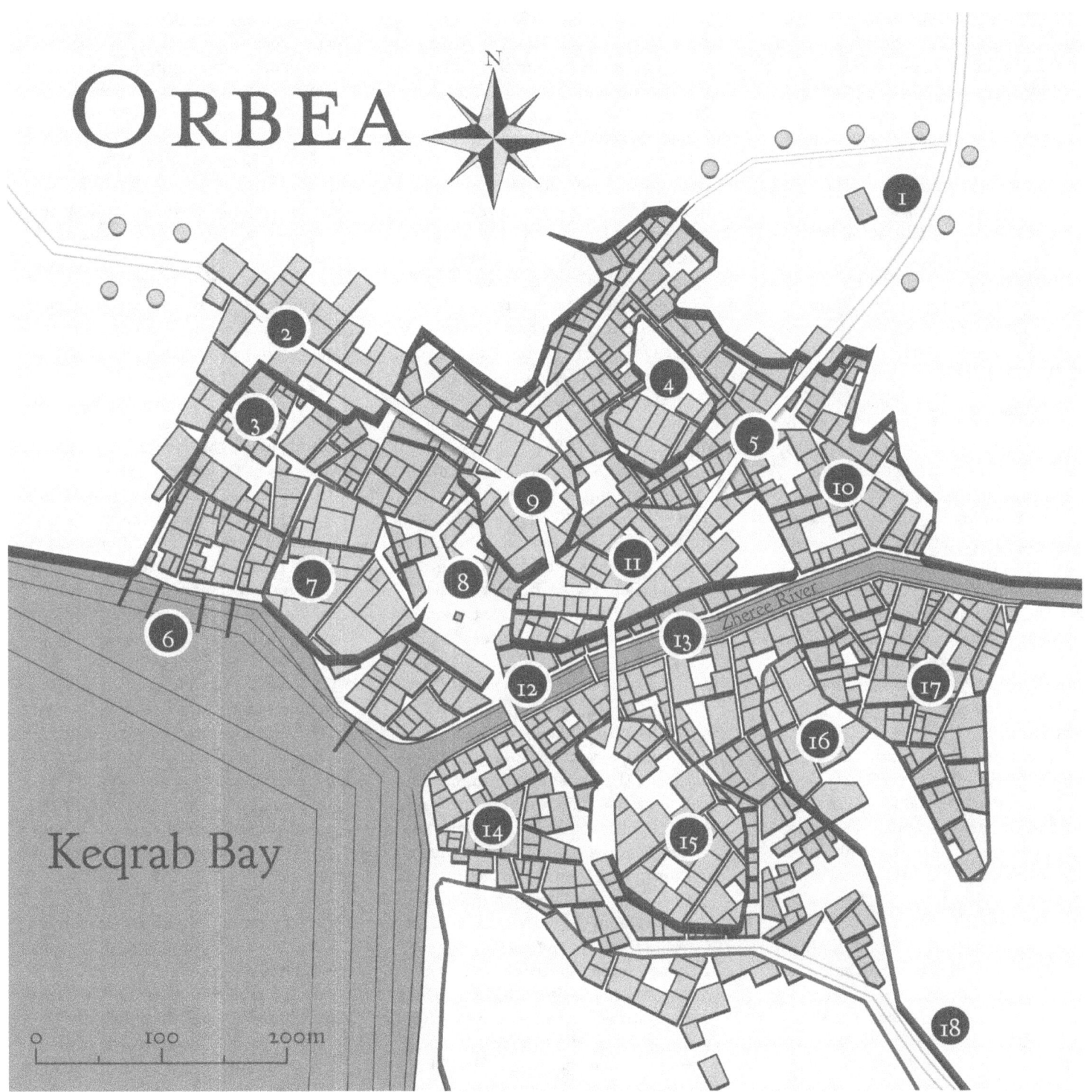

ORBEA

Keqrab Bay

Zheree River

0   100   200m

12 - The Autumn Bridge. Near the mouth of the river, 50-feet above Zheree Falls, the Autumn Bridge connects the wealthy Eight Gems Ward to the thriving Zik'thath Market. The Autumn Bridge is carved to look like one hundred Ditimayan slaves holding themselves above the Zheree. Supposedly the design comes from a legend of ancient Ditimayan nomads who used each other's limbs to create a chain so they could ford the angry river. The view of the sun setting over the Omerian from the bridge is particularly enticing. It's on this bridge that many travelers passing through Orbea fall in love with the town.

13 - Zhalruvox Channel. The Zhalruvox Channel clings to either side of the Zheree. The shops, restaurants, and inns here are a little tamer than those found in the Zik'thath Market. That said, the Channel's shops and services are not what one would normally expect to find in any other town, village, or city. Free from the prying eyes of the town's militia and the Arruquetan garrison, a black market culture thrives in the Channel. Illegal weapons, magic items, rare animals, mercenary services, and more can be bought in the Channel, usually at a steep price.

Ref Grergaz (NE male Knotsider human **veteran**) is the mastermind behind Zhalruvox. Unlike the gangs that infest the northern wards, Ref keeps his business quiet. Nearly everyone is on his payroll and he doesn't cause a stir. And thanks to contracts with powerful people all over Central Omeria, he is well-protected. Of course, you'll never actually find Ref in Zhalruvox Channel. Ref lives in a quiet mansion overlooking the Omerian in the Eight Gems Ward where he tends to his garden and spends time with his grandchildren.

14 - Eight Gems Ward. The well-to-do of Orbea live in the Eight Gems Ward overlooking the Omerian Ocean. As the pinnacle of wealth, the Eight Gems is one of the only wards that has its own standing militia. Some of the guards work for the town and are paid in taxes. Others are former soldiers hired as mercenaries. Although Eight Gems is unwalled, anyone that "doesn't fit in" is quickly accosted by the ward's defenders. A non-resident better have a good excuse or better bribe. Otherwise, they may find themselves bloodied and dragged out onto Market Road, or worse (tossed into the Omerian).

Like most people with too much money, the residents of Eight Gems spend most of their time trying to one-up their neighbors. Every year, the houses get taller and more elaborate. The parties grow more lavish and over-the-top. And the clothing is simply outrageous. A popular trend among the Eight Gems' elite is to dress as a Signature Monster. For example, a dilettante whose chosen monster was a Chimera might wear a golden lion mask, and wear golden epaulets designed to look like a ram and a dragon. Or someone whose monster was a harpy might wear an elaborate cloak made of pink and yellow feathers and not much else. The more risqué the better, darling.

15 - Gadran's Plateau. Queen Daria Emagavel of Arruqueta made a deal with Orbea: you let me collect tolls from the people traveling through the Leash and through Orbea, and you can do as you please. The Tribunal agreed and the Arruquetan Toll was built along the ramp leading off the plateau. The toll charges 1 sp for two-legs, 4 sp for four-legs, plus 1 sp per wheel. With nearly 1,200 travelers passing through the toll each day, Gadran's Toll has helped fund Emagavel's continued political and military interests.

As the toll has expanded, so has Arruqueta's presence in Orbea. East of the toll, Arruqueta maintains two huge barracks with 100 trained soldiers (**guards**) each. In addition, they have equipped the plateau with mangonels and ballistas. Plus, the Arruquetans maintain a stable of 20 **griffons** whose riders can have them saddled and in the air in less than a minute.

Overseeing the operation in Orbea is one of Emagavel's most trusted officers, Captain Santxa Goytino (LN female Ditimayan human **knight**). Goytino also oversees a unit of 10 Cords, the secret police of Arruqueta, who sniff out separatist forces in Orbea.

16 - Laris Ledge. Also called "the Thumb" Laris Ledge is the second-highest point in Orbea, second only to Sevari. Originally, it was intended to be an area of expansion for the town. Many of the Maze's greatest developers pitched it as the new Eight Gems. A few months after residents moved into Laris, an earthquake shook Orbea. The shockwaves knocked a massive chunk off the east cliff, toppling three buildings and killing not only the families within but also twenty people in Azen'qod Ward below. Since then, the project was abandoned. A few of the homes are still occupied, but overall, Laris is a ghost town, which is strange considering the congested nature of Orbea.

17 - Azen'qod Ward. There are shrines and small temples all throughout Orbea, each dedicated to a different, unique god or goddess. But if there was one spiritual center of Orbea, it would definitely have to be Azen'qod Ward. The three largest temples in Azen'qod are the Temple of Yrena, Goddess of Destruction; the Temple of Zuton, God of Good Luck (which, let's face it, is more of a casino than a temple); and Usteus, God of Judgment.

Like all temples of Yrena, her temple in Azen'qod is maintained by eight blind seers known as Yrena's Witnesses. For the most part, the seers keep to themselves. Oddly, they don't have the same freedom to perform sacrifices in honor of Yrena as other temples do. That's thanks mostly to the halfling worshippers of Usteus who've made it clear that as long as Usteus' temple stood in Orbea, there would be no unsanctioned murders (aka murders done by anyone but the halflings themselves).

Thirty percent of Azen'qod's population are wanderer halflings and most are devout worshippers of Usteus. The temple is governed by Meros Scarletfoot (LE male wanderer halfling **spy**). But Meros is more than just a holy man. He is also a criminal mastermind. By manipulating the faith of his fellow halflings, he sends them forward to commit "acts of Salvation" on behalf of Usteus. His grip on the halfling culture of Orbea has made him very wealthy. Over the last few months, the Salvation has started a bitter rivalry

with the lizardfolk gang of neighboring Khikzux Ward. Since the first incident, fresh bodies from both sides have turned up in the Zheree and Kenqrud Bay every week. The militia originally tried to get involved but was explicitly told to stay out of it by both gangs. With few resources and fewer options, the militia had no choice but to comply.

Following Vorpos' Trail

This section details the steps Vorpos took once he arrived in Orbea. While this is the best order for the characters to follow Vorpos' path, you are not obligated to run it this way. If the characters become stuck, you can offer a clue that drops them into another part of Vorpos' trail where they can pick up on the mystery once more.

The Tall Ghost (Khikzuk Ward). Through rumors around town, the characters learn that Vorpos' first stop in Orbea was at a small, out-of-the-way bookshop in Khikzuk Ward called The Tall Ghost. The Ghost's owner, Ophiar, was on an expedition in the Wallingmiota when Vorpos first came by. He still hasn't returned. Ophiar's neighbor, Mrs. Wattlesbee (N female kobold **commoner**) relayed this information to Vorpos, although, she wasn't sure when he would return.

He asked her for an inn to stay at. She mentioned The Blushing Crocodile Inn in Khikuk.

The Blushing Crocodile Inn (Khikzuk Ward). The Blushing Crocodile Inn is a ramshackle hovel with three crowded, shared rooms at the edge of a filth-ridden canal. The Blushing Crocodile's owner, Quz (N male lizardfolk **commoner**) doesn't remember Vorpos or any gnome stopping by the inn. He says it's possible the gnome stayed at another inn in the city as there are at least a twenty, most of which are upon the plateaus.

While the characters are at the Crocodile, have one of them notice a gnomish street vendor across from the inn. The sign on her cart advertisers "authentic gnomish cuisine." The street vendor's name is Spidira (NG female gnome **commoner**). She remembers Vorpos well as he stopped by Spidira's cart and purchased a vegetable kabob the day he arrived. "He didn't look thrilled by the condition of the Blushing Crocodile so was asking me where there was an inn worth staying," she recalls. "I told him to look upon Yaqut Heights." Before the characters leave, she adds, "You should probably know this, but your friend was being followed by some tall fella in a gray cloak. Didn't get a good look at him, but I didn't get the impression that he was friendly, neither."

She tells them that the quickest way up to Yaqut Heights (**Area 9**) from Khizuk Ward is through a tunnel called Teal Alley that enters the plateau in its northern face.

Teal Alley (Yaqut Heights). More of a series of winding staircases than an alley, Teal Alley connects to various passages, tunnels, and other hideaways within the heart of the Yaqut Heights plateau. Although there are easy-to-follow signs that lead up to a surface exit, it's easy to get lost within the maze.

As the characters travel through the tunnels following Spidira's directions, they are accosted by a human **bandit** named Kelvar. "Hey! Hey! Wanna buy a book? Just 10 gold pieces. Brand new... still got that smell, ya know? Take a look! Take a look!" The book is *Glyphs and Scripts* by Aruxius, the same copy Vorpos had with him. Kelvar and his brothers jumped Vorpos while he was traveling through the maze, stole his coin purse, and pilfered the book. The brothers already spent the gold on drugs and alcohol, and are now trying to offload the book. If questioned, Kelvar whistles. Just then, from the shadows, Kelvan's three older, bigger brothers appear (**thugs**).

If the characters defeat the thugs without killing them, they can ask them about the gnome. They admit that they stole the book off Vorpos, but didn't kill him. Last they saw him, Vorpos was still heading up to the top of the Heights. That's all they know.

They don't remember anything about a figure wearing a gray cloak.

Moja's (Yaqut Heights). There are four inns on Yaqut Heights: the Sleeping Bride (described in the Important Locations section), the Anxious Rhinoceros, the Deep Dandelion, and Moja's. The best move for the characters to make is to investigate each of the inns. The inns are easy to find and most Orbeans will offer directions at no charge.

Moja's is a reasonably priced inn/casino situated across a small merchant area. The person working behind the counter of Moja's, Tedd, remembers the gnome.

"He was a bloody mess when he came in. He told me he got rolled down on Teal Alley. I felt bad for the bugger and would have given him a room but we were all booked up. I recommended to him that he find one of the temples down in Azen'qod Ward. It's a rough section, but there are a few priests of Usteus down there. Just hope he didn't get all mixed up in the insanity."

If asked what he means, he explains that the Temple of Usteus is known to harbor religious extremists.

"Most folks call them a gang. But they're a little crazier than that, you know?"

The innkeeper gives the characters directions. He also mentions that shortly after the gnome left, someone wearing all gray came in asking for him. "There was something strange about the man's voice. Dialect I'd never heard."

The Temple of Usteus (Azen'qod Ward). As the characters travel through Azen'qod, towards the temple, read the following:

> Azen'qod ward is tucked between a canyon wall and the Zheree river. It appears to be one of the poorer wards, but certainly has a bit more charm to it than the canal-stricken streets of Khikzuk. The streets

are narrow and the houses are short. Von Dorals and wanderer halflings are common here, as are canids. There's even a gnome or two. Mushroom gardens, moss-and-vine covered walls, and even patches of glow grass give the location a cozy feeling like being in a shady glade.

The Temple of Usteus is a relatively tall building hewn directly into the canyon wall deep within the borough and far from the river. It's quieter here, only the sounds of halfling marms sweeping off their front porches and the occasional cough of an old-timer. The twin statues of Usteus stand at either end of the entrance into the temple. The right statue, Usteus the Punisher, holds its mighty Maul of the Guilty. The Accuser's eyes stare at the entrance to the temple as if it is waiting for someone to leave. Meanwhile, the left statue, Usteus the Liberator, kneels with its head down as if to ask for forgiveness to those exiting the temple.

Inside, you see the flicker of torchlight and hear voices.

The characters are free to enter the temple without being harmed (unless they act violently towards the Usteusian followers, of course). If the statues give them pause, have one of the temple's priests (N male wanderer halfling **cultist**) invite them in, promising that Usteus only passes judgment on his followers and enemies, of which they are (likely) neither. "Unless, of course," says the priest, motioning to the imposing right statue "You have reason to fear the Punisher?"

Once the characters enter the temple, read the following:

> The main chamber of the temple is a 40-foot-square room with 10-foot high ceilings. Thick columns carved from the same stone as the floors, walls, and ceiling support the weight of the earth overhead. Hung on each

of the columns are iron sconces with burning torches.

At the center of the columns, in a 20-foot-square opening, a dais carved like an eight-pointed star covers the floor. At each point of the star stands a halfling wearing a robe with a similar star design. At the center of the star stands two more halflings standing over a third halfling who is kneeling with his head on the ground and his hands behind his back. The halfling on the right wears a white mask with a gentle smile while the halfling on the left wears a black mask twisted in a frown. The black-masked halfling also holds a blood-stained maul, easily twice his size.

One of the halflings outside the star speaks, "Zalorin Petras. You have been accused in the eyes of Usteus of a crime most alarming: consorting with enemies of the temple. Now, as is the will of Usteus, you must present yourself to both forms of our most Holy Judge and seek Salvation. Once you have spoken, our most Holy Judge will decide if he stands before you as your Punisher or as your Liberator."

The halfling speaking is Meros Scarletfoot (see **Area 17**). The other nine halflings are all LN wanderer halfling **cultists**. And the halfling who begs for his life was an informant for Meros who is under suspicion of double-crossing the Salvation.

Meekly, the informant—whose face is already battered from his former brothers—begins to speak. Before he can say another word, the black-masked halfling representing Usteus the Punisher hits him in the face with the maul. Unless the characters intervene, the Punisher proceeds to beat the man to death.

If this happens, Meros says, "Salvation comes to our fallen brother in the form of punishment. He is saved." The others echo the sentiment in unison, "He is saved." Meros then motions for the remaining halflings to handle the body.

As long as the characters didn't intervene with the Ritual of Judgement, Meros is very welcoming to them, acting as if nothing violent or out-of-the-ordinary had just happened. Despite his devious nature, he is quite forthcoming. He remembers Vorpos and gave him a spot within the temple to rest and recover from his attack. He mentions that Vorpos shared his story with Meros.

> "The gnome told me that he was on a mission to find a friend, a bookshop owner across the river. During our talks, he shared that he had discovered something important—something that could unravel all of Omeria. Valcryn believed that his life was in danger. The poor soul would wake at night screaming.
>
> "After resting with us for two days, he told me that he was going to travel back over the river to see if his friend had returned. I could not send a messenger on his behalf, of course, as we have..." he pauses and smiles. "Well, let's just say my kind aren't exactly *welcome* over in Khikzux.
>
> "I'm afraid he never returned after that."

Meros offers the characters anything they might need. He's even willing to sell *potions of healing* at half the normal rate (25 gp each).

The Man in Gray (Anywhere). After the encounter with Meros and the Usteus worshipers, the trail goes cold. The characters can return to Khikzux, but The Tall Ghost is still closed and Ophiar has not returned.

Eventually, one of the characters notices a figure in a gray cloak watching them from 30 feet away. Once noticed, the figure bolts and the characters will have to chase them through the busy city. Refer to the rules on Urban Chase Encounters in Chapter 8 of the *DMG*. If the characters catch up to the runner or harm him, the characters learn that

it isn't a man at all: it's a female **orc**, Gluronk, Mega's first mate. Gluronk's incredible build and husky voice are easy for non-orcs to mistake her as male—a frequent point of contention for her.

At this point, Gluronk has heard that Mega escaped the Castlegraspians, of course, but she doesn't know about his fate at Qola. Hearing the information, the look of terror on the tough warrior's face is unmistakable.

> Gluronk shakes her head, "It's all because of the book, isn't it? He just had to know what was in that damned book. It's doomed us all." She spits, cursing Mega's name in orcish.
>
> "I came to Orbea to hide away after The Ghost Holm. We used to lay low here after our big jobs, let the heat die down. After Ghost Holm, he was supposed to meet me here. Then, we'd head up north to his brother's cabin on the other side of the Spine. She sighs, "Of course, he never came."
>
> "So I didn't know what to do. Most of the Odezdoz had been arrested or were scattered across the continent, and I felt this feeling like I was in danger. Like I was being watched. I know this sounds crazy, but I swear I could feel eyes on me everywhere I went. Like something dark in the corner of my mind.
>
> "Then, one day as I was walking down the streets, I saw that gnome. I recognized him right away from the images we were given by that wizard in Haver. If there was someone who knew what was going on, that I could give the book to, it was him."
>
> She pauses realizing what she's just revealed.

Unless another circumstance occurred where Gluronk didn't leave the Ghost Holm with the book, *Prime*, she's been in possession of the book this entire time.

> "Yes, I have it," she admits. "I have the unreadable book. It's not on me, of course. I've hidden it for now. But if giving it to you will help me sleep better at night, then by Suen's arms, I'll give the damn thing to you.
>
> "The gnome and I talked for a while. He didn't even want to touch the thing. That's how afraid of it he was. Said it gave him nightmares. Same ones as me. In our dreams, the skies are dark and there's something roaring in the distance. Just before us stands a... tower... or something. And at the top of the tower is a glowing green light. Brighter than any I've ever seen. I can't explain it, right, but it gives me chills just talking about.
>
> "I had a little money, so I put him up in a spot over on the Thumb, an out-of-the-way spot called the Tame Cave. It's quiet up there with plenty of escape routes. He'd be safe there. I'll bet he'll be glad to see you. Probably just wants to get home, poor bugger."

She won't tell the characters where she's hidden the book but mentions she gave it to someone in town whom she can trust to hide it for her.

"Even if you get it out of me who I gave it to, you probably won't find him. And I told them to never tell me where they're hiding with it."

She tells the characters to meet her at the top of the Killer two hours after sunset.

"Dress nice," she chuckles.

The Tame Cave (Laris Ledge). Once the characters use one of the roads, staircases, or tunnels to reach the top of Laris Ledge, read the following:

> Gluronk wasn't wrong. It's quiet up here. The only sounds are those made by crickets and the dull roar of the town in the canyons below. There are a few souls here and there on the Ledge, but overall, the place feels

old second-story windows which are now even with the ground. When the characters knock at the door, no voice comes, but they discover that the door is ajar.

> The room is 15 feet wide by 20 feet deep with 10-foot-high ceilings. A four-post bed is to your left and a large pair of windows that step out onto a ground-level balcony are directly ahead. In a chair directly in front of that window, you see a small humanoid, his back to you. He nods the back of his head to you, seemingly noting your presence in the room. But he gives no word of welcome.

If the characters call out to Vorpos, he gives no reply. Once they see his face, they quickly understand why: Vorpos is dead, a knife through his left eye. His head jerks up and down while a pair of **rats** eat the flesh around his lower jaw. A DC 13 Wisdom (Medicine) check reveals that he's been dead for close to a day. In addition to the knife wound, he has strangulation marks around his throat. The knife itself is devoid of any markings. However, in his pocket, he's carrying a small, circular stone with magic runes on it. A character who can cast *identify* on the stone will know that it's a *sending stone*. If a character uses the stone to send a message, they receive a reply from a woman with a demanding, soldierly voice:

> "This is Captain Santxa Goytino of the Arruquetta-Orbean Alliance. Identify yourself and your current position at once."

The characters can send one 25-word reply back to Goytino before the stone ceases to function. After that, it cannot be used again until the next dawn.

If the characters spend a minute to perform a DC 15 Intelligence (Investigation) check around the room, they notice that the balcony window is unlocked from the inside. Twelve-inch-long humanoid footprints lead over the

hollow. Wide, two-story mansions, lie empty, the brown, dry grass of the peninsula grows wild in what was probably once well-manicured lawns.

Regular cracks and rises in the cobblestonepaths reveal that the spot is prone to earthquakes, landslides, or potentially both. On the north side of the Ledge, the cut-in-half ruins of houses fuel this thought—looks like the Thumb was once bigger, but part of it tumbled over into the canyon below. A bronze plaque remembering the dead stands 30-feet from the edge.

You discover the inn where Gluronk told you to find Vorpos. It appears that it was once one of the mansions on the plateau, but whatever event

caused the northside to collapse also caused the building to sink six feet down into the ground, burying almost the entire first floor. Oddly, the building is still mostly intact. A flight of steps was dug and paved down to the original front door. A brightly painted sign over the door reads, "The Tame Cave. 1 sp per night."

The innkeeper is a ruddy-faced Von Doral woman named Hilga (**commoner**). She's half-asleep when the characters enter. Even at the low-price, business is slow. When asked about Vorpos, she shares that he is indeed in the inn, Room 27.

Room 27 is on the second floor. Natural light pours through the mansion's railing and away from the Tame Cave. As the prints are too large to be Vorpos', it's possible they were his killer's.

There is also an invisible *scrying* sensor in the room. A character that can see invisible objects sees it with a successful DC 15 Wisdom (Perception) check. The moment that the characters notice it, the sensor vanishes.

Hilga doesn't remember anyone else other than Gluronk (who she refers to as "that big green gal") visiting Vorpos.

The Cords (Laris Ledge). Once the characters exit the Tame Cave, unless they are careful, they find themselves surrounded by 4 Arruquetan Cords (all **guards**) led by Sergeant Simon Delgalarrondo (LN male Ditimayan human **veteran**). All of the guards are armed with light crossbows and all are mounted on **griffons**.

Five soldiers wearing dark, blue tunics and matching capes train their crossbows on you as you exit the Tame Cave. Each one has a fuschia cord of rope that dangles from the right epaulet. The leader of the group steps forward. "I am Sergeant Simon Delgalarrondo of the Cords of Arruqueta. We have reason to suspect that you have committed murder within that place of business. Drop your weapons and come with us."

The soldiers mean business. They received an anonymous tip that one of the informants was murdered by members of the Separatist movement and that the descriptions given of the Separatists match exactly the characters.

From here, the characters have a four options:

- **They can fight the Cords and will likely defeat them**. If the Cords' numbers are reduced to half or less, they make a tactical retreat with the intent of returning to Gadran's Plateau to bring additional reinforcements.
- **They can run from the Cords**. Hiding in the Thumb is very difficult as most of the buildings are empty and easily accessible. Plus, the griffons allow the Cords to maneuver quickly. The Ledge itself is 400-feet above the canyon's wards, so jumping off the cliff is likely to result in death. Alternatively, the characters can use enchantments, illusions, etc. to escape.
- **They can convince the Cords that they did nothing wrong**. The Cords are stubbornly devoted to their cause, but they *can* be convinced that the characters are innocent. Have one of the characters represent the party and make their case. Then have the character make a Charisma (Deception or Persuasion) check contested by the Simon's Wisdom (Insight) check. Simon automatically makes his check at advantage, but the party's representative can also gain advantage if the character's player did an exceptional job roleplaying the scene.
- **They can go peacefully with the Cords**. If the characters surrender themselves to the Cords, the Cords bind their hands with manacles (as in the *PHB*), then lead them to Gadran's Plateau. There, they are placed in one of the holding cells at their command center.

Should the characters escape the Cords by any means other than convincing them that they did nothing wrong, the Cords actively hunt them within the town. Each hour that the characters remain in town, roll 1d20. On a result of 13-20, a squad of 5 Cords (**guards**) led by 1 **veteran** notices the characters and moves to arrest them. You can make these rolls in place of the random encounter checks normal for this adventure.

The Cords' griffons are trained to obey only their command words. However, a character can spend 1 minute with a griffon, then make a DC 16 Wisdom (Animal Handling) check. On a success, the griffon will allow the character to ride it as if the character was its true rider (but only that character).

Cord Command Center Detention (Gadran's Plateau). *Only run this encounter if the characters are arrested by the Cords following the discovery of Valcryn Vorpos' body.*

Before the characters are interred, they are deprived of all of their weapons, armor, and equipment, including arcane focuses, spell books, and component pouches. Characters who seem particularly dangerous with free hands—such as monks—remain manacled even in the cells.

After traveling down a few flights of stairs into the heart of the plateau, they are placed into a 10-by-10 cell with iron bars. The room is well lit by *continual flame* globes placed at regular intervals in the hallway.

The ceilings, floors, and walls of the cell are made of thick, hewn stone, impossible to easily pass through, even by magical means. The cell bars are each 1-inch thick. They can be bent or pulled from their spot on the floor with a successful DC 21 Strength check. The door itself is locked with a mundane key, necessitating only a DC 15 Dexterity check using thieves' tools to unlock—although, the Cords should have taken such tools away.

A **guard** keeps watch at all times at the end of the hallway, his back to a locked door. On the other side of the door is a second guard. The two communicate via a special knocking system that changes each time it knocks. A character listening to the knocks can make a DC 20 Intelligence check to determine the nature of the pattern. Each time they hear another knock, the DC lowers by 1.

In addition to the characters, there are six other prisoners in the cellblock. You're free to detail these prisoners however you like, although, it's likely that are or are suspected of being Arruquetan Separatists.

Of course, none of this matters. Within a few minutes of them being incarcerated, read the following:

The door at the end of the hall opens and a stern-looking woman with long, dark hair wearing the blue, black, and fuschia uniform of a Cord officer enters flanked by a pair of Cord guards. One of the guards unlocks your cell and the woman stares at you. "Go," she snaps, pointing to the door. At the end of a hallway, you see a familiar face.

"How in the Obsidian did you manage to get yourselves arrested this fast?" Omnaweahl stomps over and wags her finger at you. "You're lucky I have friends in high places. Otherwise, you all would've been carted off to a dungeon somewhere in Arruquetta and fed to Emagavel's hyenas."

The dark-haired woman scoffs and steps aside, allowing you to leave.

Once the characters recover their gear, they are escorted outside with Omnaweahl. Outside, a tall, Dinzer man with gray in his beard is waiting.

A tall man with a shaved head and a grey beard wearing robes similar to Omnaweahl's stands outside waiting for you.

"So these are the ones stirring up a commotion in town, eh, little sister?" the bearded Dinzer man says while he smiles at you. However, it's clear there is sadness in his eyes.

The man is Ophiar (N male Dinzer human **mage**), the friend who Vorpos tried to meet in Orbea before he was murdered. He introduces himself to the characters and explains that he had heard the news of his friends' death from the Cords.

"How could Valcryn have possibly been an Arruquetan Separatist?" Ophiar says, shaking his head. The tears well up in his eyes once more. "He hated Arruqueta." Omnaweahl tries to comfort her brother. "I should have been there for my friend," he says, choking back sobs. "I should have known he was

friends with you," says O. "You always had such interesting friends."

If the characters are curious about how Omnaweahl knew about the characters' incarceration, she gives a sheepish look.

"I just might possibly have a crystal ball I've been using to keep tabs on you since you entered Orbea. I would have been here sooner, but I was out east handling business in Naqqad. Sorry. Anyways, if this book is as big a deal as my bosses think it is, they want to ensure that it doesn't fall into the wrong hands. After what we've seen her, it's pretty clear there's a bunch of trouble surrounding it already."

O clears her throat and puts her hands into the pocket of her robe. "So, I guess, you'll be meeting the orc woman at Sevari Tower soon? It's already an hour after sunset. If so, my brother and I will be happy to escort you there."

Whether or not the characters accept their offer (they may not trust Omnaweahl after she admits she was spying on them, Gluronk is already headed towards The Killer for her rendezvous. **The Long Shadow (Sevari Tower).** Gluronk has already made the exhaustive 500-foot climb up The Killer to Sevari Tower. However, the characters won't immediately recognize her:

A thin, dark-haired Ditimayan human woman wearing a form-fitting purple-sequin dress with a matching mask fashioned to look like a squid approaches you. "Hey," says the woman in Gluronk's familiar deep voice. "It's me. Gluronk. I'm in disguise."

Gluronk is wearing a *hat of disguise* to make herself look like a noble from the Eight Gems Ward. If the characters didn't have the opportunity to dress up, she rolls her eyes and says, "Well, may-

be they'll think you're my bodyguards."

Gluronk explains her plan to the characters. The friend who is in possession of the book is in the largest casino on Sevari Tower, the Long Shadow. Once Gluronk introduces the characters to her, she will give the characters the book. She will also have enough tickets for each of the characters to leave aboard the Red-and-Blue Gentleman, a casino blimp parked in the airfields. The casino blimp departs for Knotside the next morning.

If the characters agree, Gluronk leads them to the Long Shadow.

This impressive sloped building before you looks like it was carved from the stone of the canyon itself. Red and white wisp-lights highlight the corners, windows, and entrances of the building. Posted at regular balconies, dancers of all races invite passersby to enter. Of course, not just anyone can enter. The line to enter the casino is nearly around the block. Wealthy tourists and Orbean citizens stand impatiently waiting for the two, 7-foot-tall bugbear guards at the front door to allow them entry. All of them wear ornate tunics, cloaks, and jeweled masks fashioned to look like different types of monsters: chimeras, bulettes, woggles, basilisks, cloakers, even a dragon or two.

Gluronk, in the disguise of an Orbean noblewoman, surpasses the line and walks up to the bugbear guards, addressing them in goblinoid.

Translation: "I am the shadow on the water."

The bugbears open the doors and motion for Gluronk and you all to enter, much to the dismay of the masked nobles still waiting in line.

If the outside of the Long Shadow was impressive, the inside is even more mesmerizing. All around you, you see insane wealth being thrown around like it was nothing.

At a counter to your right, nobles exchange liter pouches full of platinum pieces for painted wooden tokens. Directly ahead games of Banzo, Bouncing Crocodile, Dragon Chess Express, and Three Dragon Ante are played by cheering winners who suddenly find themselves up for the first time in the evening and jeering losers who've sunk even further into debt.

Clustered around leather couches and chairs, drunk nobles are entertained by quick-swapping doppelgangers who encourage them to imbibe more. When one of the drunken nobles dressed in a suit of obviously-fake shining armor gets a little too handsy with a doppelganger girl, a finely-dressed orc—obviously casino security of some sort—grabs the "knight-in-shining-armor's" wrist and gives him a sobering warning in broken Common: "Next time you touch girl you get the Drop!" The noble nods.

While all of this is exciting, it's clear that Gluronk is here on business. She heads straight for the east end of the casino. There, a devilkin woman wearing all white and flanked by two ogres stands and watches everything from a balcony fifteen feet above the casino floor.

The woman is Prayer in the Morning (LE female devilkin **assassin**), the owner of the Long Shadow. Her two **ogre** companions say little, but are never more than 10 feet from her side.

When the devilkin woman sees Gluronk in her human disguise, she raises an eyebrow in amusement. "Don't you know that purple clashes with green?"

"It'll be a pity to get that fancy white outfit all bloody," Gluronk snaps back. The two then embrace and laugh. Gluronk turns to you, "This ugly devilkin wench is my friend, Prayer in the Morning. She is the owner of this casino

and many moons ago was one of the most feared pirates on the Omerian Ocean."

"Still am, snout-face," says Prayer, winking. "And it wasn't *that* long ago."

Gluronk snorts and rolls her human eyes.

Prayer leads the Gluronk and the characters into her office overlooking the casino floor.

This large room is 40-feet wide and 15-feet deep. The north end of the room has a curved wall with windows overlooking the Omerian Ocean. The twin moons linger over the dark horizon, lighting the powerful waves below you.

Expensive-looking furniture fills the center of the room. Against the eastern wall, a large, wooden desk stands in front of a cabinet covered in dozens of liquor bottles. Beside the desk, a giant lever sticks out of the floor. The top of the lever is carved to looked like some sort of multi-sided die.

Prayer walks over and snatches one of the bottles from the wall with her prehensile tail, then pours herself, Gluronk, and each of you a drink.

"Hope you all like poison," she says behind a grin. Raising her glass, she toasts, "Until the Eighth" then sips.

The liquor isn't poisoned. Prayer just likes toying with her guests.

After the pleasantries, Prayer says, "Straight to business, then!" She walks over to the wall near her cabinet and removes a wooden panel from the wall. Behind the panel is a steel panel. Prayer whispers a single magical phrase and presses her palm to the panel. The panel slides up revealing a hidden compartment with an ancient, leatherbound tome inside.

Prayer pulls *Prime* from its hiding spot, walks across the room, then offers it to the characters. Simple as that.

Just then, two of the orcs from downstairs knock at the door. One of the orcs says in broken Common, "Boss. Got another one. Keep grabbing shifter girls. What you want do?"

Gluronk hops up and down excitedly. "The Drop! The Drop! The Drop!"

Gluronk explains the situation to you: whenever people cause trouble in the casino, they're brought to Prayer's office and forced to stand over a circular trapdoor in the floor, just by the outer windows. From there, Prayer pulls that lever by her desk, and down they go, 500 feet to the ocean floor below. And because Prayer is an entertainer above all, she broadcasts the entire affair on scrying mirrors positioned throughout the casinos.

If the characters are okay with witnessing the Death by Drop, after a moment, the same orc from before drags the "knight-in-shining-armor" into the office. The knight stumbles, clearly drunk, and doesn't seem to realize the severity of what's about to happen.

Gluronk asks Prayer if she can do the honors, to which Prayer agrees. Gluronk trots over to the lever next to Prayer's desk while the orcs put the "knight-in-shining-armor" in place.

Prayer says a magic word. The *continual flames* in the ceiling increase in brightness and fully illuminate the area, revealing the office to everyone standing on the casino floor below. She picks up a magic wand and speaks into its tip: "Ladies and Gentleman of the Long Shadow!" The wand amplifies her voice. The patrons cheer.

"It's that time again!"

The patrons start chanting: "Drop! Drop! Drop! Drop!"

"That's right!" she says like a carnival barker. "Don't let the outfit fool you, my beloved children. This one decided he just couldn't keep his hands off my girls. Naughty, naughty."

The patrons boo.

"On the count of three, my 'good friend here' will remind us all what happens when you can't be good boys and girls and follow the rules in my casino."

The crowd chants with Prayer: one... two...

That's when the remote traveler drops its disguise.

The Machine

Even if the characters didn't allow for the drop to occur, one way or the other, the "knight-in-shining-armor"—which is actually a **remote traveler alpha-class** in disguise—gets into the office. Just as it looks like it's about to get the drop, its disguise ends and its true construct nature is revealed.

It is likely that it gets a surprise round on everyone in the room. In that case, it immediately uses its stored *fireball* spell to level the playing field.

The remote traveler's number one priority is to retrieve the book. It goes directly for whichever character is holding it and will not let up until the book is in its hands.

Meanwhile, Gluronk, Prayer, and any of Prayer's security force who survived the initial explosion work with the characters to fight back the construct. You can have the players run the NPCs during the combat if you like.

The *fireball* was enough to send most of the patrons running out of the casino. After three rounds of combat, 10 **guards** armed with light crossbows arrive in the casino. The

guards spend 1 round trying to assess the situation. If no one informs them who the "good guys" or "bad guys" are, they open fire discriminately, shooting at whoever looks the most dangerous—likely the characters.

After 5 rounds of combat, if the remote traveler isn't dead or close to dead (half its hp or fewer), on initiative count 20 of the 6th round, read the following:

Suddenly, the office is bathed in light from a source outside the office windows. You can't see what it is, but you hear a familiar voice come from whatever it is. "Get down, imbeciles!" shouts Omnaweahl.

Omnaweahl is piloting her Dinzer peregrine 20 feet from the office windows, 500-feet above the surface of the water. The peregrine holds an action to fire its Eldritch Cannons at the remote traveler as soon as she has a clear shot at it; meaning any characters standing in the way need to move or drop prone. While her cannons may not do enough damage to defeat the construct, it will give the characters enough time to flee the casino (or finish it off). If they run out the front entrance, Omnaweahl wheels the peregrine around to meet, them then lowers a ramp to let them get in.

If the characters agree to join her, as soon as they're all inside, she takes off, flying as far away from Orbea as possible. Otherwise, the characters will need to find another way to escape the deadly remote traveler alpha-class by either defeating it in combat or fleeing—possibly by way of *The Red-and-Blue Gentleman*.

Adventure Conclusion

More than likely, the characters are on their way north. If she is asked why they are headed that way, Omnaweahl explains simply: "Valcryn Vorpos believed that the secret of the book could be unlocked using Aruxius's old texts, right? Well, I say we go ask the man himself, Aruxius. We're going to Wallingmiotta."

Aruxius retired from scholarly pursuits twenty years ago. Tired of politics, war, and the stress of everyday life, he traveled to Wallingmiotta where he could live quietly in the Neutral Lands and has been there ever since. The only trouble is, Aruxius doesn't like visitors.

The Mysteries Continue

There are a number of mystery threads left hanging at the end of this chapter. The intent of this series is to not only surprise players once they've finally had a chance to play the game, but to also surprise my patrons and fans as they read through the adventure series. Once the entire mystery has unraveled, then they will understand the answers to the puzzles themselves. In the meantime, for GMs who hope to run this adventure before the latter pieces arrive, here are a few answers to some of the big questions.

Who Killed Valcryn Vorpos? By the end of Chapter 4, the biggest mystery is the identity of the murderer of Valcryn Vorpos. If it isn't obvious, the remote traveler alpha-class strangled Vorpos and stabbed him through the eye, then fled through the window. But who sent the construct? Why do they want the book? And if it's a remote-traveler, who is on the other end of the remote?

Why did the Cords think the characters murdered Vorpos? A *sending stone* was found on Vorpos' body connected to a *second stone* owned by Captain Santxa Goytino's of the Cords. Goytino believed she was in contact with an informant code-named Quick Badger. Quick Badger fed her valuable information on the locations of Arruquetan Separatists living in Orbea. After Vorpos was murdered, someone gave the Cords the tip that it was the characters who murdered Vorpos and that Vorpos was the real Quick Badger. But was Valcryn Vorpos the real Quick Badger? And why did someone try to frame the characters for Vorpos' murder?

What is Prime? That's the million gold piece question. In its current state, the book cannot be read. However, Valcryn Vorpos believed that the mystery to unlocking its secrets lie within the book *Glyphs and Scripts* by Aruxius. Will the characters learn the book's secrets when they speak with Aruxius? Or is it another dead end?

All will be answered by the conclusion of this adventure path. Until then, the story continues in the next Chapter, *Wallingmiotta*.

Until the Eighth. Ω

TALES OF OMERIA: THE BURNING WEB

BY DAVE HAMRICK

3rd-Level Adventure for Fifth Edition

Cartography by Dave Hamrick
Primary Art by Joyce Maureira and Rick Hershey

The Burning Web is a Fifth Edition adventure for 3-5 characters of the 3rd-level. Time is of the essence in this adventure, so there should be an ever-present sense of urgency. Otherwise, the story's antagonist could escape before the characters are even able to confront them. While much of the background and text assumes that the characters are involved in the main plotline of the Hand of the Eight, this adventure can easily be run as a one-shot adventure playable in 2-3 hours. On the same token, while this adventure adds to the excitement and story behind Hand of the Eight, it is not necessary for the overall plot.

Someone is kidnapping krigs, the spider-humanoid natives of Orbea. Despite their off-putting appearance, krigs are generally passive, intelligent creatures who've helped bring many of the Weysevain Coast's cities into the modern era of arc-technology. What would make someone or something attack the krigs? In this spin-off one-shot adventure, a group of adventurers are tasked to learn exactly that.

Adventure Background

Krigs are the spider-humanoid natives of Orbea. Nearly identical, krigs live throughout the continent of Omeria in various cities. Of the 10,000 believed to be in existence, only 2,000 are rumored to live in the town where they originate, Orbea. Recently, a group of terrorists known as The Burning Web has been kidnapping krigs within their own town. The adventure begins when a group of adventurers traveling through Orbea witness a krig abduction. After stopping the krig's abductors, they discover that the group has been working out of a warehouse in the town's seedy Salt Ward.

There, the adventurers discover that a human sage named Ament Leywood (under the pseudonym Titos Barakis) has been performing experiments on the krigs. Of course, not everything may not be as it seems.

The Burning Web

Fifteen years ago, Ament Leywood, his wife, and two young daughters moved from Murktown to the town of Jando's Arch on the Ghost Holm. Leywood had been invited to work there with a group of Knotsider sages to investigate an archaeological find on the north end of the island. A month earlier, an adventuring group found a series of abandoned tunnels that led deep into the Holm. The tunnels twisted and turned, terminating at random deadends with little-to-no connecting chambers. Von Doral engineers recognized the stonework to be at least a few centuries old, but overall, could not identify the origin of the tunnels' creators. Within the tunnels, they discovered dozens of humanoid corpses, some as old as the tunnels themselves. Sages specializing in medicine observed that the corpses lacked fatal wounds. They theorized the dead humanoids had died of starvation and thirst. Additionally, the sages discovered what appeared to be discarded insect husks, roughly 3-feet in diameter, at a concealed chamber near the center of the labyrinth. Also, the chamber had faint traces of radiant energy.

Before Leywood and the sages could investigate the location further, war broke out between northern and central Omeria. Jando's Arch, a Knotsider colony and military base, and likely a target for central Omerian offensive forces called for the evacuation of all of the island's non-essential personnel. Leywood and his family were escorted to the southern end of the island and put aboard a ship. But as their ship was leaving the harbor, three Dinzer Condor-class aircraft appeared in the skies. The condors dropped *fireballs* on the village and the arch. But then, one of the *fireballs* strayed from its path and hit the deck of the ship carrying Leywood and his family to safety.

The Original Sidequest

This adventure expands upon the side quest "Put the Krig Down" in the fourth chapter of the ***Hand of the Eight*** adventure path, ***The Secret of the Book***. If you choose to run this adventure in place of the side quest, you will replace this side quest with the section "The Abduction." The original hook has been reprinted and expanded upon here for context and convenience.

Two men in white robes are carrying a semi-conscious krig by its arms to a horse-drawn carriage 30-feet away. There is a third man, also in white, at the reins. If questioned, the men explain that the krig is sick and that they are taking him to a temple to receive medical attention. The krig, through its haze, gazes at the characters through its many eyes and weakly asks for help. If the characters intervene, the men in white robes attack. All three men are thugs who work for an organization called the Burning Web. The Burning Web believes that the krigs are all part of a vast, global conspiracy that wishes to take over Omeria by putting krigs in positions of power. They were taking the krig to a warehouse by the docks (**Area 6**) to perform experiments on it. After they save him, the krig thanks the characters, then leaves. If the characters decide to get involved, they must go down to the docks and find the Burning Web's warehouse.

Nearly everyone on board died in the explosion, including Leywood's wife and daughters. Somehow Leywood survived the blast, blown clear of the wreckage. Three days later, Leywood—barely clinging to his life—washed up on a beach near a small fishing village.

The injuries Leywood sustained in the blast blinded him in his left eye and impaired the use of his left arm and leg. And the loss of his family and his career fractured his mind. Leywood became obsessed with the idea that what they discovered in the tunnels was somehow connected to the Dinzer assault on Jando's Arch. With the war in full bloom, none of the sages or leadership in northern Omeria would support his claims. Eventually, he left the sage's guild and retreated south to study privately.

In time, Leywood noticed that there was a connection to the mysterious krigs of Orbea and the tunnels his colleagues had discovered. Although the birthing process of krigs is never seen, as large insectoids, it stands to reason they could be hatched from eggs similar in size and shape to the ones discovered on the Ghost Holm. Furthermore, the Orbean Undermaze shares many of the qualities the tunnels had, especially their austere and labyrinthine nature.

Under the pseudonym Titos Barakis, Leywood moved to Orbea to follow his conspiracy theory. He believed that the Dinzer assault on the Ghost Holm, the death of his family, the krigs, and the tunnels were all somehow connected. Leywood recruited a group of other disenfranchised Omerians who felt there was something amiss with the krigs and their expansive political reach. This group of like-minded individuals named themselves The Burning Web. Under Leywood's leadership, the Web started their research and information gathering out of a dilapidated warehouse in Salt Ward. And now, Leywood is close to getting the answers he craves.

Adventure Hook

The characters become involved while they are traveling through the town of Orbea on the Weysevain Coast. Walking down a Salt Ward street in the middle of the evening, they witness an abduction.

Salt Ward

Salt Ward is home to Orbea's cluttered docks and warehouses. Despite its proximity to the Orbean militia's barracks to the north in Shirzosh, Salt Ward is thick with crime. There is not a week that goes by where a body isn't found floating face down in Keqrab Bay. Most of the warehouses in Salt Ward are owned by wealthy smugglers and merchant houses from all over Central Omeria. They use Orbea as a place to store illegal wares. As such, the warehouses are heavily guarded by well-paid professionals. So brazen are the landlords, they put their clan and tribe symbols on the doors of the buildings they own as a warning to those who would dare enter: "you steal from here, you steal from me."

Important Locations in Salt Ward
The following locations are tied to the map on page 101.

1 - Orbea Militia Barracks. The professional police force of Orbea works out of a building at the south end of the neighboring Shirzosh district. There is a total of 150 full-time militia members operating in Orbea. The majority of the militia members are **guards**, and each squad includes a **veteran** sergeant operating as the squad's leader. The captain of the Orbea Militia is a **krig** who is only referred to as The Captain, identifiable by the tasseled epaulets it wears (and its proclivity for smoking cigars).

Although the Orbean militia is often viewed to be somewhat ineffectual within the fast-growing town, they can call upon the Arruquettan Cords if things get too heinous. Plus, there is a reserve of volunteer militia members from neighboring villages and towns.

2 - Luagru Fish Market. Fresh fish caught in Kreqrab Bay and the Ocean beyond is sold here at the Luagru fish market. Because of the way the wind travels through the canyons that make up the Maze of Orbea, the smell can be somewhat daunting for those traveling south through the ward.

3 - Zik'thath Market. From run-of-the-mill weapons, armor, and equipment to curiosities from afar, anything and everything can be purchased at Zik'thath Market. The characters can expect to find any magic item of common or uncommon value here, as well as the occasional rare magic item, too. Plus, most of the vendors are willing to haggle. On the same token, street vendors can be incredibly pushy. And with all the commotion, theft is common. Like much of Orbea, the presence of law enforcement in the market is low. If any is here, they only work if it looks like they can collect a "reward" from those they save (aka a shakedown).

4 - The Temple of Commerce. What originally started as a jest has now become something of a tradition. The 400-foot-wide, two-story range of vendor stalls that makes up the south end of Zik'thath Market is referred to the Temple of Commerce. Built by a Naqqadi trader named Ramin Atlasi in the early days of Orbea's expansion, gold-painted statues of Atlasi line the columns of the building's north-facing veranda. Each morning, superstitious merchants operating in Zik'Thath leave flowers and fruit offerings at the feet of the late Atlasi's idols in hopes to bring a day of fortune and high sales.

5 - Amazing Clock Replica. At the center of Zik'rath stands a 30-foot tall obelisk. The obelisk is topped by a replica of the Amazing Clock and is attuned to the original in Castlegrasp. Like the one in Castlegrasp, this smaller version of the eight-armed clock tells time, forecasts weather, and predicts the coming of global catastrophes.

6 - The Autumn Bridge. Near the mouth of the river, 50-feet above Zheree Falls, the Autumn Bridge connects the wealthy Eight Gems Ward to the thriving Zik'thath Market. The Autumn Bridge is carved to look like one hundred Ditimayan slaves holding themselves above the Zheree. Suppos-

edly the design comes from a legend of ancient Ditimayan nomads who used each other's limbs to create a chain so they could ford the angry river. The view of the sun setting over the Omerian from the bridge is particularly enticing. It's on this bridge that many travelers passing through Orbea fall in love with the town.

7 - The Unnamed Ramp. A steep ramp curves down the side of Sevari Tower into Zik'thath Market. Outside of a few choice expletives, no one has ever given the "ramp" (more of a cliffside, really) that ascends to the plateau at a 70-degree angle a proper name. It's climbable, certainly, thanks to steel railings placed at regular intervals up the 500-foot high path. But beyond a few ropes-and-pulley systems put in place to bring heavy objects up, it's nearly useless for delivering goods to the top of Sevari. Of course, the business owners atop Sevari prefer it like that.

8 - The Long Shadow Casino. The most famous casino at the top of Sevari Tower is the Long Shadow, a four-story building that hangs over the tower's western edge. The minimum deposit at the Long Shadow is 1,000 gold pieces. Plus, most games have a minimum buy-in of 100 gold pieces. Like most of Orbea's casinos, the Long Shadow's most popular game is Banzo. Its current Banzo champion is a Knotsider gnome named Felgim Trumda. The casino's owner, a devilkin named Prayer in the Morning is loved and celebrated (and feared) by all who enter the casino's pitch black doors. She also offers a house specialty which she extends to anyone short on luck. "1,000 gp loan. Due in one hour with ten points on top. Or? You get the drop!" In other words, Prayer loans the sap 1,000 gold pieces. The loan is to be repaid with a 10% interest on the principle in one hour. If the borrower can't pay up, Prayer's pit bosses open up a hole in the showroom floor and drop the borrower over 500-feet into the Bay below. If the borrower

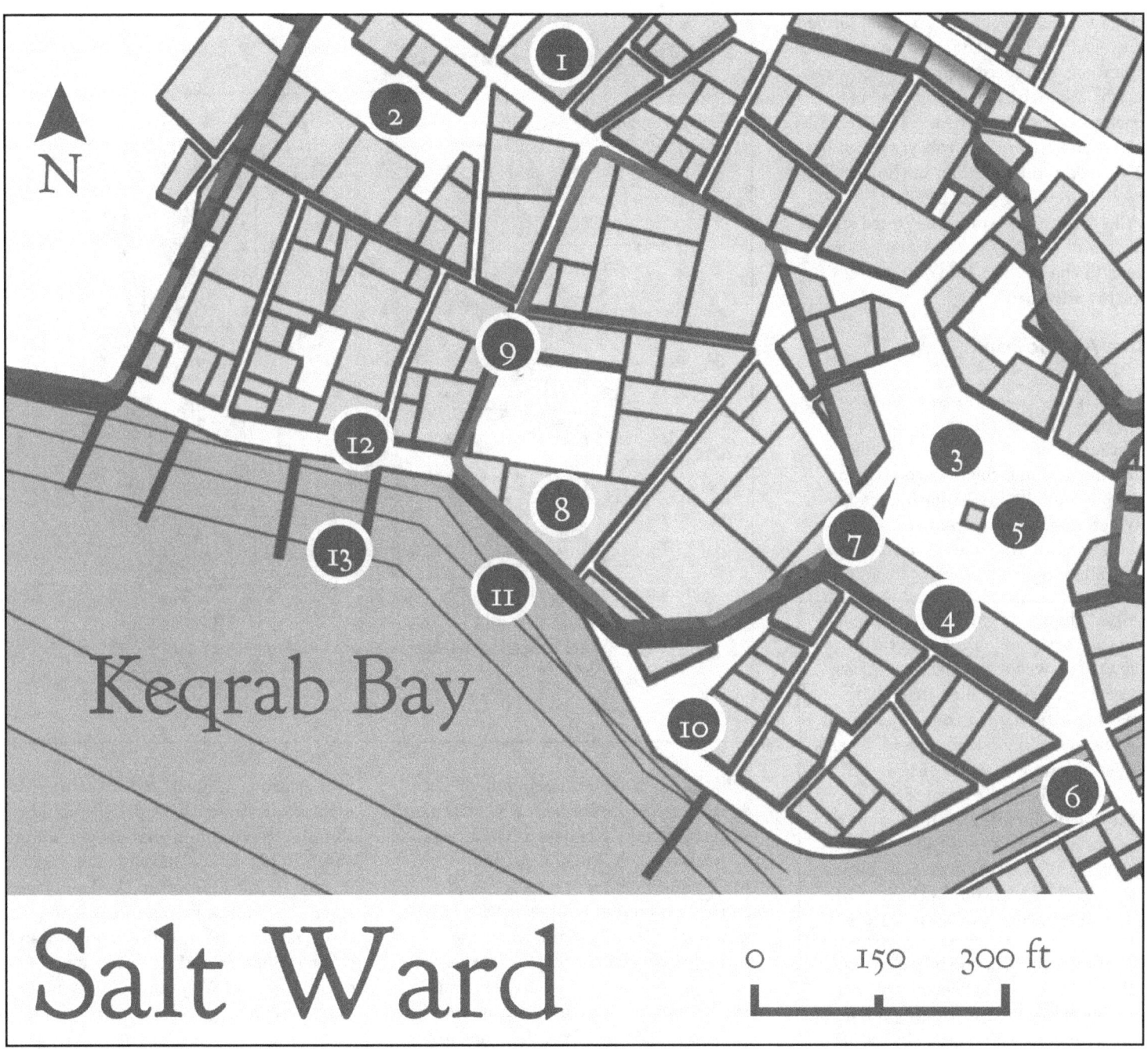

Salt Ward

Keqrab Bay

0   150   300 ft

survives, they're debt-free. So far, no one has survived.

Occasionally, people walking by on the Strand (**Area 11**) witness one of these drops occur up close and personal. It's considered unlucky to be hit by one of the Drop's "dead splashes."

9 - The Killer. If the Unnamed Ramp wasn't horrible enough, its equally devious "twin" clings to the western

wall of the Sevari Tower, a railing-free 500-foot climb of narrow stairs called The Killer. Why the Killer? On average, three to four citizens slip and fall to their death every year while trying to climb or descend the staircase.

10 - Zaxier Alley. Zaxier Alley runs east-to-west between a collection of warehouses right by the water on the southern end of Salt Ward. The krig

abduction detailed in this adventure happens here.

11 - Salt Ward Strand. Fifteen feet above the water directly in front of Sevari Tower, a narrow, 300-foot-long passage connects the southeastern and northwestern sections of Salt Ward. Although the passage has relatively low ceilings thanks to the tower's natural rock face, it's wide enough for a carriage to pass through. Continual flame lanterns are hung the entire expanse, chiefly as a deterrent for criminals who might hide within the hollowed out pockets below the tower.

12 - The Burning Web Warehouse. This location is detailed in the Burning Web Warehouse section below.

13 - Veracity. Ament Leywood keeps his small sailing ship, Veracity, tethered in the harbor. It is detailed later in this adventure.

The Abduction

The adventure begins as the characters are passing through the southeastern section of Salt Ward. They may have just arrived in Orbea via the Keqrab Bay or could be investigating leads connected to another adventure. As they walk past an alley (see **Area 10**), read the following:

> Just then, you catch something out of the corner of your eye in the alley to the west of you. Turning your head, you see two men dressed in white outfits lifting the limp body of what looks like a krig, one of the spider-humanoid natives of the town. About 20 feet in front of them, at the far end of the alley, a third man in white waits by a horse-drawn cart. "Hurry! We've only got 15 minutes to get back! Get the damn thing on the cart and let's go," yells the driver.

From the southeastern end of the alley, where the characters are, to the northwestern side is roughly 50-feet. The abductors—all three **thugs**—attacked the **krig** in the alley. Now, they hope to load it onto the cart and take it across the Strand (see **Area 11**).

If the characters call out or rush to stop them, they first try to run. If blocked, they fight. Because of the sensitivity surrounding krig in Orbea—and the Weysevain Coast in general—getting caught attacking a krig often leads to severe punishment.

If the characters stop the thugs, the

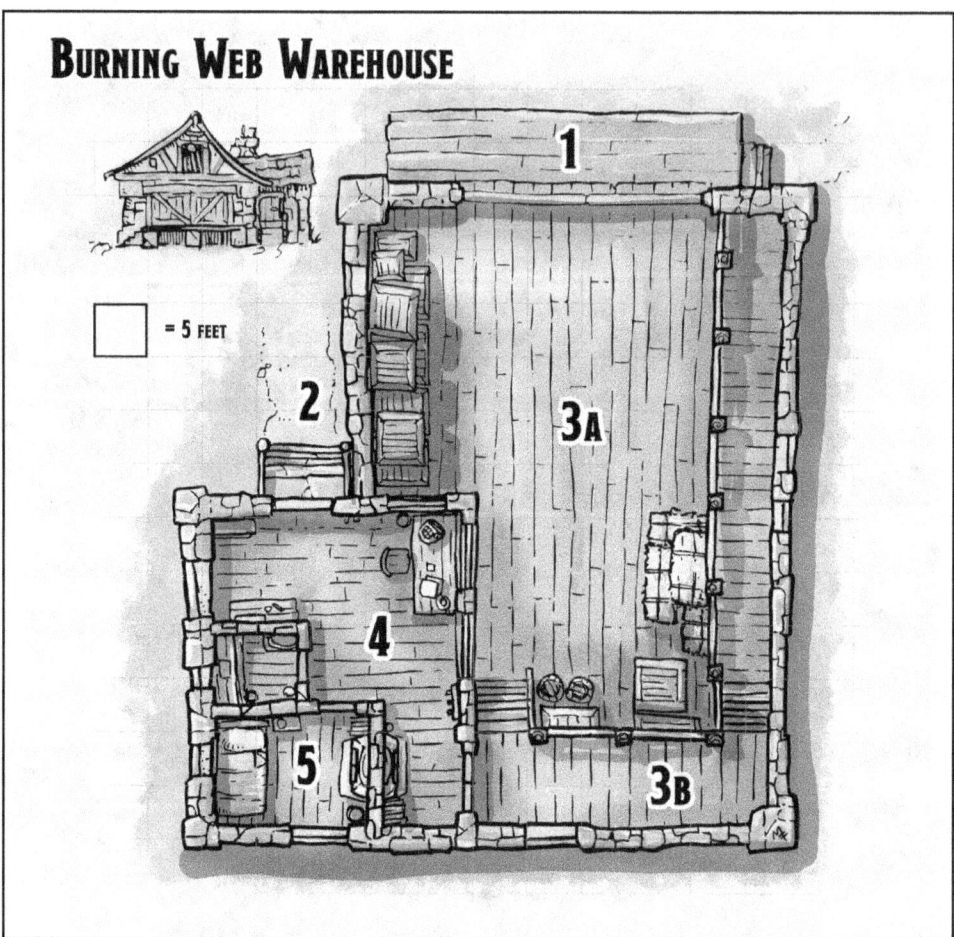

BURNING WEB WAREHOUSE

☐ = 5 FEET

1

2

3A

4

5

3B

krig thanks them and wanders off. It does not seem talkative but is not rude either. If the krig is asked why it was attacked by the thugs, it doesn't know. All it knows is that it was accosted by the two men in white while it was walking by the alley and then they turned their maces on it for no reason.

Any thugs that survive the encounter can be convinced to talk. Although they are dedicated to their cause, they are easily intimidated. They explain that they were taking the krig back to a warehouse on the northwestern side of Salt Ward and even offer the address. When asked why they were interested in the krig, they explain that their leader, a man named Titos Barakis, is performing experiments on them. However they aren't completely sure why. The thugs warn that their colleagues are prepared for such events and have

preparations in place to destroy any evidence and flee without getting caught. Finally, they explain that they must all check-in each hour on the hour. There is only 10 minutes left in the hour (the thugs were already in a hurry when they were stopped). If the group doesn't return, Barakis and the other members of the Burning Web immediately make plans to evacuate (see Plan X).

Crossing Town

The Burning Web's warehouse is roughly 500 feet from the scene of the abduction. If the characters hurry, they can cross the Strand and reach the warehouse in 1 minute. You may want to put obstacles in their way to slow them down and build a sense of urgency and excitement. Examples of obstacles are included in the section on Chases in Chapter 8 of the *DMG*.

The Burning Web Warehouse

If the characters ran across the Strand and out into the open without being stealthy about it, chances are the two **thug** lookouts working the front of the warehouse noticed them appear. A third **thug** stands guard at the warehouse's side door. While they don't jump to conclusions that the characters stopped their friends, it's likely they sense something is up.

> You see the ramshackle warehouse at the corner of the main street and the boardwalk. Two men wearing plain clothing stand on the loading dock. Their attention is turned towards the Strand. A narrow alley runs alongside the building on its east side. Twenty-five feet down, a side door leads inside. That door is protected by another guard. All three look very anxious.

If the Burning Web members get the impression that the characters are planning to assault the warehouse, instead of fighting, they retreat inside to inform Leywood/Barakis. Once alerted, Barakis immediately calls for execution

of Plan X (see page 104).

If the characters try to question the thugs, have all of the characters make Charisma (Deception) checks contested by the thugs' Wisdom (Insight) check. If the thugs win their Insight check against any of the characters, they immediately assume that they've been caught. At a minimum, one will try to run into the warehouse to warn the others.

Keyed Locations

The following locations are keyed to the map of the Burning Web warehouse (page 102).

1 - Loading Dock. As noted above, two **thug** guards stand watch here. The wooden platform in front of the doors is 3-feet off the ground, just the right level to unload a horse cart. The sliding doors are not locked. They are heavy, however, requiring a character to use his/her action to open them (no Strength check needed).

2 - Side Door. A **thug** guard stands watch here. The thug uses a knocking system (three knocks, then two knocks, then three knocks) to let the others inside know to let him in. Otherwise, the door is locked. A character can use his/her action to break the door down with a successful DC 15 Strength (Athletics) check, or the lock can be picked with a successful DC 15 Dexterity check using proficiency in thieves' tools.

3a - Warehouse Floor. Two **thug** guards stand on the inside of the door unless Barakis has given them the signal to evacuate (see Plan X).

Depending on the status of Plan X when the characters enter the warehouse, Barakis and the other members of the burning hands may still be performing experiments.

At the center of the room, a levitating platform holds an unconscious **krig** 3 and 1/2 feet above the floor. A second levitating platform hovers parallel to the krig's, likely where the second victim would have been placed. The top of the krig's skull has been removed and placed in an ivory surgical bowl off

AMENT LEYWOOD (BARAKIS)	
Medium humanoid (human), chaotic good	

Armor Class 9
Hit Points 7 (2d8 - 2)
Speed 20 ft.

STR	7(-2)	INT	15 (+2)
DEX	9 (11)	WIS	14 (+2)
CON	8 (-1)	CHA	9 (-1)

Saving Throws Int +4, Wis +4
Skills Arcana +4, History +4, Medicine +6, Nature +4
Senses passive Perception 12
Languages Common, Dwarven, Krig
Challenge 0 (10 XP)

Partially Blinded. Ament has disadvantage on Wisdom (Perception) checks that rely on sight.

ACTIONS

Dagger. Melee or Ranged Weapon Attack: +1 to hit, reach 5 ft. or range 20/60 ft., one target. *Hit* 1 (1d4 - 1) piercing damage.

to the side. Inside its head is a mess of green and purple sinew, its unusual brain.

Barakis (see the sidebar) is—or was—in the room using a *ring of mage hand* to assist in the procedure, along with two Burning Web medical assistants (**commoners** with Intelligence and Wisdom scores of 12 and proficiency in Medicine). One of the assistants regularly applies drops of red liquid from a vial (a *potion of healing*) to the krig's exposed brain to keep it alive.

The two medical assistants are non-combatants and automatically drop to the floor with their hands behind their heads, afraid for their lives. If Barakis is still in the room, he immediately flees up the stairs to **Area 4** in order to initiate Plan X.

3b - Mezzanine. Two more **thugs** stand on the mezzanine surrounding the warehouse floor. If Plan X is underway, they use their heavy crossbows to cover Barakis and his assistants as they flee.

4 - Backroom. Barakis' office/backroom overlooks the warehouse floor. The walls and desks are covered in notes and schematics detailing krig physiology. The hourglass that the Burning Web uses to time the abductors sits on top of a small bookshelf loaded with medical texts. There is a **thug** by the rear door whose job is to open the door if the correct knock sequence is given (see **Area 2**) and keep an eye on the hourglass.

The storage closet to the side contains cleaning supplies and a chamber pot.

5 - Bedroom. Although Barakis doesn't sleep much, when he does, he sleeps in this room. In addition to the small bed and armoire, there is a safe hidden in the floor. Noticing the difference in the floor panels requires a DC 13 Wisdom (Perception) check. The panel over it is easy enough to lift off the safe. However, the safe is locked and trapped. Any force applied to open its door incinerates the contents within. The combination to open the safe is 22-13-60. Otherwise, a charac-

ter can spend 1-minute listening and testing the tumblers. At the end of the minute, the character must make a DC 20 Wisdom (Perception) check. On a successful check, they determine the combination and open the safe.

So long as Barakis didn't remove the contents of the safe during Plan X, the characters find his journal (see Leywood's Journal), a *wand of magic missile*, a pouch containing 100 gp, and a dull, green gem wrapped in a piece of leather. The gem has no value.

The south window opens into an alley behind the warehouse. During Plan X, this is how Barakis escapes.

Plan X

The moment that the Burning Web suspects that the militia, Cords, or even adventurers have caught on to their activities, Barakis initiates Plan X. This is the protocol for Plan X:

- All schematics, notes, journals, and evidence, including the bodies of test subjects, are destroyed. Barakis and the thug in **Area 4** each carry a *fireball* bead (as a *necklace of fireballs*) for such an event. If Barakis has time, he will take his journal and other contents from the safe in **Area 5** with him.
- All members of the Burning Web are to make a tactical retreat to the rear of the warehouse and escape either through the side door (**Area 2**) or via the window in the back office.
- All members of the Burning Web that aren't caught are to retreat to Barakis' sailing boat, Veracity, tethered to the dock directly south of the warehouse.

All members of the Burning Web have drilled on Plan X and are ready to execute at a moment's notice.

Fire

Being made of mostly wood, the warehouse is extremely flammable. If Barakis and the thug from **Area 4** use their *fireball* beads to create a fire, the entire building immediately catches fire.

If a creature is in the burning building at the start of their turn, they must make a DC 10 Dexterity saving throw to avoid the flames. On a failed saving throw, the creature takes 3 (1d6) fire damage and catches fire. Until someone takes an action to douse the fire, the creature takes 3 (1d6) fire damage at the start of each of its turns.

And if a creature is in the burning building at the end of its turn, it must make a DC 10 Constitution saving throw to avoid smoke inhalation. A creature can hold its breath to avoid making this saving throw. On a failed saving throw, a creature takes 2 (1d4) fire damage and is poisoned. The creature must repeat its saving throw at the end of its next turn. If the creature is still in the burning building, it makes this saving throw with disadvantage. On a success, the poison effect ends. On a failure, the creature falls unconscious.

Because of the poor condition of the building, the building collapses after 1 minute on initiative count 20 (losing initiative ties). Any creature still inside when the building collapses must make a DC 15 Dexterity saving throw. On a failed saving throw, a creature takes 14 (4d6) bludgeoning damage plus 7 (2d6) fire damage and is restrained by the rubble. While the creature is restrained by the rubble, it takes 1d6 fire damage plus 1d6 bludgeoning damage at the start of each of its turns. On a successful saving throw, a creature takes half as much damage and isn't restrained.

Escape on Veracity

Barakis' small sailing ship, Veracity, is supplied and ready to leave into the bay within 5 rounds of evacuating. Using oars, the ship moves at a speed of 20 ft. per round on the water. Once its sails can pick up wind, its movement increases to 45 ft. per round.

Leywood's Journal

If the characters find Leywood's Journal in the safe in **Area 5**, the journal contains all of the details from The Burning Web section in the introduction. In addition, Leywood's Journal has the following information within, detailed below. Only Barakis/Leywood knows the information in his journal. The other members of the Burning Web don't even know his true name.

- "I've now interviewed four survivors who have gone into the Undermaze in Orbea and returned. Each one has given me the same description of the tunnels. These descriptions match the tunnels in Ghost Holm perfectly. Unfortunately, no one has witnessed the so-called Matriarch's Lair, if even such a thing exists."

- "Today, I spoke with Meros Scarletfoot at the Temple of Usteus. He shared something with me no one else has. The last time an Undermaze survivor was brought into his temple, the survivor had burn marks on his body. But not from fire—radiant energy."

- "I theorize that the krigs not only look alike, but they are all exactly the same. While they may develop their own traits and habits at later stages of their lives—nurture versus nature—upon birth they are perfect clones. I hope to capture a pair and compare their physiologies."

- "We are two weeks away from the plan. I've secured a warehouse in Salt Ward as well as a cart. There are two krigs who follow the same routine and walk the same path in Salt Ward every day. We will seize these two and bring them back to test my theory. If I'm right, this could open up a whole new world of understanding."

- "Tonight's the night. One last thought before I prepare: if the krigs are all clones of each other, who created these clones? What is their purpose? I'm both excited and afraid to learn the answer. As always, I do this for you Heather, Ailse, and Cassie."

Adventure Conclusion

The end of this adventure could go multiple ways. If Leywood/Barakis escapes on Veracity, he might turn up in later adventures as an important NPC. His knowledge of krigs and their unusual nature could play an important role in solving some of the mysteries of the ***Hand of the Eight*** adventure path.

If Barakis is stopped, he will share his story and purpose with the characters, in hopes that they will assist him on his mission. Barakis/Leywood's ultimate goal is to enter the Undermaze and discover what secrets are held below Orbea. With the help of a brave group of adventurers, he just might be able to do that. Ω

CHAPTER 5: WALLINGMIOTTA

BY DAVE HAMRICK

4th-Level Adventure for Fifth Edition

Cartography by Watabou.itch.io

Wallingmiotta is a 4th-level Fifth Edition adventure for 3-5 characters. Characters who survive the adventure should be close to reaching the 5th level by the adventure's conclusion. This is the fifth chapter in the Hand of Eight adventure path. It can be played as the kickoff for the larger adventure setting or as a one-shot adventure for your players. The campaign is intended to be set in the DMDave crowdsourced campaign world of Omeria. However, it can just as easily be inserted into any other mysterious, untamed wilderness.

A near-fatal crash. A mysterious forest filled with dangerous creatures. A machine deadset on the destruction of anyone who has come into contact with a mysterious unreadable book. A long-lost wizard. This is the setting for Chapter 5 of the **Hand of the Eight** adventure path, *Wallingmiotta*. Having just escaped from the town of Orbea, the characters must find the reclusive illusionist, Aruxius, in order to understand the contents of the book *Prime*. To do so they must search through the untamed wilderness known as the Wallingmiotta.

Background

Two-hundred years ago, Aruxius the Illusionist, a danaavrakt, was given a book as a gift from a dying friend. There was a catch, however. Aruxius had to use his most powerful spell on the book, a ritual of *perpetual illusion*, to mask the contents of the book. Of course, this confused Aruxius. The book his friend gave him did not seem that important. In fact, Aruxius considered it rather mundane. Still, Aruxius granted his dying friend the wish and masked the book with the spell. Under the effects of the spell, the only creatures who could ever read the book would have to be of fiendish or celestial descent. And only Aruxius could remove the enchantment.

In time, Aruxius started to understand why his friend asked him to hide it. A journey through the deserts north of Odonburg opened his eyes to the dangers the book held within it. Discouraged by this terrible notion, Aruxius retired from teaching and became a recluse, eventually settling down in the mysterious forests of Wallingmiotta.

But understanding why his friend wanted to mask the contents of the book wasn't the only riddle that plagued Aruxius. If the contents of the book were that dangerous in the hands of others, why not destroy it? Why give it to Aruxius in the first place?

For one hundred years, Aruxius held onto the book. Then, one day, he decided that it was time he let go of it. Aruxius traveled west across the Wallingmiotta to the gnome village of Pella's Wish. For five days, he joined the gnomes in their feasts and games and pranks. And he made friends with their mayor, a mysterious gnome named Wilgrim.

Wilgrim knew immediately that Aruxius had more on his mind than gnome festivities. Aruxius, unable to keep secrets from his new friend, revealed the book and explained what it was and what it meant. He also explained that it was time he let go of it.

"The most dangerous prank yet," said Wilgrim. Aruxius nodded in solemn agreement.

"No worries, my big friend. I have just the people to give this to." That night as the danaavrakt said his farewells he left the book with the gnome. The next morning, Wilgrim visited the home of his good friends, the Vorpos family: Orla, Lopos, and their young son, Valcryn.

Adventure Summary

The adventure starts as the characters are en route to the Wallingmiotta forest to find the wizard Aruxius. They should have the book *Prime* in their possession. As they are flying over the Basilisk's Spine Mountains in the mage Omnaweahl's magical flying machine, the aircraft starts to malfunction. Hundreds of miles from civilization, Omnaweahl brings the flyer down in the forest.

After recovering from the accident, the characters and Omnaweahl must travel through the dangerous, untamed forests of the Wallingmiotta. The characters must survive strange monsters, traps, dangerous humanoid tribes, and even rogue constructs that hunt them, all while trying to locate the reclusive Aruxius.

Adventure Hooks

For the most part, the adventure assumes that the characters have played through the earlier chapters of the Hand of the Eight adventure path. Barring that, you can still use the content within as a one-shot. Here are some ideas:

Crash Landing
The characters are traveling to another destination when the flying machine they are in (either the peregrine-class flyer detailed in this chapter, a flying ship, or something similar) wrecks. They must travel back to civilization through the dangerous forest.

Hunted
While the characters are exploring the Wallingmiotta, they discover that they are being hunted by a dangerous construct. The reason the construct hunts the characters is up to you. Similar to this story, they could have an artifact of value with them, or they could be prisoners having recently escaped custody.

The Lost Elven City
At the northern end of the Wallingmiotta is the ruins of an ancient elven city, Imfe Aiqua. It's said that no one has ever entered the city and lived to tell the tale. The characters must work alongside the magic researchers at Camp Hummingbird to uncover the Elven City's secrets and enter. This is a set up for the forthcoming spin-off adventure, *Glaive of the Revenant King*.

Dead-Stick Landing

At the beginning of the adventure, the characters are passengers in Omnaweahl's **peregrine-class flyer**, *Old Spirit*. Having just escaped from Orbea and a dangerous remote traveler alpha-class, the characters are headed to the Wallingmiotta. As they're flying over the Basilisk's Spine Mountains, read or paraphrase the following:

> Piloting the craft, Omnaweahl turns her head back to you, "Although you can't see them in the dark and cloud cover, we're over the Basilisk's Spine right now. We should be over the Wallingmiotta in thirty minutes and to Barnemouth in an hour."
>
> Fifteen minutes ago, Omnaweahl (or just "O") explained the mission to you all. You would take her flyer to the town of Barnemouth in northern Omeria. From there, you would all cross the river into the wild forests of the Wallingmiotta.
>
> Within the Wallingmiotta, you would find the danaavrakt mage Aruxius. Hopefully, Aruxius' knowledge of illusion and enchantment spells would unlock the mysteries of the book, *Prime*, which you now carry with you.
>
> Also known as the Forest of Phantasms, the Wallingmiotta is a massive expanse of forest filled with huge, dangerous creatures, illusions, and malicious fey. It's long acted as the border between the hobgoblin lands of the Garrish and the human/gnome territories of Knotside and its neighboring city-states. Before that, it was the home of the elven nation of Kelren. But those elves have been extinct for almost three-hundred years following a sudden plague. Only their ruins and ghosts remain.

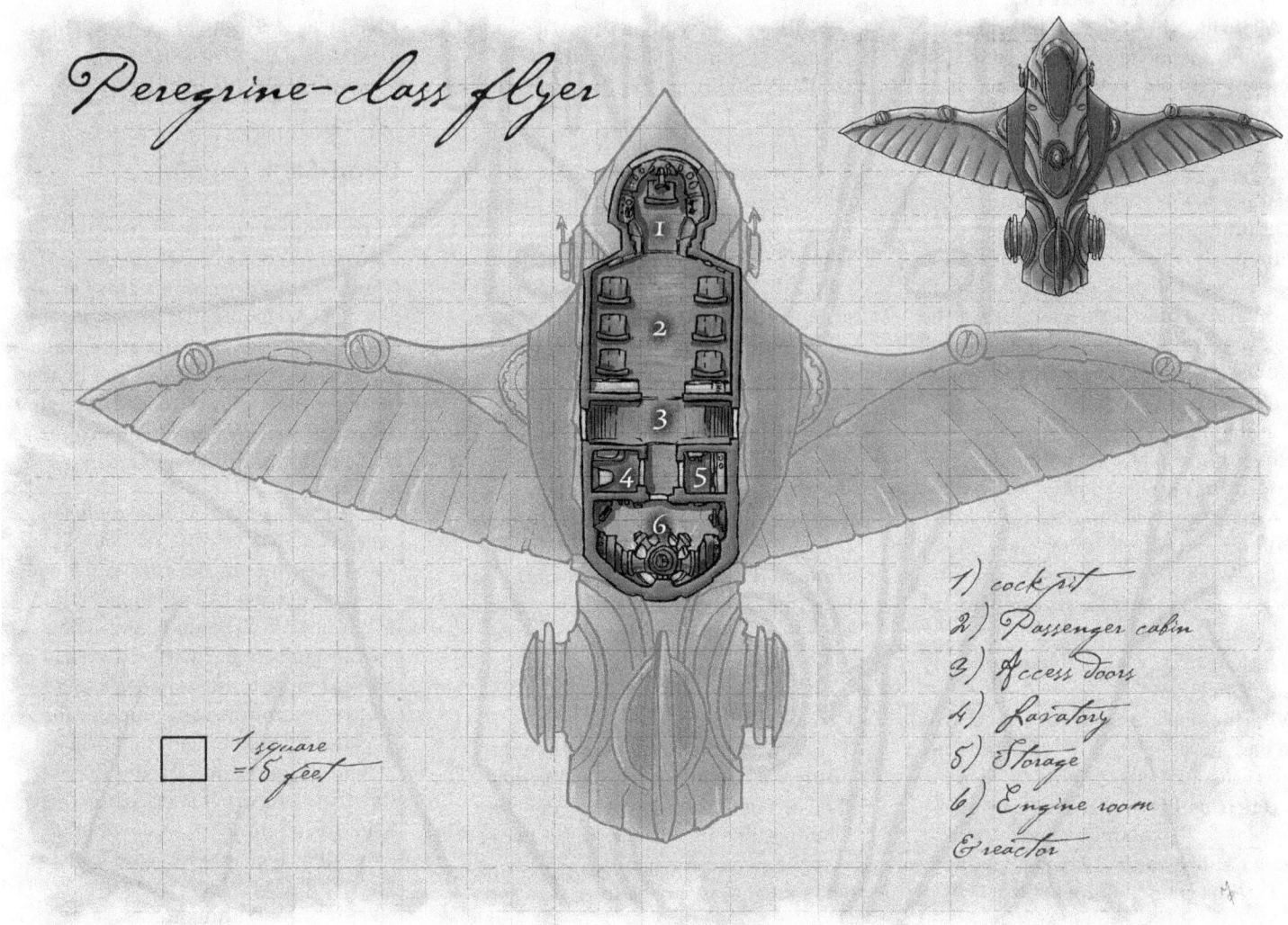

Peregrine-class flyer

1) cockpit
2) Passenger cabin
3) Access doors
4) Lavatory
5) Storage
6) Engine room & reactor

☐ 1 square = 5 feet

Omnaweahl gave the characters the opportunity to consider the mission. If the characters did not wish to help, she would give them each 100 gold pieces for the book and recruit another group to help her. The characters would be free to go wherever they please.

Old Spirit

Omnaweahl's aircraft, *Old Spirit*, is a prototype-version of the Dinzer peregrine-class flyer detailed below.

Dinzer Peregrine-Class Flyer
The Peregrine-class flyer is a single-engine high-speed multirole tactical aircraft originally developed by the Shadow Honour artificer guild of Charidge for the Imperial Navy of Odonburg. Designed as a quick-response, air superiority day fighter, it evolved into a successful all-weather multirole tactical aircraft.

A Peregrine-class flyer has the following features:

Ceilings. The ceilings in the fuselage and cabins are 8 feet high with 6-foot-high doorways.

Doors. The flyer's doors are made of wood and have AC 15, 18 hit points, and immunity to poison and psychic damage. A lock can be picked with a successful DC 15 Dexterity check made using thieves' tools, or the door can be forced open with a successful DC 20 Strength (Athletics) check. The controls at the front of the flyer can raise or lower the doors.

Lights. The interior of the flyer is illuminated by permanent *light* spells powered by the flyer's emerald reactor. The flyer also has exterior lights that can create a beam of bright light in a 120-foot cone and dim light for another 120-feet.

1 - Cockpit
The pilot of the flyer sits in the cockpit in the captain's chair. While seated in the captain's chair, the pilot can cast

the following spells:

At will: *comprehend languages, scrying* (the sensor is always located in the fuselage and cannot move), *true strike*

1/day: *find the path*

2 - Passenger Cabin

The cabin holds six chairs which can recline, allowing a passenger to rest comfortably in the chair. Each chair has a cubby of nourishment set into the right armrest. The cubby generates a soft, flavorless food tablet that dissolves on your tongue and provides as much nourishment as 1 day of rations and one pint of cold drinking water. Once the cubby generates a food tablet, it can't do so again for 8 hours.

3 - Access Doors.

At both the east and west sides of the flyer's entry, two access doors lower allowing creatures to enter the flyer.

4 - Lavatory

A soft, padded bench with a hole carved in the center fills this room. Below the bench is a chamber pot with a portable hole in its bottom. As soon as waste passes into the chamberpot, and a creature exits through the lavatory door, a *prestidigitation* spell is cast on the creature to clean and disinfect it and remove any unpleasant odors.

5 - Storage

The storage locker is protected by an iron door and has AC 19, 18 points, and immunity to poison and psychic damage. Often, weapons and magic items are stored here.

6 - Engine Room

The engine room has the following features:

Arc Propulsion Engine. The force energy drawn from the emerald Odonburgite within its emerald reactor powers the flyer's Shadow Honour Levi-tech arc-propulsion engine (APE).

Emerald Reactor. The flyer is powered by a Quickshroud 1.87 dl emerald reactor.

Tool Chests. The room includes two tool chests. Both chests act as *bags of holding*, containing enough tools and spare parts to completely rebuild the ship almost from the ground up. The only irreplaceable object is the ship's Emerald Odonburgite crystal.

Minimum Crew. It only takes one crewperson to fly a Peregrine-class flyer, a pilot. Often the pilot is a **mage** with proficiencies in Arcana and Vehicles (air).

PEREGRINE-CLASS FLYER
Gargantuan vehicle (70 ft. by 30 ft., 135 ft. wingspan)

Creature Capacity 1 crew, 6 passengers
Cargo Capacity 4 tons
Travel Pace 220 miles per hour (5,280 miles per day)

STR	DEX	CON	INT	WIS	CHA
20 (+5)	15 (+2)	18 (+4)	0	0	0

Saving Throws Dex +6
Damage Immunities poison, psychic
Condition Immunities blinded, charmed, deafened, exhaustion, frightened, incapacitated, paralyzed, petrified, poisoned, prone, stunned, unconscious

ACTIONS

On its turn, the flyer can take 2 actions, choosing from the options below. It can't take actions if it has no crew.

Fire Eldritch Cannons. The flyer can fire its eldritch cannons.
Move. The flyer can use its helm to move with its wings.
APE Move (Costs 2 Actions). The flyer can use its helm to move with its arc-propulsion engine.

HULL

Armor Class 17
Hit Points 300 (damage threshold 15)

CONTROL: HELM

Armor Class 18
Hit Points 50

Move up to the speed of one of the flyer's movement components. If the helm is destroyed, the flyer can't fire its eldritch cannons.

MOVEMENT: WINGS

Armor Class 15
Hit Points 100; -5 ft. speed per 25 damage taken
Speed (air) 120 ft. (hover)

MOVEMENT: ARC-PROPULSION ENGINE

Armor Class 15
Hit Points 200; -25 ft. speed per 50 damage taken
Speed (air) 500 ft. (on the same turn the flyer uses it action to move 250 ft. or more in one round, attacks made against it are made with disadvantage)

WEAPON: ELDRITCH CANNONS (2)

Armor Class 15
Hit Points 30 each
Ranged Weapon Attack: +8 to hit, range 300 ft., one target. *Hit*: 11 (2d10) force damage.

Flyer Descent

Round	Seconds	Remaining Altitude (ft.)	Feather Fall Distance (miles)	Events
1	60	10,000	4d4	The flyer dips below the clouds. The tree line is visible in the moonlight. O prepares to cast *resilient sphere*.
2	54	9,000	4d4	—
3	48	8,000	3d4	—
4	42	7,000	3d4	—
5	36	6,000	2d6	—
6	30	5,000	2d6	—
7	24	4,000	2d4	—
8	18	3,000	1d8	O casts *resilient sphere*.
9	12	2,000	1d6	—
10	6	1,000	1d4	The flyer crashes at the end of this round.

Systems Failure

As *Old Spirit* is flying over the Basilisk's Spine, something bad happens.

> Suddenly, the lights in the passenger cabin dim. In their place, red lights flash. From the cockpit, you hear the flyer's instrumentation buzzing.
>
> "Odon's robes," curses Omnaweahl who's scrambling. "The entire system is shutting down. I'm losing power!"
>
> She releases her harness and rushes to the rear of the flyer. Seemingly, the aircraft is on autopilot. Omnaweahl speaks a command word to release the lock on the engine room door and steps inside. A dull green glow emerges from the engine room while you watch Omnaweahl lift the cover off a device, likely the one that powers the aircraft.
>
> "Oh no," she gasps, the tone of her voice filling you with dread.

The emerald Odonburgite that supplies power to the flyer's engine is going dead. After screaming a few choice expletives, she rushes back to the cockpit.

> The lights in the cabin start to flicker. Omnweahl taps her instrumentation. "Come on!" she screams. O grabs an arcane stone from a slot next to her.
>
> "Flight control, this is Peregrine 7. Flight control, this is Peregrine 7. I'm dead in the air. Can you hear me, over?"
>
> Then: darkness. All of the lights, systems, and controls in the ship go dead. By your estimation, you're 5-6 miles in the air. If the flyer is about to crash, there's little to no no chance for survival.

Give the characters a few rounds to react. Let them come up with a plan or at least try to work with Omnaweahl on a plan. Be sure to reward creativity with success, but remind them that if they don't find a way to protect themselves in the crash they will likely die.

The flyer is currently gliding, but also descending. In 10 minutes, it will crash into the treeline of the Wallingmiotta (see the spot marked Crash Site on the map of Wallingmiotta on page 7). To add a sense of urgency to the crash, set a real timer for 9 minutes. For the final minute, switch to turn-based game time following the sequence of events detailed below.

The flyer has the following options available for crash landings.

- The flyer has two *potions of feather fall*. When a creature drinks the potion, they come under the effects of the *feather fall* spell for 1 minute (no concentration required)
- Omnaweahl has prepared resilient sphere, but it can only protect her from the crash.
- The chairs' restraints give advantage on Constitution saving throws made to avoid taking damage from the crash.

The Descent

The Descent table below gives the round-by-round sequence of events starting at 1 minute before the crash.

Round. The round is the combat round (6-second intervals) where the characters make preparations to land.

Seconds Remaining. The seconds remaining is the amount of game time the characters have until the flyer crashes.

Altitude. Altitude is the height the flyer is at the start of the round.

Feather Fall Distance. When a character uses a *potion of feather fall* or similar spell or effect and leaps from the aircraft as it descends, roll the dice listed for the round. The result is the number of miles south of the crash site the character lands in the forest.

Events. Any special circumstances that happen during the crash are detailed here.

The Crash

Once the flyer hits the tree line, it takes the flyer three rounds to come to a complete stop as the trees of the Wallingmiotta break the flyer's fall.

Round 1. The flyer must make a DC 10 Constitution saving throw. All of the flyer's components take 70 (20d6) bludgeoning damage from the trees on a failed saving throw, or half as much damage on a successful one. Any creature still inside the flyer must also make a DC 10 Constitution saving throw. A creature makes this check with advantage if they are wearing the flyer's restraints. A creature takes 17 (5d6) bludgeoning damage on a failed saving throw or half as much damage on a successful one.

Round 2. The flyer is tumbling through the trees now and must make another DC 10 Constitution saving throw. All of the flyer's components take 35 (10d6) bludgeoning damage from the trees on a failed saving throw, or half as much damage on a successful one. If the flyer's hull's hit points fall to 0, each creature within the flyer is flung from the aircraft and must make a DC 10 Constitution saving throw. A creature takes the excess damage from the crash on a failed saving throw or half the excess damage from the crash on a successful one. If the flyer's hull was destroyed, ignore round 3.

Round 3. So long as the flyer's hull has hit points remaining, it must make another DC 10 Constitution saving throw. All of the flyer's components take 17 (5d6) bludgeoning damage from the trees on a failed saving throw, or half as much damage on a successful

one. If the flyer's hull's hit points fall to 0, each creature within the flyer is flung from the aircraft and must make a DC 10 Constitution saving throw. A creature takes the excess damage from the crash on a failed saving throw or half the excess damage from the crash on a successful one.

Crash Survivor Disposition. For each creature involved in the crash (whether they jumped from the flyer or crashed with it), roll a d10 and consult the Crash Survivor Disposition table on the next page to determine what happened to them following the crash. Each disposition is described after the table. A result of "No special disposition" means nothing out of the ordinary happened.

Crashed with flyer	Leaped from flyer	Disposition
1-2	1-2	Stuck in a tree
3	3	Landed in water
4-5	-	Pinned by wreckage
6-10	7-10	No special disposition

Landed in water. The creature lands in a pond, river, or creek, and must swim to shore.

Pinned by wreckage. The creature is restrained by the wreckage of the flyer. The creature or another creature must use its action to make a Strength check to free the creature from the wreckage. The DC for the check is 2d10 + 5.

Stuck in a tree. The creature is stuck 3d4 x 10 feet off the ground in a tree from which they must find a way down. Each round that they are stuck, roll 1d20. On a result of 20, the branches snap and they fall to the ground, taking 3 (1d6) falling damage for every 10 feet they fall.

The Crash Site

It's roughly 3 hours after sunset when *Old Spirit* crashes in the Wallingmiotta. Dawn isn't for another 6 hours. Depending on the damage *Old Spirit* took during the crash, it may be in a single, heavily-damaged piece or blasted to bits all over the Wallingmiotta.

Any creatures who came down with the flyer in the crash will be found within 1d10 - 1 x 10 feet of the crash, possibly in a special disposition. This includes Omnaweahl who is likely still inside the flyer itself and unharmed thanks to her resilient sphere.

The challenge now is recovering from the crash. There is a possibility that some of the characters are miles away from the site, especially if they leaped from the ship before it came down.

After O has a moment to shake off the trauma from the crash, she encourages the characters to assist her with the following issues:

- The ship's emerald Odonburgite core must be secured. O will not compromise on this. Dinzer technology is extremely valuable and emerald Odonburgite is rare. If the flyer was completely destroyed in the crash, then the core can be found within 1d10 - 1 x 10 feet of the crash site. Otherwise, it's still in place.
- The two toolboxes kept in the engine room likely survived the crash. Each one acts as a bag of holding and contains replacement parts for the ship. If the flyer was completely destroyed in the crash, then the toolboxes can be found within 1d10 - 1 x 10 feet of the crash site. Otherwise, it's still in place.
- The storage/weapons locker of the flyer should be secured as well. It contains two wands of magic missile, two eldritch casters (acts as a light crossbow, but in place of bolts, it fires force energy as the eldritch blast spell), and a wand of fireworks.
- Being that it's night and that they are in a dangerous place, they should

try to secure shelter as soon as possible.

While they will want to find any characters who are separated from the main party, she suggests that they wait until the morning to reconnect. In the meantime, if they can recover her *wand of fireworks*, she can send a signal over the treetops.

Finding Items from the Wreckage

It will take those at the wreckage 1 hour to secure all of the items listed above. The core is the easiest to find since it glows green. Once O has it, she wraps it in leather and places it into her pack. She also insists on carrying both of the ship's toolboxes, one of the *eldritch casters*, and a *wand of fireworks*. However, there is a 10% chance that each of the characters lost one of their packs and is unable to find it.

Sending the Signal

Once O finds the *wand of fireworks*, she locates a clear point and launches it into the sky. Any creature within 20 miles of the crash site will see the blast above. Characters who see the fireworks have advantage on Wisdom (Survival) checks to track the crash site. However, the chance of random encounters also goes up. Instead of a random encounter occurring on a result of 18-20, random encounters in the night occur on a result of 16-20. See the section on Random Encounters for details.

Setting up Shelter for the Night

If *Old Spirit* is still intact, it makes a good shelter. Otherwise, O and the characters at the crash site will need to find or create a shelter. In addition, characters who have not reconnected with the other members of the party must also seek shelter.

To set up shelter, have a character make two ability checks: Intelligence (Nature) and Wisdom (Survival). If the character has a relevant tool proficiency such as Carpentry, they can substitute their tool proficiency bonus in place of one of the other ability checks. Additionally, if the characters have tents, camping gear or *Old Spirit* is still intact, he/she may replace one of their ability checks with an automatic success.

The DC for each check is 15. Consult the Setting up Shelter Results table to see how the character did.

Successes	Value
0	*Uncomfortable shelter.* The characters do not gain the benefits of a long rest.
1	*Secure shelter.* The characters gain the benefits of a long rest as normal, but there is still a possibility for random encounters.
2	*Very secure shelter.* The characters gain the benefits of a long rest as normal, and they are safe from random encounters until the morning.

Reconnecting with the Party

Any characters who were separated from the party must try to find the party. When a character starts to travel towards his/her party, make a DC 15 Wisdom (Survival) check on their behalf. The check is made with advantage if they saw O's signal.

On a successful check, the character heads directly for the crash site. Refer to the section on travel times below to determine how fast they travel.

On a failed check, the character is lost. Roll a 1d4 - 1. The result is the number of miles added to the character's distance from *Old Spirit*'s crash site. A lost character can spend 1 hour trying to reorient himself or herself. At the end of the hour, make another DC 15 (Wisdom) Survival check on the character's behalf. This time, the character won't receive the benefits of O's signal. Also, if the check is made at night, the character makes the check with disadvantage. This process continues until the character passes one of their checks.

If the distance two or more separated characters have between them is the same, there is a 50% chance each round that they find each other in the forest and reconnect.

The Wallingmiotta

Following the crash, the adventurers find themselves in the wildest part of the Wallingmiotta, just slightly north of the Basilisk's Spine Mountains.

Omnaweahl recognizes where the party is and explains the gravity of the situation. It is assumed she explains this in the morning:

> "When we crashed, we'd just finished clearing the Basilisk's Spine Mountains. The mountains are some 30-50 miles south of us," says O. She points toward the south where you can see the tall spires of the mountain range even at this distance.
>
> "To the west," she points, "probably 50-100 miles from here is Troubled Run, the river that separates the hobgoblin lands of Gar Warbrizz from the Wallingmiotta. Hobgoblins have no love for Dinzers, so it's unlikely we'll find help there. That means that we've got 150-200 miles to the east of us of nothing but forest. Our original destination was Barnemouth, and that's to the north. But that's probably 200 miles from here."

O sighs and places her hands on her hips. "No matter which we look at it, there's at least two or more weeks of travel in front of us. I cast *sending* this morning to get in touch with my brother Ophiar to let him know what's going on. He hasn't responded yet. If I don't hear back from him in eight hours, I'll try again. If any of you have similar capabilities, I suggest you do the same. I'd rather not use up my daily allotment sending messages. This is a dangerous place and I'll need all the firepower I can muster. Literally."

From there, the characters can decide on what they want to do. Despite Barnemouth being hundreds of miles away, O seems determined to reach there. She believes that Barnemouth will provide clues to help them find Aruxius' location in the Wallingmiotta. On either side of the Wallingmiotta are centaur lands. She doesn't believe that the centaurs are inherently dangerous, but are very territorial.

Hundreds of years of warring have left them wary of working with the other humanoid races. The goblinoid tribes of Gar Warbrizz, while currently in a time of peace with the other humanoid nations, don't like magic and have been known to imprison humanoids "suspected of espionage." Even if they knew where Aruxius was, they wouldn't share the information. It's possible to travel through the Basilisk's Spine, but that presents a whole new set of challenges as the mountains are nearly impassable without proper gear. Omnaweahl explains that it could take a month or more to get through the range without using one of the common passes. Even then, they'll be north of the Wound, still in dangerous territory.

How to Travel Through the Wallingmiotta

Using the player's map of Wallingmiotta, identify the hex in which the party is currently located (likely, they all start at the crash site). Don't share this information with the players if the party is lost. Otherwise, show the players the party's location by pointing to the appropriate hex on their map of Wallingmiotta.

Let the players determine which direction the party wants to go and whether the party plans to move at a normal pace, a fast pace, or a slow pace.

One of the characters must be the navigator. Each day, make a Wisdom (Survival) check on the navigator's behalf to determine if the party becomes lost.

Also, roll for random encounters throughout the day and check for food consumption. The forest is relatively easy to forage in, requiring a DC 10 Wisdom (Survival) check to secure food and water (see chapter 5 of the *PHB* for details).

Travel Distances

On the maps of Wallingmiotta, each hex measure 10 miles across. Characters moving at a normal pace can travel 1 hex per day. If the characters move at a fast pace, the easiest way to deal with their progress is to roll a d4. On a roll of 3 or 4, they advance 1 additional hex that day. Characters moving at a fast pace take a -5 penalty to their passive Wisdom (Perception) scores, making them more likely to miss clues and walk into ambushes.

If characters set a slow pace, roll a d4. On a roll of 1 or 2, they advance 1 fewer hex that day (in other words, they don't move). On any other result, their caution is rewarded, and they travel the same distance as a group moving at a normal pace. Characters moving at a slow pace can move stealthily. As long as they're in the open, they can try to surprise or sneak by other creatures they encounter.

If you prefer to track miles, you may do so. Travel times are then 10 miles per day at a normal pace, 15 miles per day at a fast pace, or 9 miles per day at a slow pace. A character with a flying speed of 30 feet can travel 4 miles per hour.

Navigation

At the start of each new travel day, the GM makes a Wisdom (Survival) check on behalf of the navigator. the result of the check determines whether or not the party becomes lost over the course of the day. The DC of the check is based on the day's most common terrain: DC 10 for fields and coasts, or DC 15 for the forests. Apply a +5 bonus to the check if the group sets a slow pace for the day, or a -5 penalty if the group is moving at a fast pace.

If the check succeeds, the navigator knows exactly where the party is on the player's map of Wallingmiotta throughout the day.

If the check fails, the party becomes lost. Each hex on the map is surrounded by six other hexes; whenever a lost party moves 1 hex, roll a d6 to randomly determine which neighboring hex the party enters, and do not divulge the party's location to the players. While the party is lost, players can't pinpoint the group's location on their map of the Wallingmiotta. The next time a navigator succeeds on a Wisdom (Survival) check made to navigate, reveal the party's actual location to the players.

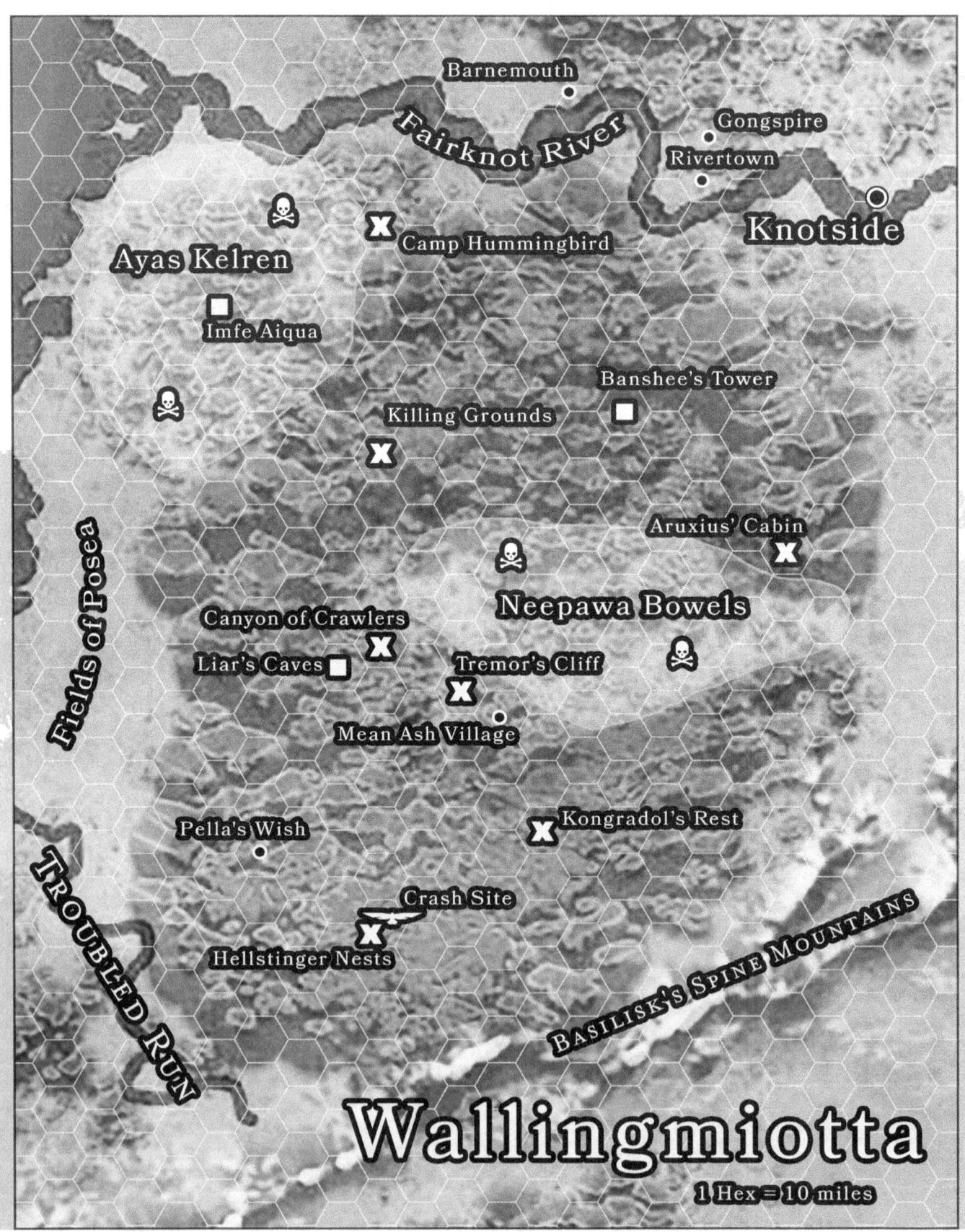

Barnemouth

Fairknot River

Gongspire

Rivertown

Knotside

Ayas Kelren

Camp Hummingbird

Imfe Aiqua

Banshee's Tower

Killing Grounds

Aruxius' Cabin

Neepawa Bowels

Fields of Posea

Canyon of Crawlers

Liar's Caves

Tremor's Cliff

Mean Ash Village

Kongradol's Rest

Pella's Wish

Crash Site

Troubled Run

Hellstinger Nests

Basilisk's Spine Mountains

Wallingmiotta

1 Hex = 10 miles

WALLINGMIOTTA MAP KEY

◉ CITY

• TOWN/VILLAGE

■ RUINS/DUNGEON

✖ POINT OF INTEREST

☠ DANGEROUS AREA

✈ OLD SPIRIT CRASH SITE

Beasts

The characters come across a nest, herd, or family of wild animals. Most animals will act indifferent to the characters, however, some may attack if desperate or it is protecting its young. Roll on the Beast Encounters table to determine the nature of the encounter.

	Beast Encounters
d6	Encounter
1	*1d4 + 1* ankhegs
2	*2d4* apes
3	1d6 + 2 black bears
4	2d4 boars
5	1d4 swarms of poisonous snakes
6	3d6 wolves

Centaur Clans

The nomadic centaurs who live to the fields east and west of the Wallingmiotta are powerful, territorial, and unpredictable. When you roll a result of a centaur clan, use the tables below to determine the details of the centaur clan. Roll on each one in turn to determine the clan's name, components, and unique traits.

The Clan Name table is set up to create three-word names. These are often the names given to them by their enemies (hobgoblins in particular) as

Random Wallingmiotta Encounters

As the characters travel through the Wallingmiotta or they are camping in a shelter that isn't very secure, roll a d20 three times per day of game time., checking for encounters each morning, afternoon, and evening or night. An encounter occurs on a roll of 18 (or 16 with *fireworks*) or higher.

Then, roll another d20 and check the Wallingmiotta Encounters table for the location appropriate to where the characters. Each day that the characters are in the Wallingmiotta after the first day (the morning after the crash), add 1 to roll (to a maximum of +5). The encounters are described after the table.

Encounter	Ayas Kelren	Fields	Forest	Neepawa Bowels
Beasts	1-6	1-7	1-7	1-10
Centaur Clans	7	8-15	8-9	—
Fey	8-9	—	10-11	11-12
Giant Beasts	—	16	12-13	13-18
Gnomes	—	—	14	—
Goblinoids	—	17-18	15	—
Kobolds	—	—	16-17	19-20
Tremor	—	—	18	—
Undead	10-21	—	—	21
Explorers	22	19-20	19-20	22
Knight-in-Shining-Armor	23+	21+	21+	24+

they may have their own name in their native tongue.

The Clan Composition table determines how many centaurs and horses the band contains. The Clan Leadership table indicates the clan's commander (if it has one) and gives a modifier to apply to the composition results: for a clan led by a unicorn, double all the results, and for a clan that lacks a leader, halve them. Commoner centaurs use the **centaur** stat block, except they only have 21 (3d10 + 6) hit points and lack the Charge special trait as well as Multiattack, Pike, and Longbow actions. Centaur druids use the **centaur** stat block, except they have Wisdom scores of 15 (+2) can cast the same spells as the **druid** NPC. Álogos

are detailed in Appendix B.

Roll once on the Special Creatures table to see which special creature is part of the clan and in what numbers.

The Clan Identifiers and Attitude tables add some distinctive flavor to the clan.

	Centaur Clan Name	
d6	Name Part 1	Name Part 2
1	Force of	Arrows
2	Hand of	Blood
3	Runs with	Fury
4	Sings with	Radiance
5	Sound of	Screams
6	Trumpet of	Thunder

Clan Leadership		
d6	**Leader**	**# Appearing Modifier**
1	Unicorn	Double
2-4	Álogo	None
5-6	None	Halve

Clan Attitude	
d6	**Attitude**
1	Friendly towards humanoids
2	Fear of magic
3	Scouts watch from a distance
4	Hostile towards orcs and goblinoids
5	Refuses to speak Common
6	Surrounds trespassers

Centaur Clan Composition	
Clan Composition	**Number Appearing**
Centaur druids	1d4 + 1
Warriors (common centaurs)	6d6
Commoners	4d10 + 10
Riding horses	4d6

Notable Characteristics	
d10	**Characteristic**
1	Elkhorn headdresses
2	Colorful mohawks
3	Faces painted red
4	Tribal tattoos
5	White handprints on bodies
6	Arms and legs dressed with feathers
7	Armor made of goblinoid bones
8	Ceremonial chanting
9	Dark brown keffiyehs
10	Camouflage bodypaint

Special Creatures	
d20	**Special Creatures**
1	1 air elemental
2-5	3d6 elk
6	1d4 elven druids
7-9	2d6 griffons
10-12	2d6 hippogriffs
13	2d6 hobgoblin prisoners
14	1d6 pegasi
15-16	2d6 wolves
17-19	2d6 wood elf scouts
20	1 young bronze dragon

Fey

Having little to fear from trespassers, Wallingmiotta fey treat outsiders with curiosity more than hostility. Often, they watch from a distance, only making themselves seen in order to remind humanoids who the true lords of the Wallingmiotta are. Roll on the Fey Encounters table to determine the nature of the encounter.

Fey Encounters	
d6	**Encounter**
1	3d6 **blink dogs**
2	2d6 **dryads**
3	1 or 3 **green hags**
4	1 **satyr**
5	3d6 **sprites**
6	1d3 **treants**

Giant Beasts

While the mundane beasts of the Wallingmiotta may react towards the characters with fear and trepidation, the same cannot be said of their larger cousins. Giant beasts see Medium and smaller creatures, humanoids especially, as rare treats. As such, they are aggressive, especially in Neepawa Bowels. Having said that, most are looking for an easy meal and will retreat at the first sign of danger. Roll on the Giant Beasts Encounters table to determine the nature of the encounter.

Gnomes

Forest gnomes are the rare exception to the Wallingmiotta's aggressive nature towards humanoids. They act as guardians of the forest and have strong relationships with many of the beasts and fey there. Even Tremor respects the presence of the gnomes. The only creatures who do not respect the gnomes are the undead elves that roam

Giant Beast Encounters	
d8	**Encounter**
1	3d6 **giant bats**
2	2d4 **giant boars**
3	3d6 **giant centipedes**
4	1d4 **giant crocodiles**
5	1d3 **treants**
6	2d6 **giant spiders**
7	2d4 **giant toads**
8	4d6 **giant wasps**

the northwestern edge of the forest. All of the gnomes that characters encounter will know the location of Aruxius' cabin and will gladly provide directions in exchange for a funny story, interesting trinket, or a warm meal.

When the characters encounter gnomes, roll on the Gnome Encounter table below to determine the nature of the encounter. Each encounter is detailed after the table.

Gnome trickster. A gnome illusionist (see the Hand of the Eight Supplement C for details) uses its illusions to trick and trap the characters as they travel through the Wallingmiotta. The gnome does not wish to harm the characters (at least not fatally) only to annoy and humiliate.

Gnome village. Carved into tree stumps, large mushrooms, or mounds, the characters discover a gnome village of 6d6 chaotic good gnome **commoners**. The gnomes are governed by a gnome mage or **druid** (50% chance for either) and protected by fey. To determine the nature of the gnomes' protectors, roll 3 times on the Fey Encounters table. The gnomes are helpful but warn they aren't fighters. However,

Gnome Encounter	
d6	**Encounter**
1-2	Gnome trickster
3	Gnome village
4-6	Gnome wanderer

if they feel threatened (such as by the presence of the Knight-in-Shining-Armor), their protectors will assist.

Gnome wanderer. A gnome **commoner** accompanied by small beasts such as a squirrel, badger, rabbit, mole, or woodpecker, greets the characters. The gnome can provide directions for the characters.

Goblinoids

A war band of goblinoids is scouting through the Wallingmiotta. The goblinoid war band consists of 6 **hobgoblins**, 2 **bugbears**, and 10 **goblins**. The war band is lead by a **hobgoblin** captain. While not outwardly aggressive towards the characters, they will try to glean as much knowledge as they can from the characters on the whereabouts of gnomes, centaurs, or other intelligent creatures in the forest.

Kobolds

Mean Ash is the ruling kobold clan of the Wallingmiotta. Like gnomes—who they hate—the forest does not act aggressively towards the kobolds. It's believed by Wallingmiotta scholars that the kobolds represent balance in the forest, bringing their tyrannical ways to the normally chaotic good forest.

A kobold war party always consists of

4d6 **kobolds** led by a kobold druid (use the **kobold** stat block except it has a Wisdom score of 15 and the **druid** NPC's spell list).

Kobold war parties are almost always aggressive towards the characters. Furthermore, their appearance is always predicated by one or more traps with the purpose of driving the characters into one of their kill holes.

When rolling a kobold encounter, roll a d6 to determine the trap that starts the encounter. Each is detailed after the table.

Kobold Traps	
d6	**Encounter**
1-2	Fake monster
3-4	Forest fire
5-6	Pit trap

Fake monster. As the characters are traveling through the forest, they spot the outline of a gargantuan creature 100 feet to the right or left of them (never ahead or behind them). The "creature" raises its arms and roars (through the use of ropes-and-pulleys and a megaphone inside the creature's head). And its eyes glow (torches). At a distance of 100 feet through the trees, a successful DC 17 Wisdom (Perception) check reveals that the creature is a construction made of logs, leaves, and untreated leather. Within 20-feet of the monster, a character can tell that it's obviously a fake. An **ogre** wearing blinders stands at the front of the creature, its body tethered to the "monster." The ogre can pull the beast forward.

If the characters move in the opposite direction of the creature, they move towards a kobold trap. The trap is a low, 10-foot wide pass that creates 10-foot high natural walls on either side of the pass. The walls of the pass are lined with spikes. A creature that tries to climb out takes 1d4 piercing dam-

age. Once the characters are within the pass, the kobolds raise hidden walls from the ground, blocking exits at either side. The walls have AC 15, 18 hp, and are immune to poison and psychic damage. From there, the kobolds attack from hiding.

If the characters don't fall for the fake monster, the kobolds command the blinded ogre to move forward to give it the appearance that the monster is attacking.

Forest fire. The kobolds light a ring 20-foot diameter of fire that surrounds the characters on all sides. The fire is carefully set to avoid catching the rest of the forest on fire. From there, the kobolds attack from hiding, firing their slings from the other side of the fire. A character can use their action to extinguish a 5 foot square of fire. Otherwise, if a character moves through or starts their turn in the fire, they take 5 (1d10) damage from the flames.

Pit Trap. Use the rules in Chapter 5 of the *DMG* for details on simple pits. The pit is 10 feet deep and spiked. Once the characters are at the bottom of the pit trap, the kobolds appear and use baskets to dump 4 **swarms of poisonous snakes** onto them. From there, they attack with their slings.

Tremor

Tremor is a 25-foot tall bear that crashes through the Wallingmiotta. While many believe Tremor is one of the Great Titans, this is untrue. Tremor was created spontaneously through fey magic. He now acts as the ultimate protector of the forest.

Tremor does not move through the Wallingmiotta quietly. He can be spotted or heard from 300 feet away as he crashes through the trees and underbrush. Any creatures he sees as hostile towards the forest—likely the characters—he attacks and fights until killed.

Because **Tremor** (see Appendix B for his stat block) is so deadly, it's unlikely that the characters will be able to fight him off without assistance. Furthermore, because Tremor is a part of the Wallinmiotta, the Wallingmiotta's natural inhabitants (namely the fey, gnomes, and kobolds) will not assist. "It is the will of the Wallingmiotta," will be the reply they give in their respective native tongues.

The best way to avoid Tremor is to flee (which is tough, considering his relative speed) or to hide from him. Once the characters have hidden for 1 minute, Tremor leaves. After 10 minutes, he is out of range.

Undead
Wallingmiotta was once home to the elven kingdom of Kelren. Centuries ago a plague wiped out the elves. Now, the ruins of this once great civilization are haunted by their undead remnants. The undead elves are automatically aggressive towards any group that does have an elf in its ranks. Roll on the Undead Encounter table below to determine the nature of the encounter.

Undead Encounters	
d10	Encounter
1	1d2 **ghosts**
2	2d4 **shadows**
3	1d6 **specters**
4-6	3d6 **skeletons**
7	1d3 **wights**
8	1d2 **wraiths**
9-10	3d6 **zombies**

Explorers
The party runs into another band of explorers, likely from north of Fairknot River. The party consists of a **mage**, a **knight**, a **scout**, and 1d6 **guards**. Roll a d6. On a result of 5-6, the explorers have been looking for the group after seeing *Old Spirit* crash land.

Knight in Shining Armor
The remote traveler alpha-class that attacked the characters at the Long Shadow Casino in Orbea appears, flying via a rocket-like device strapped to its back. Encounters with the Knight in Shining Armor are detailed in the section bearing its name below.

Locations in Wallingmiotta

The map on page 114 depicts the area the Wallingmiotta forest covers and its surrounding environs. The same map appears in Appendix C for the players to reference as they move through the wilderness. The remainder of this section describes these key locations, which are presented in alphabetical order for ease of reference.

If there is a particular site that you want the characters to discover and explore, you can move the site so that that it falls along their path, and give it a new name if necessary. For example, the kobold village of Mean Ash doesn't have to be in the location marked on your map. You can place it anywhere you want, or create another kobold village that has a similar configuration. Many other locations described in this section are just as adaptable. In addition to relocating a site, you can add or remove monsters and traps to make it harder or easier.

Aruxius' Cabin
The danaavrakt illusionist, Aruxius, lives in a small cabin at the edge of Neepawa Bowels. The encounter with Aruxius is described in the section bearing his name.

Ayas Kelren
The Wallingmiotta takes on a very different appearance once the characters enter the territory. Once home to the Kelren elves, the trees are darker and less lush, the air is cooler, and mist clings to everything. Gray clouds hang overhead during the day, blotting out the sun. While traveling through these woods, the characters will hear whispers in the wind and see shadows out of the corner of their eyes.

The region of Ayas Kelren (which translates to the "Lands of Kelren") is warped by the death of the elves, creating one or more of the following effects:

- Undead within Ayas Kelren have advantage on all of their Intelligence, Wisdom, and Charisma saving throws.
- Navigators have disadvantage on their Wisdom (Survival) checks to find their path while traveling through Ayas Kelren. Instead of rolling for a random hex, the group moves 1 hex closer to Imfe Aiqua.
- If a humanoid spends at least 1 hour within Ayas Kelren, that creature must succeed on a DC 13 Wisdom saving throw or descend into madness determined by the Madness of Ayas Kelren table. A creature that succeeds on this saving throw can't be affected by this regional effect again for 24 hours.

Madness of Ayas Kelren	
d10	Flaw (lasts until cured)
1-6	"I am overcome with great sadness and do not wish to travel any further."
7	"I believe that I am the reincarnation of an ancient elven warrior."
8	"I must go the ruins of Imfe Aiqua, City of the Elven Kings and find the Tomb of Ruehnar Kelren."
9	"I will stop at nothing to unleash the Great Titans on the land and bring about the doom of our world."
10	"I must speak with the dead of Ayas Kelren. They harbor secrets."

Madness of Ayas Kelren. If a creature goes mad in Ayas Kelren, roll on the Madness of Kelren table to determine the nature of the madness, which is a character flaw that lasts until cured. See the *DMG* for more on madness.

Ayas Kelren is detailed further in the spin-off adventure, *Glaive of the Revenant King.*

Banshee's Tower

The wail of the banshee can be heard through the forest for miles around. In the nearest gnome village, they pretend it is the call of a very persistent screech owl, but few actually believe it.

On a low rocky hill near the middle of the forest is the old tower, scorched and partially collapsed. The banshee's home is on the second floor of the tower in the room open to the sky because of the partial collapse of the third floor. However, this is not where she died. The red-haired elven daughter of the lord of this tower was imprisoned in the dungeons below when the tower fell. The same dungeons where she was forgotten and died of deprivation pining for her father, her home, and her people.

The Banshee's Tower is detailed further in the forthcoming spin-off adventure titled *The Banshee's Tower*.

Barnemouth

Barnemouth is home primarily to humans but it is also home to a considerable number of northern-based wood elves who fled the persecution of the northern orc tribe, the Drakescales. It is the largest town along the Fairknot River before it spills into the north end of the Omerian Ocean.

Barnemouth is known for its massive statue of Godefroi Barnemouth the Loving, a contemporary of Camor. The statue does not look like a paladin, but more like an older, loving grandfather. Despite his years of service for the northern armies, this is how Bar-

nemouth preferred to be remembered.

Interestingly, there are no temples in Barnemouth. At one point, the city was home to worshippers to Tholona the Dawn, but during the Cleansing that followed the War of Gnohr, the early Barnemouthers collapsed the temple. While the aggression towards religious worship isn't as strong as it was two hundred years ago, those who follow divine faiths—including paladins—are shunned by the locals.

The Drakescale orcs have once again started their march south towards Fairknot River. Already, the town of Camor has reported attacks in the forests north of their village. It's only a matter of time before Barnemouth sees action.

If the characters reach Barnemouth, they can restock, rest, and gather rumors. Barnemouth is detailed further on pages 120-123.

Basilisk's Spine Mountains

The colossal mountain range that spans the width of Omeria and divides the northern end of the continent from the central end is the nearly impassable Basilisk's Spine Mountain. The mountain range originally had many names depending on the culture that lived near it. When Duda Weysevain traveled through the mountains and along the coast that now bears his name, he noticed on his map that the range resembled a large, multi-legged lizard, hence its modern name. Many of the geographical features that Weysevain recorded around the range take its name from the Spine.

A newer mountain range, the snow-capped peaks are treacherous and difficult to cross. In addition, it is a volcanic range rife with earthquakes, landslides, and other geological calamities.

The rules for climbing and crossing through the mountains are detailed further in Chapter 6 of the *Hand of the Eight, The Fantastic Lie.*

Camp Hummingbird

One of the few human encampments in the Wallingmiotta that has remained, Camp Hummingbird is home to roughly 150 researchers from all over Omeria. The majority of the researchers are scholars (**commoners** with Intelligence and Wisdom scores of 13 with one or more Intelligence-based skill proficiencies), **nobles**, and **guards**. There are **veterans** who lead the military operations in Hummingbird, and they answer directly to Caustis Mèyor (LN female half-elf **knight**). Meanwhile, the lead scholar at Hummingbird is a neutral Dinzer human **mage** named Enuxar.

Although Enuxar leads the expeditions through Ayas Kelren, it is Mèyor's unusual nature that gives the researchers advantage. Mèyor is unaffected by the evil that permeates the ancient elven lands. While the automatic assumption is that it must be because of her half-elven heritage, research has shown that other half-elves—and sometimes even full elves—are still affected by the woods' dark call. Furthermore, the undead of Ayas Kelren ignore Mèyor, allowing her to travel freely. After some serious convincing on Enuxar's part, Mèyor will travel into Ayas Kelren with a special scrying device he equips her. Enuxar hopes to discover the ruins of Imfe Aiqua. For whatever reason, the city is not where it once stood and any who have entered the lands of Ayas Kelren with the intent to find the city never return.

Overall, the Camp is friendly to the characters, especially if O is still among them. If the characters spend at least 1 hour in the camp, they can find someone who can show them where Aruxius' cabin is located on their map of the Wallingmiotta.

Camp Hummingbird is detailed further in the spin-off adventure, *Glaive of the Revenant King.*

Continued on page 124...

Barnemouth

Humans dominate the Fairknot village of Barnemouth, but it is also home to a considerable number of northern-based wood elves. These elves fled persecution by the northern orc tribe, the Drakescales. Barnemouth is the largest town along the Fairknot River before it spills into the north end of the Omerian Ocean. The town is known for its massive statue of Godefroi Barnemouth the Loving, a contemporary of Camor. Those passing through often comment that the statue does not look like a paladin, but more like an older, loving grandfather. Despite his years of service for the northern armies, this is how Barnemouth preferred to be remembered. Interestingly, there are no temples in Barnemouth. At one point, the city was home to worshippers to Tholona the Dawn and General Ilwyn, God of Summer. During the Cleansing that followed the War of Gnohr, the early Barnemouthers collapsed the temple. While the aggression towards religious worship isn't as strong as it was two hundred years ago, those who follow divine faiths— including paladins—are shunned by the locals. The Drakescale orcs have once again started their march south towards Fairknot River. Already, the town of Camor has reported attacks in the forests north of their village. It's only a matter of time before Barnemouth sees action.

Important Barnemouthers

Like many who live along the Fairknot River, Barnemouth's citizens have known peace and tranquility for some time. Only recently with the incursion of Drakescale orcs have they had to raise arms. Outside of their hatred of organized religion, Barnemouthers are a friendly, helpful lot.

Important Barnemouthers include the following NPCs:

Dillurk Woodpeak is the town's historian and caretaker of Loving Hold (**Area 1**).

Doniana Helyn is a fortune-teller and dream reader who works from a shop in the Tangle (**Area 8**).

Mona Mèyor is the head of the town guard and militia (**Area 7**).

Oprimo Regent is the headmaster of Ebondawn, a self-proclaimed arcane guild that operates out of the Nine Sabers guildhall (**Area 4**).

Pataz of Odonburg manages a few warehouses at the docks and is known for black market dealing in goods and information (**Area 9**).

Rand Lauf is the leader of Bronzeforce, one of the three adventuring guilds that works out of the Nine Sabers guildhall (**Area 4**).

Rhibun Beshu is the owner of the Natural Hand tavern in Last Glance Ward (**Area 3**).

Sarya Moonshade is the constable and mayor of Barnemouth (**Area 6**). Sarya once wanted to become a singer but lacked the voice to do so.

Thokhim Snowbraids is the leader of the Wind Dragons, one of three adventurers guilds that makes their home in the Nine Sabers guildhall (**Area 4**).

Viciara Tortlar leads the Anorian enclave, Little Mythse Anore (**Area 10**). She is also the secret leader of the Good Will Union.

The Good Will Union

A group of roughly thirty half-Anorian Barnemouther merchants have formed a publicly known faction called the Good Will Union. The coalition meets once a week to discuss town affairs and offer help where it's needed. The Union has a secret, though: most are practicing warlocks. Some draw their eldritch energy from Vapul, as it befits those of Anorian heritage. But there is no one set god or otherworldly patron that the group's members draw power from. If anything, the secret side of the Good Will Union is for scholarly purposes. However, they have been known to use their powers on behalf of Sarya Moonshade who is well aware of their existence.

The Hand of the Eight

If playing in this setting as part of the larger adventure series, there are additional rumors that the characters can learn as it relates to the story.

Kongrodol the Worm sleeps in the belly of the Wallingmiotta Forest. They say when the Hand of the Eight appears, Kongrodol will return to avenge the fallen elves of Imfe Aiqua.

There are a few people in town who might know where Aruxius lives including the fortune teller Doniana Helyn (**Area 8**) and the Anorian sage Viciara Tortlar (**Area 10**).

The centaur clans that protect the fields east and west of the Wallingmiotta are fierce enemies of the hobgoblin hordes of

Gar Wabrizz.

A particularly nasty group of kobolds live in the Wallingmiotta. They are protected by a colossal bear named Tremor.

Terrible lizards the size of buildings roam the forest. Careful: they love the taste of humanoid flesh.

Supposedly, a Dinzer aircraft of some sort crashed in the deep south of the Wallingmiotta forest.

Barnemouth Locations

The most important locations in Barnemouth are detailed below. Barnemouth is a town of approximately 2,000 citizens. Therefore, buildings shown on the map that don't have a number and a description are up to you to interpret. Consider that Barnemouth is a large, prosperous— if conservative—town on the banks of the Fairknot river, and one of the last major civilized areas before the Fairknot bumps against the edges of Ayas Kelren and the Fierce Lands.

If you are using the town as a point of interest in the Hand of the Eight adventure path, the sections labeled "Hand of the Eight" contain details and clues for the characters to discover while in the area.

1 - Loving Hold. The old fortress of Barnemouth hasn't seen active duty in hundreds of years. While it's supposed to be the home of the constable-mayor, Moonshade prefers to live over the Drunk Spider. Instead, the hold works as a fest hall, meeting house, and even museum chronicling the Time of Triumphs and the siege of Imfe Mythse Anore.

Key NPCs. Dillurk Woodpeak (LN male Knotsider human **commoner**; Intelligence 13; proficiency in History) acts as the caretaker of Loving Hold. Woodpeak is a wealth of knowledge on the Fairknot region and even the Wallingmiotta. Expect that he knows most of the rumors and information offered in the Adventures in Barnemouth section above.

A staff of five attendants (human **commoners**) assists Woodpeak with the care of the Loving Hold.

Hand of the Eight. Aruxius travels to Loving Hold periodically to speak with Woodpeak. Woodpeak isn't sure exactly where Aruxius lives, but he suggests that the characters travel to Pella's Wish. He'll mark on a map the location of the gnome village.

2 - Black Wing Grounds. A group of rangers named the Black Wings patrol the forests north of Barnemouth. The collection of buildings at the northeast end of town is where they live, train, and operate.

At any given time, there are at least ten rangers (guards) in attendance. The other thirty to forty who operate from Barnemouth work in the Amber for weeks at a time.

Key NPCs. Their leader, Phraan Boarrider (CG male Aiquan elf **scout**) was recently injured in a skirmish with Drakescales and is recovering. Boarrider, nearly 250-years old, is one of the few living Aiquans who avoided death at the hands of the plague that killed most of the Aiquans. Boarrider is also one of the few Barnemouthers "in the know" of the Good Will Union's true nature.

Imzar Rilynate (NE male Anorian elf **spy**) is a particularly ill-spirited ranger who works with the Black Wings. Many fo the Black Wings consider him the true leader of the group. Unfortunately, Imzar's intense hatred of humans has kept him from ascending. Since Boarrider's injury, however, many suspect that Imzar will take his rightful spot at the top. Around humans, Imzar only speaks in thick Anorian Elven. Only natural Elven speakers will understand his slang and idioms—others who speak Elven will need to make regular DC 10 Intelligence (History) checks to comprehend what he is saying.

3 - Last Glance Ward. The old joke goes: "This is your last glance at civilization, enjoy it while you can." Of course, there are plenty of villages and towns west of Barnemouth. Still, Barnemouth is the largest, most populated, and best-protected town before the Fairknot slips north into the Fierce Lands.

The merchants of Last Glance Ward— many of which are half-Anorian—play on the ominous jokes and warnings given to those heading into the Fierce Lands. As such, many of the shops there serve survival gear, weapons, and wards and trinkets. Nearly every shop sells siren hooks. The black, curved claw can be worn as a talisman, a broach, or any number of creative ways. Some smiths even forge the siren hooks into the pommels of daggers. Supposedly, siren hooks ward off the legendary hollowmen, monsters reported to haunt the forests and banks of the western Fairknot region.

Key NPCs. Chi Qouyas (NG male wanderer halfling veteran) is a swordsman sells his escort services to those who seek to travel along the Knotted Road south

into the Fierce Lands. Though mostly well-liked, Chi has a bad habit of getting into other people's business. Regardless, his unique fighting style and knowledge of the flora and fauna of the Fierce Lands makes him a valuable asset.

Rhibun Beshu (CG male Knotsider human **commoner**) owns the Natural Hand tavern, a three-story building close to the town walls. Rhibun used to be a trapper who worked the amber, but after a run-in with an unfriendly owlbear has decided to settle down. He acts as a point of contact for Good Will Union, selling their services (with his 10% mark-up, of course) to those looking for assistance arcane. Rhibun is a jolly, old woodsman with a hearty laugh. It's not unusual to find him sneaking drinks behind the Hand, lest his wife Heroli catch him and ring his ear.

Rucker (LN male devilkin **noble**), for lack of a better term, is a snake oil salesman. A few years ago, Rucker nearly died in the town of Riverside. Since then, the green-skinned devilkin has started to change his ways. Still, he loves nothing more than quick coin from an easy target. Rucker always travels with a masked Garrish hobgoblin named Exter who works as his bodyguard.

Hand of the Eight. Chi Qouyas knows the exact location of Aruxius' cabin in the Wallingmiotta and will gladly lead the characters there for 1 gold piece per day in payment. With Chi navigating the party, random encounters only happen on a result of 18+, and he never gets lost in the Wallingmiotta.

4 - The Nine Sabers. One hundred years ago, the Nine Sabers Guidhall was home to a band of traveling warriors who explored and adventured throughout northern Omeria, the Fair Knot region in particular. Each a born and bred Barnemouther, they were a coalition of warriors, rogues, and rangers who used their skills to scare off many of the dangerous inhabitants north of the Fairknot. The last of the Sabers, Kaarlo Jakar died twenty years ago at the ripe old age of 99. At Kaarlo's passing, the guildhall was opened to the public. Kaarlo's granddaughter Edda Clanbloom sold off most of the valuables within the Nine Sabers' old fortress then moved to Presson's Enclave where she now lives in a sizable plot of land.

Now, three different adventuring guilds work out of the old location: Ebondawn, Bronzeforce, and the Wind Dragons.

Needless to say, none of these organizations have the talent or heroic qualities the Nine Sabers once had. Instead, they act as loan sharks for young adventurers looking to get a start in the Fierce Lands.

Key NPCs. Ebondawn's headmaster is Oprimo Regent (LE male Knotsider **noble** with the Magic Initiate feat). Regent positions himself as a sorcerer supreme of Barnemouth, utilizing tricks and deception to make the people of Barnemouth believe he holds power. Of the three headmasters in the Nine Sabers, he is the least seen, preferring to "stay in the shadows" of the hall's old wizard tower.

Rand Lauf (NG male human **guard**) leads Bronzeforce. Bronzeforce is a ragtag coalition of retired guards, wannabe mercenaries, and inexperienced adventurers. Many of Bronzeforce's members are too poor to afford their own housing, so Lauf allows them to stay in the barracks for as long as they need. Among the Barnemouthers, Bronzeforce is something of a joke. Recently a paladin named Thalia Pridemane (LG female Pressonian human **knight**) entered town looking for work and decided to stay among the Bronzeforce. Immediately, the inexperienced members of Bronzeforce were taken surprised by her talents with a blade. Unfortunately, locals learned of Thalia's devotion to the god, General Thinir. They want Lauf to remove her from her post and exile her from town. Lauf, never one for tough decisions, hasn't made a move one way or the other yet.

Finally, Thokhim Snowbraids (N male Von Doral dwarf **knight**) is the captain of the Wind Dragons. Thokhim and his four brothers, Raznoum, Norammeat, Dholgratin, and Grozas (all knights) were once members of a security force that operated in Von Doral. After the exodus, the brothers did not want to feel unneeded. Instead of retiring to a mundane life south of the Basilisk's Spine, they turned their attention to Northern Omeria and the Fairknot Region. The term Wind Dragons is actually a mispronunciation of Vindraakunz. Rough translation: drunk and disorderly.

Hand of the Eight. Members of all three of the adventuring guilds are eager for excitement. Members of the Wind Dragons and Ebondawn charge 2 gp per day for their services, whereas Bronzeforce members will charge as little as 3 sp per day for work. Thalia Pridemane will travel with the characters for free if they offer her food and company—the disdain for religious people in Barnemouth has made her time difficult there and could use an escape.

5 - Statue of Godefroi Barnemouth the Loving. The grandfatherly statue of the town's founder is found in the center of town. Once per year on Godefroi Day (roughly two weeks after the Summer Festival) Barnemouthers decorate the statue with wild flowers.

6 - The Drunk Spider. Barnemouth's most popular tavern and inn, the Drunk Spider, is where nearly all Barnemouthers end their day. Certainly, there are other drinking establishments in town, but the Spider easily consumes every six out of town coins that go towards bar tabs. Originally called Godefroi's, the Spider gets its name from an urban legend. Supposedly, when Godefroi was still alive and bartending at the Spider, the old paladin caught a spider and tossed it in a mug. The spider pulled itself out and stumbled away. Soon after, the name caught on.

The Drunk Spider's food is decent and its drinks are strong, but the real reason people visit the Spider is for the entertainment. Many traveling minstrels, entertainers, and bards end their journey along the Fairknot at the Drunk Spider. It's a tradition for them to wrap up their journeys with a festival celebrating their accomplishments, followed by a few weeks of rest before they return to the road. The first night of a traveler's return, they must tell share their favorite anecdotes as part of the Spider's Chant.

Key NPCs. The town's constable-mayor, Sarya Moonshade (LG female half-Aiquan scout) lives in one of the suites above the Spider. A bit of a night owl, Sarya loves the raucous vibe of the Spider and its citizens. Many Barnemouthers joke that if you want to meet with the constable-mayor, do so in the afternoon and be sure bring a hangover remedy.

The owner of the Spider is a descendant of Godefroi Barnemouth, Roxane Barne (NG female Knotsider **commoner**). Roxane took ownership of the bar from her Uncle Lou who passed ten years ago. While she enjoys the wealth that comes from owning the popular establishment, the decade of service has worn her out. She's hoping to sell the

place so she can retire. Currently, Roxane is in negotiations with Andreus Thurber, a retired adventurer from Presson's Enclave who sees an opportunity to expand on the concept.

Hand of the Eight. Someone at the Spider is bound to know the location of Aruxius' cabin in the Wallingmiotta. Only trouble, of course, is figuring out the truth from the lies. A character can spend an hour here gathering information. At the end of the hour, make a DC 10 Wisdom (Insight) check on their behalf. On a success, they learn exactly where Aruxius' cabin is. Otherwise, they aren't confident in the information they've been given (even if the information is accurate).

7 - The Pig Gate. The Pig Gate gets its name from the butcher shop, Osner's that's just south of the gate. Osner only serves pig at his establishment. And each morning, Osner cooks salted pork belly. Osner's pork belly can be smelled for miles around. (Some grumble that it tends to attract dangerous creatures from the Wallingmiotta, but are quietly reminded that the trouble is worth it for a strip).

Five years ago, Osner and the locals started an autumn tradition called Pig Slaughter. And that is exactly what it is. Most of Osner's providers' pigs are at their target weight and ready to be sold to the butcher. Osner, taking contracts all along the Fairknot throughout most of the summer, invites his buyers to Barnemouth. From there, the pigs are slaughtered, cooked, and served for three days as all of Barnemouth celebrates. The tradition has become so popular, already, many of the traveling entertainers that end their journeys at the spider make sure they reach Barnemouth before the Equinox so they can partake.

Because of its position on the south end of town, the Pig Gate is also where the town's standing militia keeps its base of operations. At any time there are ten guards on duty.

Key NPCs. The current head of the militia is Mona Mèyor (LG female half-Anorian **veteran**), Caustis' sister. Mora's a little friendlier than her famously uptight sister and is more than happy to help those in need.

Osner Applewhite (N male Knotsider human **commoner**) is the eponymous owner of Osner's Butcher and a beloved citizen despite coming off as standoffish. Osner is exceptionally conservative and

bigotted, too. He despises divine worshippers, mistrusts all Anorians and those of orcish descent, and thinks Dinzer technology is a danger to the world. But damn can he cook a pork belly.

Luman Nowels (LG male Knotsider human **guard**) is Mona Mèyor's right-hand man. A little more open-minded than his fellow Barnemouthers, Nowels often uses his best judgment when handling situations. Many Barnemouthers see Nowels as something of a pushover and sell out. Osner has publically called for Nowels' removal.

8 - The Tangle. The east side of town that clings to the Knotted Road is called the Tangle. The Tangle consists of the first collection of shops, food stalls, and merchant booths westbound travelers meet when entering Barnemouth.

Key NPCs. One of the more curious shops along the Tangle is Doniana Helyn's. Doniana (CN female forest gnome **illusionist**) stands outside her permanent tent fanning herself. When a particularly interesting-looking traveler enters town via the Knotted, she entices them by mentioning something of which they recently dreamt. For 5 silver pieces, she explains the nature of the mark's dream.

Hand of the Eight. Doniana is close friends with Aruxius and has frequently traveled to meet with the danaavrakt. When met with a particularly difficult dream to interpret, Doniana seeks Aruxius' advice on the matter. For 2 gp, she can mark the location of Aruxius' cabin on a map of the Wallingmiotta.

9 - Docks. Like many of the villages and towns that crowd the Knotside River, Barnemouth's docks are the town's center of trade and commerce. Because Barnemouth is the "last glance at civilization" before one enters the Fierce Lands to the west, the docks are choked with warehouses of all varieties. The docks are also home to a thriving black market thanks to its distance from cities like Knotside and Murktown. Many stolen goods are sold here, including pilfered Dinzer technology and emerald Odonburgite. Perhaps not-so-ironically, most of the transactions are managed by the Dinzer Pataz and his cadre of Odonburg ex-patriots.

Key NPCs. Pataz of Odonburg (N male Odonburg human **noble**) is the major player in Barnemouth. To some, Pataz is a crime lord, underhanded and not to be trusted. To others, he's a brilliant strategist and influencer whose reach

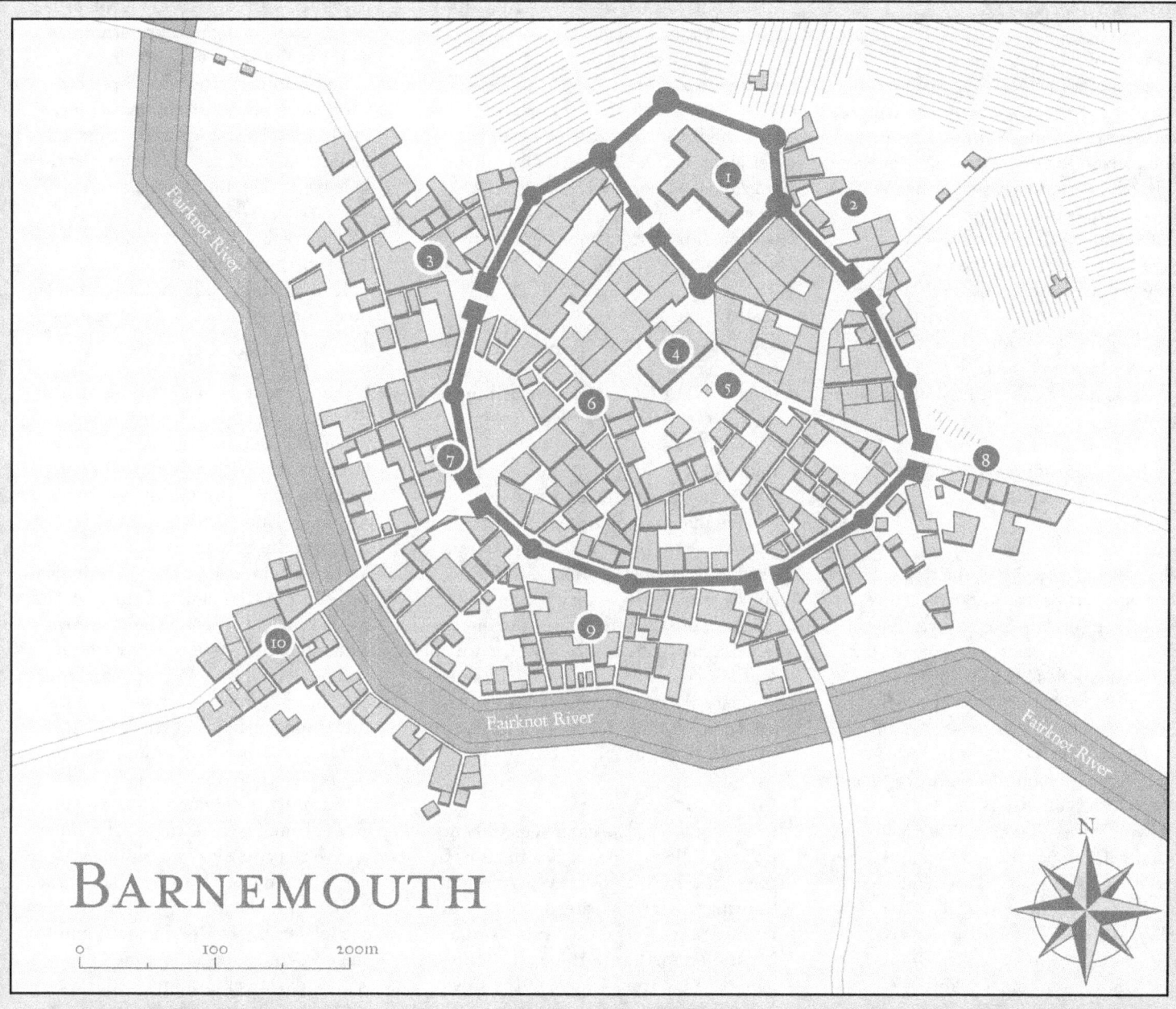

BARNEMOUTH

goes as far as Southern Omeria. Very little happens along the Fairknot of which Pataz is not aware. And although Pataz is quite wealthy from his black market dealings, his favorite thing to trade is information. Pataz, like many Dinzers, has an exceptional memory. What he learns of his allies and enemies alike he uses to advance his place in the world.

10 - Little Mythse Anore. Most of the full elves and half-elves of Anorian descent that live in Barnemouth live on the southside of the river in the "shanty town" dubbed Little Mythse Anore. While Sarya Moonshade supposedly has do-

minion over the entirety of Barnemouth, the majority of the Anorians who call the town home answer only to Viciara Tortlar.

Little Mythse Anore is nearly a village in its own right. It has its own shops, meeting hall, and even an inn for traveling Anorians and half-Anorians. The inn, Tatholg's, is the building in which the Good Will Union operates. Anyone who wishes to speak with Viciara must do so there.

Key NPCs. Viciara Tortlar (NE female Anorian **warlock**) is the warlock su-

preme of the Good Will Union, but only from behind the scenes. Otherwise, it's rare to even see her speaking with the other members. a devout worshipper of Vapul, Viciara draws her power from the severe winters that crush Northern Omeria.

Hand of the Eight. Viciara knows the location of Aruxius' cabin and will show the characters the way on a map at the cost of 10 gp. She and Aruxius don't care much for each other, but she has nothing negative to say about the danaavrakt.Ω

(continued from page 119)

Canyon of Crawlers

A series of unusual, labyrinthine canyons tear through a nearly 100-square-mile section of the Wallingmiotta. The canyon is filled with all manner of horrible creatures, including giant beasts, dinosaurs, undead, oozes, and aberrations. When the characters come across it, they have two options: they can avoid the location and travel around it, which could potentially add multiple days to their travel time. Or they could travel through it. The latter option is faster, certainly, but far more dangerous.

The Canyon of Crawlers is detailed further in the spin-off adventure, **The Canyon of Crawlers**.

Fairknot River

The southern border of the northern Omerian city-states and townships is marked by Fairknot River. The cold-water river emerges from springs in the Basilisk's Spine Range in the east and deposits into the northern Omerian ocean in the west. Notable towns and cities that dot its banks include Barnemouth, Rivertown, and, of course, Noble Knotside.

A wide river, Fairknot River is always filled with ships traveling up and down the river trading goods at the dozens of villages on either side of it. Very few bridges span Fairknot River as the Wallingmiotta has been "off-limits" to most humanoids since before the time of the Kelren elves.

Fields of Posea

The western edge of the Wallingmiotta is an expanse of grasslands, hills, and savannahs called the Fields of Poseas. The fields are dominated by the nomadic centaur clans. However, goblinoids pushing north of Gar Wabrizz have begun to encroach in the horsefolk lands. So far, the conflicts have been nothing more than a few skirmishes. However, if the goblinoids persist, it may lead to an all-out war between Posean clans and Glonklad's hordes.

Gongspire

The fortress village of Gongspire has long held the honor of never being breached. Currently, its military force—known as Spireans—are working to clear out Drakescale orc settlements in the Amber Forest to the north.

Hellstinger Nests

The first day that the characters begin traveling through Wallingmiotta, they discover that *Old Spirit* crashed in the middle of a hellstinger wasp colony. Although the wasps aren't active at night, in the daytime, they are very active and unusually aggressive.

While in the same hex as the hellstinger wasps, do not roll random encounters as usual. Instead, the characters are attacked so long as they remain within the hex during the morning and afternoon by 3d6 **giant wasps**. There are literally thousands of wasps in the area. It is impossible to kill them all off outside of major magic likely beyond the characters' level.

Imfe Aiqua

Imfe Aiqua was the capital city of the elves of Kelren. Now, it lies in ruins at the center of Ayas Kelren, permanently tainting the northwestern end of Wallingmiotta with its curse. Imfe Aiqua is detailed further in the forthcoming spin-off adventure Glaive of the Revenant King.

Killing Grounds

Bones and half-eaten carcasses litter the ground of this hex. The Killing Grounds are home to two deadly **tyrannosaurus rexes** that the natives of Wallingmiotta have named Stomp and Render. When the characters enter the hex of the two, roll random encounters as normal. But instead of the usual random encounters, the characters encounter one of the dinosaurs or possibly both. Roll d6. On a roll of 1-2, the characters encounter both dinosaurs at the same time.

The tyrannosaurus rexes are both very aggressive, but not particularly intelligent. Hiding from the dinosaurs usually discourages them, forcing them to leave to look for easier prey. However, if attacked, they automatically become reckless. While reckless, the dinosaur has advantage on its attack rolls and attack rolls made against the dinosaurs are made with advantage.

Knotside

If there was a "capital of the north" it'd likely be Knotside. The city is home to some 20,000 northerners, mostly humans, but with a fair number of gnomes, elves, and halflings as well. Although Knotside has a royal family in place, the Selfridges, Knotside is primarily a democracy. The current elected leader of Knotside is Principal Tam Netheroak (LG male half-elf **noble**), whom most Knotsiders view as fair and just. However, his six-year tenure is soon up. Representatives from the three major parties of Knotside are already starting their campaigns to replace Netheroak.

Originally, Knotside was the elven city of Imfe Mythse Anore. The Anorians were tyrannical worshippers of an ice demon named Vapul and brought hardship to northern Omeria. Under the leadership of Kelren the Blade, the elves of Imfe Aiqua joined forces with an army of humans from Presson's Enclave to rid northern Omeria of the Anorian forces and their dark god. Omeris Knot the Fair, a paladin of Presson's Enclave and leader of the humans during the Anorian Conflict, assumed leadership of the conquered city. Knot lent his name to both the city and river.

Although Knotside is a city known for its strong trade relationships with the northern city-states, its chief export is lumber thanks to the Amber Forest to the north. Despite protests from Aiqua-no elves and Wallingmiottan gnomes, Anorian converts, the survivors and descendants of the Anorian Conflict, were put to use in the forests as lumberjacks and rangers.

Knotside is a major city full of adventure and intrigue, perfect as a starting point for many adventures (see DM-Dave.com for details). If the characters reach Knotside, they can spend 1-hour searching for clues to Aruxius' whereabouts with no roll needed—someone shows them on their map where his cabin is.

Knotside will be detailed in future installments of the **Hand of the Eight** and other adventures.

Kongradol's Rest

Ten-thousand years ago, as man was just starting to discover civilization and the elves ruled the land, a race of beings called dulons lived high in the mountains of Omeria, particularly the Basilisk's Spine (or Ailmar Lura in the elven tongue). Though few, the dulons were significantly more advanced than the other humanoid races of pre-human-dominated Omeria. Many of the modern races of Omeria were created by the dulons in order to help them build their great empire. The ancient elven text, *Vulen Luxisys*, suggests that the dulons were preparing for an event they called The Eternal Day. Although the text isn't clear, it reads that, on that day, a dark force known as Poqir would bring doom to the land. To combat the coming of the dark force, the dulons created five great weapons: the Titans.

In time, the dulons vanished from the world and with them their technology and mostly their memories. Human scholars who read the elven texts and heard the stories believed that the dulons were mythological. But five-hundred years ago, a band of explorers from Knotside discovered an ancient cave at the western edge of the Wallingmiotta. The cave was unlike any ruins or dungeon they had ever discov-

ered. Strange, green crystals grew from the walls and floors, emitting radiant energy throughout the complex. The adventurers discovered the remains of the bizarre dulons and their technology. And they also stumbled upon one of their Titans, Kongradol the Worm. Fortunately, Kongradol had not risen from its slumber in 5,000 years.

Upon seeing the Titan, one of the adventurers, Oxon the Eye, entered a trance. Oxon, in a language later learned to be the tongue of the dulons, echoed the dulon fears of the Eternal Day. Odon, Oxon's brother who witnessed the trance, wrote in his journal that Oxon spoke of seven catastrophic events, each of them grave omens. Following those events, the eighth and final catastrophic event, the Eternal Day, would signal the arrival of Poqir and the end of all existence.

The Worm still sleeps, its resting place guarded by the Saigroth, a trio of ancient elven warriors who are rumored to have the blood of dulons flowing through their veins.

Kongradol's Rest is detailed further in the spin-off adventure, **Glaive of the Revenant King**.

Liar's Caves

Liar's Cave was once an elven outpost cut into the stone of the natural cave by a variety of magics. The elves that built it and lived there were outcasts among their kin and survived with just the bare necessities of a few dozen lacquered human peasants as furniture, a library of a few thousand esoteric tomes, and less than a decade's supply of finely-prepared intoxicants. Needless to say, they were desperate.

The stench of elven desperation was enough to attract other predators hunting for their arcana – the elves only ended up living here for less than a decade before the complex was completely wiped clean by something. It has been used a few times since by one group or another. For many years the lowest section of the structure was flooded

with cold water dividing the structures into two distinct mini-fortresses. It isn't known who finally drained the water, but now a series of small drains keep this area from flooding (but it remains very wet and the floor is slippery to the point of danger).

Somewhere along the way, the cave picked up the sobriquet of Liar's Cave – and most people know of it that it is up in the hills in the bush about six hours walk to the northeast. But few know anything about the history and most don't even know about the structures within.

The Liar's Caves are detailed further in the spin-off adventure, **The Liar's Caves**.

Mean Ash Village

The Mean Ash tribe are descendants of the Cold Ghost tribe that once lived in the tunnels below the Basilisk's Spine. Driven off by the Von Dorals, the Mean Ash adapted to the Wallingmiotta and eventually became a part of its environment. Like the gnomes who inhabit the mysterious forest, the Mean Ash are accepted by the fey and forest itself. The giant bear, Tremor, in particular, cherishes its relationship with the Mean Ash, who see Tremor as their great Father-Protector.

The Mean Ash village proper is home to some 500 **kobolds**. Foliage-covered nets blanketing the already-dense canopies blot out the sunlight, casting the village in perpetual darkness. The abodes of the kobolds do not resemble typical humanoid dwellings, either. Instead, the kobold homes resemble a massive beaver dam consisting of fallen logs, mud-caked walls, netting, and other oddities that creates a deadly maze filled with beasts, dark fey, monstrosities, traps, and of course, the diabolical Mean Ash clan itself. No non-kobold humanoid has entered the Mean Ash village and survived to tell the tale.

The current leader of the Mean Ash is Gurn Vumsegg, a wild magic sorcerer.

Although most kobolds live for only a handful of decades, Gurn has been alive for at least 100 years. It's rare that the kobold chief ever leaves the Mean Ash village. Instead, he prefers to work in private at the heart of the dam, sending out his forces to do his dirty work. Rumors persist that Gurn draws much of his power from the severed head of the long-deceased emerald dragon, Zedryno the Jealous.

Neepawa Bowels

The marsh-covered lands of Neepawa Bowels cut through the center of Wallingmiotta. While the bowels are not magically tainted like the cursed woods of Ayas Kelren to the northeast, they have their fair share of dangers. Giant beasts are particularly prevalent in the area, as are kobolds of the Mean Ash clan.

Travel through the bowels is particularly grueling. The characters cannot move at a fast pace through Neepawa Bowels. And to move at a slow pace and still make progress, the d4 roll must come up with a result of 4. Otherwise, the characters do not move for that day.

Pella's Wish

Second only to the Mean Ash village in terms of population, the large gnome village of Pella's Wish can be found in the southwestern portion of the Wallingmiotta. Like their natural enemies, the kobolds, the forest gnomes of Pella's Wish are well-protected by the fey of the Wallingmiotta.

A typical gnome village, Pella's Wish forms a symbiotic relationship with the trees. The gnomes create their domiciles within naturally hollowed out trees, large rabbit holes, and sometimes, below mushroom caps. Small animals, particularly squirrels, rabbits, badgers, and woodpeckers live with the gnomes, beloved like close friends and relatives.

Secretly a disguised **couatl**, Wilgrim Potts counsels the gnomes and has done so for over 500 years. Wilgrim was close friends with the Dinzers when they traveled through the Wallingmiotta. He pointed them towards many of the forest's points of interest including Kongradol's Rest, the elven city of Imfe Aiqua, and eventually the northern human city-states. These days, Potts keeps to himself, but occasionally travels to visit his friend, Aruxius to the west of the forest. During his vision at Kongrodol's Hold, Oxon foretold that Wilgrim would live to see the Eternal Day come to pass.

Tremor's Cliff

Tremor is a 25-foot tall bear that roams through the Wallingmiotta (detailed above in the Random Encounters section). When he is not hunting or protecting the forest, Tremor retires to a 100-foot-tall cliff face located south of the Neepawa Bowels. At any given time, there is a 10% chance that Tremor is resting on the cliff.

However, Tremor is not alone. A **harpy** named Yoraene lives on the cliff with Tremor in a nest made from discarded plate mail armor. She uses her song to soothe and calm the bear so he can sleep. More clever than most of her kind (her Intelligence score is 9 and she has the same innate spells as a **green hag**), Yoraene enjoys testing creatures who dare approach the cliffs. Those who pass her test will be given safe passage through the forest. And those who fail her test are instead eaten by Tremor. So far, no one has passed her test. She worries Tremor is getting fat.

Rivertown

Rivertown is an unfortified fishing town. It lies at a crossroads between Knotside, Gongspire, and Barnemouth. One of the more religious communities north of the Fairknot, Rivertown's inhabitants practice a nature religion, much like druids. The priests at the local Temple of Rebirth serve as lawmen, chroniclers, and intermediaries between the normal citizenry and a powerful goddess of rebirth. The region's original founder, a gnome named Olian Stoneberry promised the goddess that his people would respect the land in exchange for bountiful harvests and game. The region is still dangerous, in places, but there are hardly any bad harvests.

Characters who enter Rivertown that spend 1-hour gathering information will learn the location of Aruxius' tower in the Wallingmiotta.

Rivertown is detailed in the adventure *Quarantine* in *BroadSword Monthly #2*.

Troubled Run

The southwestern border of the Wallingmiotta is along the edge of the appropriately named river, Troubled Run. The Run is difficult to navigate as it is filled with white water rapids, steep waterfalls, and swirling whirlpools for almost its entire 200-mile length. At regular locations along the river, the goblinoid hordes of Gar Wabrizz have created bridges to surpass the river. However, the centaur clans that ride the Fields of Posea work diligently to destroy these whenever and wherever they are found.

The Knight-in-Shining-Armor

While it can not fly as fast as Omnaweahl's peregrine-flyer, the remote traveler alpha-class (see Appendix B) can still fly at incredible speeds. With its rocket pack, it gains a flying speed of 120 feet per round.

It took the Knight-in-Shining-Armor a full day to fly across the Desolation of Ditimaya and over the Basilisk's Spine Mountains. It immediately discovered the wreck of *Old Spirit* and searched the wreckage for survivors, salvageable goods, and the emerald Odonburgite core. Then, without hesitation, it began tracking the characters.

Each day that the characters are in the Wallingmiotta, the Knight hunts them. As a construct, it does not require air, food, water, or sleep. Nothing can stop it from finding its quarry.

Once the characters finally encounter the machine, read the following:

> Omnaweahl stops in her tracks. "Wait. do you hear that?" she gives signals to shush you all.
>
> All you hear are the ambient sounds of the forest. But then, like a low roar, you hear something approaching—it almost reminds you of the sound a fireball makes as it is loosed from the tips of a wizard.
>
> In the sky above, you see the contrail of something flying above you. And by the looks of it, it's moving towards you at breakneck speeds.
>
> "Run!" screams Omnaweahl. Before you can even ask her what it is, she arms herself with her *eldritch caster* and takes off running...

When the **remote traveler alpha-class** is within 300 feet of the characters, they can make out what it is. After two more rounds, it finally lands, skidding to a halt. Without so much as a word, it starts to attack, targeting any of the characters it suspects has the book.

The Knight-in-Shining-Armor is a dangerous combatant. Since the characters last saw the machine, it reloaded its spell-storing mechanism with a web spell. Its plan is to subdue its quarry, kill it while it is incapacitated, then take the book.

However, the weapons Omnaweahl brought from the ship should be enough to even the playing field. If the remote traveler's hit points are reduced by half or more, it retreats so it can recover from its wounds. But it will likely attack again on the same day, using stealth and guerilla tactics to catch the group off guard.

No matter how much damage Omnaweahl deals to the machine, it will not harm her. You might make this apparent to the characters during their battles with the machine. They might even suspect that she is involved with its operation (she's not).

There are certain locations that the Knight won't enter or attack the characters. The knight avoids Camp Hummingbird and it won't go into the swamps of Neepawa Bowels. While it might enter the cursed lands of Ayas Kelren, it mostly shies away from there as well.

How to Stop the Knight-in-Shining-Armor

The Knight is relentless, and once it's discovered the characters, it won't let up until they are dead or it is dead. To stop the machine, the characters will need to come up with a creative plan to stop it. Here are some options:

Prevent It from Escaping. Thanks to its regenerative abilities, the Knight wisely flees whenever its hit points are reduced below half. To destroy the machine, the characters will need to find a way to cut off its exits and then destroy it. It won't be easy, however, as the Knight's controller is highly trained and won't let it easily fall into a trap.

Find Help. There are many creatures throughout the Wallingmiotta who may help the characters defeat the remote traveler. A centaur clan may offer to help the characters in exchange for the characters helping them with trespassing hobgoblins. Similarly, Gar Wabrizz

hobgoblins might help the characters if they give the characters provide information on the centaurs. Even the gnomes of Pella's Wish might help. Extra creative characters might even get the bear, Tremor, to help them.

Aruxius

Once the characters locate Aruxius, they find his cabin at the northern end of Neepawa Bowels. Read the following:

> At the top of a great fall, a well-lit cabin stands. Something about this area makes your senses come alive. The leaves on the trees seem brighter. The water feels colder. Even the air feels both abrasive and comforting all at once. A narrow, twisting stone path crawls along the edge of the waterfall to the cabin.
>
> Before you can start your ascent, a bearded gnome trots down the steps, his fair feet smacking in the collected puddles. A corncob pipe pokes out from his thick lips and he squints at you through one, large emerald eye.
>
> "By the trees, it's about damned time. Youda thunk y'all were crossin' the Obsidian Plain or something."
>
> The gnome rubs his round gut and cracks his neck, then turns on heel and heads back up.
>
> "Well, ya comin' or not?"

It's likely the characters assume that the gnome is Aruxius. The gnome is actually the **couatl** Wilgrim in his gnome disguise (see Pella's Wish above). He's visiting Aruxius when the characters show up but is well aware that the characters and O were on their way.

If he's asked whether or not he is Aruxius, he simply shrugs.

> "Maybe I am. Maybe I'm not. Who knows who I am today?"

Wilgrim never reveals his true nature to humanoids. Only Aruxius is aware of Wilgrim's true form.

> The smell of warm, baked goods fills your nostrils. Soft yet lively music from somewhere—you can't quite pinpoint where —plays. The inside of the cabin is quaint and cozy.
>
> Plush furniture fills nearly every nook and cranny. There is furniture in the room for the gnome, smaller than what a human-sized person could sit in, and then is furniture sized for someone much larger.
>
> The gnome skips across the room, snatches a cookie off a platter on one of the small tables, and plops onto a gnome-sized couch.
>
> "Well, it's them, innit?" comes a voice with a thick Murktown accent. You don't immediately see the speaker. The gnome shrugs, taking a bite of the cookie, "I suppose it is."
>
> "Bloody hell, Wil, these hardly look like the saviors of the world!" you finally see the source of the voice. A squirrel wearing northern Omeria livery crawls onto the backside of the couch. Its thick whiskers twitch as it removes its thick, spectacles and cleans them on the edge of its tiny tunic.
>
> "Maybe they are? Maybe they aren't?" the gnome shrugs.

The squirrel isn't Aruxius either. His name is Jelbi, and he is a **fey squirrel** (see Appendix B).

The gnome and squirrel don't say much more than that. Wil answers most direct questions with cryptic answers—"maybe it is, maybe it isn't?"—

whereas Jelbi is a lot shorter in his responses—"the 'ell if I know, mate!"

The characters are free to search the cabin as they please. Overall, there is nothing of value within the cabin. All of the rooms are simple, often over-decorated—like one would expect from a grandmother who keeps every item of sentimental value—and small in some portions while comically oversized in others.

Aruxius' cabin is alive with illusions, as well. Open a drawer and out fly butterflies made of pure light. Look in a mirror and your mirror image starts singing a song back to you. Sneeze and a lamp responds, "Oh my! Bless you."

Once the characters settle in, Aruxius finally arrives.

> Finally, a man wearing a brightly colored robe enters the cabin. The man is easily 8-feet tall, with massive hands and feet. His skin has a gray hue to it, a bit like ash, and his hair is short and blonde. His eyes are golden, like a cat. Still, despite his strange appearance, he smiles warmly when he sees you.
>
> "Well," he says in a low, booming voice. "Here they are."

If Omnaweahl is still with the party:

> Omnaweahl drops to one knee. "My lord, Aruxius, you do us all a great honor by having us in your home."
>
> Aruxius laughs. "Please! Stand Omnaweahl of Odonburg. It is you who do me a great honor by joining me and my friends here."
>
> The giant man squeezes into a large armchair and crosses his feet. Still chuckling, he removes the huge sandals from his feet and sets them next to the chair. The squirrel, Jelbi crawls onto his shoulder.

Aruxius sits quietly while he waits for the characters to speak. If they fail to say anything, Omnaweahl steps in and offers *Prime* to the giant.

> "Ah!" the giant says, taking the book in his huge, gray hands. He pulls a pair of gold-rimmed glasses from the chest pocket of his robe and sets them on his nose at a loose angle so he has to tilt his head to look through them. "I remember this old book."
>
> Aruxius opens the book and thumbs through it. Wil stands and stretches, then walks over.
>
> "Is it still as boring as I remember it?" the gnome asks reading over Aruxius' shoulder.
>
> "Boring to some, maybe," sighs Aruxius. "But to most, a valuable clue."
>
> After a moment he stops looking through the book and shuts it. With the tip of his finger he traces the edge of its cover, smiling nostalgically.
>
> "Two-hundred years ago, this book was given to me as a gift from an old friend. Of course, when it was written, no one knew what it would mean for the world. They just knew it would lead to great danger.
>
> "You see—this is more than just a book, my friends. This is the chill you feel at the back of your neck when something doesn't feel right. This book is the flutter you feel in your chest when you think someone is lying to you. This book is a terrifying

doorway into a new world. One that I'm not sure mankind is ready for.

"The world is full of many monsters, friends. Some monsters have claws and teeth and attack you in the dark and fill the air with their howls. Others are small and invisible, but just as deadly, capable of wiping out entire cultures. And then there are those monsters who are more than just creatures. They are concepts and ideas that infect and spread. Those monsters use weapons of passion, fear, paranoia, and hatred. Those are the most dangerous monsters as you never notice them until it's too late. And the greater those monsters become, the more difficult they are to destroy.

"One of those monsters was spawned from this book."

Aruxius removes his glasses and places them back into his pocket. He stands.

Suddenly, the room grows dim. Red light fills the room from outside, like an eclipse.

If the characters were in Qola when the Black Bird attacked, the scene is similar.

For a moment, you see the world as it truly is: Aruxius is no longer a man, but a great, muscular creature with the features of a tiger, except its fur writhes around it like snakes. The gnome Wilgrim is replaced by a winged serpent wearing an ornate gold headdress. The talking squirrel Jelbi glows, its light illuminating its corner of the room.

The tiger-creature-that-was-once-Aruxius opens its maw. Red light

seeps out like smoke. Without moving its mouth, the creature speaks a phrase in a language you don't understand.

You watch as the cover of the book in his hands starts to melt. The unreadable words dissolve from the front of the cover, then drip onto the floor. For a moment, the phantom ink sizzles before it eventually evaporates. Once the cover of the book completely melts away all that is left is an old bundle of papers held together by two pieces of undecorated plywood and a leather cord.

The room begins to shake violently. Air starts rushing through the windows and doors. All of the furniture in the tiny cabin slides, collapses, and breaks.

The tiger-creature says something again, this time in a language you can understand, "Seek the Tower of Burshai on the tallest peak of the Basilisk's Spine. There, all will be revealed."

And then...

The characters wake, staring at a blue sky, almost as if they had woken from a strange dream. They are on the banks of the same waterfall. The cabin is still there, but it looks as if it's been uninhabited for years. The planks are rotten, the walls are overgrown with ivy, insects and small animals—none of which can speak—crawl through the remains. Even the stone path leading up the waterfall is mostly erased by time's hands. A character who makes a successful DC 10 Intelligence (Nature) check may surmise that the cabin has been like this for at least ten years.

There are no signs that Aruxius, his friends, or even the characters were ever inside.

Despite the strange illusion, one thing remains the same: the characters still have the book *Prime*. Except, it no longer looks as it once did, but as it appeared when it was originally given to Aruxius two hundred years ago.

Burned onto the plywood covers of the book is its true title:

The Journal of Duda Weysevain

Adventure Conclusion

Whether this adventure concludes after the perpetual spell cast upon the book is removed by Aruxius or following a second confrontation with the Knight-in-Shining-Armor, the characters have two major clues.

First, they were told by Aruxius in his **rakshasa** form to find the Tower of Burshai on the tallest peak in the Basilisk's Spine mountains.

Second, they can finally read the contents of *Prime*. *Prime* is none other than *The Journal of Duda Weysevain*, the first northern explorer to cross the Basilisk's Spine Mountains four hundred years ago and discover the Ditimayan people and the coast that now bears his name.

The story continues in Chapter 6 of the ***Hand of the Eight*** adventure path, ***The Fantastic Lie***. Ω

CHAPTER 6: THE FANTASTIC LIE

BY DAVE HAMRICK

4th-Level Adventure for Fifth Edition

Cartography by Dyson Logos

The Fantastic Lie is a 4th-level Fifth Edition adventure for 3-5 characters. Characters who survive the adventure should reach the 5th level by the adventure's conclusion. This is the sixth chapter in **The Hand of Eight** adventure path. It can be played as the kickoff for the larger adventure setting or as a one-shot adventure for your characters to follow. The campaign is intended to be set in the DMDave crowdsourced campaign world of Omeria, but can just as easily be inserted into any other large city overlooking a large ocean or sea.

The first part of the **Hand of the Eight** adventure path draws to a conclusion as the characters travel to the tallest mountain in all of Omeria, Trenrock Mountain in the Basilisk's Spine Mountains. There, they discover the Tower of Burshai. Within the ancient tower, the characters discover that they and nearly every person living in Omeria have all been victims of a centuries-old lie.

Background

Odonburg is a nation of five million humanoids that covers the southern portion of Omeria. Odonburg's capital, also named Odonburg, was founded in 540 AT by two native brothers, Odon and Oxon, both of the Dinzer clans that ruled Ancient Xuchaebar. Odon, of course, became the first Emperor of Odon. Meanwhile, his troubled brother Oxon became one of the first of the Seven Eyes. Oxon retired after a year on the council to begin work on his masterpiece, the Amazing Clock.

The Dinzers, as the people of Odonburg are collectively known, are recognized for two things. First, they are incredibly well-mannered and thoughtful of decorum. Even the toothy wuhlos of Jabros know how to carry themself in front of others. Second, they are by leaps and bounds the most technologically advanced nation in Omeria if not the world. Incorporating magic with modern engineering, Dinzers have turned the jungles and savannahs of southern Omeria into a true utopia. Crime is low, poverty is almost totally eradicated, and on average, Dinzers live 20-30 more years than the other Omerians.

A big part of Odonburg's success in the realms arcane is due to their monopoly of the natural resource emerald Odonburgite. Emerald Odonburgite is a glowing, green gem that emits powerful evocation energy. Energy collected from samples even as small as an acorn is enough to offer an infinite supply of charges for their weapons, vehicles, and other magic items. Unfortunately, emerald Odonburgite is extraordinarily rare. As such, the Dinzers jealously guard their limited supply.

Today, Odonburg celebrates its quincentennial. Throngs of revelers roam through the streets in spontaneous parades. Bars, inns and homes are entering the fourth day of festivities. Even the Holy Palace is alive with cheer. Dinzers all over the long continent recognize their role in creating the greatest nation in the world.

There is one, however, who is not currently celebrating. Holy Evadimus, the 17th Emporer of Odonburg sits at a table with five of the Seven Eyes, his mind troubled by the news of recent events. In addition to the council, the Emporer is joined by representatives of all the major guilds in the nation, as well as his top military strategists. While Evadimus listens to them speak, he thumbs at the tip of his walking stick. The emerald Odonburg wrapped in gold casing at the top of the stick still radiates a dull, green glow.

"Holy Emporer?" asks Qadalf the Storm, Lord General of the Odonburg Men-at-Arms. Evadimus turns his attention back to the others. Qadalf continues.

"Our man in Orbea tracked the party into the Wallingmiotta soon after we disabled her craft. As predicted, they survived. Unfortunately, they still met with the danaavrakt."

"Aruxius," Evadimus nods. "I met him once. I was young. Very tall, if I remember correctly."

"Ah, yes, sir," Qadalf uses a minor illusion spell on the war table to show where the party is currently located. "As you can see, they're still traveling with Omnaweahl the Mago-detective."

"I'm having trouble understanding, Lord General," says the Fourth Eye, Imnotosh, interrupting Qadalf. "Why was the girl not put in the loop? Or why we didn't get someone else who knows all the facts to carry out this mission? Instead, we have one of our own trouncing around through northern Omeria with a group of murderous thugs ready to undo everything that our ancestors spent 500 years to create."

"Plausible deniability, Holy Eye," Qadalf bows his head. "Despite being 'murderous thugs', her cohorts are resourceful. It was best to have someone on the inside who didn't realize they were on the inside."

The council murmurs. Qadalf bites his lip. Evadimus clears his throat.

"Then what are the next steps, Lord Commander?"

"Ah, well, Holy Emporer," Qadalf says, changing the details of the illusion spell to show a snow-covered mountain, likely somewhere in the Basilisk's Spine. "They will undoubtedly head to the Tower of Burshai."

Imnotosh scoffs. An image of a delipidated tower among the Spine's peaks appears in Qadalf's illusion.

"Then all is lost," says the Fourth Eye of Odonburg.

Silence falls over the room. The image of the lonely, snow-capped tower sits at the center of the table. Finally, the Holy Emperor leans forward and speaks.

"We are the children of Odon and Oxon, aren't we? Dinzer blood runs through our veins. Therefore, we must do as we Dinzers always do: expect the best and prepare for the worst."

An hour later, a Dinzer condor-class flyer took off from Odonburg's Skyhold

on a northern trajectory.

Estimated Time of Arrival to the Tower of Burshai: 6.8 hours.

Adventure Summary

The adventure begins when the characters start the arduous journey climbing Trenrock Mountain at the heart of the Basilisk's Spine mountain range. At the top of the mountain, they discover a long-abandoned structure known only as the Tower of Burshai. As they climb through the strange tower, they begin to unravel a vast conspiracy. Once they connect the pieces of the puzzle, they soon learn that everything that they've ever learned is untrue and that the fantastic lie has long blinded them from what is real and what is fake.

At the end of their journey, just as they learn the truth, someone they thought to be their ally appears and reveals their true nature. From there, the characters are given a difficult choice:

Do they share what they learned with the rest of the world?

Or do they allow the fantastic lie to continue?

Adventure Hooks

Following their meeting with the danaavrakt Aruxius, the party should know the secrets of the book, Prime. No longer masked by Aruxius' illusion spell, the characters are free to read the book revealed to be the Journal of Duda Weysevain. Allow the characters to read the snippets from the book presented as a player's handout in the adventure supplement.

It's a long journey from the location of Aruxius' cabin to their destination, Trenrock Mountain. You are free to fast forward to their arrival at the goblin village of Mogresz, or you can have them travel through the Wallingmiotta and Gar Wabrizz. It's ultimately up to you.

While this adventure is intended to be played as part of the Hand of the Eight adventure path, you can also run it as a separate adventure. If you do, here are some hooks you can use:

Military Activity

For whatever reason, there has been notable military activity in the Basilisk's Spine Mountains. The party has been tasked by the government of Knotside to uncover what's happening on the Spine, specifically around Trenrock Mountain.

Mountain Climbers

The party has heard that Trenrock Mountain is the tallest in all of Omeria and that no one has yet tamed it. The goblins of Mogresz are even offering a 500 gp reward to the first person or party that can summit it.

Mysterious Tower

Supposedly, an ancient mage tower sits at the top of Trenrock Mountain, the tallest mountain in the Basilisk's Spine. Legends say the tower is filled with all sorts of magic artifacts.

Mogresz

Mogrez is less a village than a permanent goblinoid encampment at the southern end of Gar Wabrizz. Jammed into the rocks at the base of an imposing cliff face known as the Walls of the Woink, Mogresz is home to 60-some goblins. It was settled a decade ago by the great goblin warrior Woink the Beard. Woink was known for collecting elven ears and placing them on a necklace. At one point, Woink's necklace was so thick with pointed ears it looked like a fleshy, rotting beard—hence the name. The majority of Mogresz's inhabitants are veterans of the Elven Wars, who now live in the village with their extended families. Far enough away from their continued aggression with the elves of Olyothyr, the Mogreszians cater to tourists and thrillseekers who hope to pass the Basilisk's Spine at its thickest point. Seeing as the mortality rate is at its highest at this point, they

always collect payment in advance.

When the players are ready, read the following:

> It's been a long journey from the Wallingmiotta to the foot of the Basilisk's Spine Mountains, but you've finally arrived in the goblin village of Mogresz. In the background, the mighty spires of the Basilisk's Spine Mountains act as a dark wall to Central Omeria.
>
> Like much of Gar Wabrizz, the goblins are comfortable around the presence of "tall ones." After all, it's their lands. And with the exception of the elves to the west, no humanoid has drawn arms against the Garrish in close to a century.
>
> Still, the squat, green and orange humanoids throw you a wary eye. Less to say, "What are you doing here?" and more to ask, "Why are you here?"
>
> A little over two weeks ago, Omnaweahl made arrangements for you to meet a guide in town named Heekt. Deemed "the best mountain guide this side of the Basilisk" Heekt came with high praise. As you walk past the wooden palisades into the mud-caked village, she motions to a

tall, narrow, thatch-roofed hut with a sign written in Goblin.

The sign reads: "Heekt's Tours for Not Smart Humans."

Heekt

Heekt's hut is a 5-foot diameter, mud-floored hovel that leaks from multiple holes in its thatching. It reeks of urine and more-often-than-not Heekt is found sleeping on a short, lumpy bed, his oversized frost-bitten feet hanging over the edge.

Once awakened (it'll take a minute), Heekt stands up, cracks his back and puts his moldy, yak-wool ushanka on his head. He then smiles and says, "Y'okay."

From there, he's all business. The charge for his services is 10 gold pieces per day to lead the characters through the Spine to the base of Trenrock Mountain. He places the gold under his hat, pats a curved dagger he wears on his hip, winks, then goes right to it.

Heekt is a **goblin** with proficiency in Intelligence (Nature) and Wisdom (Survival). He adds double his proficiency bonus when he makes checks using either of those skills as they relate to the Basilisk's Spine Mountains.

With Heekt as their guide, the party will have no trouble finding their way through the mountain pass.

Overall, Heekt is a fun, talkative NPC with plenty of quirks. He loves talking about the flora and fauna he finds along the way (whether the characters want him to or not). Although small, he's completely unhindered by the snow and difficult terrain of the pass. Frequently, he'll rush ahead, turn back, and look confused that the characters aren't moving at the same pace as he. Also, Heekt also has an irrational fear of the number eight. If Heekt, the party, and Omnaweahl number eight total people, he'll refuse to go until someone exits the group (he gladly will) or they add someone else. His friend Kaybo will join the party as a porter for an additional 10 gp per day. As a **goblin** with a Strength score of 8, Kaybo is a lousy porter. Together, the two will argue in Goblin about sports—particularly goblin footie—all the way up the pass.

Finally, Heekt's catchphrase is "Y'okay." He says it when he's happy, mad, sad, and every emotion in between.

Stocking Up in Mogresz

Being out of the way like they are, Mogresz allows the laws of supply-and-demand to rule their prices. The characters can expect nearly everything in the small, goblin village to cost twice what it normally does. Furthermore, there's a chance that the goblins will reject any non-Garrish currency given to them, especially if it's elven.

Heekt will remind the party to stock up on plenty of climber's kits as well as enough rations to last a month or two. He warns that it's roughly 5-10 days to the base camp, and then it takes another 30-40 days to summit the mountain.

If the party is low on gold, Omnaweahl can spot them whatever they need for the journey (within reason).

Basilisk's Spine Mountains

As the tallest and largest mountain range in Omeria, the Basilisk's Spine Mountains are likely to be one of the greatest challenges that the characters ever face. While passable in certain parts, the area where the characters begin their journey is known all over the continent for the danger it represents. Very few creatures that lack methods of flight have ever made it up Trenrock. Even then, the high winds at the top of the mountain make it almost impossible for flyers. Not even the stormborne vultures of the Weysevain Coast can approach the top due to its winds. Superstitious goblins—such as Heekt and Kaybo—believe that air elementals known as djinn protect the mountain from the lower folk. Only their children, the windborne, can enter the domain of the djinns without drawing their wrath.

Journey to the Base Camp

It's approximately 50 miles from Mogresz to the Trenrock Base Camp. Even with Heekt as a guide, it takes 5 days for the characters to reach the camp. Harsh weather, rugged terrain, and aggressive creatures hug the narrow passages to the base camp. As the characters travel to the base camp, roll a d20 three times per day of game time, checking for encounters each morning, afternoon, and evening or night. An encounter occurs on a roll of 16 or higher. An encounter occurs on a roll of 16 or higher. Then, roll another d20 and check the Basilisk's Spine Encounters table to determine the nature of the encounter.

On a result of "Another expedition" the party encounters 1d4 + 1 **guards** led by another **goblin** (likely a friend of Heekt's) heading back to Mogresz. They appear tired, hungry, and even have a few injured among them. They recommend that the characters turn back.

Basilisk's Spine Encounters	
d10	**Encounter**
1	1 **air elemental**
2	1 **basilisk**
3	2d8 + 1 **blood hawks**
4	1 **bulette**
5	1 **druid**
6	1 **giant goat**
7	1 **manticore**
8	1 **ogre**
9	1 **saber-toothed tiger**
10	Another expedition

Trenrock Mountain

Trenrock Mountain is 29,030 feet high. Very few humanoids have ever reached the top of the mountain. Of course, thousands of tried. Too difficult to recover, their corpses litter the mountain, especially within 1,500 feet of the mountain.

This section contains information that will help you run this part of the adventure smoothly. For each day that the party travels up the mountain, follow these steps:

- Using the Trenrock Mountain progress map, identify the mark on the map that the characters are in. If the characters have become lost or had to backtrack, don't share this information with the players. Otherwise, you can show them where they are.
- Let the players determine whether or not they wish to keep moving or to rest. While there should be a sense of urgency, the exhaustion of climbing the mountain may require them to take some time off the trail.
- Check for the mountain's weather conditions to see how difficult the DC to continue will be. If effects such as extreme cold, high wind, and heavy precipitation come up, apply the conditions for the day and make the appropriate checks.
- Let the players choose a navigator,

then make a Wisdom (Survival) check on the navigator's behalf to determine if the party becomes lost.

- Certain areas on the map have keyed encounters. See the Trenrock Encounters section below for details.
- At the end of the day, mark off rations and water the party has used.

Travel on the Mountain

Even though it's only 22 miles from the base camp to Trenrock's summit, because of the difficulty involved, characters moving at a normal pace can only travel 1 half mile per day. Each mark on the Trenrock Progress Map equals 1 half mile.

If characters move at a fast pace, the easiest way to deal with their progress is to roll a d4. On a roll of 3 or 4, they advance 1 additional half mile that day. Characters moving at a fast pace take a -5 penalty to their passive Wisdom (Perception) scores, making them more likely to miss clues and walk into ambushes.

If characters set a slow pace, roll a d4. On a roll of 1 or 2, they do not advance that day. On any other result, their caution is rewarded, and they travel the same distance as a group moving at a normal pace. Characters moving at a slow pace can move stealthily. As long as they're not in the open, they can try to surprise or sneak by other creatures they encounter.

Weather Conditions

With winter fast approaching, Trenrock is subject to all manner of horrible weather. At the start of each day, roll percentile dice and consult with the Trenrock Weather Conditions table below. For each day that the party has been traveling up the mountain, add 1 to the roll (to a maximum of 30). The effects listed are detailed in the *DMG*.

Navigation

Have the players designate one party member as the navigator. The navigator might be an NPC, such as a guide, and the party can switch its

Trenrock Mountain Weather Conditions			
d100	Weather Conditions	DC	Effects
0-10	Cold, no wind	10	—
11-45	Cold, windy	15	—
46-70	Cold, moderate winds, light accumulation	20	Extreme cold
70-98	Very cold, high winds, moderate accumulation	20	Extreme cold, high winds
99+	Blizzard conditions	25	Extreme cold, high winds, heavy precipitation

navigator day to day. At the start of each new travel day, the GM makes a Wisdom (Survival) check on behalf of the navigator. The result of the check determines whether or not the party becomes lost over the course of the day. The DC of the check is based on the day's weather conditions. See the Trenrock Weather Conditions table below for details. Apply a +5 bonus to the check if the group sets a slow pace for the day, or a -5 penalty if the group is moving at a fast pace.

If the check succeeds, the navigator knows exactly where the party is on the Trenrock Mountain Progress Map.

If the check fails, the party becomes sidetracked and lost. Roll a d4. On a result of 3 or 4, the party is lost but did not lose any progress. On a result of 1 or 2, the party goes back one space on the progress chart. Until they find their path again, they are not aware that they've lost their progress or how much they've lost.

Trenrock Encounters

Although there are no random encounters on the mountain, there are harrowing moments and points of interest along the way. Each of the encounters is keyed to a letter on the Trenrock Mountain Progress Map.

Base Camp. The base camp of Trenrock Mountain is a rocky, flat clearing. Litter is strewn about, signs that other groups have been through the pass. However, there are no other expeditions around. Heekt explains that with winter fast approaching "only fools and

madmen" dare to summit Trenrock. He offers no guesses as to which the characters are but assumes they are probably both.

Heekt warns that it's an arduous journey from the base camp to the top of the mountain, a task that will take the characters over a month to perform. Like many of the goblins of his village, he believes that Trenrock is cursed. Tales of those who've perished along the way rising from the dead to attack travelers are enough to keep Heekt from going any further. No amount of gold or non-magical persuasion will change his mind. He does hope, however, that if the characters are successful, they visit him again to tell their tale. The goblin then heads back to Mogresz.

After Heekt leaves, the party is free to rest at the base camp as long as they need it. They have a long journey ahead of them.

A - The Wailing Pass. The long narrow path that hugs the base of Trenrock is known as the Wailing Pass. It stretches for nearly 5-miles and is filled with rocky crevasses, snowdrifts, sliding rocks, and other challenges. Many who climb Trenrock fail to get past the pass. The characters are able to get through most of it without any issues until they reach the midway point of the pass. When they reach the spot marked A on the map, read the following:

> If the last few days of travel weren't bad enough, it's just gotten worse. The narrow, snow-covered path

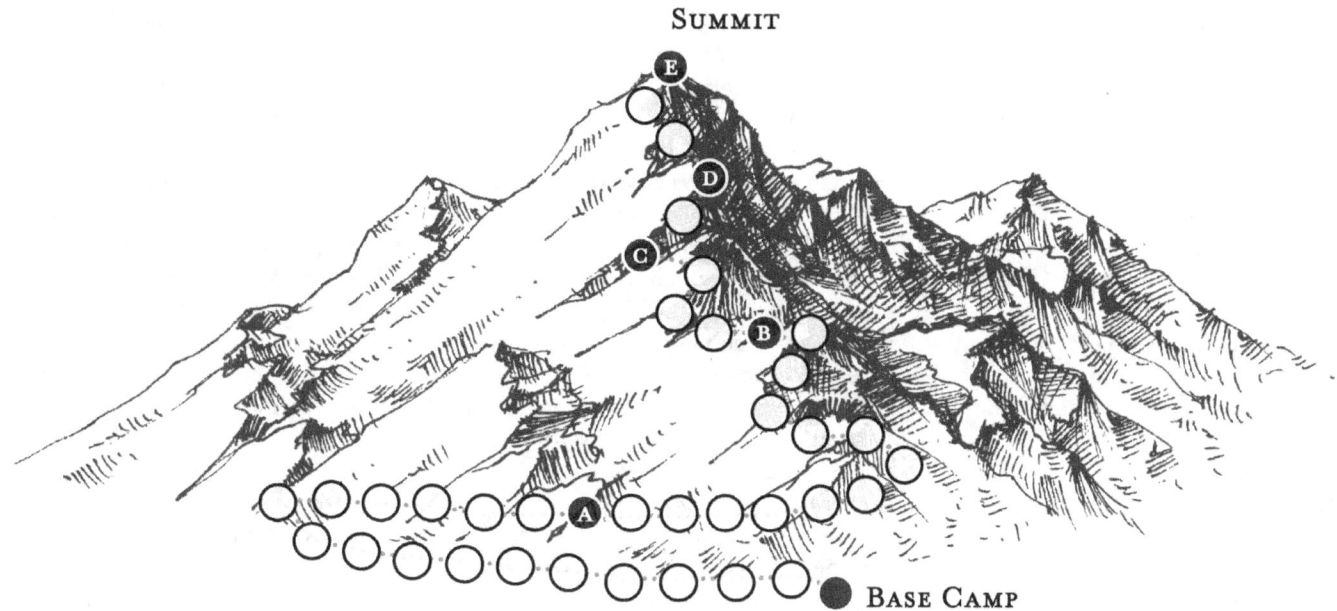

SUMMIT

E

D

C

B

A

BASE CAMP

TRENROCK MOUNTAIN PROGRESS MAP

you've sidled across for the last three days abruptly comes to an end. It looks as if the path itself slid down the mountain. The only thing between you and the far side is a sheer drop easily 300 feet down. Up above you, there is nothing but cliff face and the lumbering mountain above.

From where they're standing, it's 100-feet to the other side. The path they are on is 5-feet wide at its widest point. The drop from where they are is 300-feet straight down. They have a few options.

A character can make DC 10 Wisdom (Survival) check. On a successful check, they realize that there might be another path around. The path would take two days to get back to. From there, it takes 1d6 + 1 days for them to get back on track (however, they won't know that until the added time comes to an end).

It is possible to climb along the cliffside to the other side of the gorge. A character without a climb speed who chooses this route must make a Strength (Athletics) check at the start of each of their turns. If the character moves at less than half their movement speed (minimum of 5 feet), they add +5 to their check. Refer to the Sidling results table below to check their progress.

If the character has a rope secured to them and they slip, the creature that

is holding the rope must make a DC 10 Strength saving throw. The creature adds +5 to the saving throw for each additional creature holding the rope. On a successful saving throw, the character stops falling. Otherwise, the character pulls the creature down with them.

A creature who falls off the edge takes 1d6 falling damage for every 10 feet that they fall (to a maximum of 20d6). The gorge is 300 feet deep.

Sliding Results	
Check Total	**Result**
5 or less	The character slips and falls.
6-10	The character makes no forward progress this turn.
11-20	The character moves at half their normal movement speed.
21+	The character moves at half their normal movement speed plus an additional 5 feet.

B - Dinzer Attack. As the characters are climbing a particularly difficult stretch of the mountain, they hear the sounds of something approaching from the south. Depending on the weather conditions, they may not be able to make out exactly what it is. However, the roar of the engines should become apparent once they are within 5 miles (1 if there's heavy wind).

The characters have exactly one round to realize what's happening. If Omnaweahl is with them, she knows what it is: "Condors! Get down!"

At this point, everyone needs to roll initiative. The Dinzer condor is 1 mile away, so it's unlikely that the characters will have a mode to attack them. But at the speeds they travel, they will be within range in two rounds.

Once the condor arrives, it launches a fireball at the mountainside. Any characters that are clearly visible when this happens will be targeted by the fireball (DC 14 Dexterity saving throw). Immediately after the condor attacks, it flies out of range (moving at speeds of 300 miles per hour). If there are no visible targets, the condor fires in the general area.

Of course, the fireball isn't the only thing the characters have to worry about. The explosion triggers an avalanche.

Each creature on the mountain during the avalanche must immediately make a DC 12 Strength saving throw.

On a failed saving throw, the creature is buried under snow, taking 13 (3d8) bludgeoning damage plus 13 (3d8) cold damage as a result. The creature is also blinded, restrained and is suffocating. At the end of each of their turns, if the creature is still restrained, it takes an additional 4 (1d8) cold damage. On the restrained creature's turn, it can use its action to make a DC 10 Wisdom (Survival) check to determine which way it is oriented. On a successful check, the creature knows which way is up. On its next turn and each subsequent turn, it can use its action to make a DC 10 Strength (Athletics) check. On a successful check, the creature is no longer blinded, restrained, or suffocating.

A creature that succeeds its initial saving throw takes half as much bludgeoning and cold damage but suffers no other ill effects from the avalanche.

A creature can also search for a creature buried in the avalanche by making a successful DC 10 Intelligence (Nature) check. Once they've located their ally, they can use their action to dig the creature out (no check required).

Following the disaster, if Omnaweahl survived, she's in an extreme shock that her own people would attack her. It's clear that everything she's ever believed in has slowly started to unravel during the adventure. For the rest of the journey, she stays quiet and seems aloof.

C - The Prismatic Road. With only a few thousand feet to go before the characters reach the top, they come to the Prismatic Road, named so for the colorful banners and clothing buried under the snow and ice. The Prismatic Road is doubly cursed.

First, once the characters enter the area, they feel an overwhelming sense of dread fall over them. For whatever reason, something in the back of their minds is telling them to go no further. A creature in the area must make a DC 12 Wisdom saving throw. Creatures immune to being charmed automatically pass their saving throws. A creature that fails its Wisdom saving throw gains a curse. While cursed, the creature is stunned. If the creature leaves the Prismatic Road (it's approximately 100-feet long) the curse automatically ends for it and it is no longer stunned. A remove curse spell removes the curse and makes the creature immune to the effects of the road for 24 hours.

Second, those that have succumbed to the curse rise from the ice as zombies. Sixteen **zombies** attack. The zombies are immune to cold damage.

Any creature that dies on the Prismatic Road returns as a zombie in 24 hours.

D - The Tower of Burshai. The characters' destination is not actually at the top of the peak, but a few thousand feet before it. The Tower of Burshai is detailed below.

E - Trenrock Mountain Summit. The top of the 29,030-foot mountain offers an outstanding view of the world around it. A creature standing at the top can see over 220 miles in all directions—weather permitting, of course. Beyond the bragging rights that come with summitting the tallest mountain in Omeria, there is nothing else to be found there.

The Tower of Burshai

As the characters come into view of the Tower, read or paraphrase the following:

> Jutting out of the rock and snow like an old, broken dagger, a 300-foot tall tower made from the same black stone as the mountain stands on the path before you. Cracked and crumbling in various places, the most unusual feature of the tower is the large missing section at its center. While any mundane tower would surely collapse with such damage, the tower's upper section remains aloft, floating in space as if it was still one whole piece.
>
> This must be the Tower of Burshai.

Shortly after the founding of Odonburg, a group of adventurers discovered the abandoned tower. Although there are theories, no one is sure who or what created the original structure. However, what its new purpose would be was automatically clear. Recently appointed Emporer Odon tasked a unit of 20 Dinzers to reach the tower and convert it into an arcane amplifier. As the highest known spot in the land, its reach would be considerable.

For a time, a small group of specialists remained at the tower. And then, as the centuries rolled on, most forgot about the Tower of Burshai. Of course, records were kept of its location and purpose by the highest-ranking Dinzer officials. When those officials would step down and name their replacement, the replacement was debriefed on the Tower. For many, the tower's purpose was a lot to take in and some couldn't handle it. Those who refused to play a part stepped away from their roles. Shortly thereafter, their memories were modified to forget what they learned.

General Features

Unless otherwise stated, the tower has the following features.

Ceiling. The ceilings throughout each level are twenty feet high. They are made of the same soft, metal alloy that the doors, floors, and walls are made of.

Communication Panels. Set into the wall beside most of the doors is a screen. The screen has two uses. First, a properly credentialed Dinzer can wave their hand in front of it in order to open the door (see below). Second, the screen creates two-dimensional illusions of the areas of the tower both providing a map of the tower as well as giving access to a communication system. If a character touches an area on the map, it highlights. From there, they can speak into the panel. In doing so, their voice is broadcast into the area as if by the magic mouth spell.

Detect Magic. The entire tower exudes faint traces of illusion and transmutation magic.

Doors. Many of the doors are made from soft steel unlike anything the characters have used or seen. The doors that are still standing automatically slide open when a credentialed Dinzer (like Omnaweahl) waves his or her hand in front of the panel. Otherwise, a sealed door requires a successful DC 15 Strength (Athletics) check to pry open. Furthermore, a character can spend 1 minute examining the mechanisms to better understand how they work. At the end of the minute, they must make a DC 15 Intelligence (Arcana) check. On a success, the doors open automatically for them for the remainder of their duration in the tower.

Floors. Like the ceilings, doors, and walls, the floors are made of a soft metal alloy. Carpeting is common throughout, but much of it has rotted away from the arid conditions. In some areas, water pools from where it enters the holes in the ceilings and walls.

Light. Unless the ceiling is missing, any time the characters enter a new level or interior area of the tower, panels in the ceiling automatically light up as if affected by the light spell. The lights can detect the presence of living things, so undead and constructs won't trigger them. A creature can operate the lights by saying "lights on" or "lights off" aloud. Also, the lights automatically turn off after 1-minute passes of no living creatures in an area.

Power Cells. Many of the magic features of the tower are powered by emerald Odonburgite kept in the two columns in **Area 14**. If the Odonburgite is removed, all of the magical features in the tower cease to function.

Walls. All of the walls are made from a dense-yet-soft metal alloy that exudes faint traces of illusion and transmutation magic. A character that makes a successful DC 10 Intelligence check with a relevant tool proficiency—such as carpentry or masonry—recognizes that the architecture is unlike anything they have ever seen. It is aberrant in its design.

Keyed Encounters

The following encounters are keyed to the locations marked on the maps of the Tower of Burshai. **Areas 1** through **11** are on the map on page 138, **Areas 12** through **23** through **30** are on the map on page 141, and **Areas 24** through **30** on page 143.

1 - Entrance. As the characters approach, read or paraphrase the following:

> Just ahead you see the door into the tower. It seems to be made of some sort of steel with a seam running down its center. There are no handles or hinges that you can detect.

If Omnaweahl or another Dinzer is with the party, the door opens the moment they step within 5 feet of it. Immediately, the lights within the first level spring to life.

2 - Checkpoint. The first time the characters enter this area, read:

> Panels in the ceiling glow with dim light, illuminating this room 20-foot wide and 10-foot deep entryway. Opposite the entrance, a pair of double doors similar to the ones you just walked through are set into the wall.

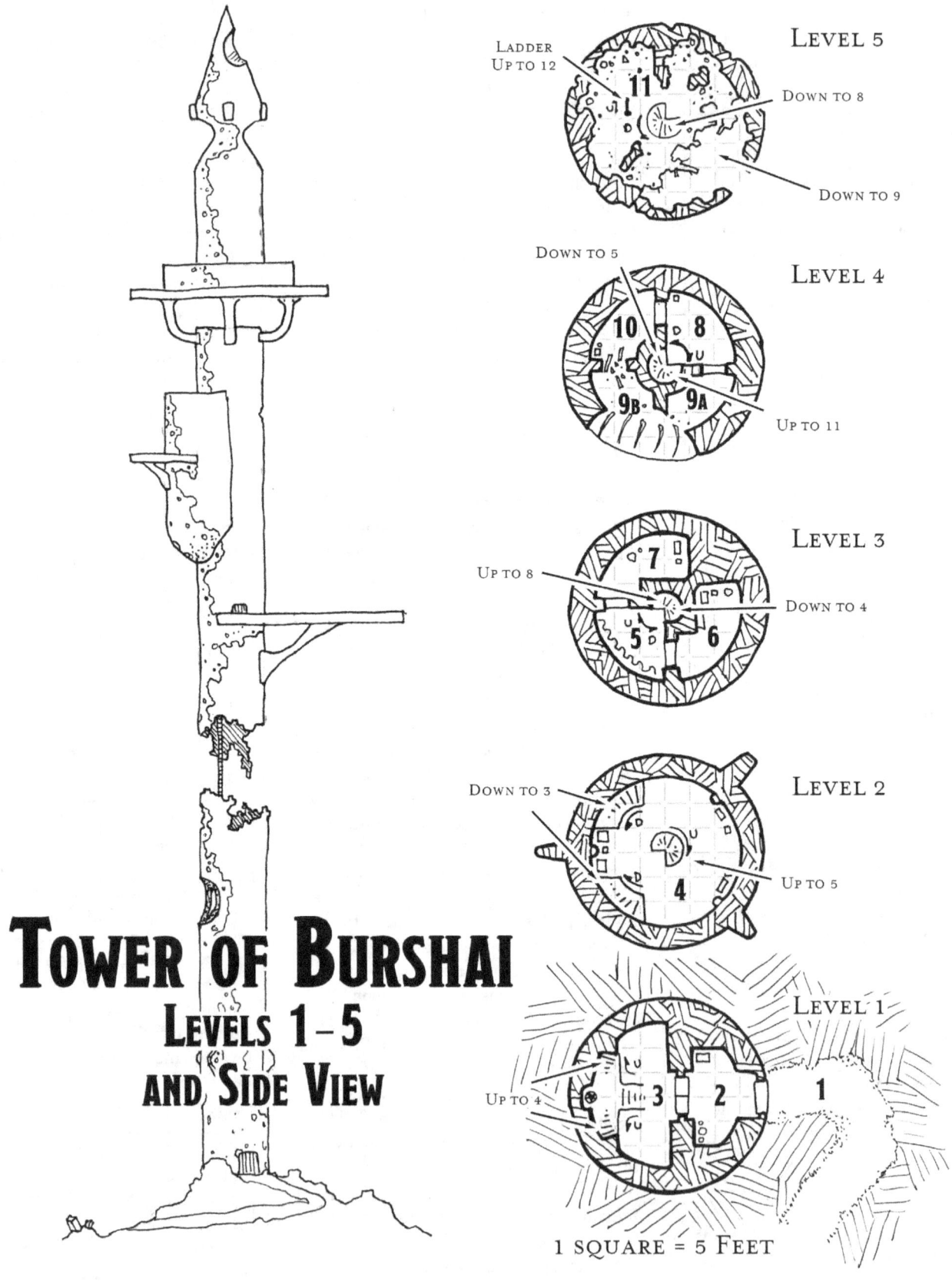

LADDER
UP TO 12

LEVEL 5

11

DOWN TO 8

DOWN TO 9

DOWN TO 5

LEVEL 4

10 8

9B 9A

UP TO 11

LEVEL 3

UP TO 8

7

DOWN TO 4

5 6

LEVEL 2

DOWN TO 3

UP TO 5

4

LEVEL 1

UP TO 4

3 2 1

1 SQUARE = 5 FEET

TOWER OF BURSHAI
LEVELS 1–5
AND SIDE VIEW

In a nook in the northern wall, a podium made of the same strange, soft steel that the doors, walls, and ceiling were made of stands. Oddly, there is no dust in the room. It's as if the tower was in use literally minutes before you entered.

Although the temperatures are freezing outside, the room you are in slowly starts to warm. Within minutes, it's at a comfortable temperature.

Originally, this area was a checkpoint for people entering the tower. A guard stood at the podium and checked credentials. The panel on the podium functions as one of the communication panels described under General Features.

3 - Gathering Hall and Stairs.

This room is 30-feet wide north-to-south and 15-feet wide east-to-west. A staircase in the center of the western wall rises ten feet then diverts at its landing. At the center of the landing set into the wall is the statue of the wizard Odon.

4 - Lower Control Room.

This room is a 30-foot diameter circle. Two staircases set into the western wall descend while a spiral staircase at the center of the room continues upward. Against the eastern wall are two large curved desk 10 feet apart. Above each desk are panes of blackened glass that seemingly float in space. The desks are covered in arcane glyphs that radiate green light.

The two panels were security panels for the tower. In addition to the desks, there are multiple chairs throughout the room.

A creature that uses the control panels can operate it as a crystal ball that projects its images on the screen. The magic in the screens ceases to function if removed from the area.

Encounter. Six remote travelers (use the **animated armor** stat block except they have the Intelligence, Wisdom, and Charisma scores of a **mage**) guard this room. They are piloted by Dinzers over 1,000 miles away. None of them will reveal their true identity, although it's likely Omnaweahl recognizes that they are Dinzer-made. In addition, she points out that they are 721 models, over three centuries old.

Treasure. Resting on one of the control panels is an old *wand of magic missiles*. Its emerald Odonburgite battery is dead, so it only has 4 charges remaining.

5 - Banner. Hanging against the southwestern wall is a 500-year-old version of the flag of Odonburg, still in mostly perfect condition.

6 - Rest Chamber.

This unusually shaped room is shaped like an "L". At the far side of a room, there is a desk with books stacked upon it. A pair of red and blue robes hang from hooks. The most unusual thing, however, is the seven-foot-tall black cylinder against the innermost wall. There is a small, rectangular glass window, allowing you to look inside it. It appears to be empty.

The cylinder is a sleeping sarcophagus. By speaking the command word "Time to Sleep" the sarcophagus opens. If a Medium or Small creature steps inside, the sarcophagus closes behind the creature and then creates a sleep effect. A creature who does not wish to be affected by the sleep effect must succeed on a DC 10 Constitution saving throw. Otherwise, they fall unconscious for 1 minute. During that minute, the interior of the sarcophagus emits a dull green light. At the end of the minute, the light vanishes, the creature wakens and the sarcophagus opens. The creature then gains the same benefits as if they had just completed a long rest. Plus, the sarcophagus' energy provides

the creature as much nourishment as if they consumed 1 day of rations and the required allotment of water. Once a creature uses the chamber, they cannot gain the benefits from the chamber again for 8 hours. Other creatures are still free to use it.

The books in the room give a little insight into the chamber's original inhabitant. The titles are A Treatise of Ettercap Biology by Onerius, Fey and their Origins by Shebaris, The Myth of the Titans by Ilrune Entumal, and The Complete History of Olyothyr Part 1. The Age of the Fey also by Ilrune Entumal (the latter two are written in elvish).

7 - Rest Chamber.

This unusually shaped room is shaped like an "L". At the far side of a room, there is a desk with books stacked upon it. A pair of red and blue robes hang from hooks. The most unusual thing, however, is the seven-foot-tall black cylinder against the innermost wall. There is a small, rectangular glass window, allowing you to look inside it. Within, you see the mummified remains of a humanoid.

500 years ago, one of the Dinzers working in the tower went to sleep in their sleep sarcophagus and never woke up. If the chamber is opened using the command word "Time to Sleep" the creature attacks as a **mummy**. However, it's been in the chamber so long, it's picked up a new trait: Regeneration. At the start of its turn, the mummy regains 10 hit points as long as it has 1 hit point remaining. If the mummy takes fire damage, this trait doesn't function at the start of its next turn. The mummy is CR 4 (1,100 XP).

Once the chamber is clear of its undead inhabitant, it functions the same way the sleep sarcophagus described in **Area 6** does.

The books in the room are *The 10th Level* by Odon (still a commonly printed book in Odonburg), *Practical Trans-mutation* by Tifarihm, and *All Living Things* by Hulay of Elsath. The latter is written in a hodgepodge of Celestial and Infernal. Unless a creature can read and understand both languages, it's exceptionally difficult to read without magic.

Treasure. Tucked into the copy of *All Living Things* is a *scroll of comprehend languages*.

8 - Fourth Level Passage. Once the characters reach the top of the steps from the level below, read the following:

> This area is cold and dark. To either side of you are sealed doors. They do not appear to be operational. A huge hole in the ceiling gives you a glimpse into the floor above which seems to be mostly destroyed. In fact, you can see outside the tower from where you stand.

The two doors in this passage leading to **Areas 9a** and **10** no longer operate automatically. Both require successful DC 15 Strength (Athletics) checks to pry open. Once a door is opened, cold air rushes into the area thanks to the gaping holes in the wall.

9a - Destroyed Office. This room was an office. Long ago, something attacked the tower, destroying the room. Now it lies in ruin. None of the magical effects that pervade the rest of the tower function in this room. Exposed to the elements, freezing wind flies in from the mountainside.

9b - Destroyed Resting Chamber. Similar to **Areas 6** and **7**, this was once a resting chamber. However, the sarcophagus was torn from the room and launched out onto the side of the mountain. A creature that gazes out of the massive hole in the wall can see for 200 miles to the south.

Treasure. Amid the rubble of the room, the characters can find a single, intact *fireball bead*, as the *necklace of fireballs*.

10 - Destroyed Study.

> This room is dark and empty. At the south end, where a door probably once stood, is a large hole in the wall. Just beyond it, there is another larger hole that looks out on the southside of Trenrock Mountain.

11 - Shattered Floor. Whatever damaged the tower years ago removed much of this level. All of the walls have collapsed. The upper end of the tower floats above. The only thing connecting this level to the next is a simple ladder, but definitely not for structural purposes. Judging by its rusted iron composition and less-than-smooth craftsmanship it was a later addition to the tower.

At the northwestern end of the room, buried in rubble, is a skeleton wearing the blue and red robes of Odonburg (albeit, a few hundred years old). Its right hand is permanently locked in a somatic component. A character with proficiency in Arcana automatically recognizes it as the hand symbol for the chill touch cantrip.

12a - Shattered Landing. The door here still functions. However, the lights and other amenities no longer work. It is cold and dark.

12b - Destroyed Work Room. The other side of the landing are the remains of an old workroom. Most of the books are burned (a combination of fire and radiant damage) but there

are still some old charts on the walls. The charts depict spider-like creatures that bear a slight resemblance to krigs although they are missing their extra arms and prominent abdomens.

13 - Record Room.

> This semi-circle room is 30 feet wide north-to-south and fifteen feet deep. A large, curved staircase hugs the way to the south ascending to the floor above. Against the interior wall next to the door are three large black cabinets each with dozens of square slots built into the faces.

The cabinets are locked exactly the same way the doors are. A Dinzer with the proper credentials need only to touch the center of a square slot and a bar slides out. The bar is two feet long and four inches wide and tall. There are six three-inch diameter balls made of dull green crystal fit into slots on each bar. In total, each cabinet holds 270 of the balls.

Each ball stores hundreds of hours of recordings. To access the recordings, a creature needs only to hold the crystal ball and say a command word—the ball then creates an illusion of the events held within its memory in a space within 15 feet of its user. The wielder can then use additional command words to pause, fast forward, rewind, or jump ahead to any point in the recorded illusion. Most of the illusions show the Dinzer inhabitants of the tower centu-

Tower of Burshai Records	
Result	Cumulative lore learned
9 or less	Nothing important learned
10-15	The Tower of Burshai was being converted into an arcane beacon. The Dinzer researchers who worked there planned to use it to cast some sort of massive illusion spell that would affect most of Central Omeria. They seemed to have trouble getting it to work.
16-20	In addition to the beacon, the tower was a research facility. The Dinzers researched fey, ettercap, and elves. They ran many experiments, especially on elves, exposing them to emerald Odonburgite.
21+	Oxon eventually came to the tower and took control of operations. Many of the researchers were nervous around the former Eye and believed that he was planning to stop the research.

ries ago recording their findings into the crystal balls. The majority of the information is dull and not useful.

However, a creature who spends 1 hour viewing the contents of the crystal balls can make an Intelligence (Arcana) check. Depending on the result of the roll, they learn one or more pieces of lore about the tower. Each piece of lore is cumulative. So if a character rolls a 16 for their Intelligence (Arcana) check they learn the lore for both the 10-15 results as well as 16-20.

14 - Seventh Floor.

> This 30-foot diameter room has four large columns at its center. All four of the columns emit soft, green light from bands carved into them. Stairs leading to the floor below and the floor above are in the southern and western walls. There is another door that exits to the east.

A careful search of a column—a successful DC 15 Intelligence (Investigation) check—reveals small trap doors in each. A Dinzer with the proper credentials can touch the trap door to open it. Inside is a single, plum-sized hunk of emerald Odonburgite. The Odonburgite is worth 750 gp when sold. Removing both powers down the station as detailed in General Features.

15 - Landing Pad. When the characters step outside, read the following:

> You step through the door and immediately you're hit with cold mountain air. It appears that you are on a large, exterior platform that is 50-feet wide on either side. It lacks a railing of any sort. You can see for miles around you. At the far side of the platform, a large, wrinkled mass clumps against the platform.

Originally, this was a landing pad for Dinzer transport ships.

The black mass was once one of those ships. Long ago, something destroyed it, melting it into a mass of black,

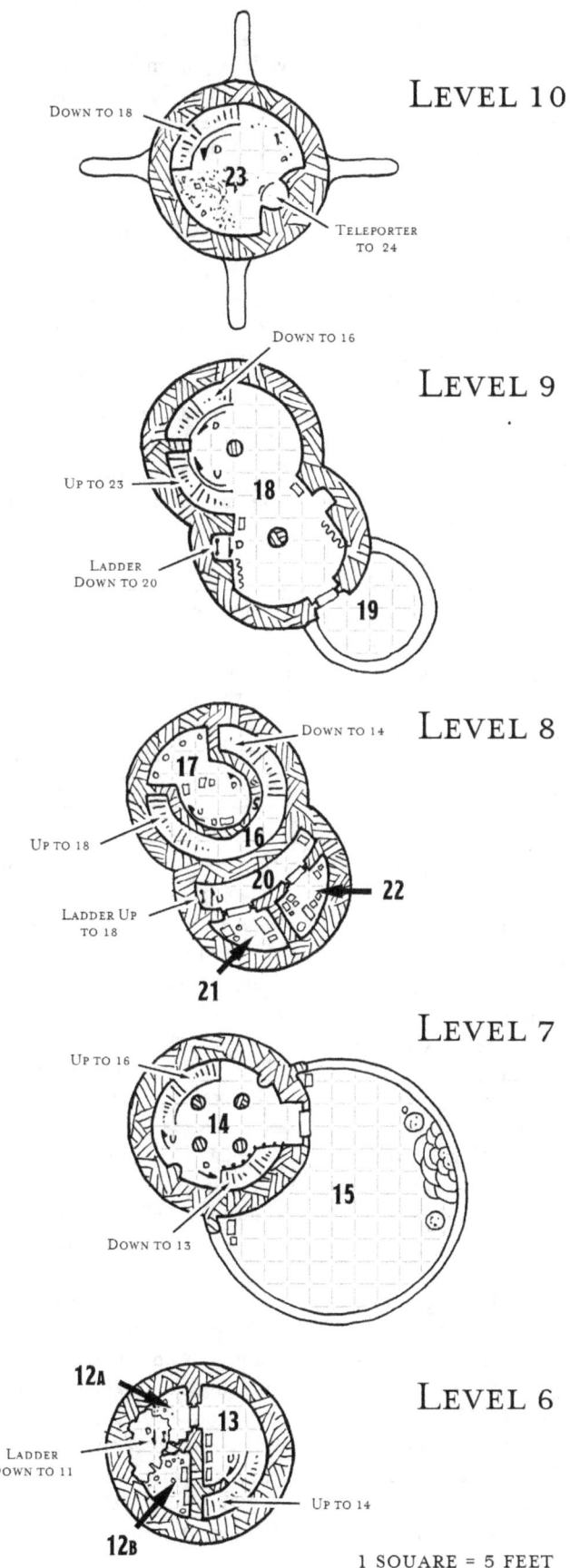

highly-radioactive rock. Any creature that starts their turn within 15 feet of the mass must make a DC 15 Constitution saving throw. On a failed saving throw, the creature takes 13 (3d8) radiant damage and is poisoned. While the creature remains poisoned, it cannot regain hit points except through magical means and its hit point maximum decreases by 9 (2d8) for every 24 hours that elapse. A creature that succeeds on its saving throw takes half the amount of radiant damage and isn't poisoned.

16 - Passage. The stairs continue around the bend. At the center of the landing is a secret door. Finding the door requires a DC 15 Intelligence (Investigation) check. It does not operate the same way that the other doors within the complex do, so the only way to open it is with a successful DC 15 Strength (Athletics) check.

17 - Core Room. When the characters enter, read:

> This room is dark except for a pale, white light that comes from the western side of the room, some 15-feet from you. It appears that this room was once some sort of laboratory. All around are alchemical vials, beakers, and potion bottles. In addition to the other alchemist's supplies, there are seemingly hundreds of dull green gems kept in steel boxes.

On the west wall are four two-foot tall steel pedestals topped with three-foot cylindrical glass cases. All but one of the glass cases are empty. The white light in the room comes from the occupied case.

The case contains a **will-o-wisp**. The case's glass is specially treated to prevent it from using its incorporeal movement to escape. If released, the wisp immediately turns invisible and flees by the fastest possible route. The glass case has an AC 13 and 5 hp. It is immune to bludgeoning, piercing, and slashing from nonmagical weapons, as well as poison and psychic damage.

If each of the cases are inspected, the characters find that there are small slots below each of them. The three empty cases have a dull hunk of emerald Odonburgite that no longer glows. Meanwhile, the fourth case has a "charged" hunk of emerald Odonburgite inside it that still has a faint glow. If the Odonburgite is removed, the wisp begins to act erratically, as if was suffocating.

The dim Odonburgite is worth 100 gp. Meanwhile, all of the dull, un-charged Odonburgite gems are useless, worth no more than 1gp all together (there are 350 pieces in all).

18 - Ninth Floor.

> This area appears to be two 20-foot wide circular rooms connected together like a figure eight. At the north end of the room are two staircases, one down to the floor below and one up to the next floor. There is a door in the south wall.

Two columns at the center of the circular rooms. The northernmost column has grooves cut into it. A trapdoor of some sort at the center of the column has been flung over. It appears that the cubby behind the trapdoor once held something—but whatever it is looks like it's now gone.

The southernmost column is carved to look like a strange clock. The clock has seven hands.

The clock is a much smaller version of the Amazing Clock in Castlegrasp. In addition to telling time, it denotes days on the calendar, as well as the weather. It has a final eighth hand that remains invisible, only appearing just before a major catastrophe occurs. Throughout the five-hundred-year history of the Amazing Clock, the eighth hand has appeared seven times. It's believed that when it appears the eighth time, the world will end. This event is referred to as "The Hand of the Eight."

A ladder on the floor on the south-western wall leads down to **Area 20**.

Encounter. A remote traveler 1015-R guards this room. It uses the stats of a **shield guardian** with a lightning bolt spell stored in it and it can use its shield reaction on itself. Also, it is being actively piloted, so its Intelligence, Wisdom, and Charisma scores are the same as a **mage**. Like the other remote travelers, its pilot is over 1,000 miles away and will command the traveler to fight until it is destroyed.

19 - Remote Traveler Landing Pad. This landing pad was created for smaller flyers, such as flying remote travelers, to land on. The panels are constantly heated to prevent ice from building up on the pad. It offers views of the southwestern side of the mountain and the lands beyond.

20 - Traveler Passage. The two doors in this chamber are open but can be shut manually by a properly credentialed Dinzer. A remote traveler 721 stands at the end of the hall. It is not currently being piloted, so it is in its default mode, acting as animated armor. It attacks the characters on sight.

21 - Remote Traveler Barracks. This small, cramped room has a 20-foot-tall "shelf" with seven remote traveler 721s placed on individual shelves, almost like they're lying on beds. Each of their "beds" exudes a dull green glow.

The travelers are currently charging and are not being piloted. As such, they are simply empty cases of armor.

If either of the power cells in the columns in **Area 14** were removed, the charging stations do not function.

22 - Remote Traveler Repair Room. This small room has a number of mechanical arms set into the wall. At the center, hung by its armpits on two hooks, is a remote traveler 751. Like the remote traveler, the mechanical arms can be piloted from Odonburg. Currently, the remote traveler and the arms are not in operation.

23 - Teleportation Chamber. This 30-foot-wide circular chamber apparently has no exit. At the northeastern corner of a room, a short flight of stairs leads up to a raised stone dais.

The stone dais is a transporter. Stepping onto the transporter and saying "Up" transports the user to transporters counterpart in **Area 24**.

Encounter. Covering the floor are hundreds of nano-engineers. As a unit, they are remote-controlled by a Dinzer pilot 1,000 miles away. They are still experimental, so their response time is poor (they make initiative checks with disadvantage). Regardless, while they fly around the room, the transporter will not function. Treat the nano-engineers as four **swarms of wasps** that are constructs and are immune to poison and psychic damage.

24 - Control Tower Entry. After the characters activate the transporter dais in **Area 23** read or paraphrase the following:

> For a moment, everything turns green and the world around you vanishes. Then, what feels like a second later, the green washes away and the world returns. You appear to be in a different, much larger room than the one you left. The room has an elliptical shape and is nearly 55 feet wide from corner to corner. From where you stand to the next week, it's 25-feet across. There are two doors in the opposite wall, each spaced roughly 10-15 feet from the corners of the room. Finally, a spiral staircase ascends up from the center of the far wall.
>
> Two, large, metallic dogs spring to life the moment they notice you. Both rush to attack.

Encounter. Both of the "dogs" are remote traveler 1043-H models that have the crude appearance of large, metallic dogs. Treat the travelers as **hell hounds**, except they are constructs with immunity to poison and

TOWER OF BURSHAI
LEVELS 11-13

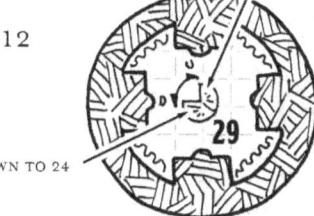

LEVEL 13

TRAPDOOR STAIRS
DOWN TO 29

30

UP TO 30

LEVEL 12

DOWN TO 24

29

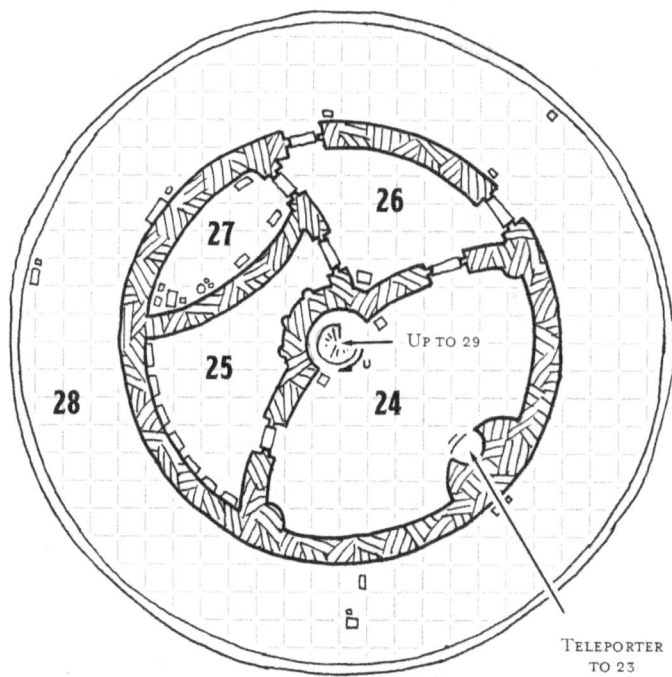

LEVEL 11

27

26

25

28

24

UP TO 29

1 SQUARE = 5 FEET

TELEPORTER
TO 23

psychic damage and have the Intelligence, Wisdom, and Charisma scores of a mage. The travelers are being piloted by Dinzers over 1,000-miles away.

25 - Control Room.

> This unusually shaped room is roughly 30-foot across and 15-feet wide at its mid-point. There are two doors exiting the room, one on its

longest wall and one at the head of its narrowest point. On one wall, seven large cabinets beset with glyphs that glow-green busily hum. Another wall has a map of Omeria on it. Pinpoints of green light mark various locations on the map. The majority of the points are in the Desolation of Ditimaya and near the mountain hold of Von Doral.

The controls operate the illusion device at the top of the tower (see The Fantastic Lie below). Destroying the cabinets (each of the cabinets has AC 15, 18 hp, and immunity to poison and psychic damage) shuts down the illusion. Also, if the power sources were removed from both of the columns in **Area 14**, the cabinets will be running on their individual backup sources. At the foot of each cabinet is a small trap door. Detecting the trap door requires a successful DC 15 Intelligence (Investigation) check. Inside each trap door, a piece of emerald Odonburgite the size of a gold coin is held in place. Removing the mineral shuts down the cabinet (so long as the main power sources were already shut off). Each of the small pieces of emerald Odonburgite are worth 150 gp.

Encounter. A remote traveler 945-S watches over the control panel. This traveler is designed for manual dexterity and has four arms, each with different fingers, tools, and clamps. It uses the suit of **animated armor** stat block except that it has the Intelligence, Wisdom, and Charisma scores of a **mage**. Furthermore, it can make four melee attacks with its Multiattack feature, instead of two. It is CR 2.

This machine does not attack right away. Instead, its focus is on keeping the controls working.

26 - Viewing Room.

> This triangular room is 20-feet long on its two shortest sides and 35-feet long on its longest side. There are five doors exiting the room: two on its long side, two on one of its short sides, and one on the last short side.
>
> At the center of the long side, a large, black piece of glass floats five feet off the ground.

When the emergency announcement comes on, the characters can view it in this room (see The Fantastic Lie below).

27 - Oxon's Chamber.

> This narrow room is 15-feet wide at its widest point and 25-feet long from where you stand to the point where the opposite walls meet at a point. On either side of the room are four seven-foot-tall black cylinders against the walls. Each cylinder has a small, rectangular glass window, allowing you to look inside it. All but one appear to be empty.

These sleeping sarcophagi are slightly thicker than the others. In addition to providing the same benefits of the other sleeping sarcophagi found in **Areas 6** and **7**, these sarcophagi also act as suspended animation capsules. Any creature that steps into one can cast sequester targeting themselves. Another creature outside of the sarcophagus can dispel the sequester early by using the control glyphs on its side. Understanding the function of the control glyphs requires a successful DC 10 Intelligence (Arcana) check.

28 - Observation Deck. When the characters first step into this area, paraphrase or read the following:

> This huge observation deck surrounds the tower on all sides. It is 18-feet wide from the tower to the railing. From where you stand, you can see for hundreds of miles in every direction.

Likely, this is where the characters encounter the remote traveler alpha-class as detailed in The Fantastic Lie below.

29 - Access Level. The stairs continue to ascend to the highest point of the tower. In this in-between level, four 500-year-old banners of Odonburg hang at all four points of the compass.

30 - Tower's Dome.

> This 30-foot wide room has a domed ceiling. Unless the cabinets were de-

Oxon of Odonburg

The occupied sarcophagus contains the suspended form of Oxon of Odonburg (CG male Dinzer human **archmage**). Oxon has been inside the chamber for nearly 500 years. He was placed within the capsule by his brother following a fight in the tower (hence all the damage). If Omnaweahl is with the party, she immediately recognizes him and is starstruck. Oxon was rumored to have died in a fatal flyer crash five centuries ago. Almost no one living knows that he is still alive.

Having adopted a vow of silence 500 years ago after he witnessed Kongradol in the Wallingmiotta and saw the future of Omeria, Oxon does not speak. Instead, he speaks with sign language. Creatures with Intelligence scores of 12 or higher will be able to easily understand his intentions from the sign language as will any creature that understands Thieves' Cant. Otherwise, a creature must succeed on a DC 15 Intelligence check to understand what Oxon is saying.

Once released, Oxon gets his bearings, then starts looking for his brother. When it becomes obvious that Odon is not in the Tower, he then heads for the control room (**Area 25**) to finish what he started 500-years ago. See The Fantastic Lie below for details.

stroyed or shut down, streaks of green energy move through grooves on the wall, disappearing into the tower's cone.

The illusion spell created by the tower emits from this area. See The Fantastic Lie below for details.

The Fantastic Lie

As the characters are traveling through the upper reaches of the Tower of Burshai (levels 11+) and they have started to unravel the mysteries of the tower, reinforcements arrive to protect the tower's secrets. A Dinzer **remote traveler alpha-class** (either the same as before if it wasn't destroyed or its replacement) lands on the observation deck (**Area 28**). Wherever the characters are, the machine approaches them with hands raised in surrender:

> The machine raises its hands in a human-like way as if to suggest it does not wish to fight. It tactfully keeps its distance, too. After a moment, its form begins to shimmer as an illusion comes over it. Although it's still obviously the construct, its face has been replaced with an illusion that makes it look exactly like Ophiar, the owner of the Tall Ghost book shop in Orbea and Omnaweahl's brother.

If Omnaweahl is still with the party, it's obvious that she is shocked. Already discouraged by the condor attack and everything she has seen in the Tower, the stress she's feeling is starting to reach critical levels.

> "Please. I haven't come to fight," says Ophiar. "I'm sorry about everything so far. You must understand: I have a duty to my country and my Emperor. You've all become tangled in something that is beyond your reach and you are putting the entire world in jeopardy just by being here. That's why we've had to make certain preparations. Please—follow me."

Ophiar's remote traveler carefully walks towards **Area 26** keeping his hands in the air. If he's attacked, he casts a stored *resilient sphere* spell on himself and uses the minute to convince the characters to go into **Area 26** to watch the viewing screen there.

Once the characters are in **Area 26**, he speaks a command word to turn the screen on.

> The black pane of glass begins to glow, clearly under the effects of some sort of illusion spell. On it, a two-dimensional image appears—it is the face of Holy Evadimus Emperor of Odonburg. He stands in an office surrounded by five of the Seven Eyes of Odonburg as well as members of his council. On the wall behind you can see the red and blue banner of Odonburg.
>
> "My fellow Omerians. This illusory broadcast is being sent out to all major broadcasting panels in Omeria. And as we speak, messengers with transcripts are arriving in cities and villages throughout our great continent.
>
> "It is with a heavy heart that I come to you today to announce the arrival of a threat to our very way of living. Recently, it's come to my attention that an anti-Dinzer terrorist organization operating in Central and Northern Omeria has begun a dastardly operation to strike at our friends and allies across the great continent of Omeria."

The image of Evadimus and his colleagues is momentarily replaced by images of the characters and (if she's still there) Omnaweahl. He mentions each of the characters by name as well as the party's name. If they haven't given themselves a name, he instead refers to them as 'The Ivory Oath.'

> "We first learned of this organization after multiple terrorist attacks in Omeria starting with piracy off the Weysevain Coast."

Images of The Ghost Holm appear on the screen.

> "Then, they destroyed a Dinzer transport blimp in the ruined town of Qola in the Desolation of Ditimaya, killing six patriots."

Images of the ship crashing into the Hole in Qola appear on the screen.

> "Shortly after that, the terrorists fireballed The Long Shadow casino in the town of Orbea."

An image of The Long Shadow comes on the screen. The entire building is burning and in ruins; likely in far worse condition that the characters remember leaving it.

> "This time, there were hundreds of deaths including the casino's beloved owner Prayer in the Morning."

Prayer's image comes on the screen with the caption "Deceased." After lingering on Prayer's face for a moment, the image returns to Evadimus and the other Dinzers. Even if she survived the battle at the Long Shadow, she's still declared dead.

> "Now I've been given word that the terrorists are operating north of the Basilisk's Spine Mountains. The news that I am about to tell you is not easy for me to share. But what they are planning could spell doom for us all."
>
> Evadimus hesitates, visibly distraught.
>
> "The terrorists have taken hold of an ancient tower in the Basilisk's Spine Mountains. We've sent Dinzer troops to stop them—"

The image on the screen shows the characters fighting remote travelers in the Tower, except the scene has been altered—instead of constructs, it looks like the characters are fighting and killing humanoids.

> "I realize that this imagery is graphic and may disturb some view-

ers and I apologize. From those brave soldiers who gave their lives, we learned the ghastly intentions of these dangerous terrorists. From the tower, they wish to cast a malicious conjuration spell on the land—magic not seen since the Unlimited Eruption. If they are successful, it will change the very landscape of our world. It will poison the land and the sky and place dangerous minerals in the ground. Those minerals will emit high levels of energy which will harm anyone that comes near them.

"Already, we have begun preparations to combat the fallout from this terrorist attack. And we've deployed are greatest soldiers to the tower. We are optimistic that the terrorists will be stopped before they can carry out their attack. But it is my duty as your Holy Emperor to inform you of the danger at hand.

"I don't know what the future brings, my fellow Omerians. But know that by the wisdom of Odon and Oxon, whatever comes of this unfortunate event, we will persevere. Good luck. And good night."

Evadimus is replaced with text explaining how to prepare for the coming emergency.

Ophiar's remote traveler speaks up again, his hands still in the air.

"Five hundred years ago, when Duda Weysevain trekked south through the Lost Dragon Pass, he discovered huge fields of glowing, green ore.

"At the time, the ore was protected by a tribe of people known as the Ditimayans. Of course, they were somewhat primitive, not like the peoples north of the Basilisk's Spine or our people. They didn't understand what they possessed. Weysevain shared this information with a pair of brothers: Odon and Oxon, the founders of our great nation.

"They learned that the mineral that

the Ditimayans called 'The Life of the Land'—what we now call emerald Odonburgite—emitted high levels of evocation magic. When applied to a magic item, the magic item instantly recovered all of its charges. The value was incredible. Within just a few years, Dinzer technology increased at exponential levels. Every magic item, every piece of technology that we have we owe to the discovery of the emerald Odonburgite.

"But it was dangerous, too. Certain types of energy—when applied to the mineral—caused catastrophic results. The Hole in Qola is the worst occurrence so far from Odonburgite becoming unstable.

"In time, our enemies learned of Odonburgite. Wars were fought. Thousands died. There was too much of the Odonburgite to easily protect and our allies proved uncooperative. They were taken by the allure of the gems. So Odon made a difficult decision: we would hide the Odonburgite from the world.

"Under the leadership of the wizard Burshai, this tower was erected to broadcast a powerful spell. First, it would cast *hallucinatory terrain* over the land. Any creature who saw the Odonburgite would not realize it was there. Instead, they would see nothing more than desert sands and wasteland. This is how the 'Desolation of Ditimaya' came to be. Second, the tower modified the memories of nearly every living creature on the continent. Not only would they forget the Odonburgite fields existed in the first place, but they would see nothing unusual about our use of the material.

"What you've learned here today—the world can't know. Our ancestors spent the last five centuries hiding the presence of the mineral emerald Odonburgite. It is our Holy mission to protect its secrets—if our enemies knew where to find it, they could use it against us. Everything we've

worked for—our way of life—would vanish in an instant.

"Peace, liberty, happiness—in a flash, all of that would be gone. The world would fall into chaos once more. Is that what you truly want?"

Give the characters time to react to the revelations. Ophiar is a zealot; very little can change his mind from the cause. He will listen to their protests and logic and eventually make an offer.

Until then, the characters may have other questions concerning the conspiracy. Here are common questions with Ophiar's answers. Any other questions that the characters have, Ophiar either does not know or is not willing to share.

Who else knows? "Only the Emporer, the Seven Eyes, and the top agents of Odonburg. And now all of you."

Why are the elves dying? "We discovered that as the levels of Odonburgite diminish, fey and creatures with fey ancestry such as elves begin to become sick. It is an unfortunate side effect."

What are the Dinzer pylons? "The pylons draw energy directly from a cache of Odonburgite and transmit the energy through air streams back to Odonburg."

Is the Desolation of Ditimaya truly a desert? "It is a desert. But some of the more dangerous parts—such as Dreadfields—are actually large caches of Odonburgite which we protect."

How is the Obsidian Plain connected? "There were many creatures who were unaffected by the spell, particularly descendants of the Striped Conjurers of Karmithyash and the few living conjurers themselves. Over the years, they've tried to rise up and take control of the Odonburgite. The worst of those events, the Unlimited Eruption, lead to the creation of the Obsidian Plain."

What are krigs? "Krigs are naturally immune to the radiant effects of raw emerald Odonburgite. We use them in the fields, quarries, and the mines."

How much Odonburgite is there?
"We estimate that there are 1.1 trillion tonnes of emerald Odonburgite in the world."

> "Now that you know what we know, you have two choices. You can reveal what you've learned here to the world and be labeled as criminals forever. Already, the world is ready for this 'disaster' to occur. And already, the full might of Odonburg is ready to handle the situation and save the world from your act of terrorism. Or, you can surrender quietly. I can escort you back to Odonburg and we can modify your memory. Because of these events, you will have to serve some time, but we can make arrangements to have you sequestered by the Stonearms in Castlegrasp. Once you've served your sentence, you're free to live your lives as you see fit."

It's likely that the characters reject this offer. Once they make the choice to reveal the nature of the tower to the world, Ophiar attacks. From there, the scene could play out a few different ways.

If the characters defeat Ophiar's remote traveler alpha-class, they must then destroy the control cabinets in **Area 25**. Doing so removes the illusion (see The Hand of the Eight below).

If the characters accept Ophiar's offer and Omnaweahl and/or Oxon is with the party, or if the characters fight Ophiar and Ophiar looks as if he's close to winning, this is what happens:

> "Stop," says [Omnaweahl/Oxon]. In [his/her] hand is a apple-sized hunk of glowing emerald Odonburgite.
> Ophiar's remote traveler looks shocked. "What are you doing?"

If it's Omnaweahl holding the Odonburgite, she looks distraught. Everything that she's learned has caused her to lose all faith in her nation, her people, and even herself as she realizes she's been implicit in the conspiracy. If it's Oxon, he is finally completing what he set out to do 500 years ago.

> "Run," says [Omnaweahl/Oxon] to you. [His/her] hand begins to glow with black, negative energy.
> Ophiar screams, "No! What are you doing! You'll kill us all!"

As the emerald Odonburgite absorbs the necrotic damage it begins to destabilize. It should be obvious that the characters need to flee or be destoryed. Below is a round-by-round break down of what happens.

Round 1. The gem begins to destabilize. Ophiar watches in horror as [Omnaweahl/Oxon]'s form starts to disintegrate along with it.

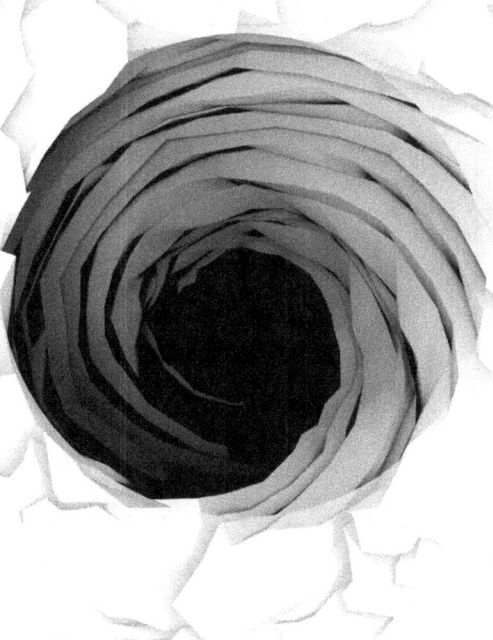

Round 2. As the gem starts to break open, high-levels of radiant energy spill out. Each creature that starts its turn this round within 20 feet of [Omnaweahl/Oxon] must succeed on a DC 15 Constitution saving throw. A creature takes 14 (4d6) radiant damage on a failed saving throw or half as much damage on a successful one.

Round 3. Finally, the gem shatters exploding outward for only a moment before it retracts and implodes inward. [Omnaweahl/Oxon] is instantly destroyed as is anything within 20 feet of [him/her]. The implosion sends out a shockwave of radiant energy. Any creature within 100 feet of [Omnaweahl/Oxon] when this occurs must make a DC 15 Dexterity saving throw. A creature takes 35 (10d6) radiant damage on a failed saving throw or half as much damage on a successful one.

Round 4. A tear in the fabric of reality opens up and begins to expand rapidly. Loose objects are pulled into the hole. At first, the objects are small: a few tools, rocks, random trinkets. Then larger objects start to drift towards the hole.

Round 5. Areas 24 through **28** are absorbed into the tear. Any creatures and objects in those areas are immediately destroyed (no save). The upper tower **Area 29** and **30** is blown 100 feet into the air. Any creatures inside those areas must succeed on a DC 10 Strength saving throw or be thrown against a wall, taking 10 (3d6) bludgeoning damage as a result.

Round 6. The top of the tower falls back down and into the tear. All creatures and objects in **Areas 29** and **30** are immediately and irrevocably destroyed. Meanwhile, the tear in reality starts to absorb the ninth and tenth levels. Any creatures in **Areas 18**, **19**, and **23** must succeed on DC 15 Strength saving throws or be pulled into the tear in reality and are immediately and irrevocably destroyed. Creatures in **Area 23** make this saving throw with advantage.

Round 7. The absorption of the tower accelerates as levels six, seven, and eight are pulled into the tear in reality. A creature in **Areas 12-17** and 20-22 must succeed on a DC 15 Strength saving throw or be pulled into the tear in reality where they are immediately and irrevocably destroyed. Creatures in **Areas 12a**, **12b**, and **13** make this saving throw with advantage.

Round 8. The entire bottom portion of the tower is absorbed as the tear devours all five levels. Any creature in **Areas 2-11** must succeed on a DC 15 Strength saving throw or be pulled into the tear in reality where they are immediately and irrevocably destroyed. Creatures in **Areas 2** and **3** make this saving throw with advantage.

Round 9. Snow and stone from the side of the mountain is absorbed into the rift. Each creature within 100 feet of where the tower once stood (which is now erased from reality) must succeed on a DC 15 Strength saving throw or be pulled 50 feet towards the rift. A creature pulled into the rift is immediately and irrevocably destroyed. A creature that passes its Strength saving throw can use its reaction to make a DC 10 Dexterity saving throw in order to catch a creature that fails its Strength saving throw, stopping them on a success.

Round 10. More snow and stone fly towards the rift creating blizzard-like conditions. Any creatures within 500 feet of where the tower once stood must succeed on a DC 15 Constitution saving throw. On a failed saving throw, a creature takes 5d6 bludgeoning damage and is blinded. The must also make a DC 15 Strength saving throw. On a failed saving throw, the creature is pulled 100-feet towards the rift. A creature pulled into the rift is immediately and irrevocably destroyed. A creature that passes its initial Constitution saving throw can use its reaction to make a DC 10 Dexterity saving throw in order to catch a creature that fails its Strength saving throw, stopping them on a success.

If a creature passes its initial Constitution saving throw, it takes half as much damage, isn't blinded, and doesn't have to make a Strength saving throw to avoid being pulled into the rift.

Round 11. The rift stabilizes. A huge, black hole measuring 100-feet across floats 200 feet in the air above the mountain. It no longer absorbs matter into it, although, it will still destroy anything that touches it.

Escaping the Tower. There is not a lot of time to escape the tower. The characters will need to find an exit and fast. The best way to escape is to leap through one of the holes in the wall to snow below. Thanks to the angle and the snow itself, falls are not nearly as dangerous. Reference the table below for the damage the characters take if they leap from levels of the tower. Once a character hits the snow, they slide 30-feet down the mountain from where they land.

Before a character leaps, they can make a DC 12 Strength (Athletics) check. On a successful check, the character only takes half damage from the fall.

Escaping the Tower		
Tower Level	Exposed Areas	Falling Damage
1st	—	—
2nd	—	—
3rd	—	1d6
4th	9a, 9b	2d6
5th	11	3d6
6th	—	3d6
7th	15	3d6
8th	—	4d6
9th	19	4d6
10th	—	4d6
11th	28	5d6
12th	—	5d6
13th	—	6d6

The Hand of the Eight

With the tower destroyed, the illusion ends and the Desolation of Ditimaya reveals its true nature. The entirety of the desert emits a constant green glow visible for thousands of miles. Fields upon fields of huge, exposed deposits of emerald Odonburgite are now visible. The Dinzer pylons, thought to be defunct, glow with radiant energy. Trails of green energy fill the sky, streaming southward. Secret Dinzer bases near the quarries, mines, and deposits appear, no longer invisible. Hundreds of remote travelers and never-before-seen-krigs toil in these areas. Millions of Central Omerians are in shock.

A few moments after the destruction of the Tower of Burshai and the dispelling of the mass *hallucinatory terrain* spell that hid the emerald Odonburgite from the Omerians, in the south section of the Orchard Park in the city of Castlegrasp, cries of fear fill the air. Hundreds of terrified Castlegraspians gather around the Amazing Clock.

Khan Hayyan-Harrak—surrounded by his Granite Nine security force—moves past his people in order to see what they see.

The Amazing Clock's eighth hand has appeared, thus signaling the final catastrophe.

"So it begins," whispers the Khan. "The Hand of the Eight."

Adventure Conclusion

This is the end of the first part of the Hand of the Eight adventure path series. If the characters survived the destruction of the Tower of Burshai, they likely find themselves stranded on the side of Trenrock Mountain. Already, the Dinzers cast them as terrorists, applying the blame for the sudden appearance of Odonburgite on them. With hardly any allies—as it's likely that Omnaweahl, Oxon, or both died in the implosion; and as it was made clear in Evadimus' illusory broadcast, Prayer is also dead—and no clear direction, they find themselves in serious trouble.

Of course, this is only the beginning. The *Hand of the Eight* adventure path returns with *Part 2: Chapter 7. The Summer Land.* Ω

APPENDICES

APPENDIX A
CHARACTER OPTIONS & NEW MAGIC ITEM

By Dave Hamrick; Eclipse Spear by The Griffon's Saddlebag; Remote Traveler by Kyle Painter
Primary Art by JD Russell, Fat Goblin Games, Dean Spencer, and Luigi Castellani

Races of Omeria

The campaign setting where the **Hand of the Eight** takes place, tentatively titled Omeria, has many of the classic fantasy races present within its world. And while the world of Omeria is still expanding with its stories, these are the races that have been introduced in the setting so far. This guide identifies how they fit into the world and how players can use them to interact with the setting. Of course, you and your players are free to interpret the races of Fifth Edition any way you like. Ultimately, Omeria is your world.

Canid

Canid are dog-human hybrids that live throughout much of Omeria. Created through magical means a couple centuries past, the original canids were developed to guard temples, keeps, and other places of import. However, the canids were smarter and wiser than their creators expected and declared that there was more to their indentured existence.

Wanderers. Thanks to their friendly attitude and ability to survive in most conditions, canids love to wander the continent of Omeria and beyond. Many canids lend their services to other groups of adventurers, instantly creating families to which they are fiercely loyal. Once a canid has bonded with a group, there is very little that will

separate it from its newfound pack.

Patient Hunters. In central and southern Omeria, many canids are trained as trackers and bounty hunters. Not only do their innate senses aid in their hunt, but its unflappable patience and determination make them terrifying foes for their targets. Canid hunters can track quarry for thousands of miles, sometimes spanning entire continents.

Canid Names. A younger race, Canid parents take their names from popular naming conventions in areas that they live, more so words than the names. Most canids do not know their father. For surnames, Canids incorporate the names of their mothers as "son of" or "daughter of" as respect for their primary caretaker.

Male Names: Apple Apple, Bee Mouth, Big Boy, Cold Paws, Dirt Head, Eagle Chaser, Funny Face, Ghost, Horse Foe, Invisible Bark, Jumpy Frog, Laugh and Laugh, Loud One, Maroon, Shepherd, Triumph, Wonder, White Flower.

Female Names: All Fangs, Afternoon Baby, Bunny, Grins, Goldie, Grass Belly, Finger Eater, Late Pup, Lucky Girl, Mud Puddle, Protector, Run Far, Runt, Skinny Thing, Smith's Friend, Sunny Day

Canid Traits. You share the following traits with other members of the canid race.

Ability Score Increase. Your Wisdom score increases by 2, and your Charisma score increases by 1.

Age. As dog-human hybrids, canids' lifespans are marginally longer than dogs. A canid reaches adulthood at the age of 5 and generally live to be 35 to 40 years of age.

Alignment. Canids have no preference toward law or chaos. However, canids do lean strongly towards good over evil.

Size. Canids average about 3 feet tall and weigh around 50 pounds. Your size is Small.

Speed. Your base walking speed is 35 feet.

Keen Senses. You have proficiency in the Perception skill.

Loyal. As an action, you can protect a creature that you can see within 5 feet of you. As long as the creature remains within 5 feet of you and you aren't incapacitated, any attacks made against that creature are made with disadvantage until the start of your next turn.

Tracker. Whenever you make a Wisdom (Survival) check related to tracking a creature, you are considered proficient in the Survival skill and add double your proficiency bonus to the check, instead of your normal proficiency bonus.

Languages. You can speak, read, and write Common and Canid. Canid is a guttural language punctuated by low growls, yelps, and barks.

Dragonborn
While no dragonborn have been seen in Omeria, it is rumored some exist across the Omerian Ocean.

Dwarves
Currently, there is only one major subrace of dwarves found in Omeria, the Von Dorals. Fifty years ago, the Von Dorals lived and toiled in the tunnels and great palaces below the legs of the Basilisk's Spine Mountains. Driven from their lands by fiends—thanks to the mechinations of the Gar Wabrizz goblinoids—Von Dorals now live amongst humans. Their presence is particularly prevalent along the western Omerian Coast. Most Von Dorals blame humans for their misfortunes. And naturally, they despise all goblinoids, going so far as to attack them on sight.

Most Von Dorals stand 4 feet tall and are stocky. Their faces are long, with strong cheekbones, and sharp chins. Their eye colors range from blue to light brown, and they tend to have wiry dark brown or black hair. Before their departure, albino dwarves—called Vundahns—started to appear with troubling frequency. In fact, one out of ten Von Dorals are born as Vundahns, with pale white skin, stark white hair, and white or pink eyes.

Von Doral dwarves use the **mountain dwarf** subrace. Vundahns also use the mountain dwarf subrace, but have the Sunlight Sensitivity feature (as a drow) and have the ability to cast one cantrip from the sorcerer spell list at will, requiring no material components. Charisma is their spellcasting ability for this spell.

Elves and Half-Elves
There are few elves left in the world. Following the eradication of the largest elven nation, Imfe Aiqua, many of the elves who are still present in the world are either of blended-heritage (typically referred to as "wood elves"), descendants of the Anorian elves of northern Omeria, or the endangered elves of Olyothyr.

Aiquan/Kelren. True Aiquan elves died as the result of a plague two-hundred years ago. Those that survived were of mixed-blood with humans. Like the conquered Anorians, Aiquan elves have no lands. Their original home surrounding the great elven city of Imfe Aiquan lies in ruins, haunted by the revenants of the dead. Unlike the Anorians, however, Aiquan elves did not all stay north of the Spine. Perhaps it's in their wild blood, but the descendants of Aiqua chose to travel the world in order to see more of it. Aiquans often have red or brown hair, fair skin, and piercing blue eyes.

Depending on how much of a "true elf" they are, Aiquan/Kelren elves use either the **wood elf** sub-race or the **half-elf** race. Almost all Aiquan elves are young, as the older, pureblood Aiquans succumbed to the elven plague in the 9th century.

Anorians. The original Anorian hailed from Imfe Mythse Anore, the ruins upon which the human city of Knotside was built. Conquered by the joint efforts of Aiquan elves and the humans of Presson's Enclave, the Anorians who weren't destroyed chose

assimilation over eradication. Anorians have pale skin and blue, green, or even white eyes. Their hair is often black, sometimes with white streaks through it. Many half-elves are part Anorian.

Anorian elves use the **drow** subrace for their stats with two minor changes. They lack both the Superior Darkvision and Sunlight Sensitivity traits.

Olyothyrians. Although they possess greater numbers than their Aiquan and Anorian kin, Olyothyrians are the elves a traveler will be less likely to encounter in Omeria. Because of a strange curse that won't allow them to travel more than a few hundred miles from Olyothyr, these tall, slender, silver-haired elves are rarely seen outside of their native lands. As such, Olyothyrian adventurers are rare. Check with your GM to see if you can play one.

Olyothyrians use the **high elf** sub-race. Olyothyrians are stubbornly opposed to inter-racial bleeding, therefore, Olyothyrians half-elf are exceptionally rare.

Gnomes
Nearly all Omerian gnomes come from the forests of the Wallingmiotta where they still thrive. A curious lot, the Wallingmiottan gnomes love to travel, get into adventure, and assimilate into other cultures. No matter where they land, these gnomes stay sharp and agile, with an innate love for illusions and pranks.

All of the gnomes of Omeria are **forest gnomes**.

Halflings
Wanderer halflings are the most prolific sub-race of halflings. Their ancestors originally came from a distant land across the Omeria Ocean. While they have no nation of their own on the long continent, they do have many villages and enclaves where they work and live together. Wanderer seers are well known for their divination powers, which they employ not only as mages,

but as fierce melee combatants.

Wanderer halflings have dark-colored, almond-shaped eyes. Their skin is pale to olive-colored and they have straight black hair. Many wanderers have a harmless skin condition called Bluedot which makes dark, blue freckles surface in symmetrical patterns over their arms, legs, and backs.

Wandering halflings have the following traits.

Ability Score Increase. Your Wisdom score increases by 1.

Intuitive Reflexes. Any time you must make a Dexterity saving throw, you can choose to make a Wisdom saving throw instead. The result of the check is treated as if you had still made a Dexterity saving throw.

Humans

The most dominant race in Omeria—at least during the current Age of Triumphs—are humans. Humans represent a wide variety of ideals and skills in Omeria. From the coldest reaches of Northern Omeria, to the hottest dunes of the Desolation of Ditimaya, to the humid temperate jungles of the Dinzer Nations, humans are adaptable and found at nearly every corner of the land.

Among humans, there are three ethnic groups who call the long continent home.

Dinzer. Dinzers stand a little taller than most of their northern counterparts, typically 6 feet or more for men and over 5 1/2 feet for women. They have lean builds with dark skin and curly, dark hair, typically shaven or kept short. Their eye colors range from deep brown to pale green. The Dinzers were originally a tribe of magically sensitive warriors who lived south of the lands that are now known as the Desolation of Ditimaya. The chief nation of the Dinzers, Odonburg, is the capital city of southern Omeria and home to thousands of magical scholars. For this reason, the Dinzers are the most technologically advanced people on Omeria.

Dinzer Names: (Male) Ador, Azurick, Cruqiohr, Elore, Egostrum, Erostrum, Ezin, Inamorn, Ugrekalis, Urokalis; (female) Enuphaen, Ditiye, Illakey, Lenydae, Ophephaen, Phithall, Umnoffaeh, Uqiohne, Uxone, Vizith

Ditimayan. Ditimayans are the ancestors of the original tribe of humans that lived in the lands south of the Basilisk's Spine Mountains. Coastal Omerians such as Castlegraspians, the Naqqadi, and Arruquettans can all claim Ditimayan heritage. Typically, Ditimayans have dusky skin, dark eyes, and thick black hair.

Ditimayan Names: (Male) Abdeslam, Ahmed, Aziz, Boutaje, Iyas, Muaz, Mujahid, Sufyan; (female) Azeeza, Azmiyah, Busr, Chaymae, Cherifa, Fathiyah, Fawza, Mahdia, Raisa, Yasmin; (surnames) Al-Ghumari, Ben Bouchta, Hachim, Hajuji, Ibn Mohammed, Ksikes, Lahcen, Laroui, Mrabet, Raihani

Knotsiders. Knotsiders usually stand between 5 to 6 feet tall and are of stocky build. It's rumored their great ancestors were dwarves. The majority of Knotsiders have fair to ruddy skin, with hair colors that range between brown to blonde (although, dark hair isn't totally uncommon, especially among the western humans). Knotsider humans live north of the Fairknot River where their villages, towns, and city-states can be found from the Omerian Ocean to the Tide of Tilldale. Most Knotsiders can trace their ancestry to the olde kingdom of Presson's Enclave.

Knotsider Names: (Male) Gif, Gom, Grardil, Mucrem, Ravul, Rezan, Vuzeuever, Zarcarth, Zuzur; (female) Inaga, Jhiluh, Kishi, Kol, Lildrielru, Sasnihmel, Useih, Tifrafu, Valmah; (surnames) Banez, Deathlight, Duskmore, Elffollower, Hasta, Haventrack, Khonon, Menzundreld, Nin

Krigs

Krigs are spider-humanoids that originate from the Weysevain Maze and, by extension, the town of Orbea in Central Omeria. Intelligent and clever, thanks mostly to their connection to their diety-progenitor Matriarch and all other krig, they quickly positioned themselves as assets throughout most of the continent. Their overall numbers are much lower than the other major humanoid races of Omeria, and it's rare to find one more than 1,000 miles from the Maze at Orbea.

The Matriarch. All krig share the same parent, the enigmatic Matriarch, who remains hidden in the unfathomable depth of the Weysevain Maze. As such, krigs are asexual, and are neither male nor female, although many, for simplicity's sake—and to avoid the stigma of being referred to as an "it"—will choose one or the other as their identifier. All krig are connected to the Matriarch and loyal only to her above all else.

Conspiracy Theories. Mostly welcome in Omeria for their insight, intuition, and ingenuity, there are those who suspect that all krig are secretly sleep agents working under the orders of the unseen Matriarch. The majority of krig operate in positions of power or close to those who have it, creating a "tangled web" of connections and allies. Extremists even go as far to connect krig to the Hand of the Eight prophecies, as they are all eight-limbed beings with eight eyes.

Krig Names. Krigs have no identity of their own, only their position. As such, they are given no names by the Matriarch, nor do they give names to themselves. Instead, close allies and friends give them names, typically to reflect their role or status, or just to help them identify the krig among its siblings.

Krig Traits. Your krig character has a number of traits in common with all other krig.

Ability Score Increase. Your Constitution score increases by 2, and your Intelligence score increases by 1.

Age. Krigs reach maturity quickly, typically within 1 or two years of hatching. Those who survive the initial culling of the krig matriarch can live long lives, typically to 150 years or longer. Some krigs have been known to live for even longer, hundreds of years or more.

Alignment. Krigs favor neutrality above all else, but tend to follow the laws of humanoid civilizations of which they become a part.

Size. Krigs stand just a little over 7 feet in height and weigh nearly 300 pounds. Your size is medium.

Speed. Your base walking speed is 30 feet.

Hivemind. As a member of the krig hive mind, you share the same bond that all krigs do: "My loyalty is always to the matriarch and the hive." As long as you are on the same plane of existence as the krig matriarch, you can seek her advice. You can use this feature to seek advice from the matriarch. You can cast the spell augury without expending a spell slot. Once you use this feature to cast this spell, you can't do so again for 30 days.

Experienced Climber. You have a climbing speed of 30 feet and you have advantage on ability checks made to climb or jump.

Eight Eyes. You have advantage on saving throws against being blinded, and you have advantage on Wisdom (Perception) checks that rely on sight.

Standing Leap. You can jump twice the normal distance, though you can't jump farther than your remaining movement would allow.

Extra Arms. You have a pair of small arms at the center of your chest. You can grasp things with these arms which have a reach of 6 feet, and you can use them to lift a number of pounds equal to three times your Strength score. You can use it to do the following simple tasks: lift, drop, hold, push or pull an object or a creature, or open and close a door or a container. Your extra arms provide a +2 bonus to all checks you use to grapple another creature but not to escape a grapple. Your GM might allow other simple tasks to be added to that list of options.

Your extra arms can't wield weapons or shields or do anything that requires manual precision, such as using tools or magic items or performing the somatic components of a spell.

Languages. You can speak, read, and write common and you can speak orb, the language of the krigs.

Orcs
The orcs of Omeria, though tribal, are not nearly as savage as one would believe, nor are they as evil. Certainly,

orcs prefer chaos, but not for the sake of destruction. Instead, they despise the rigors of civilization and the fetters of routine. Most orcs hail from cold lands, especially the lands of northern Omeria.

Omerian orcs are treated as **half-orcs** for the sake of character creation (but are considered full-blooded orcs nonetheless).

Tieflings/Devilkin
In Omeria, tieflings are called devilkin. Most were born in slavery when the Obsidian Lords conquered and enslaved the southern Ditimayan nations. Once freed by the Central Castlegraspians, they discovered that their struggle was far from over. Seen by most humanoids as no better than their forebearers, devilkin are almost always treated as a lower caste.

To free themselves of their diabolical connections, devilkin take names that represent the beauty and good in nature.

Devilkin Names: Chill above the Water, Drink from the Fountain, Eyes for the Blind, Hand of the Crows, Laughter in the Rain, Reflection in her Eyes, Roll through the Snow, Sand on the Beach, Silence in the Trees, Sun through the Heavens. Ω

Oath of the Stonearm: New Paladin Subclass

Sacred Oath

At 3rd level, a paladin gains the Sacred Oath feature. The following Oath of the Stonearm option is available to a paladin, in addition to those normally offered.

Oath of the Stonearm. Castlesgrasp was founded upon a granite quarry two hundred years ago. Today, the granite stones pulled from the quarry make up much of the city's walls, buildings, and even the Violet Qsar. But the granite did not come free. Soon after the mine was opened, the earlier Castlegraspians discovered that the terrain was inhabited by earth elementals. The elementals' queen, a might dao named Gasta the Pure, confronted the Castlegraspians, questioning their presence in Central Omeria. The city's founder, Khan Hayyan Harrak I, met privately with the dao. In a move thought unusual by many of his peers, Harrak surrendered his soul to the dao in exchange for access to the granite. Initially surprised by Harrak's offer, Gasta the Pure agreed to the exchange. Not only could the Castlegraspians mine the granite from her kingdom, but she would enchant the stone as well. Thanks to Gasta's magic, no man-made weapon would ever penetrate Castlegrasp's mighty granite walls. In addition, Gasta blessed the first

nine Castlegraspian soldiers with her touch; she turned the soldiers' right arms to solid stone. But much to their surprise, they could still move these stone arms as normal. In addition, any bladed weapon they held with their stone arms would petrify any enemy it pierced.

Years later, as the Khan grew ill, he tasked the Nine to bring him before Gasta. As promised, he surrendered himself to the dao. Gasta, cherishing her long, peaceful relationship with the Khan, placed his soul within a sky diamond. She then set the diamond next to her heart, forever keeping him close. Their souls merged and the king and the genie queen became one.

When a Castlegrapsian soldier proves his or herself during training, demonstrating immeasurable virtue, they are encouraged to take the March of the Stonearms. The soldier must enter the first mine and seek the dao Gasta-Harrak. From there, he or she must kneel before the dao and offer his or herself to the dao just as the first Khan did two-hundred years prior. If Gasta-Harrak detects the spirit of the Khan within the soldier, they are granted her blessing—an arm of stone. However, if she senses any impurity within the soldier's heart, she commands the earth to devour them.

Tenets of the Stonearm. A paladin who takes this oath repeats the tenets of Gasta-Harrak each day at sunrise and again at sunset.

Protect the City. Whether as a member of the city's fighting forces or an outbound agent, you must always work in the best interests of the city.

Bring Justice to the Lawless. Those who seek to unravel the foundations of civilization must be stopped.

Fight until the Eighth. Nothing short of death will stop you from your mission.

Respect the Land. The earth is your final home. You must respect and honor for it as you would your own parents.

Oath Spells. You gain oath spells at the paladin levels listed in the Oath of the Stonearm Spells table. See the Sacred Oath class feature for how oath spells work.

Oath of the Stonearm Spells	
Paladin Level	**Spells**
3rd	*expeditious retreat, shield*
5th	*enhance ability, enlarge/ reduce*
9th	*beacon of hope, meld into stone*
13th	*stone shape, stoneskin*
17th	*animate objects, passwall*

Channel Divinity. When you take this oath at 3rd level, you gain the following two Channel Divinity options.

- ***Blessing of the Earth.*** As an action, you can grant yourself temporary hit points equal to 5 times your Charisma modifier (minimum of +1).
- ***Stone Blade.*** As a bonus action, you can imbue one piercing or slashing weapon that you are holding with magic drawn from the earth itself. For 1 minute, the weapon you enchant counts as magical for the purposes of overcoming resistance and immunity to nonmagical attacks and damage. Additionally, a living creature made of flesh that takes damage from your weapon must make a Constitution saving throw against your spell save DC. On a failed saving throw, the creature's flesh starts to harden. The creature takes one level of exhaustion. If a creature takes a sixth level of exhaustion from this feature, instead of dying, it becomes petrified.

Aura of Stone. Starting at 7th, you exude an aura that weakens your enemies. The aura extends 10 feet from you in all directions, but not through total cover. Each creature of your choice within this aura has disadvantage on its Constitution saving throws.

At 18th level, the range of this aura

increases to 30 feet.

Stone Defender. Starting at 15th level, you no longer have a need for mundane armor or shields. While you are not wearing armor or carrying a shield, your AC becomes 19. In addition, you can use this feature to cast the stoneskin spell without expending a spell slot. When you do, you must target yourself. After you use this feature to cast the spell, you can't do so again until you complete a long rest.

Champion of Grasta-Harrak. At 20th level, you are an avatar for the dao symbiote, which gives you the following benefits:

- When you use your Stone Defender to cast stoneskin on yourself, the duration becomes 8 hours and no longer requires concentration.
- When you hit a creature using your stone blade feature, the creature takes two levels of exhaustion on a failed saving throw instead of one.Ω

Remote Traveler Pilot: New Arcane Tradition

At 2nd level, a wizard gains the Arcane Tradition feature. The following Remote Traveler option is available to a wizard, in addition to the options normally offered.

Remote Traveler Pilot

Dinzers, the demonym for the inhabitants of the Odonburg Nations of South Omeria, are known for two things. First, they are incredibly well-mannered and thoughtful of decorum. Even the toothy wuhlos of Jabros know how to carry themself in front of others. Second, they are by leaps and bounds the most technologically advanced nation in Omeria if not the world. Incorporating magic with modern engineering, Dinzers have turned the jungles and savannahs of southern Omeria into a true utopia. Crime is low, poverty is almost totally eradicated, and on average, Dinzers live 20-30 more years than the other Omerians.

A big part of Odonburg's success in the realms arcane is due to their monopoly of the natural resource emerald Odonburgite. Emerald Odonburgite is a glowing, green gem that emits powerful evocation energy. Energy collected from samples even as small as an acorn is enough to offer an infinite supply of charges for their weapons, vehicles, and other magic items. Unfortunately, emerald Odonburgite is extraordinarily rare. As such, the Dinzers jealously guard their limited supply.

Dinzers are also incredibly apt creators of constructs. Golems, shield guardians, and animated objects are all common sights in Odonburg. Outside of Odonburg, Dinzers use a mixture of conjuration magic and animated objects to travel using constructs known as remote travelers. A remote traveler is a suit of animated armor that a Dinzer mage can project his or her senses through. Some advanced versions of remote travelers can even cast spells and project the appearance of their pilot on their form.

Remote Traveler. Beginning when you select this arcane tradition at 2nd level, you gain a remote traveler suit. With 8 hours of work, a suit of plate mail armor, and 100 gp worth of emerald Odonburgite and raw materials you imbue the suit of armor with energy from the Odonburgite.

At the end of the 8 hours, the suit animates and gains all the benefits of your Traveler Bond ability. You can have only one remote traveler at a time.

If your remote traveler is ever destroyed, the magical bond you share allows you to recreate it. With 8 hours of work and expenditure of 50 gp of emerald Odonburgite, you recreate the armor. You can recreate the armor even if you do not have the original suit of armor or a new one to replace it.

If you use this ability to recreate a former remote traveler while you have a current remote traveler, your current raveler leaves you and is replaced by the restored traveler.

Traveler Bond. Your remote traveler uses the suit of **animated armor** stat block from the *MM* except the animated armor loses its Multiattack action and its movement speed is 30 ft.

The armor obeys your commands as best it can. It takes its turn on your initiative, though it doesn't take an action unless you command it to. On your turn, as long as you and the traveler are on the same plane of existence, you can mentally command the traveler where to move (no action required by you). You can use your action to mentally command it to take any action that would normally be available to you except it cannot Cast a Spell.

If you incapacitated or absent, the animated armor acts on its own, focusing on protecting you (if you are present) and itself. The armor never requires your command to use its reaction, such as when making an opportunity attack.

Your traveler has abilities and game statistics determined in part by your level. Your armor uses your proficiency bonus rather than its own. In addition to the areas where it normally uses it proficiency bonus, a remote traveler also adds its proficiency bonus to its damage rolls. Its Intelligence, Wisdom, and Charisma scores equal your own, and it is proficient in the same skills, tools, and saving throws that you are.

Your traveler does not require air, food, water, or sleep and it is immune to disease. When your traveler takes a long rest, it must spend at least six hours of it in an inactive, motionless state, rather than sleeping. In this state, it appears inert, but it doesn't render the traveler unconscious, and you can see and hear as normal. At the end of a long or short rest, it gains the same benefits as any other creature from taking a rest.

From the moment you first get your

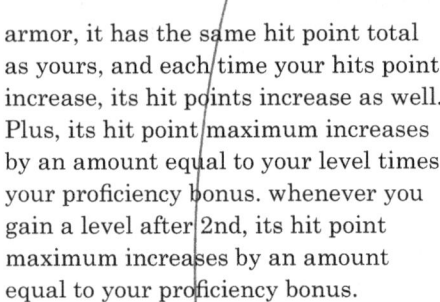

armor, it has the same hit point total as yours, and each time your hits point increase, its hit points increase as well. Plus, its hit point maximum increases by an amount equal to your level times your proficiency bonus. whenever you gain a level after 2nd, its hit point maximum increases by an amount equal to your proficiency bonus.

The remote traveler cannot wear armor. Its natural AC is 18 (it does not add its Dex bonus). A shield's benefits apply as normal while it uses its natural armor.

Your remote traveler can use and wield magic items and weapons. However, you and the remote traveler share between you the number of items that you can attune to. If the total number of magic items that you and the traveler are attuned to equal three, then any attempt to attune to another item—by either you or the traveler—fails. However, both you and the traveler can attune to a copy of an item so long as it's only one per you and the traveler.

Your traveler's alignment is always unaligned and has no personality traits, bonds, or flaws of its own.

Remote Sensing. As long as your traveler is on the same plane of existence as you, you can mentally control it. Additionally, as an action, you can see through the traveler's eyes and hear what it hears until the traveler is destroyed or you use your action to end the remote sensing effect. You do not gain the benefits of its blindsight, but you can use your own special senses through the suit's eyes (such as

darkvision, truesight, the benefits of *see invisibility*, etc.). During this time, you are deaf and blind with regard to your own senses, and you are unconscious. You can also speak through the traveler which projects your voice as if it was speaking. Each time you speak, you may choose to have its voice sound the same as yours or altered.

While the animated armor is normally immune to the blinded, charmed, deafened and frightened conditions, while you are piloting the armor via this feature, it passes any spells or effects that would cause these conditions onto you, and you must make any required saving throws in its place. If you fail the saving throw, you are affected by the spell or effect instead of the remote traveler. In addition, while the armor itself is immune to psychic damage, any spells or effects that deal psychic damage are passed on to you as if you were the target.

Finally, when you cast a spell with a range of self or you cast an evocation or abjuration spell with a casting time of 1 action, your traveler can deliver the spell as if it had cast the spell. Spells with a range of self target your traveler or you (your choice). Your traveler must be on the same plane of existence as you (at least until you reach the 14th level in this class), and it must use its action on its next to deliver the spell when you cast it. If it can't cast the spell on its turn, the spell has no effect and you lose the spell slot as if you had cast it. If the spell requires an attack roll, you use your attack modifier for the roll.

Mend. Also at 2nd level, as an action, you can expend one spell slot of 1st level or higher to have your remote traveler regain hit points equal 1d6 + your spellcasting modifier, plus 1d6 for each spell level higher than 1st, to a maximum of 5d6.

Extra Attack. Beginning at 6th level, when you use your action on your turn to command your remote traveler to take the Attack action, it can attack twice, instead of once. The number of attacks increases to three when you reach 14th level in this class.

Upgrades. At 6th level and again at 10th level and 14th level you can apply an upgrade to your traveler. when you gain a level in this class, you can choose one of the upgrades you've applied and replace it with another upgrade that you could add at that level. Unless it states otherwise in the upgrade's description, you can only choose an upgrade once. If an upgrade requires a level, you must be that level in this class to apply the upgrade to your traveler. Choose one of the following benefits:

Amphibious Mode. The traveler gains a swim speed of 30 ft.

Antimagic Defenses (10th Level Required). The remote traveler loses its Antimagic Susceptibility feature.

Arcane Detection System. Your remote traveler can cast *detect magic* at will, without expending one of your spell slots.

Defensive Maneuvers. The remote traveler gains proficiency in one saving throw of your choice.

Disguise Protocol. Your remote traveler can cast *disguise self* at will, without expending a spell slot.

Flying Mode (14th Level Required). Your remote traveler gains a flying speed of 30 feet.

Improved Suspension. The traveler's walking speed becomes 40 feet unless its walking speed is already higher, and its speed isn't reduced if it is encumbered. In addition, it can jump three times the normal distance, though it can't jump farther than its remaining movement would allow.

Protection from Energy. Choose one of the following damage types: acid, cold, fire, lightning, necrotic, radiant, or thunder. Your remote traveler gains resistance to the chosen damage type. You can choose this upgrade multiple times, choosing a different energy type each time you do.

Psychic Defenses. When the remote traveler is hit by a spell or effect that would pass psychic damage to you, you only take half damage. In addition, you gain advantage on saving throws against being blinded, charmed, deafened, or frightened from any spell or effect the remote traveler passes onto you during remote sensing.

Reinforced Armor. The remote traveler's natural AC becomes 20.

Translation Systems (10th Level Required). Your remote traveler can cast comprehending at will, without expending one of your spell slots.

Traveler Relentlessness. Starting at 10th level, when the traveler's hit points are reduced to 0, it can make a Constitution saving throw with a DC equal to 5 + the damage taken unless the damage is from a critical hit. If the saving throw is successful, the traveler drops to 1 hit point instead.

Planar Traveler. Starting at 14th level, you can mentally control your remote traveler even if it isn't on the same plane of existence as you.

Taking Out a Loan for a Suit

Creating a remote traveler requires a full suit of plate mail present during the ritual. At 2nd level, the cost to acquire a suit of plate mail can be somewhat steep, typically 1,500 gold pieces or more. To account for this cost, at the GM's discretion, the wizard may work with a local mage's guild, private investor, or some other source of capital to purchase the suit with a small loan. Typically, the wizard taking out the loan will owe the principal on the loan plus 10-20% interest due at the end of the term. Most terms are 6-months to a year. The suit itself would act as collateral for the transaction. Each suit is equipped with a "kill switch" that allows the bank or investor to disable it (as an *antimagic field*) in case the debtor fails to repay the loan. Ω

Eclipse Spear

Weapon (spear), uncommon (requires attunement)

When in moonlight, this magic spear casts bright light in a 15-foot radius and dim light for an additional 15 feet. This spear pierces through darkness to find its marks, allowing the attacks you make with it against targets obscured by magical darkness to be made without the disadvantage normally imposed by magical darkness. Attacks made with this weapon deal either piercing or slashing damage (your choice).

In addition, while holding the spear, you can use a bonus action to cast the *branding smite* spell from it. Once cast in this way, this property can't be used again until the next dusk. Ω

MONSTERS & NPCS

By Dave Hamrick; Black Bird and Remote Traveler by Kyle Painter.

Black Bird

Black Bird is a mysterious tracker who works for an unknown entity. Resembling little more than a shadow with glowing eyes, it's not even entirely clear whether or not he is human. The moniker black bird comes from the dozens—or possibly hundreds—of small, black birds that precede his arrival.

The Black Bird wields the Eclipse Spear, a magic item that can pierce through darkness and almost always find its target.

You won't escape me in the dark. You will draw me like a moth to a flame, and I can't be burned. You will be found.

BLACK BIRD
Medium humanoid (unknown), neutral evil

Armor Class 16 (Studded Leather)
Hit Points 120 (16d8 + 48)
Speed 30 ft., climb 30 ft.

STR	DEX	CON	INT	WIS	CHA
16 (+3)	19 (+4)	16 (+3)	11 (+0)	15 (+2)	18 (+4)

Skills Acrobatics +7, Animal Handling +5, Insight +5, Perception +5, Stealth +7
Senses darkvision 60 ft., passive Perception 15
Languages Common, Sylvan
Challenge 6 (2,300 XP)

Cunning Action. On each of its turns, the Black Bird can use a bonus action to take the Dash, Disengage, or Hide action.
Evasion. If the Black Bird is subjected to an effect that allows it to make a Dexterity saving throw to take only half damage, the Black Bird instead takes no damage if it succeeds on the saving throw, and only half damage if it fails.
Speak with Black Birds. The Black Bird can communicate simple concepts to blackbirds, ravens and crows when it speaks in Sylvan.
Running Leap. With a 10-foot running start, the Black Bird can long jump up to 20 feet, and high jump up to 10 feet.
Innate Spellcasting. The Black Bird's 's innate spellcasting ability is Charisma (spell save DC 15, +7 to hit with spell attacks). It can innately cast the following spells, requiring no components:
At will: *animal friendship, animal messenger, fire bolt, produce flame, speak with animals* (birds only)
3/day each: *burning hands, entangle, expeditious retreat, faerie fire, feather fall, hellish rebuke, jump, misty step*
1/day each: *fear, gaseous form, heat metal, hold person, pass without trace, scorching ray*

ACTIONS

Multiattack. The Black Bird makes three attacks with the Eclipse Spear.
Eclipse Spear. *Melee Weapon Attack:* +6 to hit, reach 5 ft., one target. *Hit:* 7 (1d8 + 3) bludgeoning damage plus 7 (2d6) radiant damage.
Summon Murder (1/Day). The Black Bird magically calls 1d6 swarms of ravens, or up to 12 individual ravens, provided that the Black Bird is somewhere with easy access to the outdoors. The called creatures arrive in 1d3−1 rounds, acting as allies of the Black Bird and obeying its telepathic commands. The beasts remain for up to 8 hours, until the Black Bird dies, or until the Black Bird dismisses them as a bonus action. While these beasts have been summoned, the Black Bird can communicate with them telepathically, and can use an action to perceive through an individual beast's senses, as with the find familiar spell.

Centaur Champion (Alogo)

The strongest and bravest of the centaur clans are the Alogos. When an Alogo rides with a clan, it is always at the front, driving its clansmen with rallying warcries. Alogos never flee combat and will martyr itself before it lets down its kin.

CENTAUR CHAMPION
Large monstrosity, neutral good

Armor Class 13
Hit Points 93 (11d10 + 33)
Speed 50 ft.

STR		INT	
STR 20 (+5)		INT 10 (+0)	
DEX 16 (+3)		WIS 15 (+2)	
CON 16 (+3)		CHA 13 (+1)	

Saving Throws Str +8, Dex +6, Con +6
Skills Athletics +8, Perception +6, Survival +6
Senses passive Perception 16
Languages Common, Elvish, Sylva
Challenge 5 (1,800 XP)

Charge. If the centaur moves at least 30 feet straight toward a target and then hits it with a pike attack on the same turn, the target takes an extra 17 (5d6) piercing damage.
Rallying Cry (1/Day). The centaur can use its bonus action to incite its allies. Each creature of the centaur's choice within 30 feet of it that can hear it has advantage on their next attack roll so long as it makes its attack before the start of the Álogo's next turn.

ACTIONS

Multiattack. The centaur makes two attacks: one with its pike and one with its hooves or two with its longbow.
Pike. *Melee Weapon Attack:* +8 to hit, reach 10 ft., one target. *Hit:* 10 (1d10 + 5) piercing damage.
Hooves. *Melee Weapon Attack:* +8 to hit, reach 5 ft., one target. *Hit:* 12 (2d6 + 5) bludgeoning damage.
Longbow. *Ranged Weapon Attack:* +6 to hit, range 150/600 ft., one target. *Hit:* 7 (1d8 + 3) piercing damage.
Hit-and-Run. The centaur makes one melee weapon attack against a target. It can then move up to half its speed without provoking attacks of opportunity.

Gnome Illusionist

Gnome illusionists take the gnomes' love of pranks to an all new level. Instead of fighting and attacked, generally, the illusionist prefers to mislead, trick, and trap targets.

GNOME ILLUSIONIST
Small humanoid (gnome), chaotic neutral

Armor Class 13 (16 with mage armor)
Hit Points 49 (9d6 + 18)
Speed 25 ft.

STR		INT	
STR	9 (-1)	INT	17 (+3)
DEX	16 (+3)	WIS	12 (+1)
CON	14 (+2)	CHA	12 (+1)

Saving Throws Int +5, Wis +3
Skills Arcana +5, Perception +3, Stealth +5
Senses darkvision 60 ft., passive Perception 13
Languages Common, Gnomish, Sylvan
Challenge 3 (700 XP)

Gnome Cunning. The gnome has advantage on all Intelligence, Wisdom, and Charisma saving throws against magic.
Spellcasting. The gnome is a 9th-level spellcaster. Its spellcasting ability is Intelligence (spell save DC 13, +5 to hit with spell attacks). The gnome can cast the following wizard spells:
At will: *dancing lights, firebolt, light, mage hand, minor illusion, shocking grasp*
1st level (4 slots): *charm person, disguise self, mage armor, silent image, Tasha's hideous laughter*
2nd level (3 slots): *blur, invisibility*
3rd level (3 slots): *fear, hypnotic pattern, major image*
4th level (3 slots): *hallucinatory terrain*
5th level (1 slot): *mislead*

ACTIONS

Club. *Melee Weapon Attack:* +1 to hit, reach 5 ft., one target. *Hit:* 1 (1d4 - 1) bludgeoning damage.

Krig

Krigs are spider-humanoids that originate from the Weysevain Maze and, by extension, the town of Orbea in Central Omeria. Intelligent and clever, thanks mostly to their connection to their diety-progenitor Matriarch and all other krig, they quickly positioned themselves as assets throughout most of the continent. Their overall numbers are much lower than the other major humanoid races of Omeria, and it's rare to find one more than 1,000 miles from the Maze at Orbea.

KRIG
Medium humanoid (krig), neutral

Armor Class 15 (studded leather, shield)
Hit Points 22 (3d8 + 9)
Speed 30 ft., climb 30 ft.

STR		INT	
STR	10 (+0)	INT	15 (+2)
DEX	13 (+1)	WIS	12 (+1)
CON	17 (+3)	CHA	9 (-1)

Skills History +4, Perception +5
Senses passive Perception 15
Languages Common, Orb
Challenge 1/2 (100 XP)

Expert Climber. The krig has advantage on ability checks made to climb.
Innate Spellcasting (1/Day). The krig's innate spellcasting ability is Intelligence. It can cast the spell *augury* without requiring material or somatic components.
Keen Sight. The krig has advantage on Wisdom (Perception) checks that rely on sight.
Standing Leap. The krig's long jump is up to 20 feet and its high jump is up to 10 feet, with or without a running start.

ACTIONS

Multiattack. The krig makes two attacks with its scimitar.
Scimitar. *Melee Weapon Attack:* +3 to hit, reach 5 ft., one target. *Hit:* 4 (1d6 + 1) slashing damage.

Red-Striped Thornfoot

Having emerged from the Obsidian Plain as dangerous, fire-breathing predators, the nomads of southern Omeria learned to train these massive creatures for us as beasts of burden. Most are muzzled while they are working to avoid their nasty fire breath.

RED-STRIPED THORNFOOT
Huge beast, unaligned

Armor Class 15 (natural armor)
Hit Points 95 (10d12 + 30)
Speed 40 ft.

STR		INT	
STR	22 (+6)	INT	2 (-4)
DEX	11 (+0)	WIS	10 (+0)
CON	17 (+3)	CHA	5 (-3)

Senses darkvision 60 ft., passive Perception 10
Languages —
Challenge 4 (1,100 XP)

ACTIONS

Bite. *Melee Weapon Attack:* +8 to hit, reach 5 ft., one creature. *Hit:* 16 (3d6 + 6) piercing damage plus 5 (1d10) fire damage.
Breathe Fire (Recharge 6). The thornfoot exhales fire in a 30-foot line that is 5-feet wide. Each creature in the area must make a DC 13 Dexterity check. A creature takes 17 (5d6) fire damage on a failed saving throw, or half as much damage on a success.

Remote Travelers

A remote traveler is a top-of-the-line suit of animated armor/shield guardian hybrid that allows its owner to operate the construct from an unlimited distance. The alpha-class is an especially durable version of the remote traveler, with improved strength, speed, and defensive capabilities.

(continued...)

Currently, the alpha-class models are in the prototype stage. Very few exist. One of the alpha class models dubbed the "knight-in-shining-armor" was spotted in Orbea attacking casino owner Prayer in the Dark.

Construct Nature. The remote traveler does not require air, drink, food, or sleep.

REMOTE TRAVELER
Medium construct, unaligned

Armor Class 18 (natural armor)
Hit Points 37 (6d8 + 10)
Speed 30 ft.

STR 14 (+2)		**INT** 16 (+3)	
DEX 11 (+0)		**WIS** 14 (+2)	
CON 13 (+1)		**CHA** 10 (+0)	

Damage Immunities poison, psychic
Condition Immunities blinded, charmed, deafened,exhaustion, frightened, paralyzed, petrified, poisoned
Senses blindsight 60 ft. (blind beyond this radius), passive Perception 12
Languages Common
Challenge 2 (450 XP)

Antimagic Susceptibility. The traveler is incapacitated while in the area of an antimagic field. If targeted by dispel magic, the armor must succeed on a Constitution saving throw against the caster's spell save DC or fall unconscious for 1 minute.

False Appearance. While the traveler remains motionless, it is indistinguishable from a normal suit of armor.

Remote Bond. The traveler follows its pilot's telepathic commands as long as they are both on the same plane of existence. In the absence of any such commands, the traveler defends itself (and its pilot, if present). The traveler does not need a command to use its reaction, for example to make an attack of opportunity.

The traveler adds its pilot's proficiency bonus to its damage rolls, and its proficiency bonus times its level to its hit point maximum (included in its statistics).

ACTIONS

Slam. Melee Weapon Attack: +4 to hit, reach 5 ft.,one target. *Hit:* 5 (1d6 + 4) bludgeoning damage.

Homunculus Cage. Melee Weapon Attack: +4 to hit, reach 10 ft., one target. *Hit:* 7 (1d6 + 4) bludgeoning damage, and the homunculus makes a bite attack against the same target.

The homunculus' bite attack has a +4 to hit, and on hit deals 1 piercing damage, and the target must succeed on a DC 10 Constitution saving throw or be poisoned for 1 minute. If the saving throw fails by 5 or more, the target is instead poisoned for 5 (1d10) minutes and unconscious while poisoned in this way.

Mend (3/Day). The traveler's pilot remotely casts mending on the traveler, causing it to regain 6 (1d6 + 3) hit points.

REMOTE TRAVELER ALPHA-CLASS
Medium construct, unaligned

Armor Class 19 (natural armor)
Hit Points 170 (20d8 + 80)
Speed 40 ft.

STR	DEX	CON	INT	WIS	CHA
19 (+4)	15 (+2)	19 (+4)	1 (-5)	10 (+0)	3 (-4)

Damage Immunities poison, psychic
Condition Immunities charmed, exhaustion, frightened, paralyzed, poisoned
Senses blindsight 10 ft. darkvision 60 ft., passive Perception 10
Languages understands commands given in any language but can't speak
Challenge 11 (7,200 XP)

Remote Controlled. The remote traveler is magically bound to an amulet, its control device. As long as the remote traveler and its amulet are on the same plane of existence, the amulet's wearer can telepathically control the traveler. While the amulet's wearer controls the traveler, the wearer can see through the traveler's eyes and hear what it hears, gaining the benefits of the traveler's special senses. During this time, the wearer is incapacitated and deaf and blind with regard to their own senses. The wearer can also speak through the traveler.

Antimagic Susceptibility. The traveler is incapacitated while in the area of an antimagic field. If targeted by *dispel magic*, the traveler must succeed on a Constitution saving throw against the caster's spell save DC or fall unconscious for 1 minute.

Armadillo Mode. When the remote traveler uses the Dodge action, it gains a +4 bonus to its AC and the number of hit points it regenerates at the start of its next turn doubles.

Regeneration. The remote traveler regains 10 hit points at the start of its turn if it has at least 1 hit point.

Spell Storing. A spellcaster who wears the remote traveler's amulet can cause the traveler to store one spell of 4th level or lower. To do so, the wearer must cast the spell on the traveler. The spell has no effect but is stored within the traveler. When commanded to do so by the wearer or when a situation arises that was predefined by the spellcaster, the traveler casts the stored spell with any parameters set by the original caster, requiring no components. When the spell is cast or a new spell is stored, any previously stored spell is lost.

ACTIONS

Multiattack. The remote traveler makes three fist attacks.

Fist. Melee Weapon Attack: +8 to hit, reach 5 ft., one target. *Hit: 11 (2d6 + 4) bludgeoning damage.*

Flame Thrower (Recharge 5-6). A jet of flame fires from the remote traveler's wrist in a 15-foot cone. Each creature in that area must make a DC 16 Dexterity saving throw, taking 10 (3d6) fire damage on a failed saving throw or half as much damage on a successful one.

Illusory Appearance. The traveler covers itself and anything it is wearing or carrying with a magical illusion that makes it look like another creature of its general size and humanoid shape. The illusion ends if the traveler takes a bonus action to end it or if the traveler dies.

The changes wrought by this effect fail to hold up to physical inspection. for example, the traveler could appear to have human skin, but someone touching it would feel the cold metal underneath. Otherwise, a creature must take an action to visually inspect the illusion and succeed on a DC 20 Intelligence (Investigation) check to discern that the traveler is disguised.

REACTIONS

Forcefield. When the remote traveler is hit by an attack or targeted by the *magic missile* spell, it can use its reaction to create an invisible barrier of magical force that protects it. The traveler has a +4 bonus to AC against the triggering attack, or it takes no damage from the magic missile spell that triggered this reaction.

Selkie

Selkies are mysterious fey creatures that live near coasts. In their original form, they appear as ordinary seals (although some claim they can tell a selkie's nature by the twinkle of intelligence in its eyes). Selkies can transform into humanoids, typically elven women. Interested in the affairs of humanoids, particularly sailors, they use their shapechanging ability to meddle in the lives of landwalkers. However, selkies have difficulty understanding humanoid customs. On more than one occasion an over-curious selkie meddled in the lives of landwalkers causing irreparable harm as a result.

Some sailors say that saving a selkie from a net can bring a good luck, while others believe it may bring a curse.

SELKIE
Medium fey (shapechanger), neutral

Armor Class 16 (natural armor)
Hit Points 13 (3d8)
Speed 30 ft., swim 90 ft.

STR	9 (-1)	INT	12 (+1)
DEX	13 (+1)	WIS	10 (+0)
CON	11 (+0)	CHA	12 (+1)

Saving Throws Dex +3
Skills Athletics +3, Perception +2
Senses passive Perception 12
Languages Common, Sylvan
Challenge 1/8 (25 XP)

Shapechanger. The selkie can use its action to polymorph into a Small or Medium humanoid or into its true form, a Medium seal. Its statistics, other than its size, are the same in each form. Any equipment it is wearing or carrying isn't transformed with it. It reverts to its true form if it dies.

Expert Swimmer (Seal Form Only). While in seal form, the selkie has advantage on ability checks related to swimming.

ACTIONS

Bite (Seal Form Only). *Melee Weaopn Attack:* +1 to hit, reach 5 ft., one target. *Hit:* 1 (1d4 - 1) piercing damage.

Rapier (Humanoid Form Only). *Melee Weapon Attack:* +3 to hit, reach 5 ft., one target. *Hit:* 4 (1d6 + 1) piercing damage.

Tremor

Tremor is a 25-foot-tall bear that dominates the Wallingmiotta. While many believe Tremor is one of the Great Titans, this is untrue. Tremor was created spontaneously through fey magic. He now acts as the ultimate protector of the forest. Tremor does not move through the Wallingmiotta quietly. He can be spotted or heard from 300 feet away as he crashes through the trees and underbrush. Any creatures he sees as hostile towards the forest he attacks and fights until killed.

When he is not hunting or protecting the forest, Tremor retires to a 100-foot-tall cliff face located south of the Neepawa Bowels. At any given time, there is a 10% chance that Tremor is resting on the cliff.

However, Tremor is not alone. A **harpy** named Yoraene lives on the cliff with Tremor in a nest made from discarded plate mail armor. She uses her song to soothe and calm the bear so he can sleep. More clever than most of her kind, Yoraene enjoys testing creatures who dare approach the cliffs. Those who pass her test will be given safe passage through the forest. And those who fail her test are instead eaten by Tremor. So far, no one has passed her test. She worries Tremor is getting fat. Ω

TREMOR
Huge fey, unaligned

Armor Class 14 (natural armor)
Hit Points 230 (20d12 + 100)
Speed 60 ft., climb 40 ft.

STR		INT	
STR	23 (+6)	INT	2 (-4)
DEX	10 (+0)	WIS	14 (+2)
CON	20 (+5)	CHA	9 (-1)

Saving Throws Str +10, Con +9
Skills Perception +6
Senses passive Perception +16
Languages —
Challenge 11 (7,200 XP)

Keen Smell. Tremor has advantage on Wisdom (Perception) checks that rely on smell.

Magic Resistance. Tremor has advantage on saving throws against spells and magical effects.

Magic Weapons. Tremor's weapon attacks count as magical for the purpose of overcoming damage resistance and immunity.

ACTIONS

Multiattack. Tremor makes three attacks: one with his bite and two with his claws.

Bite. *Melee Weapon Attack:* +10 to hit, reach 10 ft., one target. *Hit:* 17 (2d8 + 6) piercing damage.

Claws. *Melee Weapon Attack:* +10 to hit, reach 10 ft., one target. *Hit:* 20 (4d6 + 6) slashing damage.

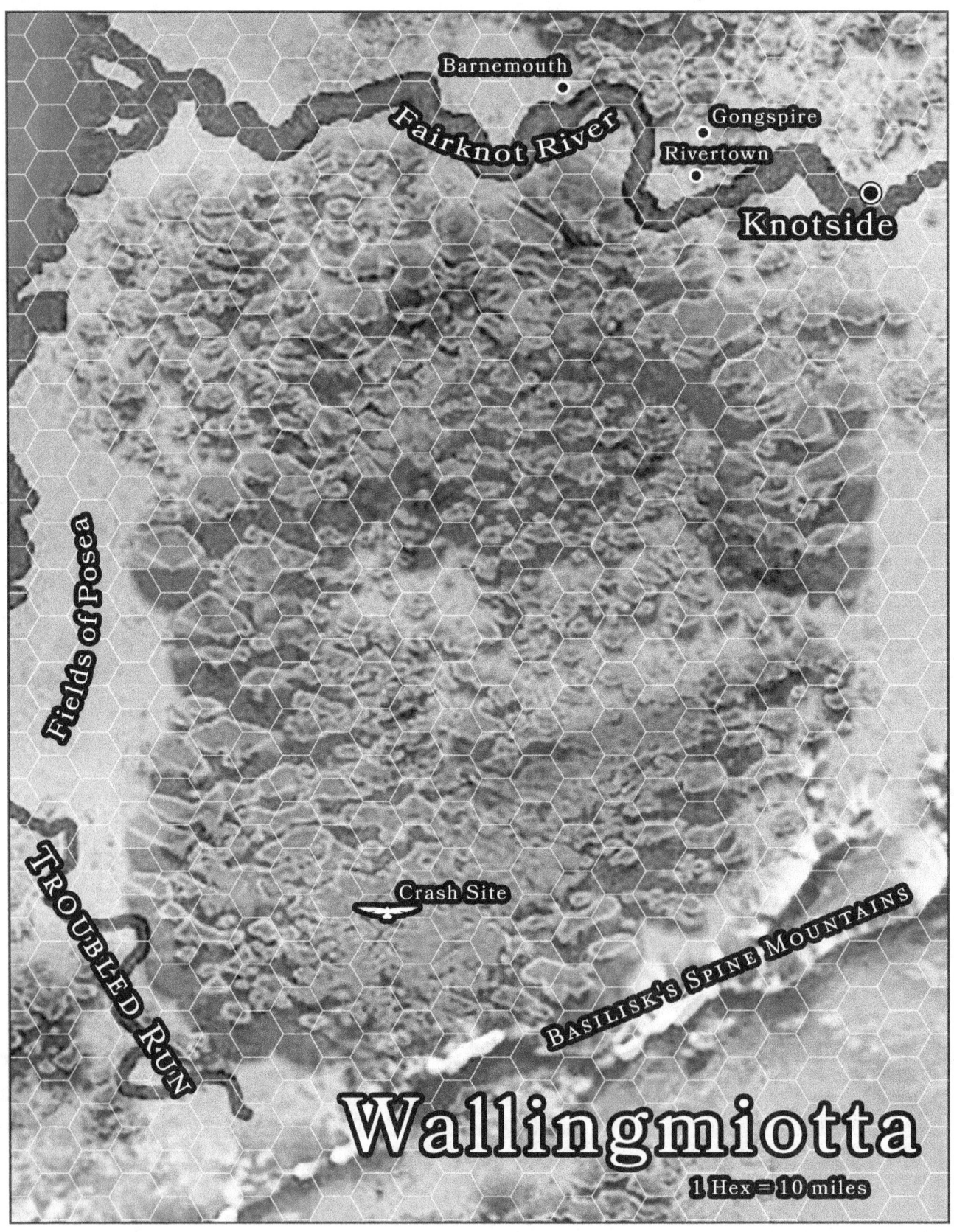

BROADSWORD #5 APRIL 2020

The Glaive of the Revenant King

Titan's Heir: The Flight of the Predator

Uncle Skeleton's Nightmare Tunnels

plus 31 New Monsters

OPEN GAMING LICENSE & SUBMISSION GUIDELINES

Send all submissions with a signed and filled-out Standard Disclosure Form to:
submissions@broadswordmagazine.com

BroadSword Monthly
Submission Guidelines:
https://bit.ly/2kIv9wn